THE ADVENTURES OF LAFOREST-DOMBOURG

VOLUME TWO

THE ADVENTURES OF LAFOREST-DOMBOURG

VOLUME TWO

THE DEVIL RETURNS

ERIC GAUTIER

Translated from the French by Roger D. Taylor

F

THE FITZROY PRESS

Cover illustration: Eric Gautier
First published as *L'Agent Double* by Editions Pen-Gan 2012
First published in English by The FitzRoy Press 2023

F
The FitzRoy Press
9 Regent Gate
Waltham Cross
Herts EN8 7AF

ISBN 978 1739214 241

ebook ISBN 978 1739214 258

A catalogue record for this book is available from the British Library

Publishing management by Troubador Publishing Ltd, Leicestershire, UK

Note: a reference list of the main characters is to be found at the end.

PROLOGUE

At one time, every naval officer, from Marine Guard or Volunteer right up to ship's commander, was required by the Royal Ordonnances to keep a personal logbook along the lines required by his vessel. When we left a ship, whether through her being decommissioned, or us leaving individually, this logbook had to be handed in to the Navy Office, where it was examined and then returned to us. My logbook forms the archive from which I can relate, more or less faithfully, the main events of which I was at one and the same time witness, involuntary actor and victim, during my campaign of 1781 to 1783. This was a campaign in which I was not supposed to participate and for which I had not volunteered; but nobody had asked my opinion.

I wrote my first logbook between the 17th July 1777 and the 29th June 1778, when I was a Marine Guard aboard the cutter *le Moucheron*. The next was begun on the 30th June 1778, the day I joined the frigate *l'Amazone*. In this second logbook I can see that I had drawn a big star at the top of the page for 20th May 1780. The officer who examined my diary after the frigate was decommissioned at Brest at the end of that year must have wondered why I had made this highly irregular addition: it was the day of my nineteenth birthday.

When I was a boy, it was not at all appropriate for a well-born person to celebrate his birthday in any way, much less have someone else do it for him. The Baron de Kermean, my maternal grandfather, would have considered it a sign of a lack of education. At the Saint-Yves College at Vannes, where I was a boarder for three years, it was thought of as a sin of pride. 'We glorify the birth of our Lord, Jesus Christ, but not that of men…' On the other hand, we were encouraged to celebrate our Patron Saints' days. And so, in the Army and the Navy, it was usual to hold an annual banquet in honour of Saint Louis. As for me, I well and truly celebrated my nineteenth birthday, but those around me did not know it, as I had invited them for another reason: I had been awarded my first epaulette.

In May 1780 I was a Ship's Ensign and first lieutenant aboard *l'Amazone,* commanded by the Comte de Galaup de la Peyrouse. Our captain had simplified his name when he was still a Marine Guard, and so was known to everybody by the name of Lapérouse. We were part of a King's squadron composed of one ship of eighty guns, two of seventy-four, four of sixty-four, two frigates, including our own, and the cutter *la Guêpe.* I well knew this last ship, a former English vessel, as I had been involved in her capture when I was still a Marine Guard. We had sailed out of the Brest harbour entrance on the 2nd May 1780 with a fleet that we were to escort to the Americas. It was made up of four King's transports and twenty-eight merchant ships carrying field artillery and twelve battalions of infantry under the command of the Comte de Rochambeau, Lieutenant-General of the Army.

I had learned that I had been promoted to Ensign while I was on leave at the end of my previous campaign. I had bought an octant[1] on my return to Brest and waited until I was once again at sea before celebrating my promotion with my shipmates. But we had had bad weather for the first two weeks of our voyage and I had been forced to postpone it. Noticing that my birthday was to be on the Saturday of our third week since leaving Brest, I decided to make use of it by having my little party. I thought that the conflux of these two events, on the one hand the celebration of a new rank, and on the other the start of a new year of my life, might be a good augur for the rest of my time on this lowly earth, somewhat like the conjunction of two planets,

---

1   Translator's note: *octant*: instrument for measuring the elevation of the sun, moon and stars; predecessor of the sextant.

and that Providence would be pleased to draw a line through my past. But if the Good Fathers of the Saint-Yves College had been there, they would certainly have told me that wishes based on superstition are never granted!

My logbook entry for the 20th May 1780 says that we had picked up the Tradewinds in 25 degrees latitude north, that the weather was fine and hot, and that we were finally making progress on our voyage, running on starboard tack. We had cast off the bad weather and contrary winds of the Bay of Biscay, and the calms south of the Azores. I remember the feeling of joy on board, and that we had to lower the t'gallant yards to slow us to the speed of the convoy. I had celebrated my promotion in the great cabin, with the captain and officers. We had uncorked several flagons of Sillery wine that had cost me a pretty packet, and which I had brought aboard with this occasion in mind. I had cooled them in a barrel of sea water before serving them.

I was a Ship's Ensign. I had always thought that this would happen, but not so quickly. It was only in the spring of 1777 that I had passed my Marine Guard examination. I had embarked immediately aboard a cutter managed directly by the offices of Monsieur de Fleurieu, officially known as the Director of Ports and Arsenals, but to those in the know his responsibilities went far beyond this. In June 1778 I was then entered on the roll of *l'Amazone,* shortly after her launching at Saint-Servan, the military port at Saint-Malo. After the declaration of war in July 1778, *l'Amazone* had first cruised around the British Isles before preparing for a campaign in the Indian Ocean. Eventually we were sent to join the Comte d'Estaing's squadron in the Americas. I had my baptism of fire at Grenada, and my first wound on the gundeck of *l'Annibal,* to which I had been temporarily detached. Shortly after this battle, and as a result of circumstances that I had neither foreseen nor wished, I was with the Comte d'Estaing at the disastrous attack on Spring Hill at Savannah, in October 1779. One can find many faults with the Comte d'Estaing, but he was brave under enemy fire and could be generous towards those who had been at his side in battle. I was surprised to learn, when we returned to France, that he had added me to the February 1780 list of promotions to Ensign.

One can move more quickly through the ranks in wartime! A Marine Guard at fifteen, I found myself an Ensign and a frigate's watch leader after only four years of service, while my commander, the man I most admired in the world, had waited eight years for this promotion. All the same, despite the flagons of wine and the good mood that I tried to put on for the benefit of the crowd, and despite the sincere congratulations of the Comte de Lapérouse and the other officers, I did not take much enjoyment in my good fortune. I felt apprehensive about the future, without quite knowing why, and this troubled me considerably; perhaps I was paying the price for so many accumulated fears and misfortunes which had been bottled up inside me for far too long.

Son of an officer lost at sea in the King's service, I had been admitted to the Marine Guard cadets despite having only dubious proofs of my nobility, and thanks to the influence of my maternal uncle at Court. There was nothing I could reproach myself about in this matter, but I knew that there would always be others, of a malevolent disposition, who would do it for me. Moreover, I owed my rapid rise to the Comte d'Estaing, of whom it would be an understatement to say that he was not liked by the officers of the Navy. As yet there was no problem with all of this, and I intended to address the situation by working even more zealously and making sure I always remained modest. But that was not the whole story.

My childhood and youth had been seriously damaged by a man who had first approached me at Brest in 1776. He had used the pretext of offering me support in a nasty duelling affair into which I had been dragged against my will. I knew nothing about him at that time apart from the fact that he was called Flaharn and that he was a Ship's Captain. He was reputed to be an excellent seaman and I had immediately fallen under his influence. It must be said that Nature had been generous to him: she had given him an exceptional physique, bodily strength and endurance, along with a noble appearance. He had a sharp mind too and was reputedly unbeatable at chess. As if that were not enough, he was highly skilled with both sword and pistol, feared nothing and nobody, and knew how to make himself feared. I learned later that he had once commanded fighters in Hindustan and that the sepoys over there had nicknamed him *Sher Sahib*, which in their language means, I think, the Lion Lord. He himself preferred to be compared to a tiger which, in my opinion, he more closely resembled.

When Flaharn took me under his wing I had just arrived as a cadet at the Company of Marine Guards at Brest. I thought that our meeting was a matter of chance, having no idea that he had in fact planned it. Nor did I know that he was interested in me because he thought I could tell him the hiding place of a chest containing treasure stolen by him during his escapades in India. This was a fabulous collection of diamonds which had been taken from him after a fight with a French officer, a Breton whom he had challenged to a duel at Chandernagore. Flaharn, who thought himself invincible, had been beaten. His adversary was the Marquis de Kersalaun, who had left India thinking that Flaharn was dead. As I would learn later, the Marquis de Kersalaun, an old comrade-in-arms of my father, had entrusted this fortune to the safekeeping of my parents. To try to find this treasure, about which my parents had never spoken to me, Flaharn had ambushed Kersalaun and his wife, and tortured them with the help of his accomplice, an Indian called Jakar Singh. Kersalaun and his wife had both died without revealing anything. Nonetheless, the two criminals had managed to discover the part played by my parents in this matter. My father was already dead, having been lost in 1771 when his ship foundered. The two monsters had kidnapped my mother in order to interrogate her, and she too had died prematurely in their brutal hands. I was therefore the only living witness and, although I did not know it at the time, I represented the final chance for those two miserable creatures. In 1776 I was of course ignorant of all this. Nobody had as yet been able to explain the sad and mysterious disappearance of my dear mother three years previously. I had therefore completely trusted Flaharn until the day I learned that it was he who had killed her. But there was no way of proving this in a court of law. Flaharn and his accomplice had eventually fallen out and killed each other during our campaign at Savannah.

And so, my first days in the Navy had been darkened by *Sher Sahib's* crimes. Everything had finished in a bloodbath at Savannah. It was all in vain. The diamonds longed for by Flaharn had been hidden by my mother in our family chapel at Kermean, in the parish of Mesquer, where I had eventually found them.

Thinking about it now, I have to admit that, despite everything, it was only because of Flaharn that I had got to know Maria Kirwan. She was the young landlady at the inn at Brest where my devilish mentor stayed. Maria and I were of the same age and from our first meeting my heart had been only for her. I had made promises to her which I had not kept especially well, having found myself unable to resist the advances of certain seductresses, first at Saint-Malo, then at Saint-Domingue. I can of course find excuses, but those are the facts and I am not proud of them, especially as each encounter almost cost me very dearly. But there was worse than that. In the hope of gaining the favour of this girl with whom I had fallen madly in love, I had promised to marry her. To keep to my word I had to ask permission from the Baron de Kermean, my maternal grandfather, who had become my guardian after the death of my parents. He liked me a lot, but he was somewhat irascible, and as yet I found myself too intimidated to talk to him about my dear Maria Kirwan. She had been born on the Île-de-France, where her mother had gone after the fall of Pondicherry. Her father, an Irish officer in the service of the King, had been killed during the siege of that town by the English in 1761. At the end of the war her mother had returned to her native Lower Brittany, only to die from the epidemic which had struck the region in 1770. Just like me, Maria had lost her parents early. She had been taken in by a maternal great-uncle, a childless widower and owner of *La Dame au Paon*, a prosperous inn on the Brest waterfront frequented by the masters and officers of merchantmen and coasters.

As he was getting on in years, he had gradually handed over the management of the establishment to his niece, and, my word, she was making a good job of it, as I was able to witness when I returned to Brest at the beginning of spring 1780.

I could imagine in advance the loud objections the Baron would raise when I told him about my marriage plans with a 'serving wench' as he would no doubt call her. I feared that eventually I would have only two choices: break with Maria Kirwan or go against the grandfather to whom I owed so much. Neither of these was attractive. Up until then I had been able to tell the girl that the regulations forbid Marine Guards to marry, which was true, but now I was a Ship's Ensign. I was only nineteen, and so there was no hurry, but it had become a question of trust between Maria and me. At the time of this second departure for the Americas I had promised to talk to my grandfather as soon as I got back. The previous campaign had lasted one year and this time I thought I would be away for longer. I was mistaken about that as *l'Amazone* was in fact going to be sent back to Brest before the end of this year of 1780. But nobody could have foreseen that, not even the Comte de Ternay, our squadron commander, or the Comte de Lapérouse.

To come back to my birthday celebration on the 20th May 1780, I very much would have liked to believe that this harmless activity could have had, in some magical way, a beneficial influence on my immediate future. Knowing now what happened afterwards, I can say it had none whatsoever. Thinking back to that time, I remember the feeling of anguish to which I was subject, without understanding its cause. I can see that it sprang from what I had just been through, but I also wonder whether this feeling was in fact more of a premonition. I had wanted to turn over a symbolic new leaf in my life and break with the past, but on the contrary, previous events were going to catch me again with a force and violence well beyond anything I could have imagined. One cannot escape one's fate.

1

On board l'Amazone, Wednesday 6th December 1780, end of the middle watch.

'Wake up please, Sir. Monsieur Laforest-Dombourg?'

I jump in my sleep and sit up in my bunk. A sudden roll throws me to one side and I hit my head against something metallic; it is hot and smells of fish oil. I open my eyes and see the little pane of a lantern held uncertainly and dangerously just three inches from my face.

I am coming out of a nightmare that has haunted me for three weeks. It is a nightmare so upsetting and so real that each time I wonder whether I have really slept and woken up.

'I'm sorry, Sir. I didn't do it on purpose.'

I recognise the voice, not yet broken, of Monsieur de Thomas, aged fifteen, one of our Volunteers. There are four on board and de Thomas is the cheekiest of the group. He helps our third lieutenant who is in charge of the middle watch from midnight until four o'clock and whom I must relieve until eight o'clock.

'Lieutenant Guillemin told me to wake you. They have already rung seven bells.'

'I didn't hear it,' I say, 'You did well to keep on at me, Monsieur de Thomas. But you didn't need to knock me out with your lantern!

Thank you…you can carry on.'

I immediately regret my outburst. I cannot understand why I am so troubled by this nightmare.

I am in a cemetery. There are no crosses. I recognise it. It is the Jewish cemetery at Savannah. Is it night-time or daytime? It is misty. I feel a presence close by and turn my head. A threatening shape is standing beside me. It speaks and I hear the deep voice of Flaharn. It frightens me. He says that he has come back from hell purely to take his revenge and that he will have the last word. I want to run off but I realise that I am buried up to my neck. Only my head is above the ground between the tombstones. I cannot move.

I always wake up at that moment, but then have trouble ridding myself of my torment. Even during the day it grips me again when I think of Flaharn, making my flesh creep. And yet I don't see myself as more impressionable than anyone else. Flaharn was certainly a pitiless enemy and I was right to be scared of him while he was alive. But he is dead! Less than a year ago I myself saw his huge carcass stretched face downwards in a sea of blood in his tent at Savannah, near the de Hainault grenadiers' camp. His unfortunate accomplice Jakar had shot him in the face with a pistol, from point-blank range. I saw Jakar himself die shortly afterwards, as he finished making his confession. Flaharn had stabbed him during their final quarrel and he had not survived. I had told a grenadier corporal about their two bodies. He had returned to camp at the same time as me after that morning's battle. I remember his *nom de guerre*: Bellerose. A survivor! He had promised to add their corpses to the common grave dug for the bodies of his comrades being collected from the Spring Hill redoubt. So why have I not found peace?

Young de Thomas has not closed the canvas curtain separating my little cabin from the false gun room where his shipmates' hammocks are slung. During the last campaign, when I was still a Marine Guard, I used to hang my own in the same place, just below the main companionway. A skylight fixed under a gundeck beam lights up the three boys fast asleep despite the constant swinging. I sit on the box at the foot of my bunk, in which my sea chest is stowed, and lean against the portside planking against which is constructed the six feet by four feet space allocated to me since becoming an Ensign. There are six of these for the ship's officers, ranged on each side around the Volunteers' quarters. Through the thick hull timbers behind me I can hear the water roaring. The sound echoes dully along the whole of the half-lit between-deck. It is like the wind in the branches of a tree, but louder, unceasing and always at the same strength. This impressive sound is punctuated with gurgles and the groaning of the steering lines in their blocks whenever the helmsman above corrects our course as we run at full speed before a following wind.

I start to feel cold. It must be freezing outside on the quarterdeck where, for four long hours without a break, I will have the sole responsibility for the ship and the two hundred men aboard. I pull an overcoat over my uniform and go up to take my instructions from the officer of the watch I am to relieve.

Lieutenant Guillemin is somewhat gruff, but I have always tried to be considerate towards him, for which he is grateful. He is of average height, well-built, with a square jaw, brown hair and blue eyes. When he talks to you in French he has a Vannes accent, otherwise he says little. He is an auxiliary officer with the rank of Frigate's Lieutenant, awarded when he joined *l'Amazone*. During our first campaign he was the fourth lieutenant while I, as a simple Marine Guard, was below him in the hierarchy. Now the roles are reversed. He is the third lieutenant, but I am a first lieutenant, having since been promoted to Ensign, being therefore a member of the Corps of ships' officers.

This Grand Corps, as it is often called, even by its detractors, has only three ranks between Marine Guard and Lieutenant-General[2]: Ship's Ensign, Ship's Lieutenant and Ship's Captain. In wartime there are not enough Grand Corps officers to meet the requirements of the navy, and so they are complemented by merchant officers given the rank of Frigate's Lieutenant for the length of a campaign. These are called Auxiliary Officers to differentiate them from the Frigate Lieutenants who have risen from the ranks of the full-time Volunteers. Frigate Lieutenants are above Marine Guards and below Ensigns. Our philosophers, in love with the notion of equality, are critical of this system. They deplore the fact that you have to prove your nobility to be admitted to the Marine Guards. I do not disagree with them. In

---

2 Translator's note: *Lieutenant-General:* Roughly the equivalent of Rear Admiral in the Royal Navy.

practice, luckily, the authorities have not been too punctilious about these famous proofs. I myself have been a beneficiary of this and my case is not exceptional. Even such famous seamen as the Comte de Lamotte-Piquet benefitted from it before me. All the same, men being what they are, this situation can sometimes create bad feeling. It would be surprising if that were not the case. To make things worse I owe my advancement to the Comte d'Estaing. Certainly, I look older than I am, on account of the scar on my left cheek, a souvenir of the Battle of Grenada, but I am only nineteen and have been at sea for just three years. Lieutenant Guillemin is at least forty, a merchant captain, and familiar with the Coromandel Coast and the Bay of Bengal. That is why the Comte de Lapérouse asked for him, as originally we were to go to the Indies, like Christopher Columbus, and like him we ended up in the Americas, though not for the same reason.

Arriving on the quarterdeck I am joined by Volunteer de Thomas. He has been to wake his replacement and they are standing in silence in front of the hourglass set up beside the little lantern which lights the compass binnacle. The man at the wheel is wearing a big, hooded cape that keeps his face in shadow. I wonder how he can hold to our course on the compass rose. Lieutenant Guillemin seems unconcerned. From time to time he leans over the compass to check our heading. This hood still concerns me. We are going at a good speed and we are nearing the continental shelf, where the ocean bottom rises. The sea can get up more easily here in a blow. To keep the wind astern in these conditions cannot be easy, but it seems that our helmsman knows his business.

Beside us an infantryman tries to shelter as well as he can in the lee of the main companionway hatch. The Comte de Ternay's squadron has been garrisoned by the de la Sarre regiment, with its white cotton uniform and grey tabling, worn in all weathers. That is military discipline. The fellow there must envy the sailors who can pull hoods or hats over their coats to protect themselves from rain and cold.

Lieutenant Guillemin lets me have a look at the ship's logbook. Since leaving America, except for the first few weeks, it has been easy for the successive officers of the watch to take over the navigation: we have normally been sailing a straight course, with the wind on the quarter or from astern. We almost always find the same notes on the logbook: *westerly wind, fresh, clear sky, compass course east…observed latitude at noon of 5th December 48 degrees 24 minutes North, calculated longitude*

14 degrees 50 minutes West of the Paris meridian…since noon yesterday corrected run of two hundred and forty nautical miles. The ship's log is regularly showing eleven to twelve knots, with the frigate running under topsails and mizzen topsail braced square. At dawn we will put on more sail. The Master Pilot has predicted that if the wind holds we will see the Iroise[3] Passage and the coast by two in the afternoon. We will be able to scrape into the Brest harbour entrance before nightfall. It will be towards the end of the ebb but at the moment there are neap tides.

The sand timer is empty. Young de Thomas taps it with his index finger before turning it, so that he cannot be accused of 'eating up sand'. He tells the infantryman to ring eight bells on the wheelhouse bell hung on the quarterdeck, at the foot of the mainmast. He looks at his officer of the watch, who says nothing, and without further ado goes off to his bunk. The ringing of the little bell echoes in the sound of the wind in the rigging. Port watch relieves starboard watch in the freezing darkness. A new helmsman takes the wheel. I am relieved to see that this one does not have a hood. Lieutenant Guillemin gives me a word of advice about the main topmast, which had to be replaced after damage sustained during our eventful departure from the Americas on the 28th October, and I am left all alone with my responsibilities.

L'Amazone plunges on into the night. When the long swell pushing us on lifts the stern, her bow throws up clouds of spray right to the waist of the ship. The Master Pilot is correct; we will certainly get to Brest this evening. But it is likely that nobody will be expecting us there and I wonder what our welcome will be like.

*

In spring 1780, after our departure from Brest, the Comte de Ternay had decided to make a long detour to the south to avoid English cruisers and to find some good weather. We were even wondering whether we would end up making our landfall in the Antilles, but eventually we headed north again. In July, after seventy days at sea,

---

3   Translator's note: *Iroise Passage:* the old name for the Mer de l'Iroise, the stretch of water to the west of the Brest harbour entrance, delineated by the island of Ushant to the north and island of Sein to the south.

we finally anchored at Newport, south of Boston, in a big, enclosed harbour rather like that of Brest: Narragansett Bay. Two weeks later the entrances were blockaded by an English squadron bigger than ours. We were not in a happy situation. The Americans who expected us to be there with a bigger force were not especially pleased by our impotence and did not hesitate to make us aware of this. It seems that the decision to send our frigate back to France was taken on the spur of the moment, after a meeting at the end of September between our two commanders and General Washington. We had taken as a passenger the Vicomte de Rochambeau, who was carrying important despatches from his father to the Court at Versailles. I do not know what was in them, but they must have been devilishly urgent. I had a suspicion that they very likely would not please the Ministers.

We had taken advantage of a gale from the north-north-west to run through the English squadron, which we understood was cruising between Nantucket Island and Cape Cod. Our three frigates left with the wind astern, in rain showers mixed with snow, which brought visibility down to just a few cables. The enemy vessels were widely spread, making our exit much easier than expected. Nonetheless they saw us and gave chase. We had managed to escape them quite quickly by piling on sail, but only narrowly escaped disaster: we had hardly lost our pursuers when without warning the main topmast came crashing down. We rigged a spare spar from our store and headed for France. The other frigates, *la Surveillante* and *l'Hermione*, were to cruise between Acadie[4] and Cape Breton before taking a break at Boston. A big repair like that is always difficult to effect at sea, and our progress had been slowed considerably at the start of our crossing because of this accident. The winds had been mostly favourable since.

*

On board l'Amazone, Wednesday 6ᵗʰ December 1780, early afternoon.

The crew has been given their dinner. The coastline rises above the frozen horizon. Through my telescope I can see the two halves of the cliffs barring the ocean. Between them is a narrow breach behind which the sea seems once more to stretch to infinity. That's how the port of

---

4   Translator's note: *Acadie:* The French colony on what is now Nova Scotia.

Brest appears, coming from seawards, as long as there is no fog.

We will not stay long in port, having only enough time to careen the ship while the Comte de Lapérouse and the Vicomte de Rochambeau take their despatches to Versailles. We will once again sail for America as soon as they return. Our captain has a sweet fiancée waiting for him, but I doubt he will spend much time with her. Will I have more luck with Maria Kirwan? I am always nervous when I see her again. She is not expecting me. I have not been able to send my letters, nor have I received any; it is only official despatches that come for our commanders, sent by the French ministry to the American Congress. At least, this time, my conscience is clean. This is not much to my credit, as the New England girls are much more restrained than the beautiful Creoles of our sugar islands. I have to admit that my desires weaken once I get to sea again and smell the heady perfume of the ocean. I have tried in vain to stay totally immune to the fiery attractions in our ports of call. I have already attempted to free Maria Kirwan from my attentions. I even wrote a letter to her, reluctantly, breaking things off, when I was at Saint-Malo, but each time that I see her again I promise I will never leave her. The worst of it is that I mean it; I forget completely that I could not stand staying in port forever. I cannot say why my feelings for her are so strong. Maybe it is because her eyes are the colour of a winter sea and that they hide in their depths a mystery which I can never fathom and which fascinates me. She seems so slim and delicate! But when I take her in my arms I can feel that she is much stronger than me and I wonder why she has chosen me, with all my faults. I am sure that it is not because of my more elevated standing, of which Maria makes merciless fun. In this too, she is different from other young girls.

I will certainly not be able to go to Kermean to see my grandfather. This gives me a cowardly reason to postpone the moment when I must broach with him the delicate subject of Maria Kirwan. All the same, I would very much have liked to have gone, if only to find out what happened to the chest of diamonds which had cost my mother her life and in the pursuit of which Flaharn had spilled so much blood. When I had left Kermean last March, to rejoin *l'Amazone* at L'Orient, the Chevalier de Kermean, my maternal uncle, had told me that he intended to take the cursed treasure to Versailles, to give to the King. I hoped that he had done so and that I would never hear about it again.

I could not even write to Kermean to ask my grandfather about it, as my uncle had stressed that I must keep the matter secret and above all not mention it in any personal correspondence. He always says that a letter risks being intercepted, and in these matters he knows what he is talking about.

The frigate brings the wind on the port beam to take the Iroise Passage. Our bow is pointing to the Brest harbour entrance, now visible to the naked eye between the Saint Mathieu Point and the high cliffs beside the Toulinget Channel to starboard. To port are the Pierres Noires rocks, behind which can be seen the island of Béniguet, a flat piece of land edged with a beach of white sand that a ray of sun lights up between two clouds. The sea seems to have been deserted by our ships on this cold winter's afternoon. I go below for the officers' meal.

After my dinner I am off watch, but like all those who have the right, I stay on deck to watch the approach of land. The Comte de Lapérouse is standing on the port side of the quarterdeck, beside the Vicomte de Rochambeau. I am to leeward of them and can hear their conversation.

The Vicomte is the Second Colonel of the de Bourbonnois regiment, whose new uniform, entirely white except for black cuffs and a few ribbons and frills, also black, he is wearing. He is twenty-five years old and seems quite thin besides the Comte de Lapérouse, his elder by fifteen years. He has just come back from the foredeck where he has been observing, with his telescope, the parts of the Brest harbour visible from our ship's deck. He says that he has not seen a single ship. The Comte de Lapérouse replies that the best anchorage for big squadrons and fleets is just after the entrance passage, but that frigates and ships can moor on coffin buoys still hidden from view by Porzic Point and Spanish Point.

'Last summer, at Newport,' the Vicomte replies, 'the French Minister had assured us that the regiments we had been unable to bring with us would be leaving from Brest with Squadron Commander de la Touche-Tréville. He even said there would be twelve ships to transport the troops due to us: the Neustrie, Auvergne, Rouergue and Anhalt regiments. At least six thousand men, plus artillery, food and ammunition! That must require a lot of merchant ships. If they have been assembling here, don't you think we would see some of them?'

'We are still a bit far off, but if you can't see anything then they probably are no longer there.'

'Do you think we may have crossed them?'

'No, I would think they are probably needed elsewhere.'

The young Colonel looked annoyed.

'The Navy is making fun of us! When my father made the observation, at the beginning of last spring, that he did not have enough means at his disposal, the King immediately doubled the number of troops earmarked for him. Everything that was the responsibility of the War department was brought to Brest with unmatched diligence. All the troops were delivered to the port in early April, the time fixed for their embarkation. And then we waited. What did the Navy department do? They had received the same orders as us but were not ready! Half the ships which were to transport us went off with Monsieur de Guichen to take some sort of reinforcements to our colonies, while Monsieur de Sartine took too long before thinking of having other ships brought from Bordeaux to replace them in time. So we had to leave half our troops in Brest. And we were told these regiments would rejoin us as quickly as possible! What's going on? When he was involved with him, Monsieur de Choiseul used to joke that Monsieur de Sartine's watch was often slow. He's wrong! I myself would say it never moves!'

'You are being unfair on Monsieur de Sartine and his department,' replies the Comte de Lapérouse. 'The War department can calculate precisely how long things take by land. I don't say it is easy, but it is always possible. While with the Navy, it is the sea and the wind that are always in control. I would add that the War department, up until now, has only had to deal with the troops for your father in New England. The last year's military operations have mainly been undertaken by colonial troops and ships' garrisons, with the Navy campaigning for two years throughout the whole world.'

Our commander continues, trying to explain that at present the war is not limited to New England. There are the Antilles and our Atlantic trade to protect, and our ally Spain asking us to help them blockade Gibraltar in exchange for their participation in the naval war, which we cannot do without. Lastly one should not forget the Indian Ocean, where Monsieur de Fleurieu had at one time intended to send *l'Amazone*.

'…Monsieur de Sartine and Monsieur de Fleurieu have done their best with the means at their disposal, I can assure you.'

'You are an honest man, Monsieur de Lapérouse, and I respect you, but I hope you will excuse me for saying that as you depend on them it is natural for you to take their defence. But I am not in that position. Moreover, I speak not for myself but my father. I am just relaying what is written in the despatches I am carrying, whose contents I know by heart. And believe me, I will tell them what's what, simple Colonel though I may be.'

*

At dusk *l'Amazone* anchored in Brest harbour. It was our fortieth day since leaving Newport. In the harbour there was just one ship, whose stern light we could see in front of the dark entrance to the Penfeld.

As soon as we had laid both our anchors, the Comte de Lapérouse had his small gig put in the water. He called me to the great cabin, along with the Master Gunner, to give us our instructions for unloading powder. He would have a lighter, built specifically for this particular task, sent out at dawn and we had to be ready to receive it.

At the same time as being promoted to first lieutenant, I had also been put in charge of the ship's guns. I had known well, and appreciated, my predecessor, Lieutenant de Tromenec, an experienced Ship's Lieutenant who had left *l'Amazone* to take up the command of a corvette. At first I had protested, saying that my years of service were much less than the other Frigate Lieutenants below me, both of them merchant captains with long experience. The Comte de Lapérouse had cut short my objections, saying that he thought I had been sufficiently battle-hardened during my time on *l'Annibal* at the Battle of Grenada and that, all things considered, I was the only one of his lieutenants who had been proven under fire on a sixty-four-gun ship.

All the officers were called, and our Captain announced that he was going ashore with the Vicomte de Rochambeau to report our arrival to the Comte d'Hector and to make preparations for us to move to the Arsenal. He would come back early in the morning to direct our manoeuvring into the Penfeld. He intended to be present when the ship was inspected by the Port Commander and his engineers, as he wanted their opinion before leaving for Versailles with the Vicomte. His hope was that a quick refit would enable us to put to sea as soon as he returned from Versailles.

At dawn on the 7th December the gig returned without the Captain. Another boat arrived at the same time, carrying a port officer. *L'Amazone* was to enter the Penfeld on the morning tide. We were expected at the artillery warehouses, just after the Arsenal gate, on the Recouvrance side. I myself was then occupied supervising the unloading of barrels of powder, powder charges and boxes of cartridges. These were lifted out of the powder store through a hatch in the gunroom planking, then passed through the stern gunports onto the lighter which was tied to our stern to receive them. They would then be taken to the powder store on the island of Arun, an islet at the mouth of the Aulne and Faou rivers, at the end of the harbour. When I went to report the successful execution of this delicate operation to the Chevalier de Jonquière, our second captain, he told me that, according to the port officer, the Comte de Lapérouse and the Vicomte de Rochambeau had decided to leave on a King's post carriage as soon as they learned that Monsieur de Sartine had been replaced at the Navy department by the Marquis de Castries. The Chevalier had asked the reason for this unforeseen change at the Ministry and was told that Monsieur de Sartine had fallen from the King's favour at the behest of the King's adviser, Monsieur de Maurepas and Monsieur Necker, the Director-General of Finance. They had both accused our Minister of having defrauded the state coffers of twenty million pounds. This news, which we had difficulty believing, caused us considerable distress. Could Monsieur de Sartine, who had previously been in charge of the Paris police before being moved to the Navy, really be so dishonest? According to the port officer, our new Minister for the Navy and Colonies was a close friend of Monsieur Necker, which is why he had been nominated for this post.

At the second hour of the flood on that Thursday morning our boats towed the ship in. I was sittin in the sternsheets of our big ship's boat. The weather was cold and damp. We passed close by the vessel we had seen the previous evening, moored to a coffin buoy in front of the Horseshoe Battery. She was *la Bourgogne,* sixty-four guns, recently arrived from Cadiz.

News of the arrival of a frigate from the Comte de Ternay's squadron must have spread, as there was a large crowd on the Brest quay, between the Chateau and the Arsenal, to watch us pass. When we were level with the big ships' water fountain, I saw Maria Kirwan in the front row of the crowd. She was looking in our direction. I lifted my hat and she waved furiously as soon as she recognised me. My heart beat more strongly and I forgot all the worries about our future and my past indiscretions.

If there were no ships in the harbour apart from *la Bourgogne*, the Arsenal was overflowing with them. A forest of masts, much denser than usual, was crowded into the narrow confines of the Penfeld. Ships were moored in three lines along the middle of the river, from the offices of the Port Intendant, above the Troulan dock, after the ropewalks, right to the end of the port. Amongst the first vessels was a three-decked ship whose figurehead portrayed a crowned lady on a throne. This was *la Ville de Paris*, which had just been copper-bottomed and whose guns were about to be increased to a hundred and four, as I would soon learn. Behind her I recognised *le Languedoc*, eighty guns, and *le Marseillois*, sixty-four, both of whom I had seen in action at Grenada and at Savannah during the Comte d'Estaing's campaign. They had just been refitted. The fourth had a familiar appearance and I would have easily taken her for *l'Annibal*, were she not brand new and completely coppered, and had I not known that *l'Annibal* was still at the Antilles with the Comte de Lamotte-Piquet. *L'Annibal* had covered herself with glory the previous year, at Martinique, in a battle opposing three French ships to thirteen English. On hearing about this I had been envious of my friend Vernon des Aulnes, who was still serving aboard her. This new ship was in fact *le Northumberland*, a sixty-four built to the same plans as *l'Annibal*. She had been given this odd name in memory of an English prize taken during the previous war. Most of these vessels, ships and frigates, were either fully fitted out or in the process of being so. There were so many of them packed so tightly that I believe we would have had trouble towing our ship any further than the Saint-Barbe warehouse. The quay where we stopped was near the entrance to the port on the second bend of the Penfeld, level with the Clocktower and the Troulan dock, that we could see opposite on the left bank.

Once we were well anchored and moored, we began immediately to unbend the sails and send them ashore along with their spares. The Comte d'Hector came aboard with the port engineers. Their visit lasted the whole day. They found that much of the copper plating at the waterline seemed damaged and in need of replacement and decided that they would take it all off to see if any planking needed renewing. The rudder supports on the sternpost were eaten away, as were the pintles.

We got their verdict in the evening: all the dry docks were full, so we would have to completely unload the frigate at the quayside and take out her ballast, to be able to inspect the planking more thoroughly, then careen her against a pontoon. That would take much longer than the two weeks envisaged by our commander! The Comte d'Hector said he would have a message sent to the Ministry.

*

Brest, Thursday 7th December, evening.

The engineers have gone, their inspection over. The quays of the Arsenal are empty. The crew has left to take up its quarters at the shore billet, above Pontaniou, further up the side we are on. The officers will stay with relatives or friends in town, at their own expense. Maria Kirwan has sent me a note to say she will put me up free of charge, along with any shipmates who need lodgings. It is very generous of her. I pass on her invitation to our two Frigate's Lieutenants, the second lieutenant de Caudam and third lieutenant Guillemin. They are from L'Orient, like me, and accept the invitation with a warmth that does me honour.

We take our chests ashore. Lieutenant Guillemin tells us to wait while he goes to the Recouvrance landing stage, on the bend in the river beside the Arsenal, to find a ferryman. He comes back with him to pick us up.

Evening falls. The rain has stopped, a cold breeze from the north-west having cleared the sky towards the end of the afternoon. The ebb tide carries us downstream. The boatman manoeuvres with a single oar over the stern between the quay and the ships lined up on the Penfeld. We run alongside the high topsides of the ships as far as *la Ville de Paris,* where we turn into the shadow of her bow, under her bowsprit and her crowned figurehead. It is already quite dark at the Arsenal, with the sun only lighting up the towers of the Brest Chateau. We hear the mallet blows of some late workers in the Troulan drydock, on the left bank. Our breath makes a light mist. My fingers and ears are frozen and I pull up the collar of my coat and pull my hat down to my eyes.

The ferryman alters course across the river with a sweep of his oar and slides skilfully between the barques and luggers rafted up on the

13

Brest quay. Their hulls knock gently together as we pass, and these light shocks of timber on timber ring out as if amplified by the cold air.

We pay the ferryman and pass our chests hand to hand onto the quay. It is now night. The windows of *La Dame au Paon* light up the paving stones between the inn and the massive fountain in the middle of the square where the coasters unload their cargoes during the day. The old sign of a Siamese lady astride a peacock swings and creaks. The wind rushing along the Penfeld swirls around the tightly packed façades of the Brest quay houses backing on to the Sept Saints quarter. It was at this spot, on a winter's evening like this, just two years ago, that my commander had told me that my grandmother Laforest-Dombourg was a Micmac Indian. The Comte de Laprouse had met her when his ship was at Louisbourg during the last war. My grandfather de Kermean is still unaware of this, as my parents had never dared to tell him. What approach should I take to get him to agree to my marrying an innkeeper? Tell him that I love her? That would be the last reason to give to the Baron! A refusal would be guaranteed! And what am I to say to Maria Kirwan if she asks me what I intend to do about this? I think once more about my parents' story and that gives me an idea. I put my chest down on the paving and sit on it to have a think. My idea is not the brightest, I know, and I even feel that if it is accepted, I will regret it.

'Is something wrong, Monsieur Dombourg?'

My two companions have stopped in front of the door of the inn and are preparing to go in when they realise that I am alone, behind them, in the dark.

*

Maria Kirwan was wearing a simple white dress tightened at the waist by a blue belt. She had on a little white hat set at an angle, and was smiling. She took my hands in hers and I plunged my heart into the depths of her sea-green eyes. Suddenly I realised that perhaps my idea was not so bad after all.

I suggested to Maria Kirwan that we present my grandfather with a *fait accompli*. For good measure, I would at the same time tell him my parents' secret.

'He will have no choice then but to let us marry. Obviously,' I added, 'I will ask for shore leave so that I can be with you until things quieten down.'

Luckily Maria was more clear-thinking than me.

'I have never heard anything so stupid! Pierre-Marie, you really want shore leave when we are in the middle of a war? And you are a sailor. What will I do with you when you are here like a miserable loafer watching the ships pass the Brest quayside? And what about this inn that I will inherit? Do you want me to give it to your grandfather as a dowry? You're not even twenty! Follow the example of your captain, the Comte de Lapérouse, and his fiancée, Mademoiselle Broudou, so good and gentle. They have decided to wait so as not to sadden the last days of Monsieur de Galaup, your commander's father. Do your duty like him. Go to sea with him. That's all I ask of you. As far as I am concerned, you can rest assured that I will wait as long as necessary.'

In one sense I was relieved that our love would remain chaste for an indeterminate time, but it bothered me a little. For Maria it seemed that this was not a problem, but for me it was different. I had fallen into bad habits when I was at the Company of Marine Guards at Brest and we were welcomed at *Les Dames de la Marine* in the rue Siam. I was reminded of Colonel Guypair, whom I had had the temerity to challenge to a duel in 1778, when he had made statements that I found insulting towards Naval officers. In particular, when talking about the Marine Guards, he had said: 'It is the worst school as regards morality! Despite having been oddly privileged by nature, these are subjects inevitably devoted to vice!' I had to admit that he was not totally mistaken. I envied the Comte de Lapérouse, who seemed to bear his situation better than me. I had learned from Maria that Mademoiselle Broudou and her mother, by a lucky chance, as far as my commander was concerned, were at Versailles, where Madame Broudou had been to take care of some business for her husband back in the Île-de-France.

Nonetheless I have happy memories of the days that followed. I passed my days in frenetic activity working on the frigate and returned exhausted to sit in front of the fire with my dear friend before going to bed – alone. Flaharn's ghost had stopped haunting my nights, although I slept in the room where I had got to know him when I arrived in Brest four years earlier. It is true that it was also in this room that I had fallen in love with Maria. I still had regular nightmares in which I saw the bodies of our soldiers shredded by English grapeshot at the foot of the Spring Hill redoubt. I think these images will be engraved on my mind for ever, although they usually passed when I woke up.

The winds stayed in the north for several days and the frosts began. The sky was clear and it grew colder and colder, but I was so occupied that I did not notice. The work on board *l'Amazone* had started at a feverish and forced pace as we had to get to sea again as quickly as possible. We were sent shipwrights and workers from the port, along with forced labourers in their red shirts and bonnets, chained in pairs and surrounded by guards. Under my supervision the cannons were lifted out one by one and lined up on the quay by the forced labourers. The rudder was replaced, the crosstrees unrigged and brought ashore, along with everything else except the oven and galley. To enable the shipwrights and caulkers to examine the interior of the planking, we had to lift out all the ballast onto the pontoon, then put it back in again for the careening. We had to kill a huge number of rats, and the smell of those who had gone to die in the planking was enough to stop us in our tracks.

We had got that far when the Comte d'Hector told us that the Comte de Lapérouse had been ordered to give up his ship to the King and take command of *l'Astrée,* another newly built 12-pounder frigate which had just been copper-bottomed and for whom this would be the first commission. She had already been towed to the General Warehouse at Brest, on the other side of the river. We had ten days to prepare her and take her out into the harbour ready for putting to sea. There was not a minute to lose. The whole crew and corps of officers of *l'Amazone* were to transfer to *l'Astrée.* The latter had a different builder from our previous ship and although she had been designed with gun ports for 18-pound cannons, her scantlings had been found to be insufficient, and so she had been reclassed as a 12-pound frigate, with twenty-six guns of that calibre on the gun deck and six 8-pound guns on the fore and after decks, like *l'Amazone.* She had exactly the same beam and draft, and almost the same length, a hundred and thirty-five feet to *l'Amazone's* hundred and thirty-four.

Our sailors were in good health and very attached to their captain who, although he did not take discipline lightly, never mistreated them and always won them over. There were no rivalries either amongst our officers and that too was down to the Comte de Lapérouse. Visitors who came aboard congratulated us on the keenness and patriotism shown by our crew in hurrying on our departure for a new war campaign. Even Maria Kirwan, who quite legitimately could have wanted me to stay with her for longer, encouraged me in this regard, following the example of our Captain's fiancée, Mademoiselle Broudou, who like her lived in Brest and had become her friend.

At the end of these two years of hostilities, many of the young Naval officers at Ponant had only experienced the Comte d'Orvilliers' disastrous campaign between Spain and the Channel. Their future held little except the blockade of Gibraltar, while they dreamed of the wide blue sea and the Americas. Every day I came across Ship's Ensigns with more seniority than me who envied me my position and would have liked to have taken it from me. I would not have given it up for anything in the world.

2

Brest, Wednesday 20th December, morning.

The wind has fallen during the night. It is very light but seems to have gone round to the south-south-west, which possibly does not augur well for our planned departure. But it is not so cold: my fingers are no longer frozen when I grasp the shrouds to climb up the ratlines. The sky is hidden behind a veil of unbroken grey. The flood tide has been running since four o'clock. The crew and our infantrymen are back on board. I brought my sea chest aboard this morning, having said my farewells to Maria Kirwan. The Comte de Lapérouse has apparently just got back to Brest and will join us at eleven o'clock. We will then go out into the harbour on the ebb tide, immediately load our powder and be ready to leave as soon as we have a favourable wind.

Everything is ready. We brought our guns aboard yesterday and we will finish bending on the sails by midday. As first lieutenant I am in charge of the foremast, a plum job as the foretopmen are the elite of the crew. They have finished bending on the foresail and all its brails, furling it in the bunt on its yard, and have now moved on to the foretopsail. This is still in its sail bag, which will be hauled up to the foretop before being unpacked. The canvas is new and stiff. The brails are set up and the sail hauled into place with tackles running through sheaves at each end of the yard. The topmen move along the footropes, fixing the head of the sail with short lengths of rope wound around the yard and tied off with a Carrick bend.

I too have climbed to the foretop. Sailors on deck are hauling on the brails to allow my topmen to tighten the sail. Once this is finished we will move on to the fore t'gallant sail. I look around me. The frigate is moored fore and aft, her bow pointing downstream, about sixty feet from the quay. It was here, at this same quay, more than four years ago, while still a Marine Guard cadet, that I first climbed the rigging of a ship. I remember my fear. So much has happened since. All that seems so far away!

At the moment there is virtually nobody on the quay, just some warehousemen tallying boxes which must have been unloaded last night. All the first-floor office windows are lit up: it's there that the Arsenal accounts are kept. I look at the clocktower rising above the warehouse to my right. It is half past nine and the day is still slow to get going. There is almost no wind, and I see snowflakes starting to float gently down. They are as light as my heart since learning that Maria Kirwan still loves me, despite me telling her that I was impatient to get to sea and the deep blue of pelagic waters, and that I would be sad if I had to remain in Brest.

'Monsieur Laforest-Dombourg!'

Leaning over I see the Bosun calling me from the foredeck below.

'Monsieur de la Jonquière wants to see you in the great cabin immediately! It's urgent! He told me to take your place to finish the work.'

I slide down the stays to the foredeck. Good heavens! What could be more urgent than being ready to sail on the next tide? I have always been on excellent terms with the second captain and can't understand why he would interrupt me before I have finished my task. Moreover, I like working in the rigging. It allows me to get closer to my topmen. When I am not officer of the watch or directing the guns, the foremast is part of my personal territory on board. In heavy weather I am amongst these men and have to rely on them, so all these are good opportunities to get to know them better.

I go down to the waist via the gangway ladders and go aft alongside the guns. The storage spot for the ship's boats is clear, as they have already been launched and are tied alongside, ready to tow us out of the port. The duty infantryman at the door of the great cabin tells me to go in straight away: I am expected.

The great cabin is wood-panelled and the red carriages of the two 12-pounder cannons stand on proper parquet flooring. Although I know the cabin well, it always surprises me. The Chevalier de la Jonquière is sitting behind the big table at which the officers will soon take their meal. Opposite him is a Ship's Ensign whom I have never seen before and who must have come aboard while I was busy bending on the foresail. They both stand when I come in. The Chevalier de la Jonquière does not introduce us and politely asks the man I thought was a visitor to be sure to be back on board before midday. The latter nods to me as he goes out. He is much older than me and I feel a hint of condescension in his manner. Or is it pity? But why?

I look at the Chevalier de la Jonquière. There is something strange about him.

'Please sit down, Monsieur Laforest-Dombourg.'

The second captain sits down again opposite me. His face is smooth, and he is always smiling, calm and immaculately turned out. His speech is always refined and elegant, even in battle or at the height of a storm. He is wearing his dress uniform and a freshly powdered wig. I personally prefer to keep my hair *au naturel*. On the table in front of him is an inkwell and quill, and a bound volume open at the first page. I recognise *l'Astrée's* roll book. It is brand new, like our ship, and *l'Amazone's* role has been copied into it. Given that the two frigates are identical, everyone has taken up the same position, but we have not yet had time to sign the new register. Ever since the 1776 Regulations did away with ships' clerks, they have been replaced on frigates by the second captain. Ours, like all of us, or perhaps even more so, has been occupied with preparing the ship for sea.

I think first that the Chevalier de Jonquière wants me to sign the register, but nobody else has done it and there will be all the time in the world for that once we are out, waiting for a fair wind for leaving. Why has he called me when I was in the middle of my work?

'The Chevalier de Karreg, who has just left, will be replacing you…'

That's what it is! I know that *l'Astrée* is short of officers: we had four lieutenants at the start of the war, but one left in May 1779 and was never replaced. The shortage of officers in the Navy is the reason why I am a first lieutenant despite my young age. The Navy office has used our change of ship to make up the shortfall. As this Ship's Ensign has more seniority than me, I will be made second lieutenant. That is normal. Besides, wasn't the Chevalier de la Jonquière an Ensign until recently? He was only recently promoted to Ship's Lieutenant and his epaulettes have not yet had the time to get tarnished.

'If it's only that, Sir,' I say, 'I understand completely and you don't have to worry about me. You can tell the Comte de Lapérouse that it won't in any way diminish my keenness to do my duty.'

The second captain does not reply immediately and takes up two documents from beside the ship's roll book. He looks at them thoughtfully then puts them down again. I look at them upside down. They seem to have headings from the Port of Brest Commander, and are without doubt orders or certificates.

'That's not what it is, Monsieur Laforest-Dombourg. The Comte de Lapérouse arrived at Brest this morning. He will be back on board before midday. But he sent me the Chevalier de Karreg in advance, along with his embarkation certificate…' the Chevalier de la Jonquière lifts one of the two papers, '…and your orders, signed this morning.' The Chevalier de la Jonquière passes me the second document. 'You are to leave the ship. But be assured that this is not a punishment.'

I take the paper from him without understanding the sense of what he has just told me. It is an official document, decorated at the top with the usual design of the King's arms surrounded by heraldic devices. Below this is a printed inscription:

JEAN-CHARLES CTE. D'HECTOR
Squadron Chief of the Navy, Chevalier of the Royal
and Military Order of St. Louis,
Commander of the Port of Brest

On the lower part of the page is a handwritten text relating to me:

Monsieur Laforest-Dombourg, Ensign of the King's Ships, is ordered to present himself at Versailles, at the Department for the Navy and Colonies, on the orders of Monsieur the Chevalier Claret de Fleurieu, Captain of the King's Ships,

I recognise the Comte d'Hector's signature, which I have seen on other documents. He is also interim Navy commander at Brest, as the Comte de Guichen is away on active service. I read it and reread it. I don't understand. Why Versailles? I have already crossed the ocean to the Americas twice, I know the coasts of France from La Rochelle to Saint-Malo, from the sea, while on land I have never been further than Nantes. The Ministry? There is nothing for me to do there. I am too young and a sailor, not a clerk. But what if it's a subterfuge so that someone else can get my place? I know that lots of more senior officers want it. Someone has had me transferred to an office where nobody ever goes, while the world's eyes are turned towards America, the Comte de Rochambeau and the Marquis de Lafayette. Glory, the Cross of Saint-Louis, they are to be found over there! Certainly not in some dusty corner at the Department of the Navy and Colonies!

'But what, Sir? What have I done?'

'I know nothing about it!' replies the Chevalier de la Jonquière. 'But I can tell you that as far as I know you've done nothing wrong! I was as surprised as you, believe me! I swear that I have always had the greatest respect for you and that I regret your leaving. I know nothing more than what the Chevalier de Karreg just told me. There are these orders concerning both of you signed this morning, hardly an hour ago, for Heaven's sake, by the Comte d'Hector.'

'This Karreg…' I say.

The Chevalier de la Jonquière stops me immediately.

'I know what you are thinking! He has nothing to do with your departure. He told me himself that even yesterday he had no idea he was to be ordered to join *l'Astrée.* His orders were signed this morning, like yours, because you had to be replaced in a rush and he was the only Ensign available at short notice. He had not been assigned to a ship as he has been on sick leave. I repeat, he only arrived at Brest yesterday. When he arrived at the Navy office they had no idea what ship he was to be assigned to. They fetched him from his lodgings at eight this morning, while it was still dark, to take him to the Comte d'Hector's office. Of course he is delighted to be sailing for the Americas on a brand new frigate. Who wouldn't be? But imagine

– he has only three hours to prepare himself, as we will be leaving the port just after midday.'

'All the same, I'd still like a word with him.'

For a moment the Chevalier de la Jonquière's calmness deserts him. It is true that I am known as a fighter, with the stories of several duelling incidents following me around.

'Be reasonable, Monsieur Laforest-Dombourg. I repeat – the Chevalier de Karreg has nothing to do with this!'

'But how do you know?'

'On my honour! It's he who told me.'

Our eyes cross for a moment. The Chevalier de la Jonquière waves his hand, as if to dispel the doubt he sees in my eyes.

'In any case he has gone to get ready. You won't have time to see him, as he also told me that the Comte de Lapérouse is waiting for you at the Hotel Saint-Pierre, along with the Comte d'Hector and an officer from the Ministry in Versailles, whose name he forgot. They will no doubt put you in the picture. You don't have a minute to lose. But first you must sign the register, otherwise there will be no record of your time aboard *l'Astrée.*'

The Chevalier de la Jonquière pushes the register across the table and hands me the quill after dipping it in the inkwell. The roll is still open at the first page, the one for the officers. Only two lines are filled in, one for my name and the other for the Chevalier de Karreg. I read that I was previously on the frigate *l'Amazone* and that I left *l'Astrée* to go to the Secretariat of State for the Navy and Colonies at Versailles. To the Ministry! My God!

I sign and stand up to leave the cabin, still stunned by the news which has just been broken to me.

'Monsieur Laforest-Dombourg. One moment, if you please.'

I turn around, hoping that he is going to tell me that perhaps it is all a mistake and that there is still hope.

'Take your personal logbook, as they will certainly ask you for it up there. And don't forget to send someone for your chest before noon.'

*

My third logbook! The previous one, which I had written aboard *l'Amazone,* had filled two notebooks covering two years of campaigning.

I had handed it in two weeks before, as did the other officers, when we learned that our frigate was to be decommissioned. I had only just started the new one, in which I had faithfully recorded the preparatory work on *l'Astrée* while still in port. In other words – nothing! I thought with some despair that I would not have to keep another one for a long time. I went below to get it from my cabin on the between-deck, wrapped it in a piece of canvas to protect it, and put on my best uniform.

Snow was starting to settle on the quay. I slipped several times when crossing the walkway spanning the Troulan dry dock to get to the railings at the Arsenal entrance. I had intended to cut across the Rampe du Commandement, which went off to the right of the Grande rue, but it was already quite white under the fresh snow, and I decided to carry on up to the square in front of the Landerneau Gate. This was not the moment to ruin my breeches and red stockings by tripping on that steep slope and presenting a sorry figure to the Comte d'Hector.

The soldiers of the Royal Corps of Marine Infantry on duty at the entrance to the Hotel Saint-Pierre had been notified of my arrival and an usher in a wig and white gloves took me to an anteroom and told me to wait. He would not have known why I had been summoned, but all the same he seemed snooty and tight-lipped. Lackeys attached to important people like to give themselves these superior airs, but I felt like a guilty person about to be dragged in front of his judges. The powdered majordomo went to tap on the Comte d'Hector's door and closed it carefully behind himself as he went in. I sat on one of the upholstered chairs lined up under the window, opposite a hearth where logs were gently burning. Sat on the edge of my chair with my hat and logbook on my knees, and my hands crossed above them, I was so apprehensive that I scarcely dared to breathe. It was the third time I had been summoned here. The first was because of the matter of a duel. The second was the result of the complaint from Colonel de Guypair that I had challenged him because I felt insulted by his public pronouncements about sailors. On that second occasion I had truly believed that my career in the Navy was about to end there and then. This time my summons was not a disciplinary matter, but I was no less anxious.

The usher came out and I jumped to my feet. He signalled to me to wait and went off again without explanation. The sound of muffled voices came from the Commander's office. I was sure they were talking about me. For a short while I imagined that these important men were arguing against the absurd decision to disembark the first lieutenant of a frigate to send him to Versailles, while we were at war and had been short of Naval officers aboard the King's ships since the start of the conflict. Then I wondered whether it might be the opposite: the Marquis de Castries, the new Navy Minister, had discovered that I was not truly noble and that I had been promoted to Ensign through the personal favour of the Comte d'Estaing, rather than through my own merits. He was having me called to Versailles to put an end to this scandalous state of affairs.

The conversation in the Comte d'Hector's office ended. The door handle that my eyes had been fixed on began to turn. I stood up immediately. My breath was short and I was sweating, annoyed with myself for feeling flustered. The two wings of the door opened and I found myself confronted by the kindly face of the Comte de Lapérouse. It was he who had opened the door. This gave some relief to me, and without thinking I held out my logbook.

'Please, Sir, I beg you, tell them that I want to stay with you. I swear to serve you as best I can, even if I am demoted back to Marine Guard.'

My commander gave me a friendly smile but said nothing. There was a moment of silence and I felt more hopeful after the anguish I had been through. It was then that I heard a familiar ironic laugh from behind the door. I entered the room, quite taken aback. Facing me, back to the window behind a big desk, I recognised the Comte d'Hector, having already seen him when he inspected *l'Amazone* on our return to Brest.

'Monsieur de Kermean,' said the Comte de Lapérouse, addressing the third man in the room 'your nephew does not seem to appreciate your insistence on interrupting his career.'

'Nor do you, Sir,' replied my uncle, 'but I'm not at all surprised at Laforest-Dombourg, knowing him as I do.'

I was so surprised at seeing my uncle in this office at Brest that I almost forgot to greet the Comte d'Hector.

'I have made you wait, Monsieur Laforest-Dombourg,' said the latter, acknowledging my greeting, 'and I hope you will forgive me. Your captain was trying to get me to cancel your orders. Unfortunately for you, that is not in my power. The interests of the Ministry, which the Chevalier de Kermean has just outlined to us, seem to take precedence. He will explain to you what it is all about, for sure. I myself would be unable since he has said nothing about it, except that Monsieur de Fleurieu and the Marquis de Castries have decided to assign to you a mission of the greatest importance which, it seems, you are the only one able to accomplish.'

I had the impression that the Comte was slightly exasperated, but there was a hint of kindliness in his eye.

'I am in the same position,' added the Comte de Lapérouse. 'For heaven's sake, Chevalier! We have travelled together from Versailles in the same carriage and it's only this morning you tell me that I must lose my young first lieutenant, who I have trained myself! And that I must find a replacement for him even though I must be ready to put to sea at midday!'

'There is nobody more regretful about this than I, Sirs,' replied my uncle, in a tone that plainly belied his words, 'and I ask you to forgive me. Unfortunately, the demands of my job sometimes impose a need for discretion that verges on rudeness. I admit that, and I find it deplorable, believe me. Now, I have to talk alone with Monsieur Laforest-Dombourg, to explain what is expected of him. Tell me, Captain, how much time can you spare me?'

'Well,' replied the Comte de Lapérouse, looking at the clock. 'I am intending to leave the port in an hour to pick up a coffin buoy, but at the moment the winds don't allow us to leave the harbour. I fear that will last all day or even several days. Alas, I believe that you will have plenty of time for coming aboard. All the same, I will fire a cannon to warn you.'

'I will put a boat at your disposition, Chevalier,' said the Comte d'Hector. 'Where would you like it to wait for you?'

'Good! I think that I will lunch with my nephew while giving him his instructions,' replied my uncle. 'Which inn do you use, Pierre-Marie?'

'*La Dame au Paon*,' said the Comte de Lapérouse on my behalf, smiling again.

'It's on the Brest quay,' said the Comte d'Hector. 'I'll have orders given immediately for a boat to wait for you there at the start of the afternoon.

'And my luggage?' asked my uncle.

'It can go with mine,' replied the Comte de Lapérouse, 'and I will have Monsieur Laforest-Dombourg's chest taken to *La Dame au Paon*.'

'No, bring it here, so that Laforest-Dombourg can leave for Versailles this evening. I have talked about it with the post people. They have a post-chaise available. That's just what's needed, as my nephew will be travelling alone and he can go more quickly in that than the carriage that brought us from Paris.'

That is how I learned that, while I was leaving *l'Astrée,* my uncle was going aboard as a passenger. This did not allay my worries. I remembered that when I was still a boarder at the Saint-Yves College in Vannes, and had decided to enrol as a Volunteer in the Navy, it was my uncle who took the initiative, without consulting me, to enter me as a cadet at the Marine Guards at Brest. This despite him knowing that to be accepted I would have to prove four quarters of nobility, which I did not have. I admit that he had eventually resolved this difficulty very cunningly, but at the start I had had a very bad moment when I learned, from a letter which he had sent me, that my candidature had been presented to the King, as required, and that 'all that remained was to present my proofs of nobility.'

*

Brest, Wednesday 20th December 1780, midday.

I am on the first floor of *La Dame au Paon,* in a small private room where I had dined once with Flaharn on a snowy day like this one, on the evening of 17th January 1777, a date I have never forgotten. That was the moment I had begun to suspect that my dangerous mentor was playing a double game. This time, it is for lunch with my uncle. Even though it is the middle of the day, it is so dark that one would hardly have known. The candles on the table have been kept lit. I go to the window to watch *l'Astrée* go past. The snow has stopped and a little breeze has got up from the west.

At last, I see *l'Astrée.* She is coming out of the Arsenal and passes right below my window, rounding the corner of the Recouvrance quay, guided in the ebb current by her sloop and big boat. Her yards are swayed up, all the halyards are taut, and the topmen are finishing casting off the foretopsail and mizzen topsail gaskets. Sailors are lined up on the fore and after decks, ready to haul in the sheets. I recognise my replacement, the Chevalier de Karreg, standing beside the small capstan forward, next to the Chevalier de la Jonquière. I see the Captain on the quarterdeck, with his Master Pilot. The Bosun is waiting on the starboard

27

gangway, loudhailer in hand. My two friends, the Lieutenants, are in the ship's boats. The big white ensign, on its stern pole, floats gently in the turbulence. The topmen come down to the deck. The frigate passes the Brest quay and goes slowly off beside the Chateau. She turns to port and I see the fore topmast staysail go up from her bowsprit. The brails are released, the fore and mizzen topsails set, and she disappears behind the last bend in the river, heading for the exit between the Rose and the Horseshoe. It's done! I have no ship and no prospect of one. It is the first time since my Marine Guard examination by Monsieur Bézout in May 1777. When will I go to sea again? When the war is over? The opportunities are so rare, and the places will be taken by those who know better than to distinguish themselves in a Versailles office. It was just as well I put back my marriage plans with Maria Kirwan!

'I know what you are feeling, but I had no choice.' My uncle has come to stand beside me. 'If I had not been ordered to leave with the Comte de Lapérouse, I would not have had to find someone to replace me, but I am glad it is you. Come! Let's eat. I will explain everything.'

A servant puts the hors d'oeuvres and a steaming pot on the table. Maria Kirwan supervises, uncorking two bottles and filling a glass that she hands to the Chevalier de Kermean.

'Is this room to your liking, Sir? We have just added logs to the fire. I will shut the door on the landing and nobody will disturb you, as you asked. If you need anything just pull on this cord and I will come up myself. I hope the wine is to your taste. I bought it from a wine merchant who supplies the Navy Commander. As for the main course, as I did not know that you were coming, it is what is left over from today's meal, reheated: rack of lamb *à l'anglaise,* with turnip and celery. I hope you will forgive me.'

The Chevalier tastes his wine with little sips.

'Ah, these sailors! They never stop complaining but they know how to choose their wine! I hope that the Comte de Lapérouse has shipped the same one. As for the English dish, you are forgiven, Mademoiselle. At the moment it is the done thing to eat the English.'

A sparkle dances in my uncle's blue eyes and his face lights up at his witticism. I myself am not in the mood for joking, and wonder why the instructions that the Chevalier is about to give me are so secret that not even my commander or the Comte d'Hector are to know of them. And I am anxious!

Maria notices this and looks at me in a deliberately questioning way.

'Will you be staying long in Brest?'

The Chevalier answers for me.

'Monsieur Laforest-Dombourg must leave Brest this evening. As for me, I will be going aboard the Comte de Lapérouse's frigate which has just passed your windows.'

So I will be setting off tonight, I think. Maybe it's for the best, as I won't have time to reflect on everything.

Maria Kirwan leaves us, closing the door behind her. My uncle takes his place and invites me to sit opposite him.

'What a pretty girl! She seems to know what she is doing, too. It seems she is in charge here. I am impressed! I can understand why you like this inn!'

I am about to explain my relationship with Maria Kirwan but change my mind. We have too little time to be able to broach such a delicate subject, and I am anxious to know what the future holds for me.

The Chevalier refills his glass and serves me too. He has taken on his serious look. He clasps his hands under his chin and collects his thoughts for a moment.

'It's all because of that cursed chest,' begins the Chevalier.

I interrupt him.

'You mean the chest of diamonds?'

'Indeed! The diamonds that the late Marquis de Kersalaun deposited with your parents...to their misfortune!'

'But surely you have delivered them to the King, haven't you?'

'No! They are still in their hiding place, which only three people know of: my father, you and me. That's one of the reasons why you were chosen to replace me when the Marquis de Castries announced that he had decided to send me to Philadelphia, following an unexpected request from Benjamin Franklin. Your grandfather would never have accepted a stranger.'

'You mean I have been taken off my ship just to go to ask the Baron de Kermean to give this treasure to the King?'

'That is part of it, I admit, but not all. Let me finish, please!'

My uncle instantly regrets having raised his voice.

'I'm sorry. Frankly, you see, I don't want to go to New England. A week ago, believe me, I was far from thinking that I would have to pass on to you a mission waiting for me in India.'

I jump. I didn't expect that!

'In India? A mission?'

The Chevalier looks at me with a smile.

'Yes indeed, in India! You didn't really think that I would have torn you away from your dear commander to let you rot in an office in Versailles? I can promise you that within the next six months you will be enrolled on a ship for a campaign in India. Nonetheless, you will have to put up with a little unpleasantness…at first.'

I scarcely hear this warning. India! My father had made several voyages there. I had dreamed of it when I embarked on *l'Amazone*. India was to be the initial destination when the Comte de Lapérouse took command.

'A small unpleasantness…I will come back to that in a minute,' continued my uncle. 'But let's begin with these diamonds. Before talking to anybody about them, I took ten or so at random from the chest left by my poor sister and took them to Paris to be valued by a jeweller. According to him I could have sold them for twenty-four thousand six hundred and ten pounds. The diamonds are all of a similar shape and size. I haven't counted them individually, but I would say there are several hundred, perhaps five hundred.'

I make a rapid mental calculation.

'That would make more than twelve million!' I say. 'You could build eight ships of the line with a sum like that.'

'Indeed,' replies my uncle. 'I made a similar calculation. Twelve million! It seems a huge sum! And it is! Even compared to the whole of Navy expenditure it's by no means negligible. As you can well imagine, Monsieur de Sartine is very interested in my proposition. The only trouble is that to raise this sum we would have to sell the diamonds.'

'Is it difficult to find buyers?' I ask.

'Oh no! Not at all! Between Paris, Amsterdam and Brussels you can find all the buyers you want, as long as the sale is guaranteed by the Crown. The problem is Monsieur Necker. He would without doubt get wind of this inflow of extra money, and the Ministry of Finance would reduce by an equivalent amount the meagre sums the Navy gets each year. At the end of the day we wouldn't gain anything.'

'Monsieur Necker? Hasn't he accused Monsieur de Sartine of siphoning off state funds?'

'That is pure slander,' replies the Chevalier, 'but it gets us to the heart of the problem. I'll tell you why in a moment, but first, let me explain the solution we have found and your role in it; a much easier role than mine would have been had Benjamin Franklin not asked for me to be sent to America.'

The Chevalier stops talking to refill our plates.

'Why have the Americans asked for you?' I ask.

'To help them fight more effectively against English spying. For Heaven's sake! What can I bring them in addition? I honestly don't see what use I can be to them, especially as I don't speak English well. But I know who is behind this idea. A Doctor Baldock. I rank highly in his estimation and Franklin hangs on his every word.'

'Who is this Doctor Baldock?' I ask.

'Edward Baldock…but eat or it will get cold. Officially he is a physician, diplomat and member of the American delegation at Paris. In reality he does for Benjamin Franklin more or less what I do for the Secretariat for the Navy and Colonies, if you see what I mean. He's very efficient, too. He has been very useful to us, on three occasions in particular. Twice at our request, which I will tell you about in a minute, but the first time he came to us of his own accord with some excellent intelligence. That's when an understanding started to develop between us. I can talk to you about it because it touches on somebody you yourself recruited but who betrayed us: Louis Duval whom you met at Saint-Malo.'

I am now all ears. I remember Louis Duval very well. He was the main object of my mission in July 1777. At that time my uncle had spoken with Flaharn, when the latter was the Comte d'Estaing's right-hand man. Flaharn had told him that Duval was able to provide intelligence of interest to the Navy, and I had been sent to meet him. His sources had enabled us to set up communications with Cornish smugglers. These had provided us with information on the movements of Royal Navy ships, in return for payments in piasters. Their messages were picked up at night on the Devon coast, by the cutter *le Moucheron*, of which I was a crew member.

'What happened with Duval?'

'Well, last June, Doctor Baldock, whom I still did not know personally, suddenly approached me to tell me – listen to this! – that one of their agents, who had managed to get himself into the offices of the intelligence services in London, had discovered that the English knew that our cutter *le Moucheron* was spying on them in the Channel. They even knew her captain's name – Le Meur. Baldock was able to give it to me. The English informer was a certain Duval, residing in Saint-Malo. Baldock could not have invented all that on his own, and the authenticity of this intelligence cannot be doubted, when you think that here, in France, those three names – *le Moucheron,* Le Meur and Duval, as well as their roles, were only known to a small number of people, all sworn to secrecy and all reliable. Except Flaharn, of course, but he has been dead for a year and so is out of the picture. According to Baldock, the English were preparing to send a corvette and a frigate to board our cutter the next time she came out. We ordered Le Meur to stay in port and kept an eye on the Channel. At the beginning of July an English frigate and corvette were seen cruising regularly off the Chausey islands. We arrested Duval immediately. At the moment he is in the Bastille on the order of a *lettre de cachet*[5]. We are waiting for the results of an inquiry to discover the extent of his treason and his accomplices. He will then be subject to the King's justice and will certainly be condemned and hanged.'

This story seems improbable, though I cannot say exactly why. Certainly, as far as I remember him, Duval had his faults. He liked his drink and he was not a paragon of virtue. Even so, could the English have bought him? I have trouble believing it. I have a feeling that there is an important element in this story which has not been considered and which I cannot quite put my finger on. I tell my uncle this, but he says that time is pressing and that I can talk about it with Monsieur de Fleurieu when I see him at Versailles.

'In the end,' continues the Chevalier de Kermean, 'it was the Comte de Broglie who found a way of using these diamonds to support the war effort without Necker noticing. As you know, we have long wanted to open a second front in our former colonies in India, to strike the English at the source of their wealth, but our means are limited and we are still concentrating on America.'

'Are you going to revive the Chevalier de Ternay's old plan?' I ask.

'Not exactly. Ternay wanted us to operate on the Malabar coast, on the north-west of the peninsula, to seek an alliance with the Moghul.

---

5   Translator's note: *lettre de cachet*: a letter signed by the King authorising someone's imprisonment without trial.

This time, it will be on the east coast, in the Carnatic and Coromandel. At the moment we have a powerful ally there, the Nabob Hyder Ali Khan. He too is at war with the English. He is a difficult ally, always complaining about our inaction, and has asked for reinforcements several times. We are thinking of sending a squadron over there soon with several battalions. We need the Nabob's support to pay and feed these troops, but he wants control of them, which we cannot accept. Our refusal could well lead to Hyder Ali abandoning the war and returning to his home in the west of the Deccan. But if we bring him this treasure as compensation, he might be more understanding. Moreover, there will be no need to sell the diamonds. They can be transported as they are. Indian princes are more used to handling this kind of wealth than we are. Before talking to the King about it we floated the idea with Monsieur de Vergennes, the Foreign Minister, who was just as concerned, and who agreed with us.'

I start to get worried. Good Heavens! I am not a Squadron Chief, nor a Ship's Captain. There cannot possibly be a major role for me in this plan.

'But uncle, you told me that I was to replace you on a mission to India, but I am only a Ship's Ensign. What is it about exactly?'

'Well, initially, the mission that Monsieur de Sartine and Monsieur de Vergennes wanted to entrust to me was to deliver the diamonds to the Nabob, while at the same time communicating our wishes and intentions. It was a real diplomatic mission!'

'But I'm not a diplomat!'

'Nor am I. But then they found a real diplomat who knows India and speaks their dialects. He was a gift from Heaven for them and they thought I was no longer suitable for the task.'

This initial explanation leaves me even more perplexed. I am just a sailor and don't know Indian languages any more than he does!

'I had actually thought about this language problem,' continues the Chevalier. 'For that I had found a very reliable fellow called Rollin, from Alsace, fifty-two years old. He had started in India as a Surgeon in the Lorraine regiment. After the fall of Pondicherry he had joined Hyder Ali Khan and been his personal physician for five years. You couldn't ask for better, could you? He had an excellent knowledge of Mysore and the Coromandel coast, and spoke Tamil and Persian better than a sacred cow! I think he had returned to France to present a paper to the Royal Academy of Sciences, having authored an essay on the animals and plants of the Deccan. That didn't happen; I don't know why. Once back in France he had resumed his Army service and ended up in Paris as the military doctor at the Gros Cailloux Hospital at the headquarters of the Gardes Françaises, where he was bored out of his mind. I had no trouble convincing him. Obviously, I didn't mention the diamonds. Unfortunately, as I just said, that was when the two Ministers found someone to replace me on this mission.'

The Chevalier pours himself another glass. I have not touched mine.

'This is what happened. Last September Monsieur de Sartine, when he was still the Navy Minister, received a note from a man called Tallebau, the so-called Chevalier de Saint-Luperce, who was asking for his help from the Bastille, where he had been held for several weeks. Take note of the name, as you might meet him along the way, and you mustn't trust him. Monsieur de Sartine and the Comte de Vergennes attach great importance to this Saint-Luperce, having sent him, about three years ago, to Poona, in the north-west of India, with the rank of King's Emissary to the Maratha Court. It seems that he had negotiated a brilliant trade and friendship treaty between the King and the Maratha Emperor. Monsieur de Sartine thought he was still in Poona and was astounded to find that his protégé had left India, then been arrested and dragged to the Bastille when he arrived at Marseilles last August. Having made enquiries, not without difficulty, of the Secretary of State for the King's House, who did not want to tell us anything, we learned that Saint-Luperce had been arrested on the request of a Bordeaux shipowner, who had asked the King's authorities to issue a *lettre de cachet* against him. This shipowner accused him of using the voyage of one of his ships to India for his personal profit. As for Monsieur de Sartine, he swore that Saint-Luperce had no personal interest in it and was acting purely in the King's interest. This Saint-Luperce speaks all the Indian languages and affects to know intimately a number of Rajas and Nabobs, including Hyder Ali Khan. He has written several memoranda for the Ministry which have been much admired by Monsieur de Sartine and the Comte de Vergennes. For them he has become the ideal person to oversee this mission. It would not have taken much for them to send him to the Baron de Kermean to retrieve the chest of diamonds still hidden in the chapel. They did not really need me then, except for one thing...'

'Forgive me for interrupting, uncle, but how can he replace you if he is in the Bastille? I'm told you don't get out so easily.'

'That's exactly why they needed me: to get him out of the Bastille.'

'You?'

'Yes! I'll explain. Saint-Luperce was imprisoned on a so-called *'petit cachet'* letter, as it was requested by a private individual. There was no reason for him to go to the Bastille in Paris, which is normally reserved for *'grand cachet'* letters. Examining things more closely, Sartine and the Comte de Vergennes concluded, rightly or wrongly, that Maurepas and Necker were behind the anomaly. If this were the case, it would be difficult for them to ask for the liberation of their rare bird. So they asked me to ask Doctor Baldock to help us. It was the last straw! I was being ordered to act against my own interests!'

Baldock again! It seems to me that this strange doctor is mixed up in lots of things. Is it because, even without knowing him, I am angry at his involvement in the arrest of Duval?

'But uncle, how can a French Minister so lower himself as to ask a foreigner, a rebel against his own Crown, moreover, to intervene in the matter of a *lettre de cachet?* I thought they were guaranteed by the King, or am I mistaken?'

'You are not mistaken and I had the same reaction. But don't forget that it was in reality no more than a *petit cachet*, in which case, to free Saint-Luperce, it only needed the original complaint to be withdrawn. And we have learned that the shipowner who sought the Royal injunction against Saint-Luperce is a keen supporter of the American cause. So Monsieur Sartine, with the Comte de Vergennes' agreement, asked me to get Baldock to contact our Bordeaux shipowner and let him know that in spite of his faults, Saint-Luperce was a valuable agent for the Insurgents and that they wanted him freed. I was not keen on the idea, as you can imagine. While secretly hoping that he would refuse, I was at the same time ashamed of having to carry out such an embarrassing task. To my great regret, Baldock welcomed my proposition, but on one condition only: that he first meet Saint-Luperce to assure himself of his honesty. Monsieur Sartine asked his friend Pierre Lenoir, who had succeeded him as head of the Paris police, to issue a safe-conduct to the American authorising him to visit our prisoner in the Bastille. Several weeks later the Chevalier de Saint-Luperce made a dashing reappearance in the corridors of the Ministry of Foreign Affairs and the Navy. But in the intervening period the Marquis de Castries had replaced Sartine, which changed things radically.'

'Had the Marquis de Castries told Necker everything?' I ask.

'Not at all. There is nothing to worry about in that regard. He has even less reason than his predecessor to reveal our plan to the Ministry of Finance.'

'I thought that the Marquis de Castries was a friend of Necker, who recommended him for the Navy.'

'It's exactly because he knows him well that he wants to keep things secret. What has changed is that the Marquis de Castries is a proper military man. He loathes flashy schemers like Saint-Luperce. Unlike Sartine, he would prefer to deal with a former colonel like myself. Moreover, I have served on campaign with him, which helps. I was in Germany with him during the last war and he knows me well. Thanks to Rollin, whose service as a military doctor was important in the Marquis's eyes, we could do without Saint-Luperce. Once again I was to leave for India. You can imagine how I happy I was, while Saint-Luperce was sulking! But then, a few days later, crash! Rollin died suddenly.'

'How did he die?'

'In his bed. Although his landlady told the police that before he died Rollin told her he had been poisoned. Her husband said Rollin's death did not surprise him, as his lodger was well known for his debauchery, and died from his excesses. The local police inspector had the body examined by a doctor, who could not say whether or not it was death by natural causes, and advised me to consult a doctor who was well versed in cases of poisoning. It happened that I had one at hand – Edward Baldock, who has written a remarkable work on natural history which includes a study of poisons. I asked him to examine Rollin's body, which had been taken to the Grand Châtelet. He again demonstrated his goodwill by responding quickly. He concluded by backing up what the landlady's husband had said: Rollin was no longer a young man and had for too long led a disorderly life in unhealthy climates. I myself had not noticed that, but as Baldock said, in order to do so I would have to have been a doctor myself. Of course, I didn't tell him why I was interested in an army doctor at the Gardes Françaises, and he didn't ask why. Once again my voyage to India was off. Saint-Luperce and Monsieur de Vergennes were happy.'

'You say you weren't going? But what about me?'

'Oh, their joy was short-lived. At that moment the Marquis de Castries received a complaint from the Bishop of Langres on behalf of one of his Abbots. The latter accused Saint-Luperce of having defrauded him of sixty thousand pounds, which the Abbot was claiming back. This complaint was related to the Bordeaux shipowner business. When Saint-Luperce was preparing to leave on his diplomatic mission to Poona in 1776, aboard one of the shipowner's vessels, he had tricked the Abbot's younger brother. Saint-Luperce had dazzled the young man with promises of a post as 'Director-General of Trading posts to be established on the Malabar Coast', or some such thing. In reality, this crackpot promise ended up persuading the elder brother to buy cheap goods and entrust them to Saint-Luperce, who said he would do his best to sell them at a good profit for the Abbot. The Marquis was roundly amused at the financial misfortunes of a cleric whose principal vocation ought not to have been commercial speculation. However, although he accepted that Saint-Luperce was competent as regards India, he questioned his morality, and asked me to make discreet enquiries about his previous activity. I did some research and even had Saint-Luperce secretly watched. I have left a file at Versailles in which you can read the reports of the tails and spies I sent after him in Paris. It is imperative that you ask Monsieur de Fleurieu to let you see these documents. They are held in a steel cabinet in his office.'

The Chevalier fills his plate a second time.

'This English *ragoût* is excellent! Eat! You will be travelling tonight.'

I force myself to swallow a few mouthfuls.

'Since we couldn't do without Saint-Luperce, we have agreed to use him. But only as an intermediary, without telling him anything until the last moment. The Marquis de Castries decided to tell him only that he was to be sent to the Île-de-France, where he would take his orders from the Vicomte de Souillac, Governor of the Mascarenes. It is only then that he will be told what is expected of him. I was to keep a close eye on him when we were in the Carnatic. But now I'm not going! The Marquis de Castries asked me to find a replacement and it was Monsieur de Fleurieu who had the idea of suggesting it should be you. The Minister thought it an excellent idea, even better than having me go; he even said that your present position gives you advantages over mine.'

My initial disquiet starts to return. None of this seems clear to me.

I cannot see what advantages my 'present position' can confer on the success of this mission. My uncle says it's only about watching Saint-Luperce. Fine! But from what I have just learned he is a skilled diplomat who knows India well, and the fact that he seems also to be something of a trickster, cunning too, does nothing to reassure me. I'm a bit young to keep an eye on a fellow like this!

'Don't worry!' says my uncle, smiling as if he has read my thoughts. 'You will only be asked to fetch the diamonds from my father's house and take them aboard your ship with your baggage. You won't have to watch Saint-Luperce. You will possibly be asked to join the delegation to carry a confidential letter from the Comte de Broglie. This letter, to the King's representative at the Court of the Nabob, will say that the French officers and soldiers forming a free-serving unit in Hyder Ali's army are not deserters but on a secret mission under the control of a Brigadier-General at Versailles. Even the Governor of the Mascarenes is unaware of this. It was the Duc de Choiseul who launched this operation in 1770. So this mission is within your capabilities. And what also pleases the Minister is that a Ship's Ensign like yourself can be sent at any time as an officer aboard any King's ship leaving for India from Brest or L'Orient without attracting attention. Moreover, you are the only one apart from me who could go to Kermean without arousing suspicion. Nobody will notice you! Apart from a few in the know, like Monsieur de Fleurieu or the Comte de Broglie, nobody at Versailles is aware that you are my nephew. You are too young for anybody watching to think that you have taken my place. However, the Minister has added a small additional cover story that could cause you some unpleasantness.'

Once again, I am all ears, as I had forgotten about this 'unpleasantness'.

'We thought it might be seen as somewhat peculiar to disembark a Ship's Ensign from his frigate to send him to Versailles when we are in the middle of a war. So, to allay any suspicions, it will be made known around the Ministry's corridors, on the Marquis's order, that you have been quarantined in an office to suppress a scandal. Nothing dishonourable, I assure you! According to this fictitious rumour, you will have issued a challenge to an Army officer serving in the Comte de Rochambeau's regiment in America. Given your history of duelling, the Marquis de Castries thought it wise for you not to return there. He will have been alerted by the Vicomte de Rochambeau. There is nothing in it, of course, but as a precaution, we have asked the Vicomte, who is still in Versailles, not to deny the rumour if asked about it.'

The things that reputations hang on! I have only once in my life wanted to provoke a duel. This was against Colonel Guypair. I had stood in front of him, issued my challenge and had hardly finished speaking before I was thrown in jail. Guypair wanted me to be hounded out of the Navy! I was lucky to be saved by the kindness of the Marquis de Langeron, the Commander of Brest, who was good friends with my previous senior officers at Saint-Malo.

'But uncle,' I say. 'Doesn't that risk having every Champion from the Versailles garrison seeking a quarrel with me?'

'And you will have good reason to turn down their challenges without appearing a coward. All the same, I cannot overstress how important it is that you go to the fencing halls religiously, so that everybody can judge your real skill at swordsmanship. If you haven't lost your touch that could dissuade any challengers. And you need to pass the time before leaving for India. You will go discreetly to Kermean to fetch the diamonds and give them to the Vicomte de Souillac when you arrive at Port-Louis on the Île-de-France. Meanwhile, nobody must suspect the existence of this treasure, and you must avoid Saint-Luperce like the plague. As you see, this mission is simple. You collect the diamonds from Kermean, take them aboard your ship, and deliver them to the Vicomte de Souillac. But it could turn dangerous, which is why we have taken all these precautions.'

Hearing that, I think to myself that during wartime a naval officer's life is not exempt from danger either, what with battles, storms and fatal illnesses. I wonder what additional dangers justify all the precautions the Chevalier is talking about.

'What is it you are really afraid of, uncle?'

'Well, if types like Flaharn get to hear that you are travelling the roads of Brittany all alone, with twelve million pounds in your saddlebags, do you think they will let such a fortune pass without trying for it? And what about spies in the pay of the English? If they get to know in advance the name of the corvette carrying such a treasure, you can be sure that two or three frigates will be watching for your departure from Brest.'

All that seems reasonable but still doesn't seem to justify all the measures they want to impose on me, especially this absurd story of a duel. I have the feeling that the Chevalier has not told me everything.

'If the Minister is so worried about my security, why doesn't he have me escorted to Brest by a detachment of cavalry? Wouldn't that be better than circulating unflattering rumours about me? And, while I understand the need for discretion, why has everything been hidden from the Comte d'Hector and my commander? Do you not have confidence in them? They are true patriots and know how to keep a secret!'

'You are right, Laforest-Dombourg. The Minister is not just worried about bandits on the road and English frigates. There is also Monsieur Necker. If he were to get wind of what was going on and asked the Comte d'Hector about it, do you really think we could ask him to lie? Better to avoid this dilemma. And what would the Marquis de Castries say to his friend who proposed him for the Navy?'

That's it then! I understand things better now. The choice of an insignificant person like me, and all these ruses, allegedly to keep me safe, were in reality no more than measures to keep the existence of the diamonds from the Director-General of the Treasury and to hide from him the fact that his great friend the Marquis de Castries was gently tricking him. I start to think that my stay at the Ministry at Versailles is not going to be much fun.

'But,' I ask, 'what sort of man is this Necker, whom I haven't stopped hearing about since getting back to Brest.'

'I'll tell you what Monsieur Necker is and what he isn't. Monsieur Necker is a banker and a humanist. He made a fortune at the end of the last war by speculating on the back of confidential information provided by friends in high places. Note that a lot of his clients were foreigners, the majority of them English. He is a fervent admirer of Jean-Jacques Rousseau and because of that wants to be seen one day as a benefactor of humanity. As for what he isn't, Monsieur Necker is not French. He is Swiss, Protestant rather than Catholic. For these two reasons he cannot have a direct relationship with His Most Christian Majesty and cannot sit on the King's Council. His representative in government is Maurepas[6], which explains a lot of things. It is Maurepas who had him brought to the Treasury. As Necker had political ambitions, he made himself

---

6   Translator's note: *Jean-Frédéric Phélypeaux, Comte de Maurepas* : At that time Chief Adviser to Louis XV1, following a long and chequered political career. He had been appointed Minister of the Navy at the age of 22, under Louis XV, a position he held for 26 years.

very visible at Court, saying he could finance the war with loans. Our benefactor of humanity now wants peace at any price. The financier is finding that the war is lasting much longer than he had anticipated. The interest on the loans he negotiated will be more difficult to repay. The banker in him regrets no longer being able to do business with London, and the Swiss in him couldn't give a damn whether the King's armies are successful or not. Having Maurepas as his main spokesman and not having access to the Council, he takes Maurepas' lies and exaggerations as Gospel. He has convinced himself that Sartine decides the Navy expenditure himself and that Louis XVI knows nothing about it. This spending, wished for by the King himself, has so far allowed the Navy to make a good showing against the Royal Navy, and has contributed to the prolongation of the war that Necker now wants to end. Not knowing how the King's Council really functions, he thought that the best way to force us to sue for peace with the English was to reduce Navy expenditure, and that to do that all he had to do was to rid himself of Sartine.'

'So his sacking was unjustified and the stories about it false?'

'It's a conspiracy, purely and simply! Contrary to what the honest Necker says, the Navy Minister has never acted improperly. On the contrary, he wrote to the King and to the Director-General of Finance to plead his cause and make them aware of his accounting.'

'But,' I asked, somewhat surprised, 'why didn't the King defend his Minister, since he was doing as he was asked?'

'For two reasons. Firstly, because Necker threatened to resign, which could have damaged Louis XVI. He softened this threat by asking for Sartine to be replaced by his friend the Marquis de Castries. The King also knew that our war expenses are largely financed by foreign loans obtained by Necker, who acts as the main guarantor for these lenders. The King also has as much confidence in the Marquis de Castries as in Sartine. Moreover, contrary to what the public think, both men respect each other and discussed matters at length during the handover. In accepting Sartine's departure, the King knew that the Marquis de Castries would maintain the same policies as his predecessor. He sacrificed Sartine, certainly, but in a letter he asked Maurepas to 'console him as best he could'. As for Naval expenditure, it will carry on in the same vein with the Marquis de Castries, as the demands have not changed. Once Necker realises this, he will demand control of the spending and again threaten to resign. We have to gain some time! That's why the Marquis de Castries himself is taking so many precautions to keep the matter of these diamonds secret. It is sad to have to say it, but our Minister fears his great friend Necker as much as the English spies, in matters relating to the war.'

The Chevalier stops talking and looks at me for a moment before asking if I have understood everything. I say that it all seemed a bit complicated at first, but I think I have grasped the gist of what he has told me…and not told me, I was tempted to add, but kept that to myself.

'Your task in this business will be very simple. Monsieur de Fleurieu will give you detailed instructions at the appropriate time.'

My uncle gets something out of his pocket and puts it on the table.

'You know what this is, of course?'

I lean closer. I see a little cloth packet, flat, in taffeta by the looks, about eight inches square. Silk ribbons twelve to thirteen inches long have been fixed at each of the four corners. I guess that these are to attach the thing around one's waist, hidden under clothing against the skin.

'It's the secret letter for our officer at the Nabob's Court?'

The Chevalier bursts out laughing.

'It's a sachet against sea sickness! You mean to tell me that you have never seen one?'

I never knew that such a thing existed, and when I tell that to my uncle, he looks perplexed. He tells me that the sachet contains a powder made up of crushed cinnamon, cloves, nutmeg and saffron, that is attached to the skin of the stomach, under one's shirt, before going on board. He has bought it in Paris, on the Quai des Augustins, from an apothecary who maintained that it was a sovereign remedy for stopping seasickness and violent vomiting.

It is my turn to laugh but I contain myself. I have trouble believing in the therapeutic value of this sachet, but if the Chevalier is really convinced of its efficacity, it could have a positive effect on him. Who knows? To reassure my uncle about my unfamiliarity with it, I tell him that I have never had any interest in remedies for seasickness, as I have never suffered from it.

3

I arrived at the Versailles post-horse stables early on the 23rd December, after two days and three nights of uninterrupted travel, except for lunch and dinner, all done at a gallop on the paving of the King's highway. The team of horses was changed at each post, of which there are nearly seventy between Brest and Paris. Since leaving, the weather had become wet and misty, Wednesday's snow having melted. It was no longer freezing but the cold was still there, damp and penetrating. A chaise is usually drawn by two horses, one in the traces and the other, ridden by the postillion, attached at the side and therefore separate and requiring great skill on the part of the latter. I had already travelled once in a stagecoach, from Vannes to Saint-Malo, in July 1777, in summer weather, stopping each evening to sleep. That was nothing like this more recent journey from Brest to Versailles in the heart of a rainy winter, shaken ceaselessly night and day, alone, squeezed into a narrow box between two big wheels.

*

Versailles, Saturday 23rd December 1780
     After a quick breakfast, I decide to present myself immediately to Monsieur de Fleurieu. When I ask the postillions at the post-house

where I should go, they say that the Navy and Foreign Affairs are housed together in a building in Old Versailles, the name of the part of town to the south of the Palace. They tell me that the simplest way to get there is to follow the Avenue de Paris, which passes in front of the staging post, and to cross a big parade ground up to the entrance of the first courtyard of the Palace. This is called the Ministers' courtyard, as it houses a wing occupied by the Ministers. From there I go round to the left of the Palace, to a street between the Ministers' wing and the north side of a big building called the Grands Communs and which houses the officers at the Court. I should then arrive at the top of the rue de la Surintendance, a road which descends between the south wing of the chateau and the west side of the Grands Communs. The War, Foreign Affairs and Navy offices are pressed together one after the other, going down, just after the Grands Communs.

The staging-post is the last building going out of Versailles on the Avenue de Paris, so I have to walk more than seven hundred yards to get to the gate of the Palace. This avenue is a windswept straight road a hundred yards wide, divided into three parades. Those on each side are lined by bare trees. The main thoroughfare, in the middle, is bordered by lamp stands carrying streetlights that are lit each evening. I am on a royal road!

I need to sleep and feel quite lost, all alone in the blustery winter cold of this grey early hour. I walk on the paved road in the middle in order to avoid the puddles. It leads to the Palace courtyard, converging with two other avenues coming from Sceaux and Saint-Cloud.

I come to the big parade ground in front of the Palace, bordered by two fine buildings. These are the Grand and Petit Royal Stables, where my maternal grandfather and uncle were both pages. My grandfather has told me all about it. I am still quite astonished to find myself here and wonder for a moment whether I am dreaming. Ahead I can see the buildings surrounding the Palace on the other side of the parade ground, a hundred and fifty yards further on. What strikes me more than anything is not so much the beauty of the whole, which I cannot yet appreciate from this distance, but its extent. It is not a Palace; it is a city!

The sky is still covered but the rain has stopped. Pale streaks of sunshine pierce the clouds behind me and light up the gilding on the gates of the Palace courtyard. A small group of people and some carriages are waiting for the opening of the gate, which is guarded by infantrymen in blue uniforms.

There is almost nobody about at this hour and in this weather, for which I am grateful as it saves me from the disapproving looks of any passers-by. Although my uncle had told me that it wasn't the done thing to wear one's uniform in Paris, either at the Court or in society, I am still wearing my regulation Navy officer's outfit. I still have in the bottom of my chest a blue cloth jacket bought three years earlier at a Nantes tailor, but I haven't worn it for a long time, and I discovered this morning that I had filled out and could no longer button it up decently. I go along the rue de la Surintendance, passing the Grands Communs and an intersecting street. Amidst these huge geometric buildings I feel as small as an inhabitant of the land of Lilliput, imagined by the Irish philosopher Jonathan Swift. I know Brest well, and the buildings bordering the Arsenal are justifiably renowned for their beauty and the harmony of their façades, but these Royal buildings at Versailles are even more imposing and majestic. Moreover, they are set off by their foundations of perfectly laid red bricks. I feel overwhelmed by this excess of grandeur and have a desire to flee.

Army invalids in blue uniforms guard the doors of the two buildings. I feel embarrassed in my Ship's Ensign uniform and hurriedly show them my order papers so as not to be taken for a ne'er-do-well. A guard takes me to a second-floor landing and hands me over to an usher. Having looked me up and down without the least sympathy, which I put down to my breaking etiquette by wearing a uniform, this self-important fellow signals me to follow him and we walk off along a wide corridor. On each side, through their open doors, I can see offices whose walls are hidden behind shelves loaded with wooden frames full of labelled documents. Clerks are writing at their desks or moving from one door to another with files under their arms. A silent feverishness, impressive to a visitor like me, dominates. Nobody raises their voice; everything is done *in a whisper*, as Ship's Lieutenant de la Jonquière would say. I know that this is where they write the commissions for the ships' commanders and where they prepare the orders for the King's Navy throughout the whole world. I have heard it said that even squadron commanders, absolute tyrants to their officers, are full of sweet talk when they come here to win the favour of these pen-pushers. The usher shows me to a room which must be an antechamber, as there is no desk and the walls are lined with chairs. Most importantly, a fire is burning in the hearth! The usher tells me to wait and goes off with my order paper. I choose the chair nearest the fire and sink with a sigh of pleasure into its padded back. It is warm and I have not felt so comfortable for a long time. I suddenly start to feel the effects of tiredness and lack of sleep.

*

Having arrived in the morning as the offices opened, I was awoken after sunset by the Director of Ports and Arsenals himself: Monsieur de Fleurieu. The corridors which were so full of life when I arrived were now deserted, cold and dark. Monsieur de Fleurieu had spent the day in a meeting with the Marquis de Castries and the Comte de Vergennes. He had returned to his office after the Ministry had closed, to find on his desk my order paper put there that morning by the usher. He was getting ready to go home, and if his private secretary had not asked the lackey who had alerted them to go and put a fireguard in front of the hearth in the room where I was sleeping, I might have spent the night all alone in the Ministry.

'Sir! A Ship's Ensign! You are Laforest-Dombourg, I presume? But what are you doing here still?'

Hearing this I wanted to leap to my feet, but my legs were so stiff from sitting down for such a time that I fell back onto my chair. I could not see Ship's Captain Fleurieu's face very well in the shadows. He talked with surprising warmth for a man occupying such a high position in the Ministry. He simply put his hand on my shoulder.

'When did you leave Brest, my boy?'

'Wednesday evening, Sir. I arrived here this morning. I think I must have fallen asleep.'

'Have you rested at least?'

I finally managed to stand.

'It looks like it,' said Monsieur de Fleurieu with a laugh. 'Well, if that's the case, and since you wanted to see me and we are both here, follow me.'

The Director of Ports and Arsenals had all the candles in his office relit. He sat behind his desk and asked his underlings to wait on the chairs in the corridor. Night comes quickly in December and I had no idea what time it was. Monsieur de Fleurieu asked me to sit opposite him. At that time he was forty-two years old. He had regular features with a straight nose, slightly narrowed eyes and a smiling mouth. This unpretentious and friendly man inspired my trust. He took my order paper from the desk and waved it in front of me to get my attention.

'The Chevalier de Kermean told you why you were taken off your ship?'

'Yes, Sir.'

'I can understand why you are so tired after this rapid journey that you weren't expecting. It's my fault as it was me who asked your uncle to get you here as quickly as possible. To be honest, we didn't really know when we would need you, so there was no real urgency, but it could be sooner than expected and we need to be ready. Did he tell you that?'

'No, Sir.'

A clock began to chime in the silence, interrupting Monsieur de Fleurieu. I counted seven strikes.

'I have spent the whole day with our two Ministers, after which we went to see the King, on account of recent events that could have consequences for the business you are involved in. That's why I came back so late. So you arrived at dawn. Where did you lunch? Where are you staying?'

I replied that I had left my chest at the post-house and that I had slept, without meaning too, on the chair where he had found me.

'I have reserved a room for you at the Grands Communs. It's only a little attic room, but the Grands Communs are full; there are a lot of people in Versailles at the moment, with Christmas approaching. The festivities will be smaller than usual this year, as the Royal family is in mourning following the death of the Empress Maria-Theresa[7] three weeks ago. You can dine with me tonight as my guest. We keep a store of town clothes for officers like you without a wardrobe. We will lend you some tomorrow. How long you will be here depends on the English and the Dutch. We have just learned that the Court at London broke off diplomatic relations with the Hague government three days ago. That is why we were with the King this afternoon. Unlike the Comte

---

7   Empress Maria-Theresa of Austria, mother of Marie-Antoinette. She died on 29th November 1780 at the age of 63.

de Vergennes, who thought that would never happen, the Marquis de Castries was expecting it. Already last Monday he had written to the Comte d'Hector to get him to prepare as quickly as possible a frigate and a corvette. These will be ready to put to sea at short notice for a sixth month campaign. I don't yet know their names, but we intend to send you aboard one of these ships with the Nabob's diamonds. You will be enrolled as a lieutenant.'

'And the Chevalier de Saint-Luperce?' I asked.

'He will travel with you as a passenger. He calls himself Chevalier as he maintains that he was awarded the Portuguese Order of the Cross of Christ, with the rank of Chevalier.'

I asked Monsieur de Fleurieu why a rupture between London and the Hague would hasten my departure.

'The bone of contention in all of this is the Dutch colony at the Cape, near the Cape of Good Hope, in South Africa. It's a necessary and important port of call for our ships travelling between the Mascarenes and France. It's also the supply point for the Île-de-France and the Île Bourbon[8]. We have been able to make use of it thanks to Holland's neutrality, but our Indian Ocean colonies risk finding themselves in a difficult situation if the English seize the Cape, which they seem intent on doing. We need to get there first and reinforce the Dutch garrison. The two fast ships we have on stand-by at Brest are first to take military advisers to the Cape to prepare for the arrival of our troops. Then they'll go to Port-Louis on the Île-de-France with the King's orders for the Governor, Monsieur de Souillac. That's why we want you to go with them. But we cannot start until the Dutch have asked for our help. Obviously, all this is confidential. You are only a Ship's Ensign, and a young one at that, but your past and the present circumstances persuade Monsieur de Castries and me to trust you. Remember never to put yourself in a compromising position as regards the King.'

The next morning, armed with a chit signed by the Director of Ports and Arsenals, I went to a tailor in the Ville Neuve, as the area to the north of the Palace was called. He immediately found a well-cut black outfit that fitted me perfectly. Monsieur de Fleurieu had also given me a ticket to attend Midnight Mass in the same pews as the Courtiers.

---

8   Translator's note: *Île-de-France*, *Île Bourbon*: the old names for the Indian Ocean islands now known as Mauritius and La Réunion.

This was a considerable favour, although I did not realise it at the time. I would soon learn that Louis XVI, who loved everything related to the Navy, had granted the Ship's Captain de Fleurieu the honour of his friendship, appreciating his competence and above all, I think, his unpretentious simplicity.

My grandfather, the Baron de Kermean, and his son, the Chevalier, had often told me about their time as pages at Versailles. They had explained that the Palace is a real town and that any subjects of the realm who so desired could pass freely through the famous rooms named after those painted on their ceilings: Apollo, Diana, Mercury, Venus. There were eight in all. I was amazed by the big gallery where I stood for a while amongst a big crowd waiting for the Royal family to come from their private quarters to the Mass. Somebody beside me asserted that the gallery of the Palace of Versailles was one of the most beautiful in Europe. Looking around me at the infinite number of mirrors reflecting thousands of candles, I could believe it.

The Queen Marie-Antoinette, followed by several ladies-in-waiting, came out first from her apartment. The King soon joined her and the procession formed up, with a page in front and two Scottish Guards bringing up the rear. At that time Louis XVI was twenty-six. Bigger than normal, he already looked like a robust, even solid, man. He walked a bit like a bear, swinging from one foot to the other. This impression of power was moderated by the friendly expression he showed to everybody and the natural goodness that shone from his clear eyes. In fact, he was short-sighted, but I did not know. The Queen carried herself in a more imperious and intimidating way than her husband. I was told that she forced herself to be like that in order to confuse the detractors who were always trying to catch her out. As they were in mourning, the sovereigns were not dressed in the festive clothes they would usually wear for such an occasion. Only the Scottish Guards wore shining coats of arms over their uniforms. The pages and officers of the guard wore blue and red outfits rather like my regulation uniform, but with more braiding. The black outfit that etiquette required I wear at least had the advantage of suiting every rank and financial situation. All the military men at the Court were dressed like this; that was how they were recognised, along with the Saint-Louis Cross worn by everyone I met. I found my outfit somewhat forlorn without a Cross and at first I envied the others, but was soon consoled by the friendly smiles of the beautiful ladies who were no doubt intrigued by my extreme youth.

I wrote to my dear Maria Kirwan, telling her about everything, except the smiling ladies, of course. I had no doubt that she would take it in the right way, but I did not dare write it in a letter.

On the morning of the 26th December, as advised by my uncle the Chevalier de Kermean, I went to see the officers of the Gardes Françaises to obtain permission to practise my swordsmanship in the drill hall close to the Grands Communs. This regiment was garrisoned at Paris, from where it sent detachments every four days to guard the King.

Going back to the Navy department, I noticed an unusually large crowd in front of the War Office. There were black suits, but also lots of uniforms with fancy epaulettes: high-ranking officers, brigadiers, infantry colonels, cavalry officers, some getting out of carriages parked in the rue de la Surintendance, others arriving on foot or on horseback. I was just about to enter the courtyard of the office for the Navy and Foreign Affairs when I thought I heard my name spoken in a loud and unfriendly way. I stopped and looked around but could see nothing happening. I thought it must have been coincidence, which was stupid, as my name is not too common. I entered the office and thought no more about it.

I asked one of the Navy clerks about this unusual collection of uniformed Army officers. He told me that they were all coming to pay court to their new Minister, but that they were wasting their time. I then learned that the War Ministry had been taken away from the Prince de Montbarrey, following various scandals, and despite the efforts of Maurepas to save him. Montbarrey had been replaced by the Marquis de Ségur, an old war-hardened soldier. He was covered in wounds and had lost an arm during the War of the Austrian Succession. It was said that he disliked intrigues and intriguers.

I started to go religiously, every morning, to the two Gardes Françaises drill halls. These strange wooden buildings were painted on the outside with *trompe l'oeil* making them look like Army tents. My uncle the Chevalier de Kermean had given me a taste for fencing at an early age, and even though I owed my real skill to Flaharn, I loved the heat and the special atmosphere in these temples of the sword, with their sounds of blade rubbing on blade and the precise, clear clicking of steel on steel. After fencing I usually stopped at the Grands Communs to change my shirt and then went for my orders from Monsieur de Fleurieu at the Navy department.

Five days after Christmas, while I was waiting in the Director of Ports and Arsenals' antechamber, a tall man came out wearing a red ribbon that I took for the Saint-Louis Cross. A little bigger than me, and well-built, he must have been about forty. He still had a trim waist and square shoulders. A great and disorderly mane of black and grey hair, worn naturally and knotted carelessly behind his neck, floated over his face. One would have thought his features to be too handsome and too regular, with his blue eyes and long lashes, were it not for his bold, rather heavy chin. His mouth was edged by two deep and vertical folds, no doubt the result of his permanently mocking expression. He was wearing a verdigris silk suit and carrying his sword. He nodded to me in what seemed a slightly ironic way as he went confidently past. His walk combined strength with nonchalance; women would like him.

'The Chevalier de Saint-Luperce!' Monsieur de Fleurieu chuckled to himself, seeing my astonished look as I closed the door behind me.

'He served in the King's Army?' I asked, still recovering from my amazement.

'Ah! The red ribbon? It's not the Saint Louis Cross. It's the Cross of Christ, a Portuguese Order. As far as I know he was never a soldier, although he makes out that he commanded Hyder Ali Khan's artillery at Kaveripattinam. We have to go and see Monsieur de Castries. He didn't say why, but we have had new information from our ambassadors and agents about developments between Holland and London, and on movements of English ships in the Channel. England is preparing a fleet of five ships for India that we are told will be commanded by Admiral Palliser. There may be two thousand men coming along with him, which is of interest to the Cape. And do you know who first gave us this intelligence, later confirmed by all our other sources? Captain Le Meur! Our Cornwall agents were surprised that the information they were attaching to the buoy in Salcombe Bay was no longer being picked up by *le Moucheron*. They asked Monsieur Régnier about it. He passed it on to us and the Saint-Malo commandant organised a meeting with them at Chausey. With our permission, Le Meur fitted out a lugger and started going back and forth across the Channel again. Unfortunately we can't use *le Moucheron* anymore.

This reminded me of the accusations made against Duval that the Chevalier de Kermean had told me about at Brest. When listening to that story I had had the impression that there was an incoherence somewhere in the reasoning leading to our former agent's arrest. This had been gnawing away at me for the whole of my solitary journey in the chaise. Once I had arrived at Versailles I had stopped thinking about it. Thanks to Monsieur de Fleurieu I now realised what it was that had upset me.

'Sir! My uncle told me that Duval was arrested because the English had sent a frigate and a corvette to cruise off Saint-Malo, and that proved that they knew about *le Moucheron's* movements because of Duval's treachery. That's the case, isn't it?'

'Yes, in effect.'

'Well then, Sir, why would they have taken the trouble to send two ships of war so close to our coast, with no guarantee of success, when they could simply have arrested our Cornwall agents and waited quietly for our cutter to come, suspecting nothing, and captured her without firing a shot? And you tell me too that the Cornishmen were not the least bit worried.'

'No doubt Duval did not know who they were and only knew about *le Moucheron's* role.'

'But with the greatest respect, Sir, Duval knew very well who they were. It was he who recruited them, it was he who told me that the Cornish smugglers were ready to sell us information, and it was to him that I passed on Colonel Dumouriez's wish to meet with them face to face. Duval was present at our meeting at Chausey. He had come on one of Régnier's luggers that he skippered.'

Monsieur de Fleurieu did not reply immediately but thought about it for a while.

'So, let's see…Baldock, or rather his agent, discovered the names of *le Moucheron* and her commander, along with that of Duval, in London. In any case, he could not have invented them. Could the Cornishmen be English agents? In that case they would give us false information and would certainly not have alerted us to English preparations for seizing the Cape. On the contrary, they would have tried to keep us in the dark. You're right. It is illogical. There is something strange going on. Since we have to go and see the Marquis de Castries, I can talk to him about it straight away.'

'I think,' I added, 'that it might be useful if I could visit Duval in prison to see if I can find out anything that may help us solve the puzzle.'

*

Versailles, Saturday 30th December 1780.

An usher announces us and the Marquis de Castries receives us into his office immediately. I am not feeling too confident at having to appear before a man reputed to be unparalleled in his capacity both to give and to refuse. I know too that he has just ordered the commanders of the Marine Guard companies to be much more rigorous as regards the proofs of nobility presented to them by prospective cadets.

The room is big. A map of the world and pictures of the main ports of France are hung on the white panelling edged in gold that covers the walls from floor to ceiling. I see too a big globe of the world placed on a pedestal table. My eye is drawn to a model of a ship on the corner of the Marquis's desk.

Our new Minister is a cavalry General and wants you to know it. He is wearing boots, and the red, silver-trimmed jacket of the King's Household Gendarmes, crossed with a blue sash. The Saint-Esprit Cross is sewn on his breast. The King's Household soldiers wear their regulation uniforms when serving at Versailles. The Marquis de Castries is not just the Navy Minister. He has remained head of the King's Household Gendarmes, as well as Lieutenant-Captain of the Scottish Company of the same corps.

Monsieur de Fleurieu presents me, then summarises what we have just learned about Duval. The Marquis de Castries has of course not summoned us to talk about that. He is friendly, but forgets to ask us to sit down while he patiently and politely waits for his Director of Ports and Arsenals to finish, all the while sitting erect in his chair. He is a handsome and distinguished man, with a regular but finely featured and energetic face. Below his immaculately powdered wig he is quite olive-skinned, with surprising green eyes. He tries to soften their effect, but I find them extremely intimidating.

'You know him well, this Duval?'

His tone is affable, calm and measured, but no-nonsense too.

'It was me who dealt with him at the beginning, Sir. I was assigned to make contact with him and was the only person he spoke with.'

53

The Marquis de Castries remains impassive, reflecting for a few moments before answering.

'I had completely forgotten about that. Up until now, as far as I know, Monsieur Duval has not admitted to anything. But if you think you can make him talk, then why not? Agreed! Do it! Go and visit Duval in the Bastille and see if you can unravel this mystery. But don't waste any time. Understood? Chevalier!' he continues, turning to Monsieur de Fleurieu, 'Prepare a letter for Monsieur Lenoir immediately. Saturday is the day he holds audience at his office in the rue des Capucines, near to the headquarters of the Gardes Françaises. We are going to ask him to have a safe-conduct prepared for Monsieur Laforest-Dombourg for visiting Duval at the Bastille on Monday. Give it to me as soon as it is ready, as we have to get it to the office of the Head of the Paris Police if we want it signed in time. Also have a letter written in my name to the commanding officer at the Gardes Françaises headquarters, asking him to provide food and a bed for Monsieur Dombourg from Sunday to Monday.'

The Marquis turns back to me.

'Ship's Ensign, you will go and see this Duval on Monday, then immediately return to Versailles. I want to see you here without fail on Monday evening. I will give you a chit authorising you to a horse from the King's stables tomorrow. I hope you can ride.'

Without waiting for my answer, the Marquis elegantly gestures to us to sit and looks at me once more with his green Sphinx-like eyes, before turning to Monsieur de Fleurieu.

'I have called this meeting because in ten days' time Monsieur Laforest-Dombourg will be sailing from Brest. I have just decided to have him appointed as first lieutenant aboard *la Sylphide,* a fourteen-gun corvette commanded by Ship's Lieutenant Corbel de Killéau. Monsieur Dombourg! As soon as you are back in Paris you will prepare to go and fetch these famous diamonds in Brittany and take them to Brest hidden in your baggage. Your mission will stop there as we have changed our original plans. *La Sylphide* will be carrying the King's latest orders for Monsieur de Souillac, on the Île-de-France. Also on board will be a Monsieur de Montigny, to whom you must immediately pass the chest. Monsieur de Montigny is our envoy to the Maratha Court at Poona. Montigny will be accompanied by this Saint-Luperce, but he will be able to keep an eye on him as he too speaks Persian and has wide experience of India. Once at the Île-de-France, Montigny will make a precise valuation of these diamonds. This is important because we will be giving them to the Marathas, but not as a gift! In exchange we will be asking them to provide pay, food and ammunition for the force we will be sending there, which will be as big as the Comte de Rochambeau's in New England. The Marquis de Bussy will be commanding it. The Marquis de Bussy and Monsieur de Montigny have convinced us that we should avoid compromising ourselves with Hyder Ali Khan and his son Tipu Sultan, who are only usurpers. If we were to align ourselves with them, we risk spoiling relations with the compliant princes, the Marathas and all the Rajas, who make up the only real force capable of seriously opposing the English in India for the long term. We will tell the Maratha Emperor and the Rajas that the King has no wish to conquer new territories at their expense but wants to help them chase out the occupying English, just as we are doing in America. I am only telling you this because Monsieur de Fleurieu has guaranteed your discretion. He has also told me how much you have suffered on account of these diamonds and that it is thanks to you that we will be able to use them to guarantee the success of the King's armies. We have of course not yet said anything to Saint-Luperce. We will let him know at the last moment. I think his abilities will be useful to us as he knows the Marathas well. But he must be kept completely in the dark. He still thinks that we are intending to make an alliance with Hyder Ali Khan, which is more than he ought to know. Nobody should have mentioned it to him. Your uncle, the Chevalier de Kermean, has complained about it, and as far as that is concerned at least, I agree with him.'

The Marquis stops talking. The meeting seems to be over. I stand up at the same time as Monsieur de Fleurieu to take my leave. My eye once more falls on the model of a ship on the corner of the desk. It is a small frigate rigged in the English style, with masts at less of a rake and with wider yards than ours. She has gunports for twenty cannons, probably eight-pounders, or nine-pounders if she is English, but half of them are missing. She has a spanker with a red and white striped American flag at the peak. Despite this last detail I have the impression of having seen this ship in real life somewhere. Forgetting myself, I lean over to read the tiny letters inscribed on the stern: *Ariel!*

I suddenly realise how impolite I am being and straighten up, mumbling my apologies. The Marquis does not seem to be annoyed. In fact for the first time he seems to lose his polite reserve.

'I had forgotten that you served under Monsieur de Lapérouse in the Americas! That's why you recognised the *Ariel.* Were you there when she was captured? Is she a good ship?'

'It was I who went aboard to take possession of her, Sir. Captain Mackenzie put up a good defence. We had twelve men killed during the action and our rig was so cut up that we had a devil of a job to launch our ship's boat. She is a pretty little frigate. Have we given it to the Americans?'

The Minister smiles openly.

'Only loaned her. To their John Paul Jones, so that he can take arms and ammunition to his compatriots. He left L'Orient at the beginning of the month. Before that he spent a lot of money re-rigging *Ariel* to his taste, to the displeasure of Benjamin Franklin who thought it a useless extravagance. When he came to Paris, Jones had this little model made, with the idea of using it to win over Franklin, who gave it to me. The Americans will give us the real one back as soon as she has unloaded her freight over there. I have sent a letter to Monsieur de La Luzerne asking him to give command of her to my nephew, who is at present a Ship's Ensign, on *le Neptune,* I think. You will know him, without doubt? He was on the Comte d'Estaing's campaign in 1779 at the same time as you, aboard *le Languedoc.*'

I can see that the Minister is happy to talk, and I tell him that his nephew was promoted to first lieutenant on the frigate *l'Hermione* who came with *l'Amazone* when we left Rhode Island.

When we are already at the door, the Marquis de Castries stops us.

'Monsieur de Fleurieu! Now I think about it, visits to the Bastille are normally held in the council room with either the Governor or his Lieutenant present. Make it clear in your letter to Monsieur Lenoir that it is imperative that the conversation between Laforest-Dombourg and Duval is totally private. The links between our Ministry and Duval are not for the ears of Monsieur de Launay, the Governor of the Bastille, and his various henchmen, who will be falling over themselves to report them to you know who… Talking about this Jourdan de Launay, I would say that although he once served in the cavalry, he can be rather capricious and pernickety. So have a letter prepared for me spelling everything out in detail. As for you, Ship's Ensign, treat Duval as you find him. I have confidence in you, but do not waste time with him! If you see that he refuses to talk, don't insist. The only thing of importance to us is what he told the English. Our inquiries and searches have yielded nothing, no clue at all. He is the only one who can enlighten us. That's why he is still in the Bastille. Otherwise, he would have been hung long ago!'

I think to myself that if Duval knew that, he would make sure he told me nothing.

As soon as we have gone out, Monsieur de Fleurieu asks me anxiously if I really do know how to ride. I reply that it is a while since I have ridden, but that my grandfather, the Baron de Kermean, had started me in the saddle when I was very young. I add that in my sea chest I still have a pair of riding boots that he gave me before I left and which I have never had the chance to wear.

'It's true that both your grandfather and uncle served in the King's Household cavalry.'

'Sir,' I then ask, 'the Minister is sending me to the headquarters of the Gardes Françaises. Isn't that where the doctor who died so inopportunely worked?'

Monsieur de Fleurieu seems surprised by the question.

'I didn't know you were aware of this story. Who told you about it?'

'My uncle. He only told me that Rollin's landlady said her lodger had been poisoned, but that wasn't in fact the case. At least not according to Doctor Baldock, apparently consulted because of his knowledge of poisons. Do you think that the Marquis de Castries may have decided to send me to the Gardes Françaises' headquarters so that I could make a discreet inquiry into the suspicious death of Rollin?'

'What on earth are you talking about? Good Heavens, no! I think the Marquis de Castries decided you should go to the Gardes Françaises' headquarters because, as he told us, it is next to the office where Monsieur Lenoir is right now. That enables us to get a safe-conduct for you straight away so you can visit Duval in prison on Monday. The Bastille Governor, Monsieur de Launay, is subordinate to the Head of the Paris police. Only the latter can give you a permit for this visit. My advice would be not to get involved in a business that was concluded some time ago. It won't bring Rollin back but it could displease the Minister. Moreover, the Gardes Françaises' headquarters is on the simplest, if not the most direct, route to the Bastille.'

4

On Saturday evening I posted a letter to Maria to let her know that I would soon be arriving in Brest to embark on a new ship, and that I hoped that contrary winds would delay my sailing for as long as possible.

On Sunday morning, after Early Mass, I went to the Grand Stable at Versailles and gave my chit to the duty head groom. Having received his orders the night before, he had already alerted the stable hands. My mount, saddled and bridled, was waiting for me in the courtyard. She was a young hunter, a bay mare with an almost black coat and a star on her muzzle, called l'Heureuse. At first sight she seemed sprightly and as soon as I was in the saddle, with her moving beneath me, I had the pleasure of finding that I was correct.

I set off towards the rising sun. L'Heureuse's hooves rang out gaily on the avenue de Paris paving stones. It was the first really fine day since my arrival at Versailles. There was no wind but the air was sharp. A fine frost covered the lawns of the gardens and the grass in the paddocks and a faint mist hung over the parks and fields stretching to the wooded hills to the east. After fifteen minutes I left the paved road and turned left to follow a winding track along the valley bottom to Sèvres. L'Heureuse had a gentle, pleasant trot which I kept up for three quarters of an hour until we reached the Seine. I put my mount at a walk to cross over to the other side on a wooden bridge supported by an island. The mist was clearing. Coming off the bridge I was met by a fine, tree-lined road leading off across the plain beside the river, now in full sunlight. I ignored it and launched into a trot along a secondary road to my left. I had decided to cut diagonally across the Bois de Boulogne, arriving at Paris by the Neuilly road. At Versailles I had heard it said that this route offered a unique view on the capital.

I went in via the south-west gate, called the Porte des Princes, as previous kings had used it to go hunting at La Muette. Once I was through the wall I found myself in a series of wide straight avenues cutting through stands of beech and oak. My hunter, who until then had stayed calm and docile, was no doubt enlivened by the familiar smell of damp moss and dead wood. She snorted noisily two or three times, bucking her head. I eased the reins and she set off like an arrow. The thick carpet of brown and yellow leaves covering the ground softened l'Heureuse's gallop. Leaning over her neck, well-balanced in my stirrups, I revelled in the riding skills that I thought I had lost after so many months at sea. Star-shaped crossroads passed one after the other. My mare ate them up so quickly I did not bother to count them. I kept straight on, heading for the sun still visible through the bare branches of the trees. At that speed, it took just fifteen minutes to reach the north-east gate of the wood.

I set off again at a walk on the road from Neuilly which rose gently towards the east. At the top of the slope I arrived at a circular plateau, about four hundred yards in diameter, on which eight avenues converged, forming a star. The capital of the realm now lay at my feet.

I went down at a steady pace until I had passed the tollgate, and then put l'Heureuse into a trot to cross an expanse planted with elms. This area had been named the Champs-Élysées, in line with the fashion of this and the last century for Greek and Roman mythology. Despite the end of December cold there were plenty of citizens out to stroll and take the air on this fine day. Noisy students were playing amongst the trees. There must have been a game of real tennis going on somewhere in the middle of the wood, as I could hear the sound of bats and racquets.

After another quarter of an hour at a trot I reached the entrance to the Garde Françaises' headquarters, with a sentry-box by the gate and above it a stone lintel engraved with the words:

HEADQUARTERS OF THE GARDES FRANÇAISES

There was no sentry in the sentry-box and the gate was open. I dismounted and, pulling my horse by her bridle, went into a deserted courtyard which opened up to a second, bigger one, as empty as the first. This was more than a little surprising and were it not for the inscription at the gate I would have thought I had the wrong address. I was about to retrace my steps when a sergeant in casual uniform came out of what must have been the guardroom. He told me that his captain had been warned of my arrival by a mounted policeman sent by the Lieutenant-General of Police, and that he was waiting for me.

Monsieur de Courteille, the commanding officer, was about to dine, and graciously invited me to join him. He had been given my safe-conduct, which he handed over to me. He explained that he was not just in charge of a simple barracks, but a school for the children of soldiers and non-commissioned officers who wanted to serve in the Gardes Françaises like their fathers. As it was Sunday and New Year's Eve, the pupils, who mostly lived in Paris, had gone home for a short break. As for the regimental band, which was usually quartered there, it had gone to play at the Court at Versailles. At that time there was just the Captain and his four sergeants at the barracks. I was surprised to learn that the future recruits of the Paris corps were learning to read and write. They were even being taught mathematics and German, which probably made their soldiers the best educated in the whole of the Army and Navy combined. In any case, I now knew why I had not seen any armed sentinels at the gate. Monsieur de Courteille went on by saying that because of all this he could not put me up here, but everything had been taken care of and he would give me a chit to stay at a boarding house in the area with which he had an agreement.

'Don't worry,' added the Captain. 'Paris boarding houses have a bad reputation, which is often justified. There is an inn close by, in the rue des Mathurins, but I'm not sending you there. The house we deal with is one of the most respectable. The owner is a well-known wine merchant and it's his wife who looks after the rooms. We have no one there at the moment, but our previous army doctor, who was a bachelor, used to lodge there.'

I asked him if he was referring to the army doctor Rollin, who died recently.

'Did you know him, then?'

I lied through my teeth, saying that I had never met him personally, but that my father had known him long ago, in Pondicherry. I asked him whether the doctor had really died suddenly from an old illness contracted in India, as people were saying.

'That's what we were told,' replied the Captain, 'but I can say it surprised us as he seemed to be in good health, which didn't please everybody.'

'What do you mean by that?'

Captain de Courteille began to laugh.

'I am talking about Monsieur Dutertre, the wine merchant who owns the boarding house. Strictly between the two of us, our doctor had well and truly brought him into the brotherhood.'

'The brotherhood?'

'The brotherhood of cuckolds! Anyway, it doesn't matter any longer. I'd advise you, though, if you see him, not to mention that your father was a friend of Rollin. The boarding house is at the end of the chaussée d'Antin, just before a private villa, on the right going towards the tollgate. It's less than fifteen minutes on foot from here but you could take a horse-drawn cab if you prefer, at the first crossroads on the left. We will have to look after your horse as it belongs to the King. You can't leave it anywhere, and there is no room for it at Dutertre's. You can come and collect it tomorrow morning.'

*

Paris, 31ˢᵗ December 1780, afternoon.

I arrive at the end of the chaussée d'Antin. I have come on foot, bringing as my sole baggage a bag taken off my horse's saddle. The sun is well down and the air is getting colder. A lot of people are walking in the same direction as me, and I am overtaken by several horse-drawn cabs. Everybody is heading for the café and dance hall at the tollgate.

The Dutertre boarding house is indicated by a small placard beside the entrance door. I bang the door knocker and am welcomed immediately by a competent-looking young housemaid in a green dress and muslin apron. I give her my lodging chit and she takes me into a little panelled room, pleasantly warmed by a fire. There is a roll-top writing desk and a couch on which a big grey cat is lolling. The maid chases it off and goes to fetch the landlady.

While waiting for the lady of the house I think about Monsieur de Fleurieu's injunction not to get mixed up in 'a business that was concluded some time ago,' which could displease the Minister. In fact, in my mind at least, I have already started to disobey everybody.

At first sight, Madame Dutertre matches the image I had formed after hearing Captain Courteille's indiscreet words about her. Thick wavy hair, held in place above her forehead by a gold-embroidered silk turban, cascades down her back. Two huge spiral earrings swing from her ears each time she moves her head. She has doused herself in lavender water and applied a hint of rouge to her cheeks, nicely setting off her dark skin. A little black blouse, drawn across her shoulders and tightened at the waist, completes her provocative look, emphasising her generous bosom and the curve of her thighs under her pink taffeta skirt. I immediately think that my uncle Kermean may well have been mistaken when he had asserted that Doctor Rollin had been 'bored out of his mind' in Paris. This first impression then fades under the clear gaze of her hazel eyes and the disarming earnestness with which she always talks, revealing her pure white teeth.

She invites me to sit beside her on the couch while she reads the chit from the commanding officer of the Gardes Françaises' headquarters.

'Monsieur Laforest-Dombourg, Ship's Ensign of the King. You are an officer?'

'A Naval officer, Madame.'

'So young! Have you already made many voyages?'

'I have been to the Americas twice and I am about to leave for India.'

I feel guilty, as I know that I have been expressly told to keep my departure for India secret, but I know where I am heading with this.

'For India! One of your predecessors here had also been in India,' she says with a sigh.

That was what I was expecting, and I take up the baton straight away.

'In fact, I have been sent here by the Minister for the Navy and Colonies to talk to you about him.'

'Oh!'

Her pretty mouth opens a little wider. It is just as well she has no means of verifying what I have just said! I take out of my jacket my order paper with the Navy Minister's heading and quickly show it to her, making sure she cannot see that it is addressed to the commanding officer of the Garde Françaises' headquarters asking him to provide lodgings for me.

'Is Monsieur Dutertre not here?'

She blushes slightly. Rollin must often have asked her that question.

'My husband is very busy today with the deliveries for the New Year festivities.'

Always the same old story, I think to myself: a pretty woman with a husband who is rich but seldom there.

'You told the local doctor that Doctor Rollin had been poisoned?'

'It was Pierre Rollin himself who told me that before he died. We were alone at the time…but the Inspector of Police thought I must have misunderstood. He thought that because my husband had told him that Rollin had been weak and ill for a long time. It's not true! I can assure you! Even that morning he was in full possession of his faculties!' She bites her lip and falls silent.

I do not press the point. I can well imagine that nobody was better placed than her to judge the good health of the late army doctor Rollin, but there is no way that she can confirm this to those making inquiries, especially in front of her husband.

'When did this happen?'

'Three months ago, in October. The fifteenth, I think. In any case, a Sunday, like today, but less cold.'

'What time was it?'

'It must have been about two in the afternoon.'

'I know it must be hard for you, but can you tell me in detail what happened that day?'

She looks at me and frowns, tightening her lips. There is no more open mouth showing her pretty teeth.

'You have nothing to fear from me. I simply want to be sure that we are not mistaken about Doctor Rollin's death. My father was his friend, you see. He knew him well in India. Rollin was the personal doctor of the Nabob Hyder Ali Khan. Did he tell you that?'

I feel somewhat ashamed of myself, but I have to gain her confidence.

She joins her hands in front of her face and closes her eyes as she collects herself.

'Yes, that's right. He spoke to me about the Nabob. So! My husband was out for the day and Doctor Rollin had stayed at home. It was a

Sunday and he was not working, you understand? He only went out at midday to lunch.'

'Where did he go?'

'To the *Porcherons* tavern, which is where he usually went. Then towards two o'clock there was a knock at the door. Toinon, my chambermaid, answered and came straight away to say that Rollin was ill. I ran to see. He was here in this room, here where we are sitting, stretched out on the couch. He was sweating and breathing noisily. He was trying to speak to us. His mouth was opening and shutting but nothing came out. I sent Toinon to get the local doctor. After she left Pierre Rollin managed to say a few words. I thought I heard 'nappel' which doesn't mean anything. Maybe it was 'appeal'. I thought he was appealing to me to help him. Then I clearly heard 'poison' and a word ending with '.andy', but I'm less sure of that. I took it that he was accusing someone of poisoning him. God forgive me! I thought first of my husband,'

That just slips out and she immediately looks at me anxiously.

'Don't worry,' I say. 'I have no intention of betraying you.'

'So I asked him if it was my husband he was accusing, but he indicated 'no' with his finger. So I asked him who it was but he could no longer speak. He just pointed to the cat that was in the room. He tried to say something like 'griffi' or 'griffé'. I don't know. Our cat is called Greffier, but why at his last moment would he think about a cat he had never cared for? After that he started to convulse and vomit. I went for a basin and towel to wash his face. His shirt was soaked in sweat, he was dribbling and had lost control of things down there, if you see what I mean. God it was horrible! He was always so clean and elegant! He bathed every day, you know? He said he had learned this from the Indians. He had the water brought himself so we would not have to pay for it. And Toinon had still not come back! This went on for almost half an hour. It looked like he was in terrible pain. He could no longer hear what I was saying and I'm not even sure he could see me, though he was still conscious. I'm sure of that as he was searching for my hand and gripped it hard when I gave it to him. After a while he became calmer and his breathing was gentler. I had the impression that he was not so feverish and began to feel hopeful. Then he suddenly died. I washed him completely and put clean clothes on him. I didn't want anyone to see my poor Pierre in that state. He was so handsome!

Soon afterwards Toinon arrived with the doctor who asked me about my lodger's death.'

She is quiet and obviously upset.

'And then?' I ask, after waiting a minute or so.

'My husband had been told, no doubt by the police. He arrived as the doctor was coming back with the inspector in the red coat to interrogate me. But when I started to say that my poor friend had perhaps been poisoned by the wine he had drunk at the *Porcherons* they objected loudly, my husband the loudest. It has to be said that for the last twenty years anybody who is anybody comes to drink at Ramponeau's and it's my husband who supplies him.'

'Who is this Ramponeau?'

'The owner of the *Porcherons*. He is the best-known innkeeper in Paris. And as he serves his wine more cheaply than anybody, even those outside the city limits, everyone goes to his place. And even high society still goes there from time to time, as his place was all the rage during the time of the late King Louis XV. He had an inn at La Courtille, further east beyond the boulevard. The great Voltaire himself once pleaded a court case for him. Can you imagine?'

'If he really was poisoned at the inn, it cannot have been too violent a poison, I would think. How far are we from the inn?'

'Oh, it is close by! Just after the neighbouring house, opposite the tollgate. A hundred yards at most. You can be there in less than two minutes.'

'And the doctor did not agree with you after you described Rollin's death throes?'

'I was afraid! I didn't dare speak about it in front of my husband. I have reproached myself for my cowardice. If you knew how grateful I would be if you could help me make peace with my conscience! You are going to look for his killer, aren't you?'

'The local doctor had no idea of the symptoms that only you saw?'

'He told the redcoat that he would have the body examined by a colleague more experienced in poisonings. He said too that his colleague would come and ask me about it. I decided that this time I would tell everything, but nobody came. And besides, if it was on account of Ramponeau's wine, there would have been others who died since.'

'Somebody could have put poison in Doctor Rollin's glass without the inn knowing about it. Did he have enemies? People who had grudges against him?'

'Not as far as I'm aware. Everyone here liked him. Except…'

She bites her lip again.

'But Pierre Rollin himself denied that,' I say, guessing the cause of her embarrassment. 'Do you know who he dined with that day?'

'No. Well, he said he had an appointment with a man he had been seeing regularly for a while. I don't know his name and have never seen him. All I know is that he was passionate about the study of natural science, as was my poor Pierre. They spent hours talking about the plants and animals in the distant countries over the sea that they had been to.'

Something occurred to me that I ought to have thought of earlier.

'Did Rollin ever talk to you about his leaving on a long military mission?'

'He was due to leave? Do you know anything about it?'

Her surprise is not feigned. She looks about to cry.

'No! Absolutely not! It was a random question, to explore all the possibilities.'

It's another lie, but there is no point upsetting her. In any case, Rollin has left for a much more distant place than foreseen. My uncle had not been wrong to have confidence in the army doctor. He really was extremely discreet.

'Have you tried going to the inn to ask the waitresses what happened during the last meal of your …lodger?'

I almost say 'your lover' and correct myself at the last moment.

'No,' she replies. 'as it would serve no purpose. They know me and hate me. Ramponeau himself has become more touchy in his old age and easily gets angry beneath his phoney high-class airs. He knows me too and could complain to my husband. My dear spouse would be doubly angry, firstly because he insisted to the police that Rollin, whom he did not like, died of natural causes, and secondly because Ramponeau is one of his biggest clients.'

I do not take it any further. She opens the writing desk to take out the register and write me into it. She tells me that she will give me the army doctor's room. I ask her if she still has Rollin's personal effects. She replies that, as yet. none of his relatives has been found and that in the meantime everything had been given to the Gardes Françaises regiment for safekeeping after a notary had made an inventory. She had just kept an earthenware stove that the doctor had had installed in his room.

I settle into the late Doctor Rollin's suite: a room and an anteroom, plus a washroom with a bath. The furniture is basic but comfortable. The hearth is sealed but at my request the maid lights the stove. As the landlady said, all Rollin's personal belongings have been taken away. Once Toinon has left I look under all the furniture. Nothing. The room has been cleaned. I stretch out on the bed, with my boots over the end so as not to dirty the bedspread, and stare at the ceiling. I try to imagine Rollins' last thoughts. I have no idea what he was like. He must have been seductive to have charmed the landlady the way he did. My uncle told me that he was about fifty, that he had first gone to India as Surgeon-General for Lally-Tollendal, and that after the fall of Pondicherry he had offered his services to Hyder Ali Khan. Many French soldiers had joined up with the Nabob at that time. During the Seven Years' War, Pondicherry had surrendered in 1761, the year of my birth. I suddenly remember what Monsieur de Fleurieu told me yesterday morning about Saint-Luperce. The latter had told Monsieur de Fleurieu that he had commanded Hyder Ali Khan's artillery in a battle whose name I have forgotten. If Saint-Luperce and Rollin had served the Nabob at the same time, they must surely have known each other. Saint-Luperce! I sit up. My uncle had told me that Rollin had died just at the moment when the Marquis de Castries had decided that, thanks to the doctor's knowledge, he had no more need for Saint-Luperce. The latter therefore could well have had a reason for eliminating Rollin in order to take his place in India. But would one kill a man for so little? The chest of diamonds has certainly caused a series of crimes, but neither of them knew of its existence, until proved otherwise. Maybe there was an old dispute between them dating back to when they were together in India. If it was Saint-Luperce who was dining with Rollin when he died I could easily find out from the people working at the inn. Since yesterday I could identify the 'Chevalier of the Cross of Christ' if someone described him to me. I jump up and decide to have my supper at the *Porcherons*.

It is Sunday and New Year's Eve. The noise of the crowd and the sound of accordions and violins extends the whole way along the street perpendicular to the chaussée d'Antin, once through the tollgate. The *Porcherons* inn is overflowing. The clients are piled in at little tables pushed close to each other the whole length of the room. There must be a few good-for-nothings and their fishwives here, but in the main I see honest folk representing ordinary Parisians: shoemakers, tailors, wigmakers, launderers and seamstresses, all in their Sunday best. Here and there in the crowd are uniformed soldiers from the five or six Gardes Françaises' barracks around the capital. Overworked waitresses rush in all directions, sliding between the benches with their trays above their heads. The kitchen is at the other end from the entrance, arranged around a huge hearth surrounded by cooking braziers. In the middle, on planking installed on one side, opposite a stage where bagpipes and violins are being played, couples are dancing gavottes, bourrées and contredances. There is an endless joyous activity.

I approach an older waitress going back to the kitchen and take an ecu out of my pocket, waving it in front of her and telling her that I would like to eat a simple meal in a quiet corner and that the money will be hers if she can arrange it.

'I'll 'ave a little round table put out for yer. As for food, there's beef terrine, bread an' a pitcher of wine. Would that do yer?' She says all this somewhat ironically.

'That's perfect.'

She had made her suggestion as a joke and is totally dumbfounded by my reply.

'An ecu jus' for that? Are yer serious, Monsieur?'

'I'd like to have a word with you.'

'You're a bit on the young side to be interested in me!'

'I'm after some information.'

'What d'yer take me for?'

'For an honest person, just as the information I need is honest.'

'That's as what you say!'

'I'm happy to give you two ecus for your trouble.'

She quickly has me installed at a table and I wait. When she puts my plate in front of me I hold out the two coins and let them drop onto the tabletop, before putting my hand over them.

'The late Pierre Rollin,' I say, 'formerly army doctor with the Gardes Françaises, came here often so you must have known him. Were you present the last time he ate here?'

The old gossip's eyes widen and I catch a brief glint. I have the impression that without intending to, I have touched a nerve.

'I 'ope I was there! What a tragedy that were, all the same!'

'I'm trying to find out who was dining with him on that day. And on the preceding days, so I'm told.'

'Well then! I guessed as much! Pardon me, Sir, but what wiv your black suit an' boots an' sword, you're one of 'em from the Grand Chatêlet[9]. Paid to sniff around everywhere!'

'You're quite wrong! I'm acting for myself. I'm in a black suit because I'm an officer of the King's ships and it's against regulations to wear our uniforms in Paris.'

'Oh, don't yer be getting' me wrong, Sir! An' anyway, jus' for once it wouldn'ave bovvered me if yer was a police sniffer. I'm 'appy to spill the beans on that geezer.'

I hold out the two ecus that she rapidly secretes in the pocket of her apron.

'And what was so special about this 'geezer', as you call him?'

'Well, at first sight, like, you'd think butter wouldn't melt in 'is mouth, with him tryin' to talk normal, like everyone else. But I can tell you, he were an Englishman!'

'How do you know that?'

'Good God! He were jabbering away in French wiv an English accent! I found that weird, like, from the start. An' sometimes, when he were tryin' to find the right word, Doctor Rollin were doing the translating for 'im.'

'Rollin was from Alsacc. Maybe the other man was a German.'

'I knows as 'ow to tell the difference, my little Sir! In the old days I were at the *Tambour Royal,* Ramponeau's old place. Full of toffs, not like 'ere, an' the English travellers knew about it. They was often there. Ah! Always drinkin' like fish an' chasin' the girls. They weren't prudes neither! One of our girls managed to catch a real Milord. He took 'er back 'ome to marry 'er. Which is all to say as I can smell an Englishman straight off, don't you worry!'

If the waitress is not mistaken, then it's a real turn of events. I cannot see Saint-Luperce passing himself off as an Englishman, especially as Rollin already knew him.

'Do you know the name of this Englishman?'

---

9   Translator's note: *Grand Chatêlet*: headquarters of the Paris Police under the *ancien régime.*

'Is that what they teach yer in the Navy, like? You think as spies give their names?'

'What did he look like?'

'Dressed discreet, like. Petit bourgeois wiv flat shoes. He 'ad a pot belly an' was a bit smaller than you. Wiv a right ugly mug under that wig of 'is.'

This description doesn't tell me much, apart from him not wanting to draw attention to himself and his not being Saint-Luperce.

'Did you listen to what they were saying?'

'Hang on! We don't do that 'ere! But seein' as 'e were a spy… They was talkin' about animals all the time, snakes an' things, in India and them West Indies. Nuffink interesting! Maybe they was doin' it on purpose so's we wouldn't know what they was really saying. Right then! If you'd excuse me, I've got to be goin'.'

'Just one more moment, please. What did they eat and drink?'

'It were a Sunday. I think the main dish were rump steak an' shallots. They was drinkin' wine, of course. An' brandy just before they left. It were the Englishman as ordered it like an' paid for it. Is that all, Sir? I'll be getting' on, now, and thanks for the tip.'

I am totally perplexed by what I have just heard. Assuming that the waitress is not mistaken, and given that we are at war with the King of England, an Englishman living in Paris could only be a spy. But why would a spy for the English Crown be interested in an army doctor from the Gardes Françaises headquarters, which in reality is a school for eleven to sixteen-year olds? Unless, through some improbable security lapse, the enemy had found out about our plans for India and Rollin's role in it. In that case the fact that Rollin had been eliminated, by means of poisoning, something which I am now sure of, seems to prove that he was not a traitor.

*

Both Monsieur and Madame Dutertre were at home when I returned from the *Porcherons*. Monsieur showed polite interest on learning I was a Naval officer. He seemed pleased that I would be leaving first thing the next day. I said my goodbyes, telling them not to bother about breakfast for me as I did not want to have anyone go to any trouble. On the Monday morning, I was about to go noiselessly out into the freezing street when Toinon stopped me and said that her mistress was up and was waiting for me in the little salon, in order to say goodbye.

My landlady was in a nightshirt with a very short dressing gown over it. With her long hair tumbling down her back, and with no rouge on her cheeks, I found her more interesting than the day before. I had to think of Maria Kirwan as hard as I could to drive out of my head the pleasant thoughts that this sight aroused.

Madame Dutertre, whose first name I never learned, had a bag made of waxed canvas under her arm.

'I hid it when the notary came to make his inventory…'

She was speaking very quietly and I had to get up close to understand what she was saying.

'I wanted to keep a souvenir of the man I loved more than any in my life, but I don't know where to hide it. I'm worried that my husband might find it, as he would certainly destroy it. You're the only person who believed me when I said Pierre Rollin had been poisoned, and since you are going to India, please take it. It will be more useful to you than to me. Just promise me that one day justice will be done and that the cowardly murderer of the finest, most honest man will be punished.'

The bag she gave me held a thick quarto notebook bound in leather and tied up with lacing. She did not give me time to open it.

'Go now before I change my mind. It's a manuscript. You can look at it later.'

It was still dark when I got to the headquarters. I had breakfast with the sergeants while my horse was saddled. I really wanted to open the package that I had been given, but as it was possible that the non-commissioned officers there had already seen it in Doctor Rollin's hands, opening it was a risk I was not prepared to take.

I rode off just after daybreak, first at a walk, then at a trot along the rows of bare trees lining the boulevard. I saw lots of signs for cafés and theatres at the top of the faubourg Temple, but they were all closed. There were few people about at that hour, but I met the carts of country folk and market gardeners who had come into the town by different gates and were now heading in the same direction as me. The boulevard curved round and I found myself heading south, with the sun now well above the horizon to my left. It was a red sun under a ceiling of grey, snow-filled clouds. The wind had veered to the south-west but it was still too cold for snow to fall.

I came to a halt in front of the towering dark mass of the Bastille, which reached into the sky across my path and blotted out all the roofs of this part of the capital, high though they were. The boulevard came to a sudden end there, at a crossroads blocked by a row of houses backing onto the mound surrounding the huge dry moat of the castle. These houses all had shops at street level. They stretched out to my right, in the shadow of the castle walls, towards what I thought was the start of the rue Saint-Antoine. To my left a road went off to the eastern suburb, beside the mound. I did not know which side the entrance to the fortress was on, so was unsure in which direction to go. All the shops were closed and there was scarcely anybody in the street. A cart came past me heading for the exit from the town, so I urged my horse on to get level with the driver and asked him how one could get into the Bastille. The poor chap looked at me as if I was the devil incarnate and lashed at his mules to get away from me. I kicked my horse on and caught up with him. I then realised how worrisome my question might be to someone from around here, especially as I was on horseback and dressed in black with a sword at my side. There was nobody else around to ask.

'Excuse me, Sir. I do not know Paris and I really am looking for the entrance to the Bastille.'

The man pulled on the reins to stop his cart.

'Take the passage towards the Arsenal, at the end of the rue Saint-Antoine. The street behind you. You'll find some of the soldiers guarding the Bastille. Ask them!'

Wheeling round, I followed the mound by the shops, which led me to an open gate at the south end of the rue Saint-Antoine. The gate was not guarded and I went through it, still on horseback, without being stopped. I was now in a passage with what seemed like barracks on the right and shops to my left. I went past them all until I could at last see the entrance to the fort on the other side of the ditch. It faced south between two corner towers. There were eight towers on all, four on my side, to the west, and four on the town side, to the east. These walls and towers were not quite as high as the mast on a sixty-four gun ship, but their solidity was enough to freeze your blood. The main gate to the Bastille was defended by a double drawbridge, for the moment raised, and approached by a stone bridge crossing most of the ditch. The dry moat was more than forty yards wide at this point. The bridge started at a little courtyard that I had to get to, and which was separated from the one I was in by a gate with another smaller double drawbridge.

The first drawbridge was lowered and guarded by an infantryman who looked at me inquisitively when I dismounted in front of him. This soldier was a good fifty and wore the blue cotton uniform, without lapels and with the red tabling, of the Invalides regiment. When a soldier could not support himself because of wounds sustained in war or because he had become too old to fight, the King did not abandon him. He housed him in his Hôtel des Invalides and if the veteran was not too maimed or worn out, kept him to carry out sedentary duties in what were called the Detached Companies. Besides checking the gates, their main mission was to watch the citadel from a circular path constructed around the moat on the inside face of the mound, in order to thwart any attempts to escape. Although it seems unbelievable, a prisoner had in fact succeeded, during the reign of the previous King, by getting down the walls with a ladder made from the sheets in his cell.

The guard called his post commander who came out of a little guardroom to the right of the gate. I explained why I was there and showed him my safe-conduct signed by the Head of the Paris Police. The old sergeant asked me to wait there and went back into the courtyard. After ten minutes he came back and asked me to leave my horse in a stable beside the guard post, and then to follow him. He would take me to the Marquis de Launay, Governor of the Bastille. It seemed that at the Bastille, New Year's Day was just like any other.

The Marquis de Launay and his family were lodged in the courtyard facing the fort's drawbridge. He had been up for a while and received us in his office. I have since learned that he was only forty, but I thought he was much older. He was thin and narrow-shouldered and did not strike me as very soldierly for a former cavalry officer, despite the Cross of Saint-Louis on his jacket. He twice read aloud, slowly and in front of us, the safe-conduct signed by Monsieur Lenoir, along with the letter of introduction from the Marquis de Castries that Monsieur de Fleurieu had given me on the eve of my departure. He told the sergeant to take me to the King's Lieutenant inside the fortress, who would then take me to the prisoner Duval's cell for a private interview, 'which in principle is not allowed' he said several times in a dry tone. He then changed his mind and decided to come with us himself.

*

Paris, Monday 1ˢᵗ January 1781.

I stand behind the Marquis de Launay, beside the sergeant from the guardroom, as we wait at the end of the stone bridge. Somebody from inside the castle must have seen the Governor himself arrive and decides to let down the big drawbridge, rather than the one for pedestrians. The heavy oak platform and the solid beams of its supporting members come slowly down with loud bangs that remind me of the clicking of the pawls of a huge capstan. The Marquis de Launay steps onto the platform before it is fully lowered. A squad of Invalides has hastily lined up to welcome us in the entrance tunnel, through which cold air is sweeping. The frozen veterans present arms as their commander passes by. He nods briefly without stopping.

We come out into a big courtyard, the Grand Cour. It is about thirty yards by twenty but seems narrow under the hundred-foot high walls of the fort. Looking upwards, only a patch of grey sky is visible. One has the impression of being at the bottom of a dark well; and it is icy cold! In front of us is a three-storey building much lower than the ramparts on each side of it. This building, which seems of more recent construction than the rest of the fort, divides the interior into two unequal parts. It is entered via a porch with five steps leading up to it. Above, at the level of the third floor, is a classical pediment with a clock set into the tympanum. I just have time to see that it is quarter to ten. I can scarcely believe my eyes: the sculpted reliefs around the dial are of a man and a woman in chains! The English would no doubt think this amusing, but for my part I don't know what to make of it. The officers in charge of the fort are lodged in this building, with their offices on the ground floor. The vestibule we go into is extended by a corridor blocked at its far end by an iron door. This is apparently the only means of access to the next courtyard. Before going there, we turn to go through the Council Room, a huge austere room with bare stone walls, where prisoners are interrogated on arrival. It is also the place where visits usually take place. The office of the King's Lieutenant is beside it. This officer seems older than his superior but has retained his military appearance. He introduces himself: the Chevalier de Saint-Sauveur, former Captain of Infantry. He too is wearing the Cross of Saint-Louis. This veteran is in charge of the prison archives, and on his walls are hung all the keys to the Bastille. God knows there are enough of them!

The Marquis de Launay asks for Duval's file and the Chevalier de Saint-Sauveur sends his clerks to find it. While waiting, he tells his superior that Duval arrived at the Bastille at the beginning of July 1780 and that he was put secretly into the Corner Tower. Once the file is brought it confirms all this. The Marquis de Launay suddenly seems annoyed, even anxious, and says that he no longer wishes to authorise me to see the prisoner in his cell but will have him brought to the Council Room to be interrogated by me in his presence. I reply that the Marquis de Castries has insisted that our conversation should have no witnesses and show him my letter of introduction signed by the Minister. The Governor still does not want to give way. I say that in that case I will return immediately to Versailles and report the obstruction to my superiors, telling the Minister that his signature and that of Monsieur Lenoir have no standing with the officers of the Bastille.

The Marquis de Launay's natural scowl darkens even more. The Chevalier de Saint-Sauveur takes hold of my safe-conduct signed by the Head of the Paris police and the letter of introduction from the Marquis de Castries and reads them carefully.

'The words are quite explicit, Monsieur, and signed by the Head of the Police.'

'Oh, come on, Chevalier! Monsieur Lenoir is a friend of Monsieur de Sartine, who as far as I know no longer has any influence.'

'That is true, Sir, but we still depend on him. It is also said that the Marquis de Castries is a close friend of Monsieur Necker.'

The Marquis de Launay thinks for a moment, lowering his eyebrows and pinching his lips into a grimace. I am wondering why my visit to Duval's cell is exercising him so much, when a few minutes ago he seemed not to know who he was.

'Right! Do it then! And afterwards send me this man whose name I have forgotten.'

'Laforest-Dombourg,' I say. 'Ensign of the King's Ships. It is written in all the letters that the Chevalier had just read to you.'

He shakes his head to underline his bad mood.

'Don't forget to come to my office before leaving, Monsieur Impertinent. And please give me these documents! I will keep them.'

Good God! He is insulting me, this man with his runtish little head!

My blood boils and I would like to throw a challenge in his face to watch it get even paler. Luckily, I remember in time that this kind of thing has nearly cost me dear on several occasions. What's more, this isn't any old person. It's the Governor of the Bastille himself!

The Chevalier de Saint-Sauveur has Duval's jailer called. The jailers are subalterns whose main task is taking food to the prisoners locked in each of the Bastille's eight towers. There are four jailers, responsible for two towers each. They are almost the only ones to have daily contact with the prisoners.

The Marquis de Launay departs and we wait an interminable time for the jailer. He arrives grumbling, having just finished his morning round and looking forward to a rest before his midday duties. He unhooks a bunch of keys considerably bigger than the others. The Chevalier de Saint-Sauveur asks me to leave my sword with him during the visit.

My guide is of normal height, rather strongly built, with greasy uncombed hair spilling out from under the three-cornered hat pulled down to his eyes and ears. He has a swollen blotchy nose and a week's growth of beard on his fat cheeks. His bulky body has been forced into a coat of dubious cleanliness with several buttons missing. I of course do not expect a Bastille jailer to be some smartly turned out gentleman, but this one goes far beyond what I could have imagined. Rather than returning to the courtyard we had just crossed, the warder goes straight to the metal door I had seen at the end of the hallway, which leads to the space behind the officers' building. We have to go through two more doors, each one opened and relocked behind us, to get to the courtyard at the back. This is called the Cour du Puits, after the well there, visible to the right as we enter the yard. The courtyard is half the size of the Grand Cour. The jailer double locks the door behind us. Here it is dark and intensely cold. The space is so narrow and the surrounding walls so high and close to each other that I feel as if they are about to close above out heads like the lid of a giant tomb. The silence is deathly. Although the rue Saint-Antoine is quite close by, any sounds from it are deadened by the ten-foot thick walls. Only the sound of our footsteps echo between the grey walls surrounding us. There are only two other doors in this courtyard, those of the two corner towers on the north side of the fort, the Tour du Coin to our left and the Tour du Puits to our right.

'Are you in charge of these two towers,' I ask the ogre, to break the oppressive silence of this sinister place.

The only reply is a kind of croak. The jailer selects another key from his bunch and turns the impressive lock of the entrance door to the Tour du Coin. As he pulls the door outwards I can see that there is a second door that opens inwards, once he has unlocked it with another key. He closes the two doors behind us, carefully locking them. We are now locked in! We are in a narrow, dark entrance hall and facing yet another door, this one in wood and studded with nails. It too has a huge lock like the others, and seems to be the door to a cell. To our left I can see a narrow stairwell leading downwards, I assume to a dungeon, and which continues spiralling upwards. That is where the jailer heads off. The stairs are lit every twenty steps by daylight coming through small square openings on the courtyard side. The sound of our steps on the flagstones is amplified by the echoing under the low vaulted ceiling which spirals up to the right just above our heads. The jailer stops at the first floor, in front of the first door we come across, unlocks it and pulls it towards himself in the narrow circular cage of the stairway. The metallic clicks of the lock, the creaking of the hinges and the scraping of the bottom of the door on the step, echo for a while in the heavy silence that envelopes us. There is of course a second door behind that one which he has to unlock before pushing it open.

We enter an octagonal space defined by the walls of the tower. The floor is bare wood blackened by time. A window with three sets of bars set progressively into the thickness of the wall, and half covered by a metal shutter, lets through a tiny amount of daylight. A man was waiting for us, standing by the door, having heard the noise of our arrival. I recognise Louis Duval. He is wrapped in a blanket that he holds like a cape over his head and shoulders, to protect himself from the cold.

'I'll leave you here,' says the jailer. 'I'll wait on the stairs. Bang the door when you've finished and I'll come and get you.'

'Ah! You do know how to talk, then!' I say.

His only reply is to go out, banging and locking the two doors behind him.

I look around me. Old pictures, each one more shocking and obscene than the next, have been drawn in charcoal on the dirty walls. The room is quite big but sparsely furnished. There is a table, a bed, a bucket with a lid that has clearly not been emptied for several days and which imparts an unpleasant smell, and two wicker chairs. One of these is close to a fireplace in which no fire is burning, although there are cinders in the hearth and logs piled alongside.

'We only get six a day. I prefer to use them all in one go before going to bed,' says Duval, who has seen what I was looking at.

He has not changed much. Still the same big nose and protruding ears. His pockmarked face is of course much paler than before, but he does not seem to have lost much weight. They can't be so badly fed at the Bastille. Of course, he can't drink alcohol like before. His breath is much less noxious than I remember. He stares at me with wide eyes, much open, as if dumbstruck.

'Do you recognise me?' I say after a while, to break a silence that is starting to unnerve me.

'The young man from Saint-Malo! I thought so! So they have arrested you too?'

His question seems anxious.

'I have only come to see you.'

His face lights up.

'You had plenty of influence in those days, if I remember. Are you going to get me out of here?'

'That is not in my power. But it's in the power of those who sent me.'

Duval goes to the fireplace.

'I'll light the fire,' he says. 'Otherwise you'll get cold.'

'Don't bother, please,' I say.

He doesn't insist, and draws the chairs up to the table, taking a flint and tinder to light a candle in a candleholder. He pushes a bowl and a pewter spoon to one side and we sit down facing each other.

'Could you at least tell me why I am here?'

This sudden jump to the heart of the business takes me by surprise. Is he making fun of me?

'Don't tell me you don't know why you were arrested?'

'Oh, I know well enough! I'm accused of treason and plotting with the enemies of the King. But why? And which enemies? If I had been accused of smuggling with the English I would have understood. But that was before the start of the war. The last time I saw the smugglers, the Sanders brothers, Jack and Michael, was when you asked to meet with them. Since introducing you to them at Chausey I haven't seen them or tried to see them. That was part of our agreement and I respected it.'

'The Sanders brothers? You mean the Cornishmen from Salcombe?'

'Ah, it's true you didn't know their names. They asked me not to tell you as one of their conditions. Same as your Captain, the commander of that pretty little cutter I often saw you going aboard. He didn't want us to give his name either, which I understood perfectly. I respected all that. I don't know your name. I didn't even try to find out the name of your ship. Oh! I often admired her from the ramparts as she went through the Saint-Malo passages. What a fine ship! If I'd had one like her I'd be king of the corsairs!'

'Really?' I exclaim. 'You didn't ask the Bastille Governor for an explanation? Haven't you been interrogated since your arrest?'

'They came to arrest me in the middle of the night. I hardly had time to dress. I was thrown into a locked carriage and ended up here. Interrogation? They only said what I just told you: that I'm a traitor! I don't know anything else. There was the one you call the Governor, that old monkey with all his decorations. All he kept saying was that if you're in the Bastille you're getting what you deserve. Since then, the only person I see here is the Toad.'

'The Toad?'

'The one who brought you here. Croak! Croak! That's all you can get out of him. He brings my meals, cuts my meat, seeing as I don't have the right to a knife or fork. He empties my buckets, but not every day. I may as well talk to the prison walls! I have no news from outside, nothing to write with. I don't even know what day it is! I was hardly a model citizen when I was free, but I tried to get the Toad to let me have Mass here. It would have been a distraction and I could have at least counted the Sundays. 'Get lost! Croak! Croak!' That's all I got.'

'It's the first of January, seventeen hundred and eighty-one.'

'Good God! Seventeen eighty-one already! And the war? How are things going with the Angliches?'

'It's going along.'

'Ah! You don't want to tell me? You too take me for a traitor, a friend of the Angliches? Well, at least tell me what they have against me!'

'Well, you are accused of having revealed *le Moucheron's* mission to the English.'

'*Le Moucheron?* Oh! I see. That was the name of your cutter? Hell's teeth! That means they must have discovered the Sanders brothers.

They'll be dead now, both of them. The Angliches show no mercy with spies during wartime. Jack and Mike, they didn't feel very Angliche. They were from Cornwall. It was their way of seeing things. I'm sorry for them. They were tough bastards but we always got on well. But it wasn't me who betrayed them, I swear! Someone else must have talked, not necessarily one of us. Maybe it happened on the other coast. Maybe the Sanders brothers weren't careful enough. Though that would surprise me. Well then? Thinking about it, I suppose that means they laid a trap for your cutter, *le Moucheron.* Is that it? Your captain was captured and hung, him too? I would understand what they have against me if I was guilty. But for God's sake it wasn't me! Tell them I'm here for nothing! They could at least question me, so that I can defend myself! If your Captain was still alive I'm sure he would understand. He was a real seaman, him. I only met him once but I felt that right away. If that's what they have against me, I'm done for! How can I prove my innocence shut up in this rat hole? I may as well die now! Damn! Damn! Damn!'

Duval puts his hands to his face. His desperation upsets me, and I want to tell him that the Cornishmen are still alive, but I hesitate. I remember that Monsieur de Fleurieu told me that it was Monsieur Régnier who had allowed the Cornishmen to re-establish relations with Captain Le Meur.

'Did Monsieur Régnier know the Sanders brothers well?' I ask.

'My shipowner? I think so! He knew them better than me. I was only his go-between in this business.'

'Did he know the name of *le Moucheron's* captain?'

'That would surprise me! All he knew was that Flaharn was with the Comte d'Estaing, and when I told him I knew Flaharn he asked me to contact him. That's how it all started. Then Flaharn sent you to Saint-Malo. You know all that better than me! As for whether Monsieur Régnier knew the name of your Captain, he could have got it from the Saint-Malo port office, but as I told you, at that time Monsieur Régnier wasn't on good terms with the authorities. That's why he had the idea of getting intelligence on the English. So that the Tax Inspector at Caen would leave him alone. You remember! The Inspector wanted to put paid to his business at Chausey. I told you that the first time we met in front of the Fort Royal at Saint-Malo. I remember it! The tide was coming in and we had to move. Oh God! Will I ever see the sea again?

I beg you, please save me, Monsieur! Or else help me to die right now. To think that just before I was arrested I had taken a good prize with the corsair lugger I commanded for Monsieur Régnier. We had been combing the Channel for months in all weathers without seeing a thing. Then a stroke of luck! A big fat Englishman straight from India! She had lost her convoy in the bad weather and only had half a crew, their Navy having pressed the rest. I'm still laughing about it! I was rich, by God! I didn't even have the time to enjoy it.'

I think about this. What Duval had just told me seems to prove his innocence. He seems to be sincere, despite being a good liar. But how could Baldock have known his name? Unless Régnier was the guilty one. But why would Régnier have turned in the captain of his own lugger?

'Did you get on well with Régnier?'

'I've always had confidence in him and I have no reason to change my opinion, if that's what you want to know.'

'No doubt there is a good reason for that?'

'He's married to one of my cousins. When I got back from the English prison ships at the end of the Seven Years' War everyone had forgotten about me. I had nothing to look forward to. I was offered third lieutenant in the India Company, but I didn't want to go back there. Régnier helped me find a ship, though he didn't have to. Second captain on a slaver. It was more than I had hoped for, but by the end of my first voyage I had had enough. It was well paid but too hard. I wanted out. The Captain of the slaver was furious but Régnier didn't hold it against me and kept looking out for me. Before I was arrested to be put in here, he gave me my first real chance in my bitch of a life: a fast lugger, his best corsair, my first command! And I didn't let him down! With a little sixty-footer I took an Indiaman! That's not to be sniffed at! Even if she couldn't manoeuvre well because of damage, and even if her crew was incomplete.'

Duval goes quiet. For a moment his eyes shine as he remembers the capture. Then he lowers his head, remembering again his present predicament. I think about what I can say to him. Our silence drags on. The sounds of the town and the rue Saint-Antoine make their way through the unglazed window. Eventually I stand up and shake his hand, signalling the end of our conversation. I have the impression that he is telling the truth, but I do not seem to have made any progress. On the contrary, the whole thing is still a mystery.

'You were arrested because someone you don't know provided the Ministry with what seems to be clear and unarguable proof of your treachery. But without realising it you have given me some new elements that may lead my superiors to reconsider this proof. I can't say more at the moment. Try to be patient.'

I bang the door as agreed to call the jailer. My eyes meet Duval's desperate look as the jailer locks his cell. I take the reverse route back, with a feeling of great relief.

The Chevalier de Saint-Sauveur is waiting for me in the Council Room, and hands me my sword.

'May I ask you something, Sir?' I say.

'Go ahead. I'll answer if I can, otherwise you will have to ask the Marquis de Launay. What is it about?'

'Well, I was very surprised at the severe treatment meted out to Duval. I have twice before met people who have been in the Bastille, and according to what I know, their treatment was nothing like what I have witnessed this morning. They kept their servants, they used their time to write memoranda, they received guests and they could communicate with the outside world. In one case this allowed one of them to get help to speed up his release.'

'Who are you talking about?'

'Colonel Dumouriez and the Chevalier de Saint-Luperce.'

'In that case I can answer your question, as the Marquis de Launay only arrived as Governor in seventeen seventy-six, and the two men you are talking about had already been released.'

'You surprise me,' I say, 'as I thought the Chevalier de Saint-Luperce was here last September.'

'That's right. He was here briefly in September, seventeen eighty. I had forgotten that. But previously he had been here for a long time, from seventy-one to seventy-four. As for Colonel Dumouriez, he was our guest from seventy-three to seventy-four.'

'Oh!' I say with surprise. 'Saint-Luperce had been on the Bastille before? May I ask what he was charged with that time?'

'I am not authorised to tell you, but you could certainly find out for yourself by asking somebody who is. In any case, you are right. Your Duval is not on the same regime as the two you mentioned. That is because he is here secretly and they were not. Prisoners held in secret are put in the Tour du Coin and the Tour du Puits. The trouble with that regime is that prisoners can be forgotten about, after which we get complaints. I often remind the Marquis de Launay that his predecessor regularly made requests to the King's Secretary of State about progress on the files of secret prisoners. Monsieur de Jumilhac never failed to do this since being strongly upbraided about it during the reign of Louis XV. But the Marquis de Launay has had so much work lately that he has not had time to think about Louis Duval. And don't forget that Duval has only been here six months.'

I appreciate the worthy efforts of the King's Lieutenant to defend his superior, Personally I have trouble believing that the workload of the Governor of the Bastille is as heavy as he makes out, but I now understand why the Marquis de Launay was so agitated when he discovered that a Minister as influential as the Marquis de Castries had sent me to find out about a prisoner whom he had not yet concerned himself with, and who was there in secret.

Having said goodbye to the Chevalier de Saint-Sauveur, and since I had expressly been asked, I go to present myself at the Governor's residence beside the entrance to the fort.

A lackey who must have had a telling off and whose hostility is palpable leads me to the antechamber of the Marquis de Launay's office and asks me to wait. After half an hour I wonder whether the Governor is making me wait as long as possible in order to punish me for my 'impertinence'. I get up and go to find the lackey who is reading some newspaper or other in his vestibule. In Paris it seems that everybody reads: coachmen waiting on their cabs, artisans waiting for business in their shops. This noisy town is probably one of the best informed in Europe, which is why the satires, pamphlets and broadsheets carry their gossip and scandal all the way to the suburbs. Having such a well-informed populace is not without problems for the authority of the King. I have often heard it said that the three men most admired by Parisians are the King of Prussia, Voltaire and Jean-Jacques Rousseau. I plant myself in front of the lackey and tell him that I am under orders to be with my Minister before the end of the afternoon and that I cannot wait any longer. I ask him to present my apologies to the Governor and go out.

*

I already had a foot in its stirrup when the lackey caught up with me and took me straight to the Governor's office.

'I would like to know why the Marquis de Castries has sent a young man to visit a prisoner who has been held secretly for only six months,' the Marquis de Launay asked me.

I replied that Duval had covertly helped the Navy at the start of the war, that before summer we had received what seemed like convincing intelligence that suggested he was a traitor, but that we now had doubts about his culpability. I had been assigned to the task because I was the only person in Versailles who knew him personally. I added that we were not yet sure enough of his innocence to change his regime, but it would be helpful to soften it somewhat. I suggested increasing his allocation of logs. The Marquis de Launay replied dryly that the number of logs per prisoner was decreed by the Bastille rules in order to meet a precise need and could not be changed on a whim.

'Otherwise, where would we be? As far as I know the Bastille is a Royal prison, not a holiday resort!'

It was late morning by the time I left the Bastille. To save time I cut across the most crowded parts of the capital. I found the streets inside Paris dirty and extremely narrow, with extraordinarily high houses. The noise of the crowd and its movement gave me a headache. I had never before seen so many people crowding into such a tight space. I admit that the deck of a ship of the line is hardly devoid of people, but at least they are not constantly racing around on foot, on horseback or in carriages. There is no need for a daily shovelling up of the mud and droppings. The sea air, too, stops any miasmas from collecting.

I did not dare stop to eat and arrived before nightfall at the Versailles stables. I handed over my mare who, like me, had not eaten since the morning. Without losing any time I ran along the rue de la Surintendance to present myself to Monsieur de Fleurieu at the Navy and Foreign Affairs offices.

Once I was in Monsieur de Fleurieu's office I said straight away that I had found some new and important information. I had expected him to take me immediately to the Marquis de Castries, as I had not forgotten the Marquis's insistence that I tell about my visit to the Bastille as soon as possible. Monsieur de Fleurieu did not seem to want to go anywhere and explained that my situation had changed.

'The Marquis de Castries was in a hurry because *la Sylphide* was due to sail in a week and you were supposed to go aboard with the chest of diamonds before handing them over to Monsieur de Montigny. But everything has been cancelled. You won't be leaving.'

In a flash I saw myself condemned to finishing my career in a Versailles office. I must have made a sorry sight, as Monsieur de Fleurieu went on quickly.

'Don't worry! We are only awaiting another opportunity to get you aboard a ship more discreetly, but it won't be with Monsieur de Montigny, who is still going on *la Sylphide*. We will still be keeping Saint-Luperce here, so that he can act as your guide and adviser if there is nobody else available when the time comes.'

'You said that you were waiting for an opportunity to send me off 'more discreetly'?'

Monsieur de Fleurieu rested his chin on his hands and sighed.

'Do you know Colonel Guypair? It seems that he is the one behind this setback. He seems to have a lot against you. Could you explain why?'

Guypair! It was a long time since I had heard his name and I had no idea what had become of him since the incident between us at Brest. What had he to do with what was now happening? It was my turn to sigh.

'A little over two years ago, at Brest, I challenged him to a duel because he had publicly defamed, in my presence, the officers of the Navy Grand Corps in general, and the Marine Guards in particular. He had had me put into prison and demanded that I be thrown out of the Navy. In fact everybody took my side, in particular Monsieur de la Rozière, who was the Military commander, but had been also commander at Saint-Malo, before becoming Chief of Staff for the Duc de Broglie, on whom Colonel Guypair's regiment depended. Monsieur de la Rozière had taken account of confidential work I had done for him at Saint-Malo. He had not been in a position to tell the Colonel exactly what this was. The Colonel, it seems, had been very angry when he learned that not only had I not been dismissed from the Navy, but I had not even been punished. I have not seen him since and I really don't understand how you got to hear about it. I had completely forgotten it myself.'

Monsieur de Fleurieu tried to look severe.

'Colonel Guypair is a famous officer. As commander of the Neustrie regiment he came the other day to see the new War Minister the Marquis de Ségur. He recognised you as you were passing to come here. Since then he has done everything possible to find out what you are doing, asking several clerks at the Navy Department, who told him about the little rumour that the Marquis de Castries now regrets circulating. I'm talking about the supposed duel business with one of the Officers of the Comte de Rochambeau's expeditionary force. From what I've been told, Colonel Guypair was furious on learning that you have already been on two American campaigns and that you have been promoted to Ship's Ensign. This despite him having apparently written several reports against you which he sent to the Navy command.'

Monsieur de Fleurieu cannot withhold a little smile.

'I can understand poor Guypair's disappointment! The Neustrie regiment that he commands was part of the second half of the expeditionary force that the Comte de Rochambeau had to leave behind and ought to have joined him last year. He had even embarked with his regiment on the fleet that was leaving for the Americas, with an escort commanded by the Comte d'Estaing as far as Cadiz. Guypair was finally going to have the opportunity to put into practice all the brilliant theories outlined in his famous books on military tactics. Unfortunately for him the Navy's orders were changed once they were under way. The Comte d'Estaing's fleet was kept at sea off Spain and for Guypair the voyage stopped at Cadiz. He and his regiment were sent back to Brest on two or three transport ships. His adventure was over before it had begun. So instead of finding glory in the New World, he has ended up champing at the bit in a garrison he detests, and close to the Navy that he dislikes. He wanted to take advantage of the change of Minister to present his grievances and what does he discover? That you have already been twice to the Americas! No wonder he is railing!'

I was stunned on hearing this. I saw again Guypair's bull neck and his wide, bulging forehead. He was in the prime of life, a Colonel, holder of the Cross of Saint-Louis, admired for his works on military tactics, worshipped in the Parisian salons by philosophers and women alike. And I, an insignificant little Ship's Ensign, what was I by comparison? I was no match for him. Oh, how I regretted having made an enemy because of an unconsidered moment of anger.

'I would find it funny,' continued Monsieur de Fleurieu, 'were it not that the Marquis de Castries is not at all happy. I haven't told you the most important part. As commander of a regiment that was originally to be part of a force under the Comte de Rochambeau, Guypair knows his son, the Vicomte, very well. Guypair went to see him to ask about you. The Vicomte, who had not really understood why he had been asked to play along with the story of your alleged duel, told Guypair that it was just a smokescreen to hide something else, but he didn't know what.'

I told Monsieur de Fleurieu that I had not liked the idea at all when my uncle had first told me about it at Brest, and asked him whether it was my uncle or the Marquis de Castries who was behind it.

'I think it was both of them, but principally the Marquis de Castries. Anyway, that's not all! As you may know, Guypair had served at the same time as your uncle under the late Comte de Saint-Germain when he was Minister for War. So he knows about your uncle's links to the Comte de Broglie, and all that implies…'

'So he knows I am his nephew!' I exclaimed. 'And through Monsieur de la Rozière he also knows that I was working undercover at Saint-Malo.'

'In fact,' added Monsieur de Fleurieu, 'unlike the Vicomte de Rochambeau, Guypair had immediately cottoned on that this lie about your supposed punishment meant that you were involved in some secret Navy plan. All it then took was for him to meet Saint-Luperce, who told him about his aborted departure to India with the Chevalier de Kermean.'

'Saint-Luperce!' I thought. 'That's all we need!'

'And to crown it all, I now get to the best bit! As you no doubt know, Guypair is addicted to writing and for a while has been one of the pillars of Madame Necker's and her daughter's literary salon. In these salons they chat about philosophers. So this morning, when we were at Court for the New Year celebration, Monsieur Necker mentioned you by name to the Minister and asked, in a falsely joking tone, why he was so keen to send his 'young swordsman' to India. The Marquis de Castries, who up until then was unaware of all Guypair's scheming, was of course taken completely unawares. He pretended not to remember your name and said that he therefore could not have decided anything about you, and that therefore there was no question of sending you to India or anywhere else.'

I thought that this time my future in the Navy had sudden become quite uncertain, despite Monsieur de Fleurieu's initial assurances.

'The Marquis de Castries thought you must have talked and was very angry with you. He wanted to keep you here in Versailles as a punishment. Luckily he changed his mind when I told him that in my view it all stemmed from Guypair's enmity towards you, and it was not your fault. The Marquis de Castries had no more idea than me why Guypair had so much against you. I will have to tell him how you challenged Guypair at Brest.'

'Is that really necessary?' I ask anxiously. 'Doesn't that risk getting him angry again and setting him against me even more? The Marquis de Castries is an Army man, like Colonel Guypair.'

I had had a few close calls, as they say, and I really wanted to be more careful in future, and more respectful to my superiors.

'On the contrary, it will amuse him. Don't forget that the Minister is primarily a cavalryman whereas Guypair has the misfortune to be an infantryman. What's more, Guypair has always been very public about his criticisms of the Navy, and so is well known for it. His disappointment at not going to America has increased his bitterness. He has written fiery articles against Monsieur de Sartine which were of course read at Madame Necker's famous salon, just when her husband was looking for every excuse to get rid of the Minister. Despite his politeness and his friendship with Necker, the Marquis de Castries did not appreciate these attacks against his predecessor and against the Navy. You have nothing to worry about. Now, tell me about Duval.'

I gave an account of my visit to the Bastille. Having patiently heard me out, Monsieur de Fleurieu agreed with me that Duval's replies seemed to invalidate Baldock's assertions. As long as Duval was telling the truth, which I believed he was. In effect, Baldock's accusation was based on three elements: the name of Captain Le Meur, the name of *le Moucheron,* and the name of Duval himself. There was never any mention of the Sanders brothers or Salcombe Bay.

According to Duval, his shipowner too had no idea of *le Moucheron's* captain's name. Remembering that Monsieur de Fleurieu had told me that Régnier had been the intermediary when the Cornishmen had recommended their operations, I asked him whether Régnier had gone directly to my old commander. Monsieur de Fleurieu replied that as far as he knew, the Granville shipowner had simply approached Monsieur de la Rozière's successor in order to propose a meeting on Chausey between Le Meur and our agents. It was therefore the military commander at Saint-Malo who had alerted Le Meur. He had then gone to Chausey to meet the two Cornishmen whom he already knew, having met them once before. Régnier had not come to that meeting.

'That doesn't mean that Régnier did not know Captain Le Meur's name, but nor does it prove the contrary either,' continued Monsieur de Fleurieu. 'All the same, the English could easily have had a hold over him by threatening the Chausey islands. Le Meur is controlled directly by my department. I will write to him to get his opinion on all this.'

'If Régnier is the traitor,' I reply, 'that would mean that the Sanders brothers were from then on collaborating with the English and that the intelligence they sent us was arranged by their London offices.'

'Whereas I believe the reports and intelligence sent by Le Meur are excellent and have always been confirmed by our other sources. But if neither Régnier nor Duval are guilty, how did Baldock get hold of this information? We always come back to this! I think I need to talk to Baldock, but it is difficult matter as the Insurgents are our allies. Maybe that won't last forever and we must just remain careful.'

Carrying on with my report, I talked about the discovery I had made at the *Porcherons* inn about the mysterious Englishman who dined with the late Doctor Rollin. Having first admonished me for not having obeyed his orders, he immediately recognised the significance of this.

'I will let the Marquis de Castries know immediately.'

'I hope he won't be annoyed with me.'

'If he is it will be just for show. I know he will take this information seriously. It gives us another reason not to send the Indian treasure on *la Sylphide,* as what you have told me could indicate a small chance that the English know at least something of our plans for India.'

In fact the Minister would later decide to have *la Sylphide* escorted by *la Bellone,* a 32-gun frigate.

Lastly, I reported to Monsieur de Fleurieu that I had learned that Saint-Luperce had been in the Bastille from 1771 to 1774. Monsieur de Fleurieu was unaware of this. He told me that he himself had been appointed an adviser to the Navy Minister at a time when Saint-Luperce was already working there, on account of his extensive knowledge of the East Indies, having been appointed by Bourgeois de Boynes, Monsieur de Sartine's predecessor.

With the Marquis de Castries' permission, Monsieur de Fleurieu asked for an audience for both of us with the Minister of the King's Household, the Marquis de Chaillou. Two days later the latter confirmed that Saint-Luperce had been imprisoned in 1771 on a *lettre de grand cachet* signed by Louis XV himself. This had been annulled by the King in 1774 after a joint request from the then Ministers Turgot and Bourgeois de Boynes. The Marquis de Chaillou reminded us that once somebody arrested on a *lettre de cachet* had been pardoned, his file was destroyed so as not to stain his future honour. The Marquis de Chaillou was insistent on this point, as it was the difference between a *lettre de cachet* and a guilty verdict under due legal process. The Minister would reveal no more than that Saint-Luperce had been imprisoned in the Bastille at the request of the authorities in the Île-de-France and the Île Bourbon.

'These islands are the responsibility of the Navy and Colonies office.' Monsieur de Fleurieu said to me as we left the meeting. 'We'll go back to my office, as we ought to be able to find the details in the department's archives.'

We discovered that in 1771 the Governor-General of the Île-de-France and the Île Bourbon was the Chevalier des Roches, a Naval officer since promoted to Rear Admiral. The Governor of the Île Bourbon at that time was Monsieur de Bellecombe. He had distinguished himself during the unsuccessful but heroic defence of Pondicherry, as a result of which he was promoted to Field-Marshall and Commander of the Royal Military Order of Saint-Louis. The two men had returned to France, the former retiring to his estates at Kerlaudy in Brittany, while for the latter, the latest address we could find was the Hôtel de Bretagne, rue de la Croix des Petits Champs, in Paris. I was all ready to return to Paris to try to meet with Monsieur de Bellecombe, while Monsieur de Fleurieu went to see the Marquis de Castries to have an order signed in my name. However, in the meantime, the Marquis de Chaillou had mentioned our visit to Monsieur de Vergennes, who was most put out that the Director of Ports and Arsenals should take it on himself to start making enquiries about the private affairs of a diplomat employed by his Department. The scheming Saint-Luperce had managed to charm the Minister of Foreign Affairs with his story of having been for three years the King's representative at the Maratha Court.

We were officially told to cease any investigations in that direction. I firmly intended to disobey. I had already forgotten the fear I had felt when learning of the Colonel Guypair's moves against me, which had almost caused the cancelation of my voyage to India. I therefore asked for a day's leave at the end of the week, on the pretext that I wanted to visit the Academy of a famous fencing master in Paris.

For a while I had been hearing the praises of this Monsieur Danet from the officers of the Gardes Françaises with whom I kept company in Versailles. I took this decision on learning that his fencing school was situated in a little street off the Place du Louvre, not far from the rue de la Croix des Petits Champs. As it turned out I was wasting my time, as I was told at the Hôtel de Bretagne that Monsieur de Bellecombe and his young wife had left Paris the previous autumn to go and live at their property near Puymirol. From Paris to Puymirol was more than three hundred miles, and so it was impossible for me to find a pretext to get there. As for writing to Monsieur de Bellecombe, that was impossible too without the agreement of my superiors. That just left the Chevalier des Roches. Kerlaudy was not far from Landerneau, and I thought that if ever I were to embark at Brest, I may just have the time to make a discreet visit.

This Saint-Luperce business both intrigued and worried me. I had a strong feeling that it could be important for me to know what he had been accused of at that time. It was no small matter that our authorities in the Île-de-France and the Île Bourbon had asked for him to be arrested, considering that those islands were our antechamber to the Coromandel Coast and the Bay of Bengal. What could Saint-Luperce have done in this part of India, where he maintained that he had commanded Hyder Ali Khan's artillery? What was held against him? For sure, our Chevalier de Christ, if that was what he was, despite my uncle's doubts on the matter, had returned to India and accomplished a successful mission, although once again not everybody was convinced of this. And he had been sent to the Malabar coast where he was less well known. He had been arrested and once more imprisoned in the Bastille, but quickly released thanks to the intervention of Monsieur de Sartine and the Comte de Vergennes, aided by this Doctor Baldock.

I remembered about the file that my uncle had said he had left for me in Monsieur de Fleurieu's steel cabinet. I asked Monsieur de Fleurieu whether I could have a look at it, which he quickly agreed to, as he himself had not had time to examine it, given how busy he was making preparations for the sending of a new Naval force across the Atlantic. He was also preparing a smaller force for the Cape of Good Hope, which the King wanted to be ready to put to sea as soon as the Dutch asked for it. We were therefore sending forces to the East and the West simultaneously, and orders had to be prepared so that their commanders could take decisions in line with the King's wishes. The Marquis de Castries had already written to the Comte d'Hector, ordering him to prepare four copper-bottomed ships for an imminent departure, without specifying that it would be for the Cape and India. In these despatches the Minister also signalled the arrival in Brest of an envoy who would be going to the Île-de-France to announce the British government's declaration of war on Holland. He would be carrying the latest King's orders to Monsieur de Souillac and would be going with *la Sylphide* and *la Bellone*. These frigates would be stopping at the Cape to land an officer whose secret mission was to prepare for the arrival of French troops. The Dutch had yet to ask for military help but had not yet fully realised that the English had declared war on them. They had not expected it and were in no position to defend their colonies.

*

Versailles, Monday 8th January 1781, afternoon.
Monsieur de Fleurieu has given me the contents of the box folder left by the Chevalier de Kermean. There I find several carefully labelled cardboard files and what seems to be a wrapped and tied octavo volume. I have been given an office where I can work on my own, back to the hearth, and examine in comfort this treasure that so piques my curiosity.
I start by unwrapping the package, which indeed turns out to be a cardboard bound book. A hand-written note from my uncle says that it was at his request that Doctor Baldock, the book's author, gave it to him:

AN
ESSAY
ON THE
NATURAL HISTORY
OF
GUYANA
IN SOUTH AMERICA

I see first that this 'Essay', printed in London in 1769, contains a detailed description of Guyana: its natural riches, its agriculture, its flora and fauna, the habits of its people, its illnesses and how to treat them and so on. Its author presents himself as a gentleman of the Faculty of Medicine.

Unsurprisingly, one of the files is on Edward Baldock. I learn that he is thirty-six years old, that he was born and raised in Massachusetts, and that he studied medicine firstly in New England, then in a hospital in London. He had twice served as a plantation doctor in Surinam. He had met Benjamin Franklin in London and the two had become friends. Franklin has sent him to France to make contact with the King's secret service. Baldock had returned to London several times to put in place a network for spying on the English for the benefit of the Insurgents in Paris. He communicates with his agents by messengers who travel via Belgium. The Chevalier had learned all this by talking to Baldock, and also by means of the letters sent by Baldock to Silas Deane, which had been intercepted and copied by our own secret service operatives. In the course of this he had learned that Baldock often used the name Griffiths when travelling on secret business.

I then open a file on Hyder Ali Khan. It is filled with descriptions of the Nabob's personality and how he organises his government, army and so on. All of this information was given to the Chevalier de Kermean by Doctor Rollin, prior to his death.

The part relating to Saint-Luperce is composed of ten or so reports, in the form of letters, signed 'Binet', an inspector in the 'Sixth Office of Public Security'. This police officer works for both the Paris Police and the Secretary of State for Foreign Affairs. His job is to keep an eye on 'foreigners' in the capital, for which he has at his disposal a small army of agents and spies. Given the recent reaction to our investigations on matters concerning the King's Household, I wonder how my uncle had been allowed to use this Binet to have Saint-Luperce followed, which is in effect what had happened. Doubtless he had been able to do it prior to Saint-Luperce coming to the notice of the Comte de Vergennes. I notice that the two most recent letters have not been unsealed, which seems to indicate that they have arrived after my uncle's departure for Brest.

The reports are filed in chronological order. The first tells me that after his release from the Bastille, at the end of September 1780, Saint-Luperce '*age 43, born in Lyon, took lodgings in the rue Neuve Saint-*

Eustache, at the Strasbourg hotel run by the widow Moreau'. Looking at the dates, I also see that contrary to what my uncle has told me at Brest, he had not waited for Monsieur de Castries' order to have Saint-Luperce watched. The latter had been watched systematically and the first detailed reports simply record his movements between Paris and the rue da la Surintendance at Versailles. I have to wait until the sheet dated October 1st to find anything unusual.

> *'The subject came out of his lodgings at nine o'clock in the morning and went off in the direction of the rue Montmartre, which he crossed to go along the rue des Fossés Montmartre to the Place des Victoires. He walked as far as the statue of Louis XIV crowned by Victory. He stopped beside the iron railing surrounding the plinth and tied a handkerchief to the corner bar pointing towards the Rue de la Croix des Petits Champs. He returned immediately to his lodgings by the same route.'*

The Inspector from the 'Sixth Office' had not skimped on his resources, as it seemed he had several men trailing Saint-Luperce simultaneously. One had stayed on the spot all day and confirmed that nobody had touched the handkerchief. The next day, the 2nd October…

> *'at half past nine, the subject came out of his lodgings and went to the Place des Victoires. He seemed pleased to see that his signal was still there and went to stand at the junction with the rue de la Croix des Petits Champs. At ten o'clock a fiacre arrived via the rue de la Croix des Petits Champs, with a passenger inside. The fiacre stopped in front of the subject, who got in. The fiacre then went off at a trot along the rue de la Feuillade.'*

The Inspector had underlined 'at a trot' to show that he was unable to have the fiacre followed, but his agent had taken its number. The Paris fiacres are in fact marked with numbers and letters, so that if anyone leaves anything in them, they can use the number to reclaim their belongings at the carriage management offices. This had enabled the Paris police to find the driver quite easily. He told them that he had been hired at his usual stand near the Aguesseau market. His passenger was of less than average height, in middle-class dress and spoke with a strange accent *'that according to the coachman did not seem to be French'*, as Binet had written. Having picked up Saint-Luperce at the Place des Victoires, his client had told him to drive around at will, without stopping, before depositing Saint-Luperce in the same place he been picked up. The report said that on descending from the fiacre, the subject had removed the handkerchief from the railings around the statue of Louis XIV. As for the original passenger, the coachman had taken him back to the carriage stand at the Aguesseau market. This same circuit happened twice more, always with the same mysterious client hiring a fiacre at the stand close to the market at the junction between the rue Royale and the rue du Faubourg Saint-Honoré.

I then get to the two letters that my uncle has not opened. They are dated the 15th and 20th December 1780. The 20th December letter does not say much. There are simply a few lines from the Inspector of the 'Sixth Office' apologising for the fact that the Minister of Foreign Affairs has ordered him to halt immediately the surveillance of Saint-Luperce.

The letter of the 15th, on the other hand, is extremely interesting, as well as surprising. It also raises new questions which I was not expecting. On Tuesday 13th December, Saint-Luperce had gone to wait at the junction between the Place des Victoires and the rue de la Croix des Petits Champs. However, this time it was towards the end of the day and he had not needed to put his usual signal on the railings around the statue of Louis XIV. Quite logically, the Inspector deduced in his report that the rendezvous had been fixed in advance. Another novelty was that the fiacre had not returned to the Place des Victoires; the agent there had waited in vain. The subject had returned to his lodgings on foot after dark. When the coachman was questioned, the police had learned that at the request of his client he had set down his two passengers in front of a small hotel for people of quality near the Palais Royal. The police have a register of all these places and the Inspector soon found it. He interviewed the owner, giving him descriptions of Saint-Luperce and the unknown man with the strange accent. He learned that the two men had met up with two travellers who had stayed at the hotel for several days, and that their meals had been taken up to allow the four to dine together in one of the rooms. The two guests at the hotel had of course filled out the forms required by the police, declaring themselves as John

Mathews, a wine merchant from Connecticut, and Jean Declercq, a shipowner from Brussels. They had shown papers written and signed by Benjamin Franklin and countersigned by a high-ranking official of the Department of Foreign Affairs, who had added his seal. The hotel owner's description of John Mathews indicated that he spoke French very badly, that he was below average height, aged about forty, with blue eyes and a determined, tough demeanour. As for the Belgian, he was about fifty and very tall. The innkeeper had particularly noticed the patch over his left eye, which did not completely cover an impressive scar. The Inspector was conscientious enough to have gone to the office of the Ministry of Foreign Affairs in Versailles to check that the certificates were authentic. It was confirmed to him that the visit to Paris of these two supporters of the American cause had been authorised by the Comte de Vergennes at the request of Benjamin Franklin. The latter had even said that they would not come to his residence at Passy in case they drew the attention of English spies. Inspector Binet had not made any commentary on this typically puzzling statement from the 'Good Franklin' but had not been able to resist putting three exclamation marks after it.

I no longer understand anything. What could Saint-Luperce, who has always been exclusively involved in Indian affairs, be doing with these Americans? The only American he knows is Baldock, since my uncle had told me that the doctor had asked to visit Saint-Luperce when he was in the Bastille. Could the mysterious passenger in the fiacre be Baldock, then? If the two men got along well together, there was nothing wrong with that, but why take so many precautions in order to meet? And why should Saint-Luperce be involved in a meeting of the secret organisation run by Baldock? The Americans have enough on their plate with their war of independence, without concerning themselves with India.

I take the files back to Monsieur de Fleurieu and show him Inspector Binet's report on the secret meeting between Saint-Luperce and the American agents. He is as puzzled as I am by it. He finally comes up with the hypothesis that Saint-Luperce may be acting as a liaison for the Comte de Vergennes, without the knowledge of the Marquis de Castries or their mutual friend Necker. That could explain why the Ministry of Foreign Affairs had summarily cut short our investigations into Saint-Luperce.

I wrote to Maria Kirwan to tell her that there had been a change of plan and that my arrival at Brest had been delayed. I thought that having missed one sailing I would need to be patient while waiting for the next and could use the delay to try to unravel the puzzles of Duval and Saint-Luperce. I was wrong.

An extremely well-timed message from Captain Le Meur, who had decided to resume his crossings to Salcombe despite our doubts about the Cornish agents, gave some intelligence that was quickly confirmed by other sources. The first piece of information did not surprise Monsieur de Fleurieu, who was expecting it: Vice-Admiral Darby was preparing to cross the Bay of Biscay with twenty-nine ships of the line and a hundred transport ships in order to blockade the Spanish at Gibraltar. The second piece of news was more disconcerting for the Navy Department: Captain Johnson of the Royal Navy had been promoted to Commodore and given command of a division. He was to accompany Darby to Gibraltar and then carry on to seize the Cape of Good Hope. The English threat to the Dutch colony was now clear, but we could do nothing until the Dutch government asked for our help. For the moment they were content to ask for support from the League of Armed Neutrality.

Since the start of the conflict the Royal Navy had seen it as its right to intercept any lone merchant ships it came across at sea. The English captains considered that a neutral ship was a valid prize if its cargo was of economic benefit to their enemies. On the other hand, Louis XVI had forbidden his Navy and corsairs to bring in any ships from neutral powers, even when coming from, or going to, enemy ports. The Russian Empress had used the French model to found the League of Armed Neutrality, in which members pooled their warships to escort their convoys and maintain their right to free trade with other countries. The Dutch, although invited to join the League at the start of the war between France and Britain, had at first declined the offer, believing that their long-standing friendship with the English would be enough to protect them. Later they had wanted to join the League, but Catherine II had told them that it was too late, and that they were no longer neutral, since the British Crown had declared war on them. It was not long before alarming news of Dutch vessels being captured by English ships of the line reached Versailles.

At the end of January, a diplomatic despatch from the Hague informed the Comte de Vergennes that representatives from the Dutch East India Company had approached our ambassador to ask for armed help from France. Nothing could yet be decided without a proper formal approach from the Dutch government, but the King ordered his ministers to start making preparations. This decision had immediate consequences for me which arrived without warning on the 8th February 1781. That morning, as I was arriving for my fencing training at the Gardes Françaises drill hall, a clerk from the Navy Department told me to go immediately to the Director of Ports and Arsenals' office.

'You are leaving tomorrow,' Monsieur de Fleurieu told me. 'Follow me, the Minister is waiting for us.'

*

Versailles, Thursday 8th February 1781.

For the second time I find myself in front of the Marquis de Castries, together with Monsieur de Fleurieu. The Minister invites us to sit down while a secretary gives him some papers to sign. Once the clerk has left he raises his head.

'Monsieur Laforest-Dombourg, I think that we can at last rid ourselves of you.'

I don't quite know how to take this opening statement.

'You will leave tomorrow, you will go to the Baron de Kermean, your grandfather, to collect the diamonds, and then you will go straight to Brest. We have found a solution which, I hope, will guarantee both your safety and the necessary discretion for this voyage. Monsieur de Fleurieu will explain all that in detail.'

I appreciate the 'necessary discretion', but above all I have the pleasurable thought that I will soon see my dear Maria Kirwan again. I cannot help smiling, which seems to unnerve the Minister.

'Now, listen carefully! This is very serious! Nothing that I have to tell you will leave this room, including the name of the ship to whose crew you have been added, or at least not until you have joined her. We have had enough trouble because of Colonel Guypair. Swear solemnly, here and now, that you will hold your tongue.'

If I dared, I would remind him that it was not my fault that Guypair had so easily had suspicions about the real reasons for me being in Versailles. I turn towards Monsieur de Fleurieu, who remains completely impassive. So I stand up.

'I solemnly swear here and now that I will hold my tongue.'

The Minister seems surprised, and with a gracious wave of the hand, signals me to sit down again.

'Good!'

I look once more at Monsieur de Fleurieu, who this time seems somewhat amused. The Marquis de Castries then hands me one of the documents he has just signed.

'Once you have the diamonds you will join *l'Annibal* at Brest.'

Have I heard correctly? *L'Annibal* has returned to Brest and I am to join her officers? I will see my friend Vernon des Aulnes and we will be sailing together! I cannot hide my joy. The Marquis de Castries notices this and for a moment drops his distant, formal air and questions me in a kindly tone.

'That seems to please you. Do you know *l'Annibal?*'

'I was on her main gundeck during the Battle of Grenada. I have friends aboard her and I'm truly happy to learn that I will have the chance to serve under the Comte de Lamotte-Piquet. Along with Monsieur de Lapérouse, he is the man I most admire in the whole world!'

I immediately bite my lip, suddenly realising that my words may be wounding to them, but the Marquis maintains his smile.

'My nephew has told me about the Battle of Grenada. It was a bloody affair I think.'

'We had fifty-nine killed aboard *l'Annibal,* Sir, and many wounded who died later.'

'Laforest-Dombourg has kept a personal souvenir, Sir,' added Monsieur de Fleurieu. 'You can see it on his left cheek.'

'A sabre blow?' asks the Marquis de Castries, having looked at me.

'No, Sir, it was a piece of skull,' I say.

'Skull?'

I explain that a gun captain had been struck by a cannon ball and half his skull and brains had hit me full in the face. The Marquis shakes his head.

'I went to war when I was very young and have seen plenty of battles, but anyone who is not a sailor would have trouble imagining what a naval combat is like.'

He once more adopts his serious air.

'I am sorry to disappoint you, but the Comte de Lamotte-Piquet has given up command of *l'Annibal.* Your commander will be Ship's Captain de Trémigon.'

Trémigon. I seem to have heard that name somewhere, or was it Trémignon? In any case, I am disappointed.

'Captain de Trémigon was for a long time a Captain in the India Company. He knows the seas beyond the Cape extremely well. That is where *l'Annibal* is going, along with three other ships currently being prepared. But nobody yet knows in Brest, apart from the Comte d'Hector. This mission must remain secret until the last moment.'

The Marquis de Castries picks up a folded paper lying in front of him and hands it to me.

'Once you get to Brest you will give this to Captain de Trémigon. He has been forewarned that a Ship's Ensign is coming from Versailles to join his officers but as yet he does not know why we are recommending you. This letter contains a summary of your service.'

The Marquis de Castries smiles again.

'Looking at you I think this will be useful and will reassure your new commander. I have also mentioned the existence of the diamond treasure and your role in this business. Be careful not to lose this letter. It absolutely must not fall into the wrong hands before you get to Brest.'

'I will defend it with my life, Sir.'

This time the Minister laughs heartily.

'I hope it won't come to that! We are going to give you a strong steel coffer with two keys. You will give one to your Captain and keep the other one yourself. Captain de Trémigon will keep the coffer in his cabin, but that is not the end of your mission.'

He takes several sheets of headed paper off his desk.

'These letters are for the Vicomte de Souillac and the Comte d'Orves. I explain to them how the diamonds will be used and outline our new policy for India. I'm going to summarise their content so that you can pass it on to Captain de Trémigon. Monsieur de Fleurieu tells me I can trust you to be discreet. I hope he is not mistaken. We are sending four ships and a small transport fleet carrying twelve hundred troops, some of whom will be reinforcing defences at the Cape of Good Hope. It is what follows that concerns you. After disembarking the troops at the Cape, this small squadron will carry on to the Île-de-France and join a bigger force which combines all our resources out there. This force will sail to the island of Mahé off west coast of the Deccan, then to Chaul[10] where the battalions will be disembarked. In the meantime, Monsieur de Montigny will have had the time, I hope, to have prepared our operational plans with the Marathas. The rest of our troops will arrive later with the Marquis de Bussy. Once our forces are combined we will have eight thousand men in place. We want all our efforts in India to be allied to the Marathas. As I think I have already told you, Hyder Ali Khan is not a suitable ally for us. Moreover, the west coast of India is much more sheltered in winter than the Coromandel coast. Your mission will consist firstly of guarding the chest of diamonds to Brest and then to the Île-de-France. Secondly, Captain de Trémigon will pass this letter to the Vicomte de Souillac, who will give you new instructions for guarding the treasure until it is unloaded at Chaul. You will then, of course, remain aboard *l'Annibal* and your mission as regards the diamonds will be over. Do you have any questions?'

'What about Monsieur de Saint-Luperce?' I ask.

'He will also be going aboard *l'Annibal* as a passenger from the department of Foreign Affairs. Given his knowledge of the Marathas, he will be very useful for our Chargé d'Affaires at Poona. He of course knows nothing about your mission or the existence of this treasure. Don't misunderstand me. I am telling you all this so that you can explain the position to Captain de Trémigon. Otherwise, considering your youth, I would have said nothing. Circumstance forces me to be open with you. Don't let me down!'

The Marquis hands over the letter for me to read, and also gives me a purse containing fifty gold louis and a safe-conduct signed by the King.

Louis by the Grace of God King of France and Navarre
M. Laforest-Dombourg is charged with my secret orders.
The discretion and speed of their execution will provide the most pleasing
proof of his zeal in my service.
At Versailles today, the seventh of the month of February
Seventeen hundred and eighty-one.

---

10 Translator's note: *Chaul:* Port in what was Portuguese India, south of Bombay, now Mumbai.

The document ends with the usual way: 'In the name of the King' and signed 'Louis'.

'This is to counter any unforeseen hazards. Monsieur de Fleurieu tells me that you have already benefitted from this kind of measure and have been able to make use of it with total honesty. I have no choice but to trust his opinion and ask you to continue. Her Majesty would have liked to have received you. She likes young sailors. But we told her it would not be helpful to draw attention to you.'

I feel the shadows of Monsieur Necker and Colonel de Guypair passing by.

'This safe-conduct will also give you the necessary authority to ensure that Monsieur de Souillac will listen to you, if need be. Read the letter carefully so that you can summarise it for Captain de Trémigon. I have to sign and seal it now. You are the only ones who know of its existence, at least until you arrive at the Île-de-France. Excuse me for being so insistent. If you had not already had the experience of doing secret work at Saint-Malo, I would not entrust you with anything. I tell you all this to be sure you tell Captain de Trémigon and nobody else but him! I will be going to Brest soon myself but to keep matters discreet I will not be communicating all this directly to Captain de Trémigon. These directives also deal with other activities that will unfold in due course but there is no point in revealing them yet, especially as we have so many other orders to give to our squadron commanders before they leave Brest.'

I hand the letter back to the Marquis de Castries, who pulls a bell cord. The clerk we saw just before comes back to seal the package for the Île-de-France. I am conscious of the confidence that the Minister is placing in me, even if it is a case of him being forced by circumstance, as he has tried so hard to explain. I tell him that this departure for India reminds me of my first voyage in the Navy, aboard the frigate *l'Amazone*, which was supposed to have sailed to the Malabar coast under the Chevalier de Ternay.

'Did you know the Chevalier de Ternay well?'

I reply that I had the honour of being presented to him several times, as he and the Comte de Lapérouse were very close.

'No doubt *l'Amazone* was recalled to Brest because of the mutual trust between the Comte de Lapérouse and the Chevalier de Ternay,' I add.

The Marquis looks at me sadly, shaking his head.

'I'm sorry to have to tell you that the Chevalier de Ternay died just after you left Newport. We learned this last week. He succumbed to a malignant fever, it seems.'

I see again the Chevalier de Ternay on the quayside by the Brest Arsenal when he was inspecting *l'Amazone* and *la Gentille* before their proposed departure for India. This expedition was to have been the highpoint of his career and its cancellation was a fatal blow from which he never recovered. I think about the distress that the Comte de Lapérouse must have felt on hearing this news, loving him, as he did, like a father.

The meeting finishes there, as the Marquis de Castries has to go to the King's Council. Monsieur de Fleurieu asks me to go back to his office with him so that he can give me all the details of my mission.

The door to Monsieur de Fleurieu's office is still open and a visitor is waiting inside. He holds out his hand, without rising, to greet Monsieur de Fleurieu. Even sitting, he seems huge. His town jacket, decorated with the Cross of the Order of Malta rather than the Cross of Saint-Louis, is half unbuttoned over a massive belly that is bursting the buttons of his waistcoat. His face is brick-red with a double chin melting into his neck, a thin-lipped mouth framed by jowls which swell his cheeks and hang down each side of his face. His imposing nose is worthy of a Roman emperor; his eyebrows arch in semi-circles. It is above all his eyelids that impress me: half-closed over light brown eyes filled with intelligence and wickedness, they give him a look of authority over the world, at first amused when he talks to Monsieur de Fleurieu, then suddenly disdainful when he sees me. He wears his hair *au naturel,* pulled back from his narrow forehead into a ponytail. The hair above his ears has been hastily curled with irons in honour of his visit to the Court, but it is clear that this is done rarely. At first glance I would say he is about fifty.

'Monsieur de Fleurieu, I am happy to see you. The Minister ordered me to come. I've come post-haste from Brest especially, I've got a sore backside because of the bad suspension, the meals at the Relays are atrocious and I won't even mention their wine!'

He has a nasal voice with a very strong Provençal accent.

'We were expecting you, Sir, but did not know that you had already arrived. I can assure you that Monsieur the Marquis de la Croix de

Castries will see you before this evening, but he has gone to the King's Council.'

'Monsieur the Marquis de la Croix de Castries! Good God ! At least he's not from Brittany, with a name like that! That's one thing in his favour! But he's still a foot-soldier.'

'A cavalryman.'

'Ha! Ha! I've never liked horses. Dirty beasts with a mouth that bites at the front, and hooves that try and break your leg at the back! Good! Enough joking! Fleurieu, send this pen-pusher back to his scribbling and let's talk sailor to sailor. Is he going to let me raise my ensign at last?'

'Monsieur de Laforest-Dombourg is not my secretary. He's a Ship's Ensign,' replies Monsieur de Fleurieu.

'In that case he should be aboard ship, not at Versailles!'

In normal times these words would have caused me to react and perhaps reply impertinently, but this man had really intimidated and attracted me at the same time; behind his apparent good humour and southern volubility, he seemed to me like a huge tamed boar whose brutal and irresistible force could be awakened at any moment.

'Laforest-Dombourg departs on a mission tomorrow and I have to give him his orders. Would you mind leaving us alone for a moment?'

'Fleurieu! I am a Ship's Captain, Commander of the Order of Malta! I went to sea at fourteen, had my baptism of fire at fifteen, have thirty-eight years of service and have come hoping you will give me a squadron! Get rid of your little Court peacock with his spindly legs and let's talk man to man and sailor to sailor!'

'Now then, don't get annoyed. I can tell you that the Minister wants to see you but you will understand that I can't say why. I will leave that to him.'

The big Captain jumps to his feet with surprising agility, given his corpulence. He is a little taller than me and as wide and round as he is high. He fills the room on his own. I feel like pressing myself to the wall to escape his sudden fury. His naturally red face has turned scarlet.

'Thank you, Fleurieu! I fully appreciate your sense of comradeship! As for your minion,' he adds, looking at me, 'if ever he has the misfortune to cross my path again, he had better watch out! I'm off to see my friend Blouin. At least he will tell me what's being hatched against me in this damned building and why nobody wants to give me a squadron when I see on the new list that, after Brovès, Marin has been promoted. Marin! You hear me? And du Breil de Rays! Two useless cretins with no experience!'

He goes out, banging the door behind him. Monsieur de Fleurieu shakes his head and looks at me sadly. He settles in behind his desk and invites me to sit opposite him.

'Who is he? And who is Monsieur Blouin?' I ask.

'The Chevalier de Suffren-Saint-Tropez. Commander de Suffren! And Monsieur Blouin is the Head Clerk at the Officers' Bureau. He knows all the Navy officers' files inside out and whenever the Commander comes here he goes to butter him up. Monsieur de Sartine had already proposed the Chevalier de Suffren for a provisional commission as squadron commander, but the King thought it was too soon. He appreciates his merits and wants to encourage him, but he is fortieth on the list and we are fully at war. He's not the only one fighting for a commission and now's not the time to create bad feeling. What can one do? The Chevalier de Suffren has always been like this. He approaches you with his heart on his sleeve, offering you Maltese oranges, and the next minute he is in a rage, with no warning, and nobody can calm him down. I'm worried for you. Have you met him before?'

'No, it's the first time I've seen him up close. He commanded a sixty-four gun ship, *le Fantasque*, in the Comte d'Estaing's squadron. He was head of the line in the Battle of Grenada. The Comte de Lapérouse holds him in high esteem. But why did you say you were worried for me?'

'Because I know why the Marquis de Castries has called him. He wants to offer him command of the division with which you will be going to India. But first the Minister wants to make an evaluation of him, as he does not know him. Keep this to yourself! If de Suffren refuses, it will be Captain de Trémigon who commands the division. But it would be better if it were Suffren. He is more proactive despite his awkward character.'

'I remember hearing about a Trémignon who was court-martialled after the Battle of Ushant.'

'That's him. Trémignon, Trémigon, it's all the same. An old Breton family, in any case. In July 1778 he had *l'Alexandre*, a sixty-four, third in line in the blue and white squadron. He was following *le Duc de*

Bourgogne, eighty guns, commanded by the Vicomte de Rochechouart. The night before the Battle of Ushant the Admiral had ordered the fleet to tack to keep the windward advantage. Trémigon didn't see the signal and so didn't relay it to *le Duc de Bourgogne,* who continued straight on in the dark. The next day we were two ships short for the battle. The King had de Trémigon court martialled for this, but he was acquitted. In his defence the Comte d'Orvilliers had said that it was an involuntary mistake due to his lack of experience in squadron manoeuvres. In fact, Captain de Trémigon had begun his career in the India Company, only joining the Navy after the company was closed down. He is an experienced seaman and an excellent ship-handler, but not as good in battle as Suffren.'

*

After the Chevalier de Suffren had left, Monsieur de Fleurieu explained to me that the India division would leave Brest at the same time as another fleet commanded by the Comte de Grasse which would be restarting our actions in the Antilles and the Americas. The four ships and the transports destined for the Cape of Good Hope would separate from the main convoy once at sea. It was hoped that this stratagem would hide our true objective from the eyes and ears of any English spies. *L'Annibal* and her accompanying ships were under orders to pile on sail in order to arrive at the Cape first, and to avoid combat with any enemy ships encountered en route, as this would slow them down. In this way, Monsieur de Fleurieu explained, the precious coffer of diamonds would be safer than aboard a lone frigate. He added that he did not think my safe-conduct would be of much use, but the King had insisted on signing it personally, remembering the one he had issued before the war for my mission at Saint-Malo. It was also perhaps compensation for the fact that he had not been able to receive me, when he would have liked to have talked informally with a young sailor like me who had already seen action and who knew nothing about the Court. But the Marquis de Castries had insisted so strongly that it would be unwise that he had abandoned the idea. Monsieur de Fleurieu said that the Minister would probably choose de Suffren to command this little division, but that he would not tell him immediately that it was destined for the Cape and India. Only Captain de Trémigon and

I would know of the new operational plans in India, contained in the sealed letters entrusted to me. It was the Marquis de Bussy who asked for this additional precaution. The general rumour was that we would be offering help to Hyder Ali Khan, and the Marquis de Bussy was happy with that, as the English would easily believe it and the element of surprise would be greater. In any case, prior to our arrival at the Île-de-France it was of little importance if everyone thought we were heading for the Coromandel coast. The Chevalier de Suffren's orders only concerned the Cape, which was of itself an objective of the highest importance. The new policy towards India was not even mentioned in the despatches which the frigate *la Fine* had to carry to the Île-de-France before our division left. A frigate could be attacked by a bigger enemy, while the four ships we were sending should be strong enough to evade combat, holding themselves back for a better occasion. Monsieur de Fleurieu added that Saint-Luperce would greatly appreciate this change of plan, given that the treaty he had signed, or purported to have signed, at Poona on behalf of the King was the main source of his support from the Comte de Vergennes.

As for Louis Duval, his case was still a mystery, given the quality of the intelligence being provided by our Cornish agents. Monsieur de Fleurieu promised to do his best to have Duval's regime at the Bastille softened while he tried to throw some more light on the matter.

5

I set off at dawn on the 9th February. On the previous evening I had returned my black suit to Monsieur de Fleurieu and had with great pleasure donned my old regulation uniform: the fatigues that I normally wore at sea – blue, bordered with six gold lines and with a single braided epaulette on the left shoulder. Its colours had already faded in the ocean winds.

I had been provided with a carriage hired from a civilian carter. Along with my personal chest I loaded it with the marvellous contraption envisaged by the Marquis de Castries: a forged steel box bound with riveted strips and armed with a secure lock protected by a secret mechanism. Its hinged lid was secured by a nine-bolt lock that was impossible to break open. As I was yet to put the diamonds in it, I used it to hide the sealed letters from the Minister, the purse containing the fifty gold louis, and my safe-conduct. I kept my embarkation orders in my jacket in case I had to show them while on the road. I had been given two identical keys that I attached to a string knotted around my neck under my shirt collar. I would give one to Captain de Trémigon. I was escorted by two bodyguards, one masquerading as the head coachman, the other as his foot valet. In fact, they were two long-serving soldiers in their prime, well-armed with pistols, sabres and muskets. At the age of twenty both had been dragoons in the Autichamp regiment and had distinguished themselves in a dangerous engagement in Lower Saxony, under the command of a dragoon Captain who would subsequently become famous for other reasons: the Chevalier d'Éon[11]. The latter took note of them and subsequently recruited them for more covert, but no less dangerous, operations, after the end of the Seven Years' War. They said little and did not ask questions. Everything had been done not to attract attention. We were to travel as simple civilians, with postillions as far as Nantes, and then hired horses to Kermean. The journey passed without incident.

My grandfather was by then in his sixty-seventh year, and thus far had been spared illness. He was still occupied with his agriculture and his horse breeding, but his morale was low and he suffered from loneliness. The news that my uncle was to leave for America had affected him badly. Even though he hid the fact, he was keen that the war should be over so that his son could come and replace him in running the estates. Moreover he was disappointed that my little sister, whom he loved dearly, and whom he hoped to see again, was still at the Chevalier de Kermean's parents-in-law's property, south of Nantes, along with the latter's wife and children.

'Can you believe that they have not even come to show me my two grandsons? It's not for me to travel to them! I know it's not Anne's fault, the poor child. It's on account of my daughter-in-law.'

I would have liked to have left immediately, to see Maria Kirwan again, but hearing this kind of comment I thought that it was not the time to further disappoint the Baron by telling him that I had decided to marry an innkeeper. I was even more grateful to Maria for having in a way freed me by choosing of her own volition to follow the example of Mademoiselle Broudou. In any case, there was no hurry to fulfil my duties, as on the morning of my departure Monsieur de Fleurieu had told me that my ship was still being prepared for sea in the Penfeld and that she would not be taken out into the harbour before the first week of March. The plan was to put the chest immediately into safekeeping in Captain de Trémigon's cabin aboard *l'Annibal* and so he needed to be installed there first.

Despite my impatience I decided to prolong my stay at Kermean. I

___

11 Translator's note: *Chevalier d'Éon de Beaumont (1728 – 1810)*: soldier, diplomat and spy. He spent much of his diplomatic life in London and is buried at St. Pancras Old Church. He was famed for his transvestism and at one point the London Stock Exchange took bets as to whether he was a man or a woman.

took advantage of the extra time to order six strong leather purses from a craftsman in Mesquer. These were for better storing the diamonds in the steel chest, which had a greater volume than the wooden Indian box they had been put in by Flaharn twenty years previously, before his departure from Chandernagore.

Winter seemed to soften during the second half of this month of February 1781. I went on long horse-rides with my grandfather. Like good soldiers my two former dragoons settled in well to this unforeseen break. They became great friends with Ottmeyer, the head groom at the manor, who had also fought in Germany during the Seven Years' War, with the Dauphin's cavalry.

I also took advantage of this forced interlude to immerse myself in the manuscript of the late Doctor Rollin, given to me in Paris by his former mistress. The text was both a story and a diary, entitled simply *A Memoir of Hindustan.*

The first part described, in an often obsessively detailed and fastidious way, the climate, geography and riches of Hindustan. Or rather the regions of the Indian peninsula, where Rollin had lived: the Coromandel Coast, the Carnatic and Mysore. I skimmed quickly through the chapters entitled *The Fertility of Hindustan, Fields and Harvests, Fruit Trees, Vegetables and Flowers,* and *Animals* – everything was there – quadrupeds, birds, reptiles, insects and so on. There were also chapters devoted to craftsmen, industries, measurements, morals and beliefs, Indian religions and, of course, to diseases and their local cures.

I found something familiar about this encyclopaedic description of the East Indies, as if I had already read it. I eventually realised that it reminded me of the *Essay on Guyana,* written by Edward Baldock, another doctor, this time describing the West Indies.

In the second part Rollin painted the political picture, with the Nabob Hyder Ali Khan taking pride of place. I had a vague hope that the manuscript may perhaps provide some clue that would shed light on the puzzle of Rollin's death and the role played by the mysterious English spy described by the waitress in the *Porcherons* inn. I turned page after page impatiently and in fact I made a surprising discovery, but not at all what I had expected.

The final part of the manuscript was a sort of chronological story written as a diary, in the first person, in which Rollin described his stay in India from the moment he left France. It began thus:

*In November 1756 I was surgeon-in-chief of the Lorraine infantry
when the regiment was sent to India under the command of the Comte
de Lally. I presented myself at L'Orient on the 21ˢᵗ December 1756 and
we sailed on the 30ᵗʰ, with 1020 men from our regiment and 50 from the
Royal Corps of Artillery. This advance detachment was commanded
by the Chevalier de Soupire, Field-Marshall. I was accompanied by
a young man called Joseph Alexis Tallebau, son of a Lyon wigmaker,
who was in search of adventure. He had begged me to take him as my
assistant. I had agreed wholeheartedly as I thought that his intelligence
and lively mind would enable me to train him as a surgeon's assistant
during the long voyage ahead…*

Joseph Alexis Tallebau! I had almost forgotten the remark made by
Monsieur de Fleurieu about Kaveripattinam and the suspicions it had
aroused in me when I had thought about it in Rollin's former bedroom.
Rollin's memoir described Lally's arrival in Pondicherry in 1758,
the capture of Cuddalore and Fort St. David, Lally's confused and
contradictory orders, our soldiers' tiring marches and counter-marches
through the Indian countryside, the heat, the torrential monsoon rains,
up to our disastrous defeat at Madras at which the Comte d'Estaing
had been taken prisoner. Once he was there Rollin spoke again about
Tallebau. The wigmaker's son had shown a remarkable aptitude in
learning foreign languages and had already mastered Tamil to the extent
that this was noticed by the commanding General. He had been sent
over to the English side on a secret mission, or at least that is what
he maintained when leaving his employment as a surgeon's mate with
undisguised pleasure, it being work which he considered beneath him.
The doctor had then lost track of him, until he was surprised to hear
that he was amongst the first wave of heroic attackers, sabre in hand,
to scale the Fort St. David defences, despite the fact that Rollin knew
he had been by his side for the whole action, caring for the sick and
wounded in the regimental hospital. This was followed by the English
siege of Pondicherry. The town surrendered on the 16ᵗʰ January 1761.
Many of the sick and exhausted soldiers were brought straight to the
hospital, while the people of the town were dying of hunger. Lally had
left as a prisoner, booed by the civilians for his obstinacy in continuing a
pointless resistance. The victors razed to the ground the Fort St. Louis,
the fortified enclosure, the Governor's residence and a good portion of

the White Town. Rollin, along with many French soldiers, had taken advantage of the brief confusion following the surrender to escape. He had offered his services to Hyder Ali Khan and been taken on as his personal physician. The story continued with the Nabob's campaigns and his rivalry with Mohamed Ali Khan, who was supported by the East India Company. This lasted until 1769 and the reappearance of Tallebau. But now he was called the Chevalier Tallebau de Saint-Luperce. Rollin had seen him arrive at the Nabob's camp with a fake Cross of St. Louis on his chest, presenting himself as a former artillery captain on his way to Pondicherry.

> *…Lieutenant Colonel Hügel, who was in command of the French hussars, did not for a second doubt the qualities of the Chevalier who, along with the Cross he had the effrontery to wear, was also possessed, to the misfortune of many, of an engaging and seductive appearance… unfortunately Tallebau could not resist committing one or two frauds for which he was arrested and imprisoned.*

Rollin was less than clear in his description of this episode.

> *…I interceded personally with Hyder Ali in order to save the life of my former assistant…the Nabob gave his permission for him to leave his army and make his way to the Coromandel Coast along with some English officers. These had surrendered during the capture of a redoubt on the Ambur road and had been liberated by Hyder Ali and given permission to return to Madras, as he intended to negotiate a truce with the English.*

There was nothing more said about Tallebau right up to the end of the doctor's story, which finished when he embarked to return to France. What was to be made of the fact that he had saved Tallebau's life? Was this literally or figuratively? And what was the significance of the decision to free him at the same time as the English prisoners?

In any case, I said to myself, Tallebau de Saint-Luperce would have yet another reason to be happy that he was not being sent to Hyder Ali, but rather to the Marathas, with whom he had excellent relations. With what I had just discovered, I even wondered how he had willingly accepted to be our emissary to the Nabob.

*

Kerlaudy, Tuesday 6th March 1781

It is eleven in the morning and I will soon arrive at Kerlaudy. I am alone. I have hired a mount for the day at Morlaix. Sometimes the road runs alongside the river Penzé, which I can see lower down from time to time. It is neap tides but the current upstream is still strong as we are close to the strongest time of the flood. The wind is light, varying from south to south-west. A few isolated oaks stand here and there on the flat countryside. It is very mild for the time of year.

We left Kermean three days ago and arrived yesterday here at Morlaix. We kept the team of horses we had hired at Nantes, as there is no post-house between Mesquer and Morlaix. This forced us to travel at a walk and a slow trot and to stop every evening to attend to our draft horses, led by the reins by my former dragoons. My bodyguards expected to continue on the main highway via Vannes and L'Orient; this detour towards Léon was not mentioned in their orders. The one who was playing the head coachman, and who controlled the purse strings for our running expenses during the journey, even dared to show his surprise. I shut him up by showing him the safe-conduct signed by the King. Neither Monsieur de Fleurieu nor the Marquis de Castries would have foreseen me using it in this way. I have left my two guardian angels at the inn we are staying at in Morlaix. They are guarding the impenetrable chest. They have no idea what it contains, otherwise I would perhaps be less relaxed. My grandfather and I had gone alone, during the night, into the Kermean chapel, to retrieve the diamonds from my grandmother's tomb where my late mother had hidden them just before going to Port-Louis, where Flaharn and Jakar were to kill her.

The Kerlaudy manor house stands imposingly on a hillside overlooking the Saint Pol de Léon Bay. To the east, on the slope towards the Penzé, it is bordered by the only woods visible as far as the eye can see. A wide straight avenue, lined by majestic trees, leaves to the right of the road towards the enormous rectangular building which stands out before me against the blue-green background of the sea. There beyond the waves, beyond the line of the horizon, lies England, less than a hundred and twenty miles away. The owner of this property could only be a sailor.

A servant has me wait in the vestibule and Squadron Commander du Dresnay, the Chevalier des Roches, soon arrives. He seems to be of the same age as my grandfather de Kermean, but he is much less dashing. It is obvious that he has behind him more than forty years of sea, war and colonies. To save having to make explanations that I might find embarrassing, I show him the safe-conduct made for me on the King's orders. Without asking any questions the master of the house invites me to follow him up to his study on the first floor. Two large windows give a magnificent view over the bay to the north-west, while a smaller one, set into the southern gable of the manor house, allows in the beneficent light and heat of the midday sun.

The Chevalier des Roches politely invites me to sit facing him. He seems to be considering my Ship's Ensign uniform with a kindly air. My youth does not seem to disconcert him in the least. What a wonderful thing it is to have the use of a safe-conduct signed by the King's hand! Without any preamble I can ask the former Governor of the Îles de France and de Bourbon what he really thinks of Monsieur Tallebau de Saint-Luperce and why he had him sent to the Bastille in 1771.

His eyes light up. My question seems to please him. I suspect that he was not in the least happy, on his return to France, to learn that the man he had had arrested was not only at liberty but was ruling the roost for the Minister of State for the Navy and Colonies.

'I am delighted, Monsieur, that at last someone at Versailles is concerned about the actions of this charlatan. He had disembarked from an English ship that had made a stop at the Île de Bourbon in 1770. Monsieur de Bellecombe had been intrigued by the influence that this so-called chevalier had rapidly achieved over the island's notables with tales of all sorts of extraordinary exploits he claimed to have made in India. Our Commander at Bourbon had wondered whether this Saint-Luperce was a spy in the pay of the English and reported it to me. I told him to keep the fellow under strict surveillance, while I myself sent a letter asking for information on him from Monsieur Law de Lauriston, who was then in command at Pondicherry. I have retained his letter in my archives and, as you will see, it is instructive.'

The Chevalier des Roches gets up and searches in a writing desk for an old letter, which he hands to me.

'Here. Read it yourself. No commentary is necessary.'

I have learned, Monsieur, that a certain Chevalier de Saint-Luperce is either at the Île de Bourbon or even the Île-de-France and that you, as well as Monsieur de Bellecombe, would be pleased to know what I think of him. All I can tell you is that he is an adventurer who has more strings to his bow than he has names. His real name is Tallebau. I knew him for the first time in 1761, under the name of Winslow. He is a man with talents, ambition, and a taste for intrigue. He started in India as a surgeon's assistant off a ship, after which he served in the last war as a Volunteer. I know for certain that I had no wish to take him with me when I left for France. He disappeared into India with a crowd of others.

It is to this Monsieur de Saint-Luperce that we owe the desertion of the European contingent with Hyder Ali Khan in 1767, without which Hyder Ali Khan would never have gone over to the English. It is down to Saint-Luperce that in 1767 and 1768 I lost a lot of men through desertion...

In his letter, Monsieur Law de Lauriston formally accused Saint-Luperce of having been paid by the English authorities in Madras to encourage the desertion of Hyder Ali Khan's European partisans and of French and foreign soldiers in the Pondicherry garrison.

The Chevalier des Roches showed me a copy of the memorandum he had prepared to justify the arrest of Saint-Luperce. At the time of the fall of Pondicherry, Saint-Luperce was with the English. At the end of the war he returned to France and began scheming at Versailles, presenting himself as a former honorary Volunteer in Lally's forces and claiming participation in imaginary military exploits. He also attempted to capitalise on his knowledge of Hindustan by writing several memoranda on the political situation in India, with the object of obtaining state funds to pay for his sea passage. In particular, he had asked Monsieur Law de Lauriston, who had just been named as Governor of Pondicherry, to take him as an adviser, but without success. In desperation he had been forced to return to Hindustan at his own expense, travelling via Persia and offering his services as a doctor to the courts of the Shah and the Mogul, as well as perfecting his command of Persian and different local languages. Eventually he had offered his talents to the English who had used him as an agent and spy against French interests in India.

'How could Monsieur de Sartine have trusted this individual?' I ask.

'Not just Monsieur de Sartine. Before him there were Monsieur Turgot and Monsieur Bourgeois de Boynes. While imprisoned in the Bastille, Saint-Luperce wrote a number of memoranda on the political situation in India, that his friends had shown to the Ministers of the time. They were so impressed that they petitioned the King to have our man released.'

I knew the rest, having been told it by my uncle and Monsieur de Fleurieu.

*

The Chevalier des Roches would have liked me to stay to dinner, but I declined as politely as I could, saying that by coming to Kerlaudy I was already behind schedule. To be frank, I would willingly have stayed a little longer with this kind old sailor, but I feared that he would ask a lot of questions which would have been difficult to answer while still respecting the demands for secrecy which had been impressed on me on leaving Versailles. Moreover my detour to Kerlaudy was not part of the Marquis de Castries' plans and I was not sure whether my superiors might consider it a bad mistake, or a serious misuse of my privileges, should they ever hear of it.

We arrived at Brest on the 7th March, towards two in the afternoon. I left my bodyguards with the chests and the carriage in front of the Hôtel du Grand Turc, with instructions to find a handcart to take my baggage down the Grande Rue. I went on foot down the rue de Siam in order to report my arrival to the Brest Navy Commander. I knew that the Comte d'Hector had held this post officially since the 1st February and I was somewhat anxious about appearing in front of him as I had not been told in Versailles whether or not he was to be kept in the dark about the ins and outs of my mission.

Luckily the Comte was busy elsewhere and I was dealt with by a Ship's Captain whom I did not know and who was happy simply to stamp my orders for embarkation aboard *l'Annibal*. He told me that my new ship would be taken out to the anchorage on the following morning's tide, and that at that moment she was moored in front of the General Warehouse, with her officers, crew and garrison from the Royal Roussillon regiment all aboard. She was just finishing loading her guns, to be ready to move out at dawn, as soon as it was light enough to manoeuvre. Low tide would be at half past nine in the morning. He also told me that *l'Annibal* was part of a division with three other ships: *le Héros*, seventy-four guns, commanded by the Chevalier de Suffren Saint-Tropez, Commander of the Order of Malta, along with *le Sphinx* and *le Vengeur*, both of sixty-four guns. This division was to leave at the same time as the three squadrons of the Comte de Grasse's fleet but would remain under the orders of the Chevalier de Suffren. Its destination was still secret. According to the Ship's Captain, even its commander did not know the details of his future mission.

*

Brest, Wednesday 7th March 1781, early afternoon.

The weather is calm, the wind having gone round to the east towards midday. The sky is cloudless and the sun's warmth on this fine day could almost have us forget that winter is not yet over. A porter hauls the handcart loaded with my two chests. I have rarely seen so many people in the Grande Rue and as we get to the bottom my escort has to push aside the crowd to enable us to get to the gate of the Arsenal. Man and women, even children, press against the railings of the Navy enclosure, in front of the Administration and the Troulan dry dock, handing over a final parcel or exchanging last words through the bars with their close ones, able seamen or soldiers, about to embark for God knows how long. If only they will come back alive from this adventure. All the same, I don't feel any sense of desperation amongst all these people, rather the opposite.

I see two ships of the line pass one after other in front of the clock tower. They are being towed towards the port exit, using the gentle flow of the first hour of the ebb tide. I recognise *la Bourgogne*, a seventy-four, which we had seen on a mooring buoy in front of the Horseshoe when we had arrived at Brest with *l'Amazone* in December. The other is *le Scipion*, also of seventy-four guns. They have finished loading and are on their way to the anchorage to wait until the other ships in the river are ready to join them for the big departure. One or two are taken out every day. They are mainly the ships I saw lined up in the Penfeld when I disembarked from *l'Astrée.* The Comte de Grasse is preparing to leave for the Americas with twenty-one ships of the line, several frigates, a sizeable fleet of transports, as well as the Chevalier de Suffren's division. Sailors, workmen, forced labourers with their guards, overseen by halberdiers, come and go incessantly. The last bails of merchandise and sacks of victuals are rolled or carried along. It being high tide, wheels are up to their axles in water as carts are reversed onto the slipways, the easier to pass their loads onto the lighters, as the cranes are constantly in use, with not enough to match the flow of goods. It is said that the commander himself, the Comte de Grasse, is present on the dockside every day from six in the morning, despite a bad fever he brought back from the Îles.

I arrive in front of the General Warehouse. *L'Annibal* is moored fore and aft on two port anchors, her bow facing downstream. She is at the same spot as *l'Astrée* when I left her but is much bigger: a hundred and sixty-eight feet on deck, forty-four feet in beam, two thousand nine hundred tons. She is a 'purveyor of sudden death', as our corsairs call the English equivalents: twenty-eight 36-pound cannons on the lower deck, thirty 18-pounders on the middle deck and sixteen 8-pounders on the quarterdeck and forecastle. Her chamois-coloured topsides, along the rows of gunports on her two decks, are elegantly highlighted by the three black bands of her two rubbing strakes and the quarter and gunwale. This ship is an old friend. When I saw her for the first time, in 1778, she was fresh out of the shipyard, built by the engineer Sané, and had been given by the King to the Chevalier de Ternay to lead an expedition to India. This was the expedition of which *l'Amazone* was to be part, and which the now departed Chevalier had prepared with such zeal. He had wanted his ship to be coppered immediately, but there were not enough copper sheets at Brest, so only the lower part of the hull was covered, the four top strakes receiving provisional studding that was to be replaced at the Île-de-France. Nothing has been changed since. *L'Annibal* sailed as she was for the Americas, under the Comte de Lamotte-Piquet. She had been hammered at the Battle of Grenada, when I was aboard, and at the Battle of Fort Royal at Martinique, where she achieved glory, and she is just the same now.

Her topmasts and t'gallant masts have already been swayed up, along with her yards. Her running rigging has been reeved and her sails bent on. The last cannon has just been taken aboard and the lower blocks of the two tackles used for this still hang straight down from the main yard, swinging gently besides the outboard ladder, level with the lower deck gunport through which the barrels have been passed. The gunports are open and I can see and hear, on the gundeck where I was injured in the Battle of Grenada, sailors hauling on the tackles to move the nine thousand pound monsters to their numbered stations. The 18-pounders of the middle deck and the 8-pounder deck guns have been moved into place from a pontoon which had brought them out to the middle of the river. Their lined-up barrels already point outwards from the great ship.

I tell my two guards to look after the chests and pay the porter while they wait for me. A gangway links the quay to a pontoon moored beside the ship. I go down it, climb the fourteen steps of the outboard ladder and go through to the ship's side deck. I turn right, taking off my hat to salute the flag, put my hat on again and walk towards the quarterdeck, watched by an infantryman from the garrison dressed in a white uniform with sky blue tabling and a red collar. He is on guard at the base of the mainmast, that being the point past which the sailors are not allowed to pass unless called to work the ship. Everything has been painted, changed or redone like new and the smell of hemp, paint, vegetable tar and linseed and wood oils is everywhere. On the quarterdeck I see two Ship's Lieutenants, a Frigate's Lieutenant and two Ensigns. One of the Ensigns is wearing a gilded pewter collar embossed with the arms of France, indicating that he is the officer of the watch. It is normally to him that I must first present myself. He is standing beside the hatch of the main companionway, at the bottom of the stairs leading to the poop deck. He is about my age and is talking to a Ship's Lieutenant about forty years old, seated on the watch bench. I stop in front of them and give my name, handing over my order of embarkation to the Ensign. He hands me over to the officer he is talking to, the ship's second captain, Monsieur le Chevalier Morard de Galles. He raises his head towards me. He has a slightly curved nose and a pinched mouth. His gaze is open and direct under gathered brows, and I sense an iron will in those eyes. I have the feeling too that they do not look upon me with much friendliness.

'Welcome, Monsieur Laforest-Dombourg. It's at least two weeks since Versailles warned us of your arrival and we have been waiting for you. We didn't think you'd get here before we sailed.'

I reply respectfully that I am carrying a letter from the Minister that I have to give directly to Captain de Trémigon and explain the reasons for only arriving now. I ask the officer of the watch to have my two chests brought aboard, saying that the steel chest should be given to *l'Annibal's* commander.

Lieutenant de Galles gets up and asks me to follow him. We enter the darkness beneath the forward end of the poop deck and go through the wheelhouse, now deserted and guarded by a single rifleman from the garrison. We go around the double wheel and along a passageway to the great cabin. It is bigger than those of *l'Amazone* or *l'Astrée,* that I know well. As on a frigate, the ship's sides are hidden behind panelling decorated with mouldings and painted grey, but there are no cannons here and the bulkheads are never taken down. There has therefore been no skimping on the varnish and, the supreme luxury, this 'drawing room' opens to a gallery the whole width of the poop deck, on which the Captain can take the air out of sight of everyone on board. As this place is the exclusive reserve of the ship's Captain, it is here that he takes his meals, either alone or with his guests. His sleeping cabin, to starboard, has its door opening into the great cabin, while the second captain's, built symmetrically to port, is always closed on this side. Lieutenant de Galles must use another door from the wheelhouse.

Ship's Captain de Trémigon is sitting at a fine table set in the middle of the great cabin. It is his own furniture, made from Indian or Madagascan rosewood, but expertly decorated by a French cabinetmaker who has inlaid it with the usual symbols of Victory and Love: a torch and two quivers.

The new master of *l'Annibal* is immersed in the study of the ship's roll. Lieutenant de Galles introduces me. My commander is a little bigger than me, from what I can judge, given that he is seated. He must be approaching fifty, with a face weathered and tanned by years of sailing under the sun of the tropics and the equator. He would be a perfect buccaneer were it not for his round cheeks and double chin, which give him an easy-going air. I hand over my order of embarkation and the two sealed envelopes that the Marquis de Castries gave me to bring. The Captain examines, with undisguised surprise, the packet addressed to Monsieur de Souillac and Monsieur d'Orves. He takes off his spectacles and shows it to his second-in-command.

'Look, Chevalier. This confirms what we both thought after

calculating the amount of victuals and water we had to bring on board. Our final destination is the Indian Ocean, then. But I don't understand. Captain de Saint-Félix will soon be sailing for the Île-de-France. The Minister himself will soon be delivering to him in person His Majesty's orders for the Governor of the Mascarenes. Why have I been entrusted with this mail? *La Fine* is a fast ship and leaves before us! And why give it to me and not the Chevalier de Suffren?'

'The Marquis de Castries has given me a summary of the contents of this letter, so that I can share it with you verbally, but it must remain secret until our arrival at the Île-de-France.'

I force myself to speak with as much humility as I can muster when saying this, but I understand the extent to which the oddness of my position could shock the sensibilities of my superiors. Lieutenant de Galles, in particular, has trouble hiding his annoyance. Since the start of this affair, my uncle and the Marquis de Castries have not stopped landing me in embarrassing situations that I could well have done without.

The Captain puts on his spectacles again and opens the letter addressed to him, in which the Minister has explained my position and my terms of service, if I am to believe what he told me about it. I see Captain de Trémigon frown several times. He stops for a moment to look at me carefully over his glasses before returning to his reading. I have the impression that he is going back over several passages. Lieutenant de Galles and I wait in silence.

'Good! I think I only need to put that chest in my cabin. I hope it will fit in my wardrobe. Where is it, by the way?' the Captain asks.

'I left it on the quay with my personal chest, Sir. I was given two bodyguards to escort me here and they are keeping an eye in it at the moment. I asked the officer of the watch to have them brought on board,' I add.

'Who's on duty?'

'It's Ensign d'Aché,' replies Lieutenant de Galles.

'Young d'Aché? Go and ask him to have the steel chest brought by our new Ensign delivered right here, if you please, Chevalier, and… wait! Monsieur La Forêt, will these two guards be shipping aboard?'

'No, Sir. They are in the personal service of the King, two former dragoons. Their mission stops once I am aboard. They are waiting for me to release them to return to Versailles.'

'That's a pity. I'm short of men and would happily have taken them.'

Captain de Trémigon waits for his second captain to leave. The latter seems to be in a very bad mood. I have the impression that I have made an enemy without wishing to. That saddens me, especially as he seems to be a direct and honest man.

'I am listening, Monsieur La Forêt.'

'Laforest-Dombourg, Sir…'

I repeat what the Marquis de Castries asked me to say about the package addressed to Messieurs de Souillac and d'Orves, and then continue on to the Marquis de Bussy's preference for directing our Indian policy to the side of the Emperor of the Marathas rather than Hyder Ali Khan. I make clear that for the moment we are the only ones in Brest and the whole fleet to know the contents of this letter. I say nothing about the Cape or the fact that the Minister had it in mind for him to replace the Chevalier de Suffren if the latter had refused the command offered to him.

'I believe that the Chevalier de Suffren has learned today that he will be leading us to India,' declared Captain de Trémigon with a smile, after hearing me out. 'And you know why? Because over the last few days he has asked me about it several times, on account of my experience, and each time we agreed that it could only be India. This morning, the last time I saw him, he swore blind that he still didn't know where we were heading, but that it certainly wasn't India! His insistence seemed suspicious to me, and then I heard that an important package from the Minister had arrived this morning at Brest, at the Comte d'Hector's. Just as well that the Chevalier de Suffren isn't aware that you knew his secret before him. I have a word of advice for you. Keep that to yourself and never boast about it, or the Commander will hold it against you. He can be vindictive. Moreover, he is prejudiced against Breton officers, as I well know. As for me, you can count on my total discretion.'

This made me remember the incident I had endured with the Chevalier de Suffren in Monsieur de Fleurieu's office, and the unpleasant words heaped on me that time by the Provençal Ship's Captain.

*

Captain de Trémigon had the treasure I had brought stored in the wardrobe of his cabin – a small hanging space behind a door by his bunk recess. I opened the forged steel chest in his presence, to show him the leather bags filled with diamonds and with his permission added the letter addressed to the authorities in the Île-de-France and my precious safe-conduct signed by King Louis XVI. I shut the chest as soon as possible and wanted to give him the copy of the key. I explained that I kept mine attached to my neck under my shirt but he was repelled by the idea of having something metallic permanently by his skin. He didn't want to keep it in any of his cabin furnishings either, saying that it would be a mistake to keep the key close to the chest. If the ship was boarded it would be too easy for pillagers to find it. After some reflection I said that I would wrap this second key in a handkerchief and hide it at the bottom of my personal chest. Nobody apart from him would have any idea of looking there if something happened to me before our arrival at the Île-de-France. I said nothing to him about the purse with its fifty gold louis. As yet I had not had any need to use any of them and I hoped not to have to, but I preferred to keep them with me.

I gave my two dragoons permission to leave. It was the first time they had been aboard a ship and they wanted to have a tour of it before setting off. With Lieutenant de Galles' permission I took them down with me to the main gundeck. The cannons had been put in place but the gunports not yet closed. They were very impressed by the size and number of 36-pounders and asked me if I had ever seen them in action. This led me to tell them how I had lived through the Battle of Grenada on this same lower deck of *l'Annibal*. Several sailors who were thereabouts and who had also been at Grenada recognised me and came to greet me, giving some substance to my story.

L'Annibal had returned to Brest at the beginning of January and the Comte de Lamotte-Piquet had handed her over to the King in order to take *l'Invincible*, a brand-new three-decker of a hundred and ten guns, built at Rochefort, whose fitting out was expected to be completed at Brest by April. The Comte de Lamotte-Piquet had taken with him all his officers and some of his quartermasters, but most of the crew had re-embarked on *l'Annibal*. They therefore had only had a very short leave, insufficient for them to recuperate properly before going to sea again. In this third year of war the Navy had insufficient sailors in reserve. The other ships of this light division for India were in a similar situation and the Chevalier de Suffren had complained about it so vigorously to the Comte d'Hector that we got to hear about it. This did not stop our Commander, who was never short of contradictions, and who was once again angry with the Comte, from having all the Provençal sailors from his previous ship brought aboard *Le Héros*.

As per the Regulations, the officers of a ship like ours comprised, apart from the Captain and second captain, five lieutenants, each with an Ensign to assist him. Aboard *l'Annibal*, the first lieutenant was Ship's Lieutenant Huon de Kermadec, a thirty-four-year-old Brest man, married with no children. He was also the officer in charge of the ship's internal management and maintenance. The second lieutenant was Ship's Lieutenant de Boissauveur, from Paimpol, thirty-seven years old and unmarried. He had the same length of service as Lieutenant de Kermadec but had not come through the Marine Guards. He had begun his career as a Volunteer, then spent some time as a merchant officer trading with Saint Domingue before returning to the King's service as a Frigate Lieutenant. He had been promoted to Ensign for his conduct in battle and made a Ship's Lieutenant in 1779. The third lieutenant was a Ship's Ensign with a little more service than me who had been a Marine Guard at Toulon. The fourth lieutenant was the Chevalier d'Aché, Ship's Ensign and former Flag Guard. He was from a Normandy family that contained a number of Ship's Captains and even Squadron Commanders. These 'lieutenants' had as quarters four proper cabins with a recessed bunk and an English-style writing desk, situated partly under the poop deck and partly under the wheelhouse. The fifth lieutenant, Monsieur de Gualez, was a Ship's Ensign from Brittany, a little older than me.

I was Lieutenant Kermadec's assistant. The four other 'Ensigns' were full-blown Frigate Lieutenants or auxiliaries. The six of us, including Ensign de Gualez, slept in English-style hammocks in single canvas cabins rigged at night between the four 18-pound cannons in the wardroom. Everything was taken down and stowed in boxes each morning.

The rest of the officers slept on the deck below us in the gunroom, along with the chaplain-almoner, Father Tiburce. It was there that I myself had slept when chance brought me aboard *l'Annibal* on the eve of that unforgettable and bloody battle in which I received my first war wounds.

At battle stations, aboard *l'Annibal,* the first lieutenant commanded the lower gundeck and Lieutenant Boissauveur the middle gundeck. I would normally have been assigned to the lower gundeck with Lieutenant Kermadec, but the Captain preferred that I command the ten 8-pounders on the quarterdeck. In this capacity I would have as my assistant a master gunner's mate, and each day would have to train twenty-five sailors and five ship's boys in gunnery, once the crew had been assigned to their posts.

On the 8th March the winds were easterly, and the weather was fine. We began to unmoor at seven thirty in the morning. Our Captain was grumbling that had the wind been from the north or even the north-west he would not have needed to have his ship towed, but with this east wind he could not exit the Penfeld under sail, on account of the wretched Rose Rock, that he had to pass to starboard. Coming from anyone else, this remark would have been thought of as boasting, or ignorance, but Captain de Trémigon was a marvellous ship handler. Once we were level with the Horseshoe we made sail, raising the foretopsail, mizzen topsail and inner jib. By ten o'clock we were lying to two anchors in eight fathoms of water, astern of *le Héros* and the two other ships of the Chevalier de Suffren's division, which had come out before us: *le Vengeur* and *le Sphinx*, both of seventy-four guns. During the afternoon a boat brought out our powder, which was taken on board. On the 9th March the weather was very calm with variable winds. In principle everyone was required to stay on board until we sailed, but we knew this would not be until after the visit from the Marquis de Castries, which was announced for the following Tuesday. As a result, I was able to squeeze permission from Captain de Trémigon for a day's shore leave on the Sunday. This was despite the second captain taking a dim view of it, but I was not required on watch, as I was working with Lieutenant de Kermadec. At anchor it is the custom that the officer overseeing the ship's fabric is excused watchkeeping, which I benefitted from, being his assistant.

*

Brest, Sunday 11th March 1781.
It is eleven in the morning, misty with no wind. The gently undulating surface of the harbour resembles that of a lake, an impression strengthened by visibility of less than two cables. Captain de Trémigon

has to go to see the Navy Commander and has allowed me to go ashore with him in the small ship's boat. I will return with him this evening. I am sitting beside the Captain in the stern, on one of the boxes in the boat's 'cabin'. We are the only passengers, with the seven thwarts occupied by the fourteen oarsmen. The dark shapes of the ships at anchor or moored to coffin buoys emerge out of the mist then disappear behind us. The Bosun uses them to guide him whenever he can see them. When two ships are too far apart from each other it would be possible to think we are moving through nothingness, were it not for the constant noise from the fleet around us: shouts, the echoing sound of heavy objects being moved on deck or the sound of pump water pouring into the sea through the scuppers. From time to time, above our heads, the raucous cries of marauding gulls ring out.

The mist starts to lift as we near the mouth of the Penfeld. The sky is still grey but the glow of the sun is evident through a screen of thin cloud. A pleasant spring softness envelopes us. We are at the bottom of one of the biggest tides of the year. The barques and coasters usually moored beneath the Chateau and the Dajot promenade are all aground and listing sideways. Men, women and children scurry like ants along the shoreline fishing for shrimps and collecting crabs and shellfish.

As we enter the river between the Chateau and the Horseshoe the sky continues to clear. The boat enters the military port and goes to tie up at the bottom of the steps coming down to the water below the General Warehouse. I thank Captain de Trémigon and exit the Arsenal on foot.

On this Sunday there is a big crowd drinking and dining in the main room of the inn, despite it being Lent, but I cannot see my dear Maria Kirwan anywhere. Behind the counter I can only see a man of about fifty whom I do not know, and who seems to be directing operations with some authority. I go closer, and seeing my uniform he calls out to me.

'What can I do for you, Sir?'

'I am looking for Mademoiselle Kirwan.'

'And what do you want of her?'

'I'm a friend.'

'I do not have the pleasure of your acquaintance, Sir. I am the new legal owner of this establishment. Mademoiselle Kirwan will soon be engaged to my son. She is an honourable young girl and, with respect,

Sir, I would prefer that you Marine Guards stop buzzing around her.'

I immediately dislike him. He seems smaller than me, red-faced, with dull blue eyes, a pot belly under his jacket and a bald pate fringed by a crown of greying but still thick hair which falls past his ears to his shoulders. It is the first time I have seen this fellow and my hair seems to stand on end just looking at him. In any case, I don't believe a word he has just said. I look at him carefully to make sure he is not joking – but no! His hostility and confidence are not feigned.

'I am a Ship's Ensign, Sir, not a Marine Guard.'

'It's all the same to me!'

Without giving me time to reply, he starts berating the crowd.

'These gentlemen of the Grand Corps carry a sword! Their women are better dressed than ours and they don't need to work, them! But that's not enough for them! They still have to come trying to debauch our honest and humble young girls! But there are laws in this country and everyone has to respect them, the nobles just like the others!'

All conversation has stopped. The inn's customers seem somewhat embarrassed, not knowing what to say. Most of them are merchant and coasting officers and petty officers. We are at war and they well know that without the King's ships to escort them they would not be able to put to sea. But there is grumbling all the same, at the back of the room, for the townsfolk of Brest do not much like the Marine Guards, for which I admit they have good reason.

'May I know whom I have the honour to address, Sir?' I ask this aggressive speaker.

'Monsieur Le Gall! And not at your service, Sir!'

I recognise the surname. It is the same as Maria Kirwan's great-uncle Claude whom I have met a few times – a fine old man of seventy at least, very kind but worn out. He adores his great-niece and has always been good to me.

'May I at least speak with Mademoiselle Kirwan, simply to show you that my intentions are honourable?'

'Sir! If you insist I will complain to the law. I know the best magistrates in Brest and I am a friend of Monsieur Le Normand!'

I think that the mayor of Brest is in fact called Le Normand. The town council does not have much influence, in truth. Here it's the Navy that controls and commands everything, but my superiors would certainly not appreciate me getting into a quarrel with the town's notables.

Still, I have a strong urge to grab this Le Gall by the collar and drag him over the counter, but I suspect that is just what he is waiting for and that he would be quite happy for me thus to put myself in the wrong. While I am wondering what to do, my eyes meet those of one of the inn waitresses whom I know. She moves her eyes towards the end of the room and then stares at me insistently. I move off without saying anything to this Le Gall, who immediately looks triumphant. I go and quietly lean against the wall that the waitress had indicated. She is called Daniel, Françoise Daniel, but I remember now that everyone here calls her Soizic. She is a real little Bretonne – well-built, determined, not devoid of charm, and always smiling. I watch her as she serves the tables, casually getting nearer to me. When she gets close she straightens up while appearing not to look at me.

'He knows who you are and he's lying. Don't believe what he says.'

She had spoken very quietly. I reply the same way, still turned towards a window to my left to maintain the pretence.

'Would you like me to put him straight?'

I think I hear a stifled laugh.

'Not on your life! I'd love you to, but it would only make things worse. Maria has left and given me letters for you. I can't get away yet. Wait for me in an hour at the bottom of the King's House steps in front of the Toulan dry dock.'

I leave the inn and go up the rue des Sept Saints in order to kill time on the Dajot promenade. I have not eaten but I am no longer hungry. I am sad, disappointed, desperate, but at the same time keen to know what has happened to my Maria. Having passed the entrance to the Chateau I walk under the trees to the end of the promenade, where I had fought a duel with a sub-lieutenant of the Enghien regiment when I was a Marine Guard cadet. The first buds are appearing on the branches. The wind has come up from the north-east and the sky has completely cleared. The harbour, bathed in light, is full of moored craft. With all the ships, frigates, flutes and transports, there are a hundred and thirty ships ready to put to sea once the order has been given and the wind and tide favourable for exiting the entrance.

At one o'clock I am at the rendezvous opposite the main gate of the King's House. The square in front of the Arsenal entrance is almost deserted. It is dinner time and there are no longer any sailors' families watching their loved ones through the railings, as all the ships destined to sail have left the port, with their crews confined on board. That is better for me, as it means I can check that nobody is following Françoise Daniel. A rifleman in the blue and red uniform of the Navy marches back and forth in front of the gate to the Arsenal. The river above the clocktower is almost empty and the last ship in the Troulan dry dock must have been taken out last night or this morning at dawn. There are many merchant ships moored downstream, beyond the military port, between Brest and Recouvrance; a convoy from Bordeaux arrived yesterday. All the same, this calm will be short-lived; the Army regiments have not yet all embarked, and the day after tomorrow the whole garrison will be armed and out on the town's streets for the visit of the Marquis de Castries.

The servant from the *La Dame au Paon* gives me two folded letters. The thicker one is sealed with a twelve-sol coin and my name written on the back. I recognise my beloved's handwriting. The other letter has nothing written on it, only the arms on the seal, something like *gold with three trees vert*, if my memory of my lessons in heraldry from the Rector at Mesquer is correct. I look questioningly at Françoise, who shakes her head and says that maybe it is a copy of a document from a notary or advocate, for my information.

'What the Devil!' I say to myself. Notary or advocate? I am intrigued, but the coat of arms vaguely reminds me of something. I seem to have seen it before. However I am so impatient to see what Maria has written that I slip this letter into the pocket of my jacket and open first the one from my dear and tender friend.

Reading the first few lines I feel the taste of honey and breathe more easily. I was not mistaken: my Maria still loves me. It brings tears to my eyes. The rest explains what has happened. Old Claude Le Gall, her great-uncle, died while I was at Versailles, but with enough time to write a new will designating his great-niece as his sole beneficiary. It was then that a distant cousin of Maria's late mother, one Louis Le Gall, contested the will. Maria's maternal great grandfather, also called Claude, had in 1695 inherited the inn where his father had put up part of the Siamese ambassador's retinue nine years earlier. This innkeeper Claude Le Gall had a younger brother, François, who had received a dowry in compensation. Maria's great-uncle Claude was the eldest son of the 1695 Claude. He had inherited the inn in his turn but had not had children. His brother Jean, of whom he was very fond, had married and gone with his wife to the Indies to seek their fortune. These were Maria's grandparents, her mother being their only child. She had married Captain Kirwan, of Lally's Irish regiment, who had been killed at the siege of Pondicherry in 1761. Jean Le Gall and his wife also died in India. Louis Le Gall, whom I saw at the inn, is the grandson of François Le Gall. He maintained before the court that his grandfather had been duped, as he had never in fact received his dowry. He also argued that Maria's great-uncle was not of sound mind when he rewrote his will, not only because his sole beneficiary was a young girl who had not yet attained her majority but, above all, the Le Galls for her were only maternal ancestors, whereas Louis and his son were the direct descendants of the great-grandfather Le Gall. In the first instance Louis Le Gall won his action, but my friend tells me that she had been invited to Nantes by Mademoiselle Broudou and her mother, and that she is preparing a case to defend her interests. I can write to her via the Post at the Parish of Saint-Croix, near Nantes.

'She doesn't mention this story of her getting engaged,' I say to Françoise Daniel.

'That's part of the reason she went to hide at Nantes. Louis Le Gall was harassing her to marry his son. It's because he won the first hearing based on lies, as his grandfather did get his dowry. Claude had kept written proof, which he gave to his great-niece, but Louis Le Gall didn't know this. That's why he wants to force Maria to marry his son.'

I thank Françoise Daniel and tell her that I am about to leave on a campaign to the other side of the world, but that I know people who live near Nantes who may be able to help Maria. I then go to a tavern in the Grande rue, where I borrow writing equipment while I am dining. My plan is to ask my sister Anne, who is at Vertou, at the house of my uncle's parents-in-law, to get in touch with Maria. I write two letters, one for Maria and one for Anne. I consider that with a little luck the Vicomte de la Croix de Lornes, my uncle's father-in-law, might involve himself in this business, as he loves the Navy and does not share the prejudices of my grandfather the Baron de Kermean.

Having put addresses on my two letters I immediately go up the Grande rue to deposit them at the Post, prepaid for Nantes and Vertou. I then go straight back down to the quay in front of the General Warehouse and settle on a thwart in Captain de Trémigon's boat to wait for him. I am disappointed at not having been able to take my Maria in my arms and would have liked to have been able to stay to help her, but it is impossible. There is nothing left for me to do in Brest. The future is as uncertain for Maria as for me. All the same, she has shown that she has the strength to defend herself and I think that Louis Le Gall may be in for a surprise. As for me, God only knows what awaits me over the seas: we are at war! The smell of adventure is intoxicating, for sure, but I know that there is always a price to pay that fortunately we mere mortals can never foresee. I completely forget the second letter buried in my jacket pocket.

*

On Sunday evening, having dined with the officers in the Great cabin, I remembered that I still had a letter in my pocket and withdrew to my niche between the two cannons to examine it. It wasn't at all a letter from a notary, as Françoise Daniel had suggested, but a letter from my friend Vernon des Aulnes. He had left it with Maria Kirwan so that she could give it to me when I passed through Brest and had sealed it with his ring carrying the family arms.

I learned that he had been given three months' leave and that he had gone home to his parents. He had not returned to France since our departure on campaign with the division commanded by the Comte de Lamotte-Piquet on the 2nd May 1779. He would come back to Brest at the end of March to help prepare *l'Invincible* for sea. She would be sailing in April.

I would therefore not see my comrade before our departure, which saddened me a little. Suddenly, a passage in the letter caught my eye…

…When we had left Savannah for Port Royal I spoke with a Corporal Bellerose of the Hainaut grenadiers, who had come aboard l'Invincible to go with us to Martinique. He told me how he had met you at Savannah and how you had told him to bury the body of Ship's Captain Flaharn. But he had realised that Flaharn was still alive when he threw him in the common grave. According to Bellerose he may as well have been dead: he was unconscious but he no longer looked human, with half his face destroyed by a pistol shot. But he was still breathing. Bellerose had him carried to the hospital at Thunderbolt. All the same, Bellerose thought he had little chance of surviving…

Vernon was talking about a plantation at a place called Thunderbolt, where we had a field hospital where we had left those too badly wounded to take aboard when we retreated from Savannah. I read and re-read this passage in my friend's letter: ... *Bellerose thought he had little chance of surviving...*

I would have liked to ask Bellerose myself about this, but it was impossible. I read further on that the corporal had been killed when reinforcing *l'Annibal's* main battery during the famous Battle of Martinique, which brought immortality to the Comte de Lamotte-Piquet[12], and of which our Navy is still proud. In any case, I have nothing to worry about. If Flaharn had survived – and according to Corporal Bellerose that was unlikely – he would be a prisoner of the English and waiting for a truce in order to be exchanged. Maybe he has stayed in America, while I am going the other way, beyond the Cape of Good Hope.

We had yet more fine weather and easterly winds for the following days. The Marquis de Castries arrived on the 13th. He was welcomed on land with a twenty-five-gun salute and a review of all the troops still in the town. The commanders of all the ships in the fleet were invited to the Hôtel Saint-Pierre to meet the Minister. The next day at nine in the morning we all dressed ship. The wind was still from the east and the sun was in harmony with the celebrations. The Marquis de Castries attended a big dinner in his honour abord *la Ville de Paris*. At three in the afternoon every ship took to battle stations and fired five broadsides, with all the resultant noise and smoke in the anchorage. As the Marquis de Castries left the flagship he was again saluted with seventeen cannons and all the crews lined up on the upper decks shouted *Vive le Roi!* three times.

One of the guests at the banquet given by the Comte de Grasse was that evening to embark as a passenger aboard *l'Annibal*. He was

---

12 Translator's note: *...brought immortality to the Comte de Lamotte-Piquet*: Lamotte-Piquet's conduct during the Battle of Martinique so impressed the British Admiral Hyde Parker that he sent him a congratulatory letter when a truce was called: *The conduct of your Excellency in the affair of the 18th of this month fully justifies the reputation which you enjoy among us, and I assure you that I could not witness without envy the skill you showed on that occasion. Our enmity is transient, depending upon our masters; but your merit has stamped upon my heart the greatest admiration for yourself.*

to make the voyage with us to India. He introduced himself as the Chevalier Tallebau de Saint-Luperce, still with the same self-assurance and still with the Croix du Christ sewn conspicuously on his jacket. I could have well done without his presence and was not the only one. He showed our Captain an order signed by the Comte de Vergennes which gave him the right to occupy the cabin under the poop deck assigned to Ship's Ensign d'Aché, our fourth lieutenant. The latter was sent down to sleep in one of the niches between the wardroom cannons, whose occupant, Frigate's Lieutenant d'Amphermet, had in turn to go down and sleep in the gun room.

6

On the 14th March 1781, the frigate *la Fine* left port, watched by the Minister and carrying the most recent despatches for the Île-de-France. The next day, the Marquis de Castries received a letter from Versailles, sent by the Comte de Vergennes, telling him that the English had increased Johnstone's division to six ships. As a result, the Marquis decided to switch *l'Artésien,* sixty-four guns, from the Comte de Grasse's fleet to reinforce the Chevalier de Suffren's division, of which we were a part, and which now had five ships instead of four.

On the 15th, the last military detachments embarked. The Chevalier de Suffren's division was to transport the whole of the Pondicherry regiment, along with its colonel, the Comte de Conway, as well as the first battalion of the Austrasie regiment and an artillery company: about twelve hundred men in all. The Captain commanding the Austrasie company, and his Lieutenants, were installed in the Great cabin, and I in my turn was sent to the gun room to make space for them.

The Minister waited until the last moment in order to witness our departure. On the Saturday, conditions seemed favourable and *la Ville de Paris* fired a leaving cannon, but by Sunday evening the wind had gone round to the west. We then had several calm days, followed once again by fog.

Finally, on Thursday 22nd March, a light north-easterly and clear weather coincided with a fair tide. At seven, *la Ville de Paris* gave the signal to unmoor, and we began to weigh anchor. This took until ten o'clock. We took the ship's boat on board and at eleven the Admiral signalled us to put to sea. A hundred and thirty ships under sail began to manoeuvre together, turning in circles while waiting their turn to pass through the exit channel with the ebb tide. This was not without confusion; the harbour suddenly seemed too small. *Le Héros,* in whose wake we were following at a distance of half a cable, collided ahead of us with *l'Hercule,* a seventy-four-gun ship from the Comte de Grasse's fleet. Luckily the two ships disentangled themselves straight away, without any damage. If they hadn't, even a ship handler like Captain de Trémigon would not have been able to avoid hitting them. Passing through the exit channel we could see that a large crowd had gathered on the cliffs to watch the spectacle of our departure. By four in the afternoon the last of the huge procession had passed the Mingan Rock without incident. The sky was clear and the wind had got up to a fresh and well-established north-easterly. Once round the Pierres Noires we had to brail up the topsails to allow the tail of the convoy to catch up with the leaders. By sunset the white sails of the squadrons and the fleet stretched across the Iroise Sea as far as the eye could see, heading west, settling to the task.

The fine north-easterly lasted for a week, regularly pushing us to five knots and allowing us to make a hundred to a hundred and twenty miles a day to the south-west, against the swell of the open ocean. Most of the time we had to reduce sail to stay at the speed of the convoy. Our under-canvassed ship pitched and rolled in the rough sea, forcing us to keep the gunports permanently closed on the lower deck, where the eighty riflemen of the Austrasie regiment were housed, along with their sergeants, corporals and drummers.

The sailors soon adjusted to the routine of life aboard a ship on a long passage. Time passed in a rhythm fixed since time immemorial by the Regulations: day watches, dog watches, night watches, exercises in clearing the ship for action, all the necessary work to keep the ship in good condition. The officers settled in and observed each other, as we all came from different ships and different backgrounds. In the wardroom our meals were presided over by Lieutenant de Galles, who was usually sea-sick at the start of a voyage and who tried to hide it. This, I think, exacerbated his natural severity. Nonetheless, his indisputable authority, along with the respect we had for his previous service, in which we knew he had distinguished himself, imposed a certain restraint on all of us except Saint-Luperce. The latter's brilliant conversation, witty observations and high spirits soon became the focal point of our little society. As the only one who knew his real past, I could but secretly admire the skill with which he gradually came to dominate us all.

I soon had the feeling that I was not well accepted by my new shipmates. This was a novel situation for me, and at first I thought that it stemmed from me having arrived late into the group, or from Lieutenant de Galles' prejudice against me, or from the kindness shown to me by our Captain, which some could find irritating.

It was only the surgeon's mate who seemed to appreciate my company. He was called Roblet, was two years older than me and was soon my only friend on board. Having studied medicine at the military hospital at Besançon, his taste for travelling had led him to continue his education at the Navy hospital. He had arrived at Brest at the end of 1778, and had chanced to meet Monsieur le Choquet, *l'Amazone's* surgeon, when we had arrived there to prepare our departure for India under the Comte de Ternay. In 1780, after our first return from the Americas, Monsieur de Choquet had been promoted to the rank of surgeon-major and appointed as director of the hospitals on shore. There he had met again his disciple Roblet and had warmly recommended him to Captain de Trémigon, with whom he had already made voyages to India and China. Thanks to the Captain's influence young Roblet, who was only a surgeon's mate on forty pounds, had been allowed to dine with the officers. This was lucky for me, as Monsieur le Choquet had been kind enough to speak well of me to him. He had also given to my new friend a copy of his journal of his voyage to India and China, which he had had printed and bound. Inspired by this example, Roblet had himself started to write a record of his voyage aboard *l'Annibal.* As he knew nothing about navigation, I was happy to explain anything he asked about. Medical men's diaries differ from those of Naval officers. Certainly, in the same way that sailors carefully note every detail of the progress of their ship, doctors and surgeons, for their part, record their observations on the diseases that confront them, along with their symptoms and development. But their curiosity is not limited simply to their medical art: zoology, botany and humanity interest them just as much. This is no doubt due to the fact that they have more free time and do not have to stand watch at sea or do guard duty when their ships are moored. Roblet was happy to read aloud extracts from Monsieur de Choquet's *Voyage to India and China.* The writing reminded me of the other two doctors whose works I had read: Edward Baldock's *Essay on Guyana* and of course Rollin's *Memoir of Hindustan.* Talking about them with my new friend ended up confirming my suspicions about the death of the former doctor at the Gardes Françaises.

'I have a similar narrative,' I said, 'but it has never been printed. It was written by an army doctor, an old friend of my father, who like him had been to India. I'm happy to lend it to you.'

Roblet interjected.

'He left you the original?'

'No! Not really. I never met Doctor Rollin, as he died in strange circumstances. The person who found his work, a woman whose name I won't tell you, out of discretion, gave it to me when I told her I too was going to India.'

This brought me to describing to my companion the circumstances of Rollin's death, such as they were related to me by his former mistress. He made me repeat several times Madame Dutertre's description of the poor doctor's final moments. When I quoted Rollin's final words, as I understood them from the pretty landlady, Roblet interrupted me.

'Napel? She really said 'napel'?'

'Yes. She thought he was asking for help: *un appel,* d'you see?'

'I don't believe it! The dying man was a doctor. Without doubt he wanted to say 'napel' as it was a word he knew well. I'm sure of it. Wait a moment, you'll soon understand.'

Roblet went off to look for a treatise on medicine and surgery in his chest.

'Listen to this,' he said, a few minutes later. 'Napel, or *Aconitum napellus*[13]…is a plant found in the mountains of France, Switzerland, Italy and also northern India. It is bitter, caustic and considered a dangerous poison. Its venomous roots are used by the people of India to poison the tips of their weapons. It is widely traded.' I'll ignore the botanic description, but listen to this: '…a small dose of *Aconitum*

---

13 Translator's note: *Aconite napellus:* Monkshood, also known as Wolfsbane.

napellus can produce a raging thirst, vomiting, dizziness, delirium, sleepiness, paralysis, convulsions, cold sweats and death…' The lady was right: the symptoms she described to you correspond well to a poisoning with *Aconitum napellus.*'

About a week after our departure the sky grew cloudy and the wind dropped. This continued for the following days. On the 29th, at nine in the morning, *la Ville de Paris* sent up a signal flag, with *le Héros'* number and the instruction for her to come up astern. I watched our division chief advance in the Admiral's wake. An hour later, *le Héros* left the convoy and sailed off, signalling us to follow her. The Comte de Grasse had authorised the Chevalier de Suffren to leave the fleet, along with his division and convoy: five ships, a corvette and eight merchant ships carrying twelve hundred troops. To these were added five merchantmen for Senegal escorted by the cutter *le Clairvoyant.* Our Commander signalled to us to heave-to while the Navy ships and convoy bound for America sailed off, calling the Captains aboard *le Héros* to give them our orders. Apart from *l'Annibal's* Captain, none of them knew what was the mission or destination of our little division.

Returning on board, Captain de Trémigon called us together in the Great cabin to explain the situation. Commodore Johnstone had left before us with five ships and a fleet of transports carrying troops to take possession of the Cape, which was poorly defended by the Dutch. Our mission was essentially to get to the Cape before Johnstone and land the Pondicherry regiment. Unfortunately we were already late, as the Chevalier de Suffren had learned, from a Spanish ship that had crossed paths with us six days before, that Johnstone had left Portsmouth on the 14th March, six days before we left Brest. However, if our original intelligence was correct, Johnstone was supposed to go first to Gibraltar with Admiral Darby, which might delay him.

At midday our observations showed us to be at 39 degrees 36 minutes latitude north and we estimated our longitude at 19 degrees 10 minutes west of the Paris meridian. At four in the afternoon, *le Héros* got under way again and signalled us to steer south-south-west and make all sail. The sky had cleared, the sun had returned and in the distance to starboard we could still see the Comte de Grasse's convoy along the line of the horizon under the blazing splendour of the setting sun.

The next morning, unfortunately, the Comte de Grasse's fleet was still visible twelve miles to our west. It was fine and hot but the north-east wind had weakened and our progress across the limitless ocean had become desperately slow, with the transports dragging behind. Over the following days the wind was a little fresher but still variable and unreliable, with an overcast sky, flat calms, squalls and rain. It remained like this until the 2nd April. In the evening the sky cleared and in the distance we saw a high mountain rise slowly from the sea, directly ahead, in the blue dusk mist. We knew that it was Madeira. The Admiral signalled to us to pass it to starboard. On the 3rd March, at dawn, we saw a fishing boat under our lee, and *le Vengeur*, who was sailing in our wake, changed course to intercept it. The Chevalier de Saint-Luperce, who was taking the air on the poop deck, hurried down to the quarterdeck to tell Captain de Trémigon that he spoke Portuguese fluently. He was so insistent that in her turn *l'Annibal* manoeuvred to come up to the fishing boat, which was waiting for us, dancing on the swell in the morning light with all her sheets eased. After a brief exchange, Saint-Luperce told the Captain that a small English squadron had passed well off the island, without stopping, five days earlier. He then wanted the Captain to launch a boat and insisted that he be taken immediately aboard *le Héros* so that he could pass on this important news to the Chevalier de Suffren. Our Captain pointed out *le Vengeur*, which had passed us to get within speaking distance of *le Héros*. We could clearly hear Captain de Forbin giving the same information to the Admiral. Saint-Luperce insisted in vain, saying that the officers of *le Vengeur* had not understood everything and that only he was able to give the fine details of such useful intelligence on the situation. Captain de Trémigon was unmoved, saying we would waste time for no reason, that we had to go on as quickly as possible, and that nothing was more important.

Having taken our departure from the western end of Madeira, we headed south. We had a favourable current and a fresh north-east wind but despite this were still only making five knots, as our two convoys, ours and the one for Senegal, were slowing us down considerably. At dawn on Friday 6th April, we could make out the island of Palma twenty miles ahead under a low, grey sky. At midday Lieutenant de Kermadec, alerted by the lookouts, sent me to the top of the mainmast. From there I could see the summit of Tenerife lost in the clouds twenty-five miles to our south-east. For four days we advanced at a slow pace of about sixty miles per day, with the Canary Islands to port. The ships rolled gently on a leaden-coloured sea under a dark sky, the sails hung down the masts, the yards groaned and the sheets chafed in their blocks. The wardroom was stuffy and hot at mealtimes, and I could now feel an open hostility towards me. Faces went blank when I came near, nobody spoke to me at table, I had to insist to get anyone to pass me a plate or the wine bottle. I was treated so unkindly that I began to feel myself guilty. The first real incident happened on the Sunday evening.

'I am talking to you, Sir,' I said to the officer next to me, the young Chevalier d'Aché, whom I was asking for the third time to pass the pitcher beside him.

The Chevalier turned to me and looked me straight in the eye.

'And I am not answering you, Sir.'

'May I ask why?'

'You have no honour!'

'Monsieur d'Aché,' I said, forcing myself to keep calm. 'I can do nothing about that, since we are at sea, but once we touch land you will answer for it!'

'If that's what you want!' he replied.

Lieutenant de Galles told us to stop arguing. To be fair, he rightly admonished the Chevalier d'Aché for having provoked me and demanded that we resolve our difference.

On Monday morning the sky was just as grey and the island of El Hierro was still in sight twenty miles to our north-east. At six o'clock the Chevalier de Suffren released Monsieur de la Tullaye, commander of the cutter *le Clairvoyant* escorting the Senegal convoy, and they all left us, heading south-south-east towards the coast of Africa.

Over the following days we made little progress. We were concerned for the Chevalier de Suffren, as it seemed our mission was under threat of failure. We imagined that Johnstone had long since passed the Cape Verde Islands and was already on his long traverse to the coast of Brazil. Thanks to Lieutenant de Galles' keeping a close eye on matters, my relations with my shipmates seemed to improve, or at least I was not subjected to any more provocation. My friend Roblet told me that he had heard Lieutenant de Galles tell the Chevalier d'Aché that he should thank him for having enabled him to avoid the challenge I had thrown him, as he would never have survived it. Lieutenant de Galles had served on *l'Orient,* which in 1778 was to be part of the Comte de Ternay's division for India, along with *l'Amazone,* and he must have heard about my 'exploits' of the time. The Chevalier d'Aché was a fine man and normally a friendly officer. I would have liked to have known the reason for his attitude, but the circumstances made it difficult for me to raise the subject again.

I asked my friend Roblet about it, but his position as a humble surgeon's mate did not allow him to share confidences with the officers. He did however promise to talk about it with the ship's surgeon, a good man despite a troublesome surname for someone of his calling: Boucher[14]!

On 10th April, the wind settled into the north-west, the sails filled and the rigging began to sing. The sun shone strongly but the air stayed pleasantly cool. The familiar sound of water rushing along the hull could once more be heard throughout the whole ship. We were finally in the Trade Winds. The Chevalier de Suffren ordered *le Sphinx* to tow *la Sainte Anne*, a merchantman that was slower than the rest, having had her cutwater and bowsprit carried away in a collision with *l'Espérance*, another ship in the convoy. We were soon recording seven knots on the ship's log – more than two leagues an hour. The foaming white wakes of our ships shone on the deep blue of the sea. We estimated the Cape Verde Islands to be three or four days ahead, slightly to starboard, and the Chevalier de Suffren kept our course at south-south-west, so as not to pass them to leeward before launching across the Atlantic. Our good mood was revived. We were certainly behind schedule, according to Lieutenant de Galles, but all was not yet lost.

We still had a long way to go. There were two choices for getting to the Cape, but the quicker of them was to sail over to Brazil, crossing the Equator on the way, before sailing south to seek out the south-west winds. However, as the English had a colony at Saint Helena, on the more direct but slower route, we hoped that Johnstone had been ordered to call in there.

On Thursday 12th April, *le Héros* signalled the fleet to heave-to, for the burial of the Vicomte de Sourches, commander of the first battalion of the Austrasie regiment, who had died of an illness at seven the previous evening. He was given the honours due to a full-time Colonel. The health of the crews was in fact deteriorating, with new men laid low each day. Roblet told me that he had several cases of malignant

---

14 Translator's note: *Boucher:* Butcher.

fever on board. When off duty I went with him to visit the sick in the infirmary, amidships on the lower gundeck. I was able say a few words to them in their native language and was moved to see how touched they were by this simple act, which cost me so little.

My friend had asked his superior about me, and Monsieur Boucher had told him that, behind my back, Saint-Luperce had told anyone who would listen that I had presented false certificates of nobility in order to be admitted to the Marine Guards, and that the Comte de Lapérouse had severed relations with me on account of my misconduct. Saint-Luperce maintained that nobody at Versailles had wanted to say what was held against me, for fear of besmirching the reputation of the Navy. He had added, lowering his voice hypocritically, that only Captain de Trémigon was willing to take me, and that was because I had agreed to ship aboard some valuable goods for trading on the side, the secret profits of which I would share with him. No other Naval officer would have agreed to something so dishonourable, but I was simply following my father, who was known in the India Company as a great trader on his own account, and Captain de Trémigon was his accomplice at the time. At that point, Monsieur Boucher had told my friend, Saint-Luperce had perhaps gone too far, as the upright Lieutenant de Galles had not at all appreciated accusations against his Captain in his presence. That is doubtless why he had defended me during my quarrel with the Chevalier d'Aché.

'Sir!' Saint-Luperce had then asked our second captain. 'In that case, can you explain why Captain de Trémigon did not want to tell you, his second captain, what was in that mysterious steel chest brought to him by Monsieur Laforest-Dombourg, and which he immediately hid in his cabin?'

This was on the evening of the 14th April. I asked to see the Captain, and related to him everything I had just heard from Roblet. I also told him everything I had previously learned about Tallebau de Saint-Luperce. I wanted to challenge the so-called Chevalier to a duel. Despite his anger, Captain de Trémigon dissuaded me.

'These are incredible lies! For a start, I never met your father. During his time with the India Company he was always in Bengal whereas I sailed mainly in the Sunda Straits to the Moluccas and China.'

He was also annoyed with his second captain, despite my having told him that he defended me during my argument with Ship's Ensign d'Aché.

'Lieutenant de Galles is an honest officer and I have a lot of time for him, but he could at least have told me himself! This Saint-Luperce is not just slandering both of us, and besmirching your father's name, he is spreading unrest amongst my officers!'

The Captain, enervated, paced up and down the Great cabin.

'I think the circumstances mean that we can no longer stick to the secrecy demanded by the Marquis de Castries. Today is Saturday. Things will be quieter tomorrow after Mass, as the men will be resting. We'll take advantage of it to launch the boat and go to see the Chevalier de Suffren. We will give him the Marquis de Castries' letter for Messieurs Souillac and d'Orves and pass on everything you told me about our future aims in India in general, and as regards the Marathas in particular. I will show him your letter of recommendation from the Minister, by way of introducing you, as well as the safe-conduct signed by the King. Above all, we will put the chest into his safekeeping. Don't forget to bring both the keys. This will put a stop to all these stupid and vile rumours about trading on the side. After that I'll get the officers together to bring them up to date.'

Captain de Trémigon also intended to ask the Chevalier de Suffren to take Saint-Luperce on his ship, thinking that the commander's sometimes violent authority would do him a lot of good. I objected that this would make things worse, as Saint-Luperce was quite capable of carrying on with his plotting once aboard *le Héros*. As for me, I was wondering how Saint-Luperce had found out that my father had spent several years with the India Company. Nobody in Versailles knew this apart from my uncle and Monsieur de Fleurieu. They could well have spoken about it to the Minister, but not to Saint-Luperce. Therein lay yet another inexplicable mystery.

On Sunday morning at nine, *le Héros* gave the signal to bend on the anchor cables and to sail west a quarter north-west while preparing to anchor. Ship's Lieutenant de Lusignan, commanding *la Fortune*, who had got the orders from the Admiral's poop deck, having hove-to in his wake, shouted to us that we were breaking off to take on water at Santiago, in Cape Verde. This was because *l'Artésien* risked running out, having been at the last moment switched to us from the fleet bound for the Americas, without time to take on enough water to reach the Cape. The stop would also be used to repair *la Sainte-Anne* and *l'Espérance*. The wind was fresh and still from the north-north-east. All the ships of the division and the convoy hauled their weather braces to bring the wind on the quarter. The sails now pulled better and our speed increased considerably. *Le Sphinx* was ordered to let go *la Sainte-Anne,* which she was still towing, and take *l'Espérance* instead. A sailor is always happy when his ship goes faster, but our pleasure was tempered by the fact that we were making a detour, which reduced even more our slim chances of reaching the Cape before Johnstone. There was no longer any question of launching a boat to go aboard *le Héros*; it was impossible. Captain de Trémigon decided to wait until we were at Santiago before going to see the Admiral.

By the middle of the afternoon I could see the island of Boa Vista about ten miles ahead to starboard, clearly visible from the poop deck. I estimated it was about eighteen or twenty miles long. With my eyeglass I could make out huge beaches and dunes, and hills rising to a thousand feet in the interior. From this distance everything seemed empty and dry. Soon afterwards the lookouts pointed out a very wide and high island about twenty-five or thirty miles away, along with a smaller, lower island closer to us. These could only be Santiago and Maio. *L'Artésien,* who had hauled her wind to reconnoitre Boa Vista, returned and took her place in the division.

In the evening we eased off and once more ran south-west, past the east side of Maio. Although this was not the most direct route, the Chevalier de Suffren wanted to be sure of avoiding a chain of rocks that ran out from the northern point of the island, according to the *Navigational Instructions* of Monsieur d'Après de Mannevillette. Before sunset, the Admiral signalled that by the next morning we would be in the Porto Praya roadstead, the usual anchorage for Santiago.

*

Cape Verde Archipelago, Monday 16th April 1781.
I am on watch from eight until midday with Lieutenant de Kermadec. When I come out of the gun room, the hammocks on the lower deck have been taken down. There is only the infirmary amidships, forward of the main hatch. Usually this area, surrounded by canvas, does not interfere with manoeuvres, but at the moment it is overflowing, as we have many sick men on the beds.

Last night Monsieur Boucher told the Captain that we have an excess of invalids because at Brest we took on board able seamen who had only just finished an exhausting campaign, and who would normally have been allowed to go home, had their basic rights been respected. Captain de Trémigon replied in my presence that the Navy lacked the manpower to put an end to this war and that it was probably with the suffering of his sailors in mind that the Admiral had decided to stop here, despite the risks it posed to his mission.

'We will be able to buy fresh meat,' added the Captain. 'They usually have lots of guinea fowl, sheep and cattle. We can also stock up on fresh water; there is an inexhaustible supply a hundred paces from the beach to the west of Porto Praya Bay.'

Despite my prejudices against the Chevalier de Suffren, I could not help but think that what I had just heard spoke in his favour.

The gunports have been opened to let in the cool of the morning. The weak glow of the new day lights up the dark shapes of the line of 36-pounders. At the forward end of the lower deck, in the half-light, the Bosun and his men are hauling the main anchor cable and laying it out, with a turn around the bitts, ready to anchor in ten fathoms. These are the Admiral's last orders. The crew's Chief Petty Officer, standing on the main hatch, orders his men to start lifting onto the lower deck the barrels which will be used to fetch water ashore. He is also having the water hoses and pumps prepared, for filling the casks in the hold once they have been emptied beforehand. To lose as little time as possible, everything has to be done in a single day. Nobody will have any rest. I cross paths with Lieutenant de Galles as he finishes his morning round. His face is dark and he does not seem to be appreciating this stop, which will certainly slow us down. I imagine that he is picturing the English ships, faster than ours, tearing across the Ocean. As for me, on the contrary, all this commotion makes me happy, as this unforeseen stop at Porto Praya will allow Captain de Trémigon and me to present our case to the Chevalier de Suffren and put a stop, once and for all, to Saint-Luperce's subversive scheming.

Coming on deck, I can hear Father Tiburce reciting the morning prayer on the poop deck. The sky is clearing and I can see the globe of the sun rising above the horizon behind us to port. Even in the tropics, where this happens very quickly, it is a sobering moment. The hammocks have been stowed away behind the netting, and the men not occupied with handling the ship or preparing to anchor or collect water are washing down the decks with sea water. The wind is still from the north-north-east and the weather is fine, with the heat of the day yet to come. We are making six knots, heading for the south-east point of Santiago. We reckon this big island to be about twenty-five miles ahead on the starboard bow, behind the island of Maio, whose southern point is slipping us by less than a mile to starboard. Maio is bare, with no vegetation apart from a few shrubs; a piece of the Sahara lost in the ocean. Like Boa Vista, it is edged with wide beaches of sand battered by the swell, and even flatter than the former, with just a few low hills at its centre. As the ship progresses, we can make out more and more of the bigger island of Santiago behind the southern point of Maio. Its coast stretches to the north-west as far as the eye can see. Unlike Maio and Boa Vista, Santiago is very high and mountainous. Its shore is still hidden in the mist but I can clearly see its tall peaks piercing the clouds, seemingly suspended in the sky.

The Chevalier d'Aché has commanded the watch since four this morning. I still respect him, despite our argument, but for the moment I try to avoid him. I am impatient for our arrival at Porto Praya, to clear up the misunderstanding between us caused by Saint-Luperce's slanders.

L'Annibal is at the head of the line. The Marine Guard assisting the two officers of the watch announces from the top of the poop deck that *le Héros,* sailing a cable's length astern of us, has just sent two signals to the masthead: a red pennant above two flags giving *la Fortune's* number, and two other flags ordering the corvette to sail on ahead to reconnoitre our proposed anchorage at Porto Praya. Day signals are composed of a number of flags, pennants and streamers and, occasionally one or two cannon shots. The Chevalier de Suffren uses a system based on that of the Chevalier du Pavillon[15].

---

15 Translator's note: *Chevalier du Pavillon:* Jean-François de Cheyron, Chevalier du Pavillon (1730 – 1782). Distinguished French Naval officer. Following his participation in the disastrous Battle of Quiberon Bay (see Volume One of the Laforest-Dombourg series) he wrote a treatise on naval tactics which included a new system of inter-ship signalling. Despite strong opposition from the likes of Monsieur de Sartine and the Comte d'Estaing, his ingenious system was gradually adopted by the French Navy. He was killed by a cannonball at the Battle of Dominica.

Each of our ships has two identical sets of fifteen flags, along with three pennants and four streamers. Each flag has a different colour or design, each one representing a number. It makes no difference where in the rigging the flags are hoisted. The flags are sent up in pairs, the relationship of which can denote two hundred and twenty-five different orders or pieces of information.

Before leaving Brest I have, like all the officers, created a table cut out of strong paper, on which I have drawn and coloured the flags and grille for this campaign. I have also copied out in several notebooks the general orders represented by the numbers, along with the additional orders indicated by the streamers.

La Fortune, who was following in *le Héros'* wake, can scarcely catch up with her, despite having put on more sail after getting her signal. This corvette, carrying sixteen 8-pounder cannons, has none of the qualities necessary for this type of ship. She is slow and difficult to handle and has been dragging her feet since we left Brest, much to the annoyance of Monsieur de Lusignan, her Captain. Eventually *l'Artésien* sways up her topsails, which have been half-brailed, easily overtakes our poor little corvette and comes up astern of *le Héros* to ask to go on ahead herself. The Chevalier de Suffren agrees immediately and *la Fortune* is sent to the rear guard, with orders to tell the ships of the convoy to keep well apart so as not to get in each other's way while anchoring.

L'Artésien sprints off like a racehorse, setting her t'gallantsails and studding sails as she overtakes us under our lee to starboard. She looks superb with all sail set. Her progress creates a white furrow on the indigo surface of a sea lit obliquely by the morning sun. At first she follows the same course as us towards the south-east point of Santiago, before coming up onto the wind, starboard tacks hard in, and sailing faster and faster straight for the east coast of the big island directly to our west.

Le Héros sends up the signal: *prepare to anchor*. This is followed by the command to lay out a second bower anchor. The Chevalier d'Aché orders the main anchor to be prepared at the catheads and sends a Marine Guard to report to the Captain.

The sun is rising over the horizon; it will soon be eight o'clock. The little bell in the wheelhouse sounds eight bells and the big bell on the foredeck replies with one strike of the bell to signal the start of the new watch. While Lieutenant de Kermadec and the Chevalier d'Aché exchange instructions, I have to make a routine inspection of the ship and check whether the ship is making water. When I return to make my report twenty minutes later, I find Lieutenant de Kermadec watching *l'Artésien* through his telescope.

Our advance guard has reached Santiago at a cape from which the coast curves to the south, along which she is sailing on a parallel course to ours, running before the wind like us. She is about five miles to starboard of us and seems small, being so far away, but we can appreciate how quickly her sails are moving against the hazy shoreline.

L'Artésien is quickly gaining on us. Behind her I can make out, with my telescope, and through the mist which is starting to dissipate in the first heat of the day, the rockbound cliffs at whose base the swell creates a permanent foamy fringe. Above them, the whole coast is composed of rocky slopes, with mountain peaks behind.

'Monsieur de Cardaillac is being sensible,' Lieutenant de Kermadec says to me. 'If there are enemy ships in the anchorage, they won't see him coming.'

He turns and looks astern.

'I wonder why the Admiral hasn't ordered us to keep close to the coast too.'

We have in fact been maintaining a course that, if we don't change it, will bring us into full view three miles off the south-east point of Santiago.

We are in front, a cable's length ahead of *le Héros,* ready to follow her orders. The other ships are now further apart, as directed. *Le Vengeur* is a mile and a half astern of *le Héros,* while another mile and a half further back the convoy is struggling along, in three approximate and widely spaced columns. *Le Sphinx* is at the head of the starboard column, with *l'Espérance* in tow. *La Fortune* is at the rear.

'But, Sir,' I say, 'the anchorage belongs to the Portuguese, who are neutral. If they are not our enemies, where's the risk?'

'I'm not talking about the Portuguese,' replied the Ship's Lieutenant. 'I'm thinking of the English.'

Although Lieutenant de Kermadec knows nothing about my meeting with Captain de Trémigon and the intention to see the Chevalier de Suffren, I am annoyed that he can be so calm about a possible enemy presence at Porto Praya, which could well upset my plans.

'I don't understand, Sir. Apart from Commodore Johnstone, who everyone says is far ahead of us, I thought there were no reports of English ships hereabouts.'

'You are no doubt correct, but all the same, you can never be too careful at sea!'

I know he is right, but despite this I feel myself going red with annoyance, and I am afraid that the Lieutenant will see my bad mood on my face. Luckily he does not notice, as he has his telescope fixed on *l'Artésien*. Monsieur de Cardaillac's vessel has now reached the south-west point of Santiago, which hides the Porto Praya roadstead from view. In a few minutes she will confirm that the anchorage is free of ships, as I hope.

I also raise my own eyeglass. *L'Artésien* has taken in her studding sails and is sailing close to the wind, starboard tacks hard in, to round the southern end of the point.

'Look!' says Lieutenant de Kermadec.

My heart seems to skip a beat. *L'Artésien* has suddenly worn ship to port tack, coming right across the wind, and is now sailing diagonally to meet us, hard to windward on port tack, at the same time raising all her staysails.

'She is signalling something,' I say.

'That's what I was telling you!'

Coloured rectangles are flying from the t'gallant masts of Monsieur de Cardaillac's ship, but we cannot decipher them until *l'Artésien* has covered half the distance between us.

I take my table and notebook out of my pocket. I still hope that Monsieur de Cardaillac's manoeuvre is no more than a show of zeal.

'On the fore t'gallant mast: a red pennant above a flag with horizontal red, white and blue stripes – number four, above a red flag with a white cross – number one. It's a numeric signal, meaning four. On the main t'gallant mast: a red and white chequered flag – number seven, above a red flag – number nine.'

I look for the signal corresponding to numbers 7-9 in my notebook, and check them twice, hoping I am not mistaken. I read aloud: 'The newly sighted sails are enemy'.

'Go quickly and warn the Captain,' Lieutenant de Kermadec replies. 'Four 'sails'. I think they are at anchor, otherwise he would have signalled their movements. Note it in the log.'

He pulls out his watch.

'It is three quarters after eight.'

I go down to the quarterdeck and run through the wheelhouse, where a Second Pilot is assisting the man at the helm. Captain de Trémigon is taking his breakfast on his rosewood table, over which lies a clean white cloth. He gets up straight away to join Lieutenant de Kermadec on the poop deck. I stop for a moment to make a note in the ship's log, which is kept in the binnacle forward of the ship's double wheel. When I get back to the open air of the poop deck, I can see *le Héros* overtaking us to port, taking our wind. I recognise the corpulent Chevalier de Suffren standing forward of the main companionway hatch. Beside him an officer with a loudhailer shouts that they are going to have a look themselves to confirm what we have just been told, and to follow at a distance. *Le Héros* makes all sail, bears round to starboard tack, cutting across our bows, and passes close to *l'Artésien,* who speaks to her with a loudhailer before tacking to take her place a cable's length astern of us.

Captain de Trémigon goes down again to the quarterdeck to oversee any changes to our course directly from the officer of the watch's bench in the wheelhouse. The Chief Petty Officer positions himself in the waist, loudhailer in hand. We are advancing in the wake of *le Héros,* followed closely by *l'Artésien,* but the rest of the convoy is a long, long way astern.

We have arrived close to the south-east point of Santiago, which we have been keeping a mile and a half to starboard. *Le Héros,* which has got well ahead of us, spends a few minutes passing it, then comes up to windward, apparently to keep herself under cover of the coast. She sends a signal to the masthead: *Reverse order of battle,* before altering course to steer straight for the cliffs to the north of the point.

'Ready about!' Captain de Trémigon tells the Chief Petty Officer, who repeats it with his loudhailer.

'Fish the anchor!' he adds. 'We won't be anchoring for the moment and if we have to fight it will be a nuisance to have the anchor hanging from the cathead. I know the Porto Praya anchorage well, and if the Admiral and *l'Artésien* have seen four ships anchored outside, that's because there's no more room in the bay, and since it's big, that means that there's a whole English squadron and the fleet it's escorting inside there, just behind this headland. So it can only be Johnstone.'

'The Admiral is signalling!' announces Lieutenant de Kermadec, who has kept his eyeglass fixed on *le Héros.* 'He's sending up another… No! There's just one flag: quartered white, blue, red and yellow…it's the *as you were* flag.'

The *as you were* flag is the sixteenth flag, not signifying a number, placed at the top left of the signal table. It is usually sent up to cancel an order which has just been given, and in fact it is quickly replaced by four new flags. The first two signal: *Natural order of battle*, the other two: *Close up the line.*

'Good!' says Captain de Trémigon. 'Whether natural or reverse, it's just an order of battle. We'll have to come beam on to the wind at least to hold it and since we are not far from the coast it'll have to be on the other tack, heading east, to have enough room to manoeuvre while *le Vengeur* and *le Sphinx* catch us up. Since the Admiral has ordered normal order of battle, I imagine we're going to wear ship. Prepare to clew up the mainsail and the mizzen! It won't be long before he turns to port. We'd better be ready to follow him…'

In Naval tactics, forming a battle order is achieved by abandoning the cruising order to form one continuous line, each ship sailing in the wake of the ship ahead at just a third of a cable's distance[16]. If all the ships turn together – which for reasons of convenience is usual done by tacking through the wind – so that the ship which was last in line is now first, that is termed the *reverse order*; whereas if the original order is maintained, that is the *natural order.* But in all cases, it is necessary to sail somewhere between hard on the wind and with the wind on the beam, in order to be able to maintain a short distance between ships of different sailing qualities. On this point of sail, the sheets can be eased or hardened to slow down or accelerate, without changing course, whereas with the wind free a ship is pushed on without being able to regulate its speed to that of the others.

'It seems to me that reverse order would have been wiser,' continues the Captain. 'It would have kept us out of sight of the enemy and allowed us to get our forces together more quickly, while guaranteeing the safety of the convoy. Well, Lieutenant de Galles, we won't get our stop today, but good can come out of misfortune. We have caught up with Johnstone and we may be able to get ahead of him. No doubt they've seen us, but if they want to attack us they'll have to slip their cables, abandoning their anchors and losing time later coming back to retrieve them. Start preparing for action, but leave the 36-pounders secured for the moment to give the surgeon time to get the sick down to

---

16   Translators note: *a third of a cable's distance*: about 70 yards.

the orlop. Get a petty officer and a team to arrange the barrels. There's no hurry. If they decide to slip their cables, they'll need some time to clear the bay and form a line of battle. I'd be surprised if we attack them at the anchorage, especially as Porto Praya belongs to the neutral Portuguese. In any case, we can't do that until *le Vengeur* and *le Sphinx* have caught up, which gives us some time. All the same, have the gun room and wardroom bulkheads knocked down and tell the Master Gunner to be ready to distribute cartridges and powder horns as soon as they've begun to unlash the cannons on the main gundeck. Also tell the Captains of the Austrasie regiment and our garrison to position their riflemen on the fore and after decks, without getting in the way of the ship handling.'

The second captain goes below to execute the order for clearing the ship for action and Lieutenant de Kermadec, overseeing the main gundeck, follows him. My battle station at the ten 8-pounders on the quarterdeck means that there is no reason for me to move, and I am joined by the second Master Gunner, my assistant on the ship's battle roll. He is called Gravier and comes from L'Orient. With his help I organise my five gun crews – five because only one set of guns is used at a time and there are five on the port side and five on the starboard side. I have thirty men under me, six per cannon: a Gun Captain, four sailors and a boy. The boys are there to bring the powder. We know each other well and they know what to do, as we have trained for half an hour almost every day since leaving Brest.

Le Héros continues to windward, straight towards the coast to the north of the point. She clews up her lower and upper sails, keeping just her topsails, mizzen, mizzen topsail and inner jib. We do likewise, coming up to within a third of a cable of her stern. *L'Artésien*, who is much faster than both of us, stays a cable's length astern. The cliffs get closer and we can see ahead the great clouds of spray bursting along their length and cascading down each time a swell breaks at their base. The Chevalier de Suffren sends a new signal: *make all sail.* This order is clearly directed at our two other ships, as at the same time *le Héros* loosens her topsails to reduce her speed. Astern of us, *le Vengeur* had not expected this order to put on more sail, but she is still a good mile and a half away. As for *le Sphinx,* she has cast off *l'Espérance,* but must still be slowed down by the towline, which she has not yet had the time to fully retrieve and which is probably still dragging in her wake.

We can now hear the surf breaking on the shoreline. We will have to go about soon if we don't want to end up on the rocks. That will enable the two ships at the rear to rejoin the line more easily as we will be on the other tack. Monsieur de Cardaillac has been skilful enough to keep himself fully hidden during his approach and has suddenly tacked to keep himself out of sight behind the south-east point of the bay. The English have only seen *le Héros* and with luck think there is only one ship. We will sail a board due east, in order to create some distance, then resume our course, neither seen nor recognised, and ahead of the English. The Chevalier de Suffren has once again a chance to fulfil his mission.

Ahead of us, *le Héros* is starting to ease off the wind to port. We think that in a moment she will brail up her mizzen to clear her stern and wear ship, but instead she lowers her topsails a little to slow herself down, lets fly her mizzen topsail and hoists some more signals. It is the Chevalier d'Aché's job to decipher them, that being his role in battle.

'It's for *la Fortune*,' he says. 'The Admiral is ordering him to keep to windward with the convoy and to get it to heave-to.' The Ensign shakes his head doubtfully. 'I shouldn't think they can see much from there. Do you want me to repeat it?'

'Wait until we've gone onto the other board,' replies Captain de Trémigon.

But *le Héros* does not turn. As soon as she has lowered her signals she bears off around the headland, and once more comes up to windward, still on starboard tack and increasing her speed. Captain de Trémigon, taken by surprise, gives new orders to the helmsmen from the watch officer's bench, on which he is now standing to get a better view of things. We follow the Admiral, as does *l'Artésien*, and lose sight of *le Vengeur* and *le Sphinx*, who are still at least a mile and a half to the north-east of the headland.

'I don't understand! Why does he want to cross the mouth of the bay?' asks the Captain. 'We know they are there. Why show ourselves? We're surely not going to attack them without waiting for the others. Unless he simply wants to fire at them from a distance as we go past. But we'll be out of range as we have to keep well off to avoid the reefs off the Tubaron Point south of l'Île aux Cailles[17]. Moreover, if they

---

17 Translator's note: *l'Île aux Cailles:* Quail Island, now known as the Ilheu de Santa Maria.

decide to slip their cables to attack us, we'll be cut off from the convoy and our rear guard.'

He turns to a Marine Guard who is waiting for orders at the leeward rail.

'Run and tell Lieutenant de Kermadec to prepare the lower gundeck now! Immediately! And tell the Master Gunner to start handing out powder. I hope they've got all the casks and the sick down to the orlop! I should have known!'

The south-east point of Santiago, high and steep, but with no offshore hazards, passes quickly beside us to windward. The Porto Praya Bay opens up on our right. Opposite, at the other end of the anchorage, we can see another headland ending in reefs and breakers. This is Tubaron Point, which extends far out to sea from a hill of reddish earth which rises from a plateau of the same colour. In front of it is a much lower island, its top parallel with the surface of the sea: l'Île aux Cailles.

To the right of the red hill, where a valley comes down, palms and coconut trees bend in the wind. Houses with tiled roofs line a beach overlooked on the north end by a small flat hill with a fort on top. A big Portuguese flag is flying above it. I see all of this without really paying attention: what takes my eye are the masts and rigging of the enemy ships anchored inside the bay, at least forty of them, all yawing around their anchors in the north-north-east wind. They have anchored randomly, their bowsprits pointing towards a semi-circular range of hills and plateaus forming the limits of the anchorage, with high mountains behind and a pointed summit against a sky so blue that it almost hurts my eyes to look at it.

Le Héros keeps heading for the Tubaron Point. About two and a half cable lengths directly ahead of her I can see four ships at anchor, amongst which are a ten-gun cutter, a bomb ketch and a twelve-gun frigate; easily recognisable warships with their red flags quartered with the Union Jack flying above their poop decks. *Le Héros* will be on them in less than five minutes. I wonder why they have anchored there, almost outside the bay. They are going to regret it.

The main body of Johnstone's division is gathered inside the anchorage in several columns, in front of the Île aux Cailles and the beach below the fort. They will be outside our cannon range, except perhaps for a two-decker ship anchored on her own, a little further to the south. She is more or less in line with the column, but is a good cable length astern of the ship ahead, so that if we were to sail a little higher, to starboard, we could rake her stern before easing off again to get round the south-west point and its reefs, and exit the anchorage. I examine her with my telescope and count two rows of eleven gunports on her starboard side. With her deck guns that makes fifty cannons in all, probably 24-pounders on her lower gundeck and 12-pounders on the upper gundeck, but she won't be able to bring them to bear, being at anchor. We will be on her in less than ten minutes, but unfortunately our 36-pounders won't be ready by then.

My calculations are interrupted by a roar of thunder as *le Héros* releases a broadside on the frigate. A ball of dark smoke forms around her and drifts off towards the open sea. Seabirds take to the air everywhere in the anchorage.

'He's only using his upper gundeck, probably to keep his 36-pounder broadside to blast the 50-gun ship,' says the Chevalier d'Aché, standing beside me.

In fact, *le Héros* hardens up to go further inside the bay. Captain de Trémigon send a message to Lieutenant Boissauveur, in charge of our 18-pounders, to hold his fire, so as to keep his broadside for the ship, as our 36-pounders probably won't be ready once we are in range, and the frigate is already in a pitiable state. She's already had more than enough, one might say. I read her name as we pass: *Diana*. We keep on, a cable's length astern of *le Héros*, as the distance to the lone ship reduces rapidly.

This 50-gun ship is in line with another warship moored a cable ahead of her. The latter is bigger and carries two rows of twenty-six gunports on each side: sixty-four guns including those on deck. Another 50-gun ship is anchored further on, as well as a 26-gun frigate. After that come the merchant ships of the East India Company, the *Indiamen*, recognisable by their rows of yellow-painted gunports, designed to make them look like warships. They are lined up opposite the shore. The rest of the vessels of the English fleet are anchored close together in three columns roughly parallel to the east coast of the Île aux Cailles. That's where their Commodore is, his ship recognisable by his pennant at the masthead. He is on a ship of just fifty guns, but ahead of him is a 64-gun ship, and astern are a 32-gun frigate and three or four *Indiamen*. These are merchant ships but despite that each one carries a battery of about twenty 18-pounders, and four or five cannons on deck.

Between the group anchored around the 64-gun ship and the column lined up on the first 64-gunner, there is a stretch of open water forming a kind of semi-circular fish trap a cable or so in radius.

Le Héros keeps on to windward. It becomes clear that the Chevalier de Suffren wants to pass between the 50-gun ship and the sixty-four.

'We're going to have to turn right off the wind to clear the point afterwards!' says Captain de Trémigon. 'There won't be much room. We'll have to brace the yards round and go astern…'

I think that he is regretting not having foreseen his commanding officer's manoeuvre, instead of giving the order to prepare the lower gundeck. But who would have thought we would be throwing ourselves at the English when outnumbered three to one, without waiting for *le Vengeur* and *le Sphinx*?

The Admiral passes at a cable's length ahead of the 50-gun ship's bowsprit and gives her a complete broadside from his port battery. The explosion is much louder than the previous one. The prow of the English ship disappears in a thick cloud borne by the wind, and almost immediately *le Héros* releases a broadside from her starboard battery at the stern of the sixty-four. The smoke spat out by her windward battery hides her from us for a few moments. When it clears, rather than seeing the head of our line bearing off to port, as we expected, we can see her starboard side, on which we are bearing down at great speed. She has suddenly luffed up to starboard, her bow pointing into the bay, and putting herself right across our course. Her momentum carries her forward into the wind, allowing her to let go her anchor, which was still at the cathead, before falling back, head to wind.

'Helm down! Starboard all!' screams Captain de Trémigon as loud as he can.

L'Annibal narrowly misses *le Héros,* pivoting to starboard, level with the stern of the English sixty-four, which we hadn't even had the time to fire at as we went past.

'Helm amidships! Prepare to anchor!'

Having shouted his order to the helmsman behind him, Captain de Trémigon leaps off his bench towards the Chief Petty Officer to grab his loudhailer and direct the manoeuvre.

'Furl the inner jib!'

The ship is head to wind, with all her canvas taken aback.

'Clew up the topsails!'

L'Annibal is still has way on and is running alongside the English sixty-four. We are so close that I think that the yards will tangle. I see sailors in shirts or bare-chested and red-coated riflemen gathered on the fore and after decks, just a few metres from us, their rifles pointing at us. They watch us pass, open-mouthed, without thinking of firing, as if dumbfounded. Friends and enemies hold their breath, waiting for the inevitable crash. In an overwhelming silence, our great ship heads towards the stern of the 50-gun ship anchored off the sixty-four's port bow. I can even read her name: *Jupiter.* It vaguely reminds me of something, but I don't have the time to think about it.

'Helm up! Helm to starboard! Ready the anchor!'

L'Annibal, still with way on, just misses the port side of *Jupiter* and stops beside her, slotting herself in ahead of *le Héros.* It was only Captain de Trémigon's skill that has allowed to avoid two collisions. He has gauged the speed and inertia of his great ship and given the necessary orders at the right time, neither too soon nor too late.

'Let go the anchor! Square off the mizzen topsail! Mizzen amidships! Helm to windward!'

We start dropping astern, heading straight for the bow of *le Héros,* who has to let out more cable in a hurry to stop our stern gallery from impaling itself on her bowsprit as we fall back on our anchor.

'Brail up the mizzen!'

Captain de Trémigon's last order rings out in the surreal silence. I look around me in disbelief. We have thrown ourselves right into the fish trap I spotted just a few minutes ago, right in the middle of the English fleet, with the enemy on both sides and ahead of us. The worst possible position imaginable as regards naval tactics!

The calm is brutally broken by *le Héros'* guns, which start firing at will from both sides simultaneously. Our upper gundeck soon follows suit. On the quarterdeck I organise things so that we too can fire from both sides at the same time. The principle is simple and outlined in the Regulations: two men to each gun look after the loading and firing, ten to port, ten to starboard, while the others cross the deck from side to side to run out the guns. Certainly it takes time, which is reflected in the firing sequence. My second Master Gunner oversees the port side while I look after the starboard. In the din I can hardly hear the sound of the English rifle fire, answered by the infantrymen of the Austrasie and Royal Roussillon regiments. Musket balls hit everywhere, carving out grooves in the ship's sides and the decks, sending shards of wood flying. They hit men too, in the arm, the leg, the head, the chest. Some are pierced right through. The fire is especially deadly at the beginning, as we are so close. The fore and after decks are soon strewn with bodies of the wounded and dying, that we try to evacuate towards the hatches. My gunners start to fall too and I soon have to aim some of the guns myself and help the crews. Everybody has to lend a hand. This helps me forget my fear. The Chevalier d'Aché, who can no longer read *le Héros'* signals, lost as she is in the smoke behind us, also helps us out. We haul on a gun tackle, shoulder to shoulder. Luckily our main gun battery finally opens fire at a remarkable rate. This soon creates thick smoke which darkens the sky and greatly reduces the efficiency of the English riflemen, who can no longer see their targets. They continue firing blindly, but the musket balls come in at an angle or from ricochets and are less deadly.

The Chevalier d'Aché staggers beside me. I hold him up. He says he has been hit in the forearm. I look at his sleeve and find two holes on opposite sides, a smaller one and a bigger one. They are just below his elbow, and suggest that the ball has gone right through. He says it's nothing and that he can stay at his post. It is true that it is not bleeding much. I help him to make a temporary bandage by tying our handkerchiefs together.

The English now start firing their cannons. We bear the full brunt of 24-pound and 18-pound cannonballs from the 64-gun English ship to starboard, and of 18-pound and 12-pound cannonballs from the *Indiaman* to port, which is firing at almost point-blank range. Orange flashes then appear through smoke from where *Jupiter* was positioned. Up until now she has been silent, as her stern was facing us. Her Captain has now managed to pull her round by means of a spring to her anchor cable, bringing her beam on to us. She can now bring all her guns to bear. The men on our foredeck have the best view!

Captain de Trémigon goes up onto the poop deck several times to see what the Admiral is doing. He is not even angry at our commander for having dragged us into this fatal trap. We are not going to be able to stay like this for much longer. Sooner or later we will have to get out of here, but our only route out is blocked by *le Héros.* We will have to wait until she withdraws before slipping our cable. For the moment all the Captain can do is to try to prepare for what follows and bolster us with his calm and self-assurance. From time to time he leans over the port and starboard rails and shouts to us. He tells me he is wondering what happened to our other ships. *L'Artésien* has passed to leeward of the English 50-gun ship, fortunately, otherwise she would have collided with us. As for *le Sphinx* and *le Vengeur*, the thick smoke makes it impossible to know where they are.

The Captain comes down again to the watch officer's bench. At that moment I am buffeted brutally by a gust of air and a whistling sound that deafens my ears. I turn round and see the Captain lying full length on his back. The cannonball that just missed me has taken off his left leg at the thigh. His leg is no longer connected to his body. I am surprised to see that no blood is coming out of the murderous purplish wound at the end of the remaining stump. Then I see in the middle of it a tiny red tube, several inches long, pointed and pulsing. It's the end of his femoral artery, cut off and cauterised by the cannonball that was still burning hot at such a short range. This delicate little sealed tube is pushed out horizontally by the blood pumped there by his heart. Captain de Trémigon is still conscious, his eyes wide open. He is making no sound but seems to be in a deep stupor. I dare not move him and send a boy to fetch the surgeon. Monsieur Boucher himself comes running as soon as he hears that the Captain has been hit. He immediately ties off the end of the artery, to make sure it does not burst and drain the Captain's blood, then has him taken down the main companionway. I pick up the leg and throw it overboard.

Lieutenant de Galles, having been informed, comes running from the foredeck to take command. The din of the battle has become unbearable and I think I am going deaf. The smoke is limiting the efficiency of the fire from the English soldiers, but the cannonballs and grapeshot are much more deadly than the musket balls. The ship's rail flies into little pieces when struck. One of my guns is hit fair and square by a 24-pound cannonball which destroys its carriage and lays out two of my gun crew at the same time. They are no longer moving and are dragged by their feet to the ship's waist. Our rig has been torn apart everywhere and suddenly, with a crack that can scarcely be heard over the general racket, our mizzen mast collapses. Its stays are so cut up that it falls overboard by itself, pushed along by the wind filling the brailed up mizzen topsail. Five men go up to the poop deck to cut away the remaining ropes that are still holding it.

The smoke is so thick that the light of the midday sun has gone. It is impossible to identify the different detonations amongst the continuous and stupefying roar of explosions. Only the unceasing flashes of the shots makes it possible to know that the firing is not easing. We are in the tropics and the hellish heat is unbearable.

A helmsman who has stayed at his usual post in the wheelhouse comes in a panic to tell us that there is a fire in the Great cabin. I immediately think of the chest of diamonds in the Captain's wardrobe and start heading off to see what is happening, but Lieutenant de Galles stops me and shouts at me to stay at my post. He will go himself. He comes back almost immediately to take two of the buckets filled with seawater that are kept beside each gun to cool the barrels when they get too hot from firing. I realise that I am not yet deaf!

'It was nothing,' he shouts to me when he comes back. 'A hot ball had come through a window and fallen on a chest of cartridges and set fire to their wrapping. I put it out with your buckets.'

Some of the crew's rifles are usually stored on two racks in the passageway which leads to the Great cabin. When the ship is cleared for combat, cases of cartridges are put there so that sailors assigned to take a rifle can make use of them. 'It was nothing,' for sure, but the whole thing could have blown up in his face when he leaned over them to empty his buckets of water.

It is hardly half an hour since the battle started but we already have more than a hundred dead and wounded. The deck that the men had been happily washing with seawater in the cool of the morning is now scattered with pieces of broken timber, severed ropes tangled up with their blocks, and bodies that have not yet been carried off. We are wading about in blood and human remains. A cannonball hits the main companionway hatch which is carried off with a crash. The stairs up to the poop deck are still in place, but the watch officer's bench is gone and the flag locker has been gutted, its flags scattered around the deck. The Chevalier d'Aché, who has narrowly avoided being killed by this last shot, gets down on his knees to gather them up, helped by the Master Pilot and some of his assistants. When I look forward through the smoke to assess the situation I see that the mainmast is wobbling and leaning towards the stern. I warn everyone and we just have time to run for shelter in the wheelhouse. Everything lets go at the same time: topsail, t'gallantsail, yards. The whole lot falls onto the poop deck bulkhead, which holds up against the shock. When we come out I have to use an axe to clear my guns to be able to aim them. Lieutenant de Galles climbs up to the poop deck to see what is left of the mast and hurries down again. The topgallant mast has parted from the topmast and fallen in the sea to starboard, taking our flagstaff with it. We are no longer flying a flag. It has to be replaced otherwise the English will think we are surrendering. The Chevalier d'Aché shows him what spare flags we have. They were found trapped under a spar which had fallen on deck and have been put together with the other flags. They are stained with blood and torn where the Pilot's helpers had tried to pull them out.

'We need a white flag!' roars Lieutenant de Galles.

I think of the immaculate white tablecloth on which Captain de Trémigon had been quietly breakfasting this morning, just as everything started. I ask the Master Pilot to cut me two lanyards and I go into the Great cabin, leaving those of my gunners still alive to free up our remaining guns under the direction of the Second Master Gunner Gravier. Let's hope it hasn't been burned! No! It is still there, still just as white. I fold it quickly and take it to Lieutenant de Galles.

'Come with me!' he shouts, climbing up the steps leading to the poop deck from the remains of the main companionway hatch.

I get the two lanyards I had asked for, borrow a rigging knife from one of my men and rejoin the second captain. The poop deck is covered with pieces of yard and part of the main topsail, but is deserted. All those who had to stay here at the start of the battle have been either killed or wounded. Because of the musket fire they have had to be dragged along the deck rather than carried, leaving bloody tracks. Amidst this shambles I see white shapes moving behind the bars of the two chicken coops. Someone has forgotten to move the poor birds when clearing for battle.

The English riflemen quickly get us in their sights and despite myself I flinch each time I feel, rather than hear in the noise of battle, the unpleasant sound of musket balls hitting the timber around me. Luckily there is yet more smoke and the shots are not very accurate. With the knife I cut two holes in the shorter side of the tablecloth and slip the two lanyards through them, so that we can fix it to the trunk of the mizzen mast.

'Climb up and attach it higher up,' shouts the second captain. 'I can't use my left arm anymore.'

I see that his left sleeve is torn and drenched in blood. I pull myself up what is left of the mizzen mast and fix the lanyards. I have time to remember not to pull on the flag as I slide down before feeling a violent blow in the back and a terrible pain in the middle of my chest. I let go and fall at the feet of Lieutenant de Galles. I try to get up straight away but cannot manage it. The second captain grabs me with his uninjured arm and drags me to the stairway. I am in pain but it is bearable. I don't know whether it's because I have been hit by a musket ball or whether I have broken a rib when I fell. I feel stunned but I am still conscious. I feel myself being carried, then plunged into the suffocating heat of the gundecks in full action, then taken down further into the depths of the ship. The din of the fierce battle up there is partly masked by deafening rolls of thunder. I realise that this infernal sound comes from the wheels of the gun carriages of the 36-pounders recoiling at each shot along the planks of the lower gundeck, just above our heads.

They take off my coat and waistcoat and slide me onto the bloody planking of the *theatre*. Someone cuts open my shirt to get it off more easily. It is soaked in blood. I recognise surgeon's mate Roblet's voice saying that I am not dead and clearly hear the reply of the Surgeon-Major.

'It's unbelievable that his heart is still beating, but with this wound he is done for. I know he's your friend and I'm sorry to say it but we can't waste time on him. In any case, the ball has passed right through. There's nothing more to do. Take him away!'

Arms grab me again to take me off the planking and I hear the surgeon-major's voice again.

'Stay with me, Monsieur Roblet. I need you!'

'If you like I'll put on a dressing and a bandage,' says another voice that I can't identify but which I seem to know.

My friend Roblet thanks whoever it was who just spoke. Surgeon-major Boucher says again that it is a waste of time. I don't hear the rest as I am losing consciousness. I am laid down on the orlop planking. Someone roughly rips off the key I have around my neck. I am not in too much pain; in the long run it is easy to bear a serious wound. I drift off from the sound of battle, with just the time to think that today not everybody will be as lucky as me.

7

On board l'Annibal, Tuesday 17th April 1781.

I don't know how long I have been lying, unconscious, on the deck of the orlop where I have been abandoned. I felt a little better when I was moved again onto a softer and more comfortable surface. It was night-time, peaceful, and I fell asleep again.

I am woken by the sound of rifle fire, followed by cannon shots. I wonder whether the battle has started again, but I can recognise the sound of 8-pounders firing on the foredeck, one at a time at regular intervals. I am no longer in the orlop but on the lower gundeck, where the cannons have once more been lashed in place. I am lying on a cot in the infirmary, which has been set up again on the lower deck, although without the canvas partitions that usually enclose it. A bandage goes right round my torso. I feel as if I am wounded in the chest, somewhere near my heart, as that's where my torn flesh hurts when my ribs expand as I breathe. All the same, it is bearable; my wound must not be too serious. My bed is fixed along the axis of the keel, with my feet facing forward, and I can see in front of me the two sets of ladders leading to the deck above. Sunlight is coming from my left, straight through the open gun ports. It must be the middle of the morning.

The cannons are firing once a minute. I count nine shots before they stop.

I look around me. It seems there are not enough cots to accommodate all those injured in the battle. Many are lying on temporary mattresses on the deck. They are everywhere and I can't see them all. It's as if the whole gundeck has become a hospital, which is no doubt why they have not put up the canvas partitions. A loblolly man comes into my field of view and I speak to him.

'Why are they firing cannons?'

He jumps and almost drops the bowl he is carrying.

'You are still alive?'

'Of course I am still alive! Why would I have been brought here otherwise?'

'It's Monsieur Roblet as insisted, Sir, but pardon me, Sir, they was all sayin' as you was pretty much dead, an' it were a waste of time an' you was taking up a place. If you don't mind me sayin'! I'll go an' find 'im. An' Monsieur Boucher too!'

'You haven't answered my question!' I say.

But the man has already turned his back and is heading for the ladder leading to the upper gundeck. I can see to my right that the surgeons' usual place is empty. Apart from the invalids and the make-shift nurse who has just left me there is nobody on the lower gundeck. I hear the odd groan or quiet complaint from the wounded, but the ship is quite silent. It is unusual; even the rigging has stopped singing. There is nothing but the sound of water running along the hull. This quiet continues for about twenty minutes, before I start to notice a general noise returning, as if the ship has come to life again, and I see men coming down the ladders.

Monsieur Boucher and my friend Roblet immediately come towards me and stand by my cot. I ask what is going on.

'Talking doesn't tire you?' asks the Surgeon, rather than answering my question.

I reply that I can talk normally.

'Why were they firing cannons?' I add.

'Can you breathe easily? Yes, he is breathing without effort! It's incredible! Can you sit up? Help him, Monsieur Roblet, I beg you.'

My friend helps me to sit up.

'We were giving the final honours to Captain de Trémigon. He died last night.'

This saddens me but is not a surprise.

'Have we lost a lot of men?' I ask.

'He's bled a lot, do you see? His bandage is soaked in blood. But it looks like the flow has stopped itself at the right time – a good sign!' continues Monsieur Boucher. 'Take his dressings off, Monsieur Roblet.'

'Seventy killed and a hundred and thirty wounded,' says my friend while rolling up the bandages wrapped round my torso. Monsieur de Thiolaye was killed, and the second captain of the Austrasie company. If you survive this, you'll have your place back in the wardroom.'

Roblet lifts off the final dressings. Putting my chin right down I can see that I have a huge gaping and swollen wound on the upper left side of my chest, level with my heart.

'That's where the ball came out. Not a pretty sight, is it?' says Monsieur Boucher. 'There is still some suppuration, but no haemorrhaging. That's encouraging! Could you lean forward, Monsieur La Fôret?'

The two surgeons examine my back.

'Look!' continues the Surgeon, addressing my friend Roblet. 'That's where the ball entered. The hole is smaller and very clean. The entry hole corresponds precisely to the infraspinous cavity of the scapular bone. Logically, the chest ought to have been crossed from one side to the other. The heart and lungs should have been totally destroyed, but that's not the case. It's probably because the ball hit obliquely, crossing only the integuments covering the deltoid muscle and, continuing its trajectory at this angle, it must have pierced the teres major muscle before hitting the chest wall. Having met resistance from the ribcage, it changed direction, which is why it came out below the left breast, at the spot where the pectoralis major covers the cartilage of the sternal ribs, making this nasty hole on the way. There's no other explanation. Oh! It really is an interesting case! I have heard of similar cases, but this is the first time I have had a real one!'

It wouldn't take much for him to kiss me.

'Well, then! Monsieur Roblet, you will dress these wounds with lint soaked in alcohol and you will change them for me twice a day, morning and evening. And be sure to call me each time! I don't want to miss this! And you must keep a close eye on them to make sure they don't get infected. I hope the ball has not introduced bits of cloth. They will be difficult to get out and it would be a pity to lose our patient after such a good result.'

'I'm hungry,' I say.

'But of course, Monsieur La Forêt! We are going to spoil you. To start with, have someone bring him some chicken soup with a little wine from my personal store.'

'What time is it? How long have I been unconscious?' I ask.

'You were brought to the *theatre* towards midday, just before the end of the battle. It's now ten in the morning. We kept the ship cleared for action all night. It was only this morning after dawn that we were able to bring the wounded back up here.'

'I had a key round my neck. I'd like to have it back.'

'That's right. I remember it,' says Monsieur Boucher. 'It was probably taken off by the man who bandaged you. You just need to ask him. He made a good job of it too. Was it you, Roblet?'

'No, Sir. If you remember you asked me to stay with you. It was one of our passengers who was helping us. The Chevalier Tallebau de Saint-Luperce.'

Have I heard properly? This alarms me.

'Tallebau de Saint-Luperce?' I say. 'What was he doing here?'

'The Chevalier de Saint-Luperce,' replies Monsieur Boucher, 'came to offer to help us at the start of the battle, saying he has some knowledge of surgery acquired in India. I can tell you that I was doubtful at first, but he surprised me with his ability. We were very happy to have him, as even with my five assistants we were run off our feet.'

Of course! Saint-Luperce arrived in India as surgeon's mate to Doctor Rollin of the Lorraine infantry. He was well trained.

*

The second Master Gunner Gravier came to visit me as soon as he knew I was still alive. Apart from Roblet he was the only one to show some friendliness towards me at this time. He told me that half our gun crews had been killed and related how the terrible battle ended, something which Roblet would not have been able to do.

Not long after I had been taken down to the orlop, Lieutenant de Galles had seen *le Héros* slip her cable at last, falling off to starboard. He ordered the same manoeuvre for *l'Annibal*, but just at that moment our sole remaining mast, the foremast, went by the board. Despite that, the wind and current were strong enough to push our sad wreck towards the exit of the anchorage where *le Sphinx*, who was sailing back and

166

forth between the two headlands of the bay, skilfully took us in tow. The English had then put to sea to pursue us, forcing us to form a line beam on to the wind, south of Cape Verde, to enable us to confront them while our convoy, escorted by *la Fortune,* escaped seawards. Luckily for us, Johnstone decided not to attack us during the night and at dawn, to our great relief, we found ourselves alone on the ocean. We stood down from action stations, but we had no news of the convoy. *L'Annibal* was still being towed by *le Sphinx* while our shipwrights got busy constructing a jury rig. They were helped by their opposite numbers from *le Héros,* sent over by the Admiral, along with caulkers and other tradesmen.

I would have liked to have got my key back immediately from Saint-Luperce, but he was no longer on board. At his request he had been allowed by the Chevalier de Suffren to transfer to *le Héros.* I thought that he had stolen the key around my neck thinking that it was for my personal chest. Moreover, if he had actually known that it was for the chest in Captain de Trémigon's wardrobe, which to me seemed unlikely, he would never have been able to use it. To do that he would have had to enter the Captain's cabin, which can only be accessed by passing through the wheelhouse, where a rifleman from the garrison was permanently posted. In any event, I was still convinced that Saint-Luperce knew nothing about the diamonds. Both my uncle and Monsieur de Fleurieu had on several occasions asserted this and I had no reason not to believe them. For sure, Roblet had told me that Saint-Luperce had mentioned a steel chest, which was concerning, but he could well have heard talk about it from the officers who were there when I arrived on board *l'Annibal* at Brest.

I of course did not think that Saint-Luperce had launched his conspiracy against me purely by chance. I had only crossed paths with him once at the Ministry but, thanks to the Comte de Guypair, he knew who I was and he had reason to believe that I had links with the King's secret service. He had certainly made the connection between my presence on board *l'Annibal* and the mission that had been considered for my uncle relating to Hyder Ali Khan. I concluded that he had just intended to search my personal chest, which was accessible to all in the corner of the gun room. When Saint-Luperce had stolen my key, I was not conscious enough to recognise him, but I clearly remembered the brutality of the gesture. He had ripped it off forcefully, without the least consideration, doubtless because he thought, as did everybody, that I would not survive my wound and that I would not be able to complain later. For the same reason, he would not have been careful when searching my chest, which would easily be obvious to me. I was keen to be on my feet again to be able to check my things. What did he hope to find there? According to the Marquis de Castries, the letter given to him outlining his mission said simply that he had been sent by the Comte de Vergennes to advise the Comte d'Orves and the Vicomte de Souillac on Indian matters, with no further details. The Minister for the Navy had confirmed to me that Saint-Luperce did not yet know that an agreement had been reached between his department and that of the Comte de Vergennes to seek an alliance with the Marathas rather than Hyder Ali Khan. This change of policy was outlined in the sealed letter I had to deliver to the Vicomte de Souillac and the Comte d'Orves. Now that Captain de Trémigon was dead, I was the only person at sea within the Chevalier de Suffren's division who knew the contents of this letter. As long as he had not received any other intelligence regarding our mission to India, Saint-Luperce must still believe, like everybody, that we would be dealing with Hyder Ali Khan. Although he had not mentioned it, I knew that he had good reason to be very concerned about this, given the serious dispute between him and the Nabob. Maybe he hoped that I would have in my baggage a letter of introduction or some sort of private message from the Marquis de Castries to the Governor of the Mascarenes, which would have given him more idea of what was expected of him. If that were the case, he won't have found what he was looking for, as all the important documents were in the steel chest in the Captain's wardrobe. There was a good chance, unfortunately, that he had laid hands on the purse containing the fifty gold louis that the Minister had given me along with my safe-conduct from the King. I could always complain, but I had no proof that this money was mine.

I had thought that I would very soon be able to get up, but I was taken by a fever that lasted several days before the pus which was infecting my wound began to drain off, giving me some relief. I was feeling much better but was still very tired, when Monsieur Boucher came to tell me that I had been summoned to the Great cabin. He had protested but had been overridden.

*

My legs are still buckling beneath me, and Roblet has insisted on helping me as far as the Great cabin. We go along the lower gundeck towards the main companionway at the aft end, by the entrance to the gun room. This companionway is reserved for officers, and has a welcome banister that I can hold on to. The healthy sailors have been allowed to sleep at night on the fore deck and poop deck, as a large part of the main gundeck has been transformed into a hospital. There are wounded everywhere, lying on cots or makeshift mattresses between the guns. Some never stop groaning, others die in silence. They stretch from aft of the main mast as far as the main capstan. Despite the daily fumigations and the washing of the decks with seawater, the air under the deckhead is rank with the smells from the soiled bandages, vomit, excrement and all the odours that go with suffering and death. The crew of *l'Annibal* has paid a high price for this questionable battle. Monsieur Boucher is angry with the Chevalier de Suffren, on account of the accusations he has made against Captain de Trémigon, which have been reported to us. The Admiral has compared the number of killed and wounded on *le Héros* – ninety men out of action, including twenty-three killed – which is already a lot, with the much heavier losses aboard *l'Annibal.* He has roundly accused Captain de Trémigon of being responsible for these losses, by dint of not having obeyed his orders. But what orders? 'It is annoying that the total dismasting of this vessel and such heavy losses are due to Captain de Trémigon only partially clearing for battle.' These are the exact words of the Chevalier de Suffren. Our losses were greater because we were in the front line, more exposed, ahead of the Admiral, in the very depths of the trap into which he had thrown us totally unexpectedly and without warning. Moreover, I consider that his criticisms are in poor taste, given that Captain de Trémigon is no longer here to defend himself.

I catch sight of the sea through the gunports, which are still open. It is deep blue again. The wind is light and the sky clear; the heat has returned. Yesterday the sky was overcast all day. After rain in the morning, we had violent storms and towards five in the afternoon even saw an eclipse of the sun. For a while that cooled the air but is now no more than a memory.

I go up the steps on my own, pass the upper gundeck and come out onto the quarterdeck in full sunlight, under the burning rays of the sun.

It is the first time I have been outside since that awful 16th April. The main companionway hatch has already been completely repaired and repainted. The flags are once more carefully arranged in their lockers, but we only have one mast on which to hoist signals, and that is only a spare mizzen topmast erected in place of the mainmast. The Chevalier de Suffren has sent over a yard that the topmen are now rigging. That will allow us to sail unaided, but for the moment we are still under tow. Today it is *le Héros* at the other end of the cable, but we are no longer making progress: the wind is dropping away completely. The five ships of the Chevalier de Suffren's little division are becalmed on the wide ocean under a molten sky, at 5 degrees North, the limit of the northeast Tradewinds. We are entering the area of variable winds, with no idea what has happened to *la Fortune* and her convoy, or whether the English have overtaken us in the race to the Cape.

Lieutenant de Boissauveur is officer of the watch. He sends his assistant to announce us and we pass through the wheelhouse, between the two rows of muskets stored vertically in their racks on either side of the passageway. I am sweating under my bandages in my braided coat, having thought it a good idea to put on my dress uniform for this summons. Roblet went to fetch it for me.

Lieutenant de Galles is waiting for us, standing in the middle of the Great cabin. He points to the boxes beneath the after windows by the gallery, so that I can sit down.

'You may leave us, Surgeon's Mate, if you please.'

Lieutenant de Galles paces up and down, his hands behind his back. He is wearing his working uniform in light linen. I suppose that he too has a bandage underneath, but he does not seem too troubled by his shoulder injury.

'Monsieur Laforest-Dombourg, believe me that I would have preferred to come to you, but I wanted to interview you without witnesses. How is your wound?'

'Thank you very much, Sir. I'm a lot better. I believe I will soon be able to resume my work.'

Hearing that the Ship's Lieutenant sighs deeply and sits on one of the chairs set around the late Captain de Trémigon's rosewood table.

'When I pulled you from the poop deck, I truly believed your wound was fatal. The Chevalier de Suffren thought you were dead, too. It was only yesterday he learned you were still alive.'

'That is very kind of him to be concerned for a simple Ensign.'

'It's not what you think! He called me aboard *le Héros* to tell me to have you put in irons while waiting to be court martialled when we get to the Cape. If we arrive there before the English.'

Has my wound made a philosopher of me? Is it the fact that I have heard several times that I was going to die? What I have just heard seems of such import and so incredible that I have no idea whether it should worry me or not.

'Is this a joke?'

Lieutenant de Galles does not look like a man about to laugh, but I feel no hostility towards me.

'I objected, on the basis of Monsieur de Choiseul's Regulation, which is still current, that no officer can be court martialled without an order from His Majesty. He replied that once we have rounded the Cape of Good Hope, he will have all the prerogatives of a Squadron Commander, and the Regulation I had just quoted, provides that in cases where speed is of the essence, he can still, as an Admiral, call together a court to question you and hear relevant witnesses for the case against you. He is only obliged to wait until he has made a subsequent report to the Minister of the Navy before carrying out the punishment he has decided.'

'But what exactly am I supposed to have done?'

The Ship's Lieutenant gets up and goes to stand by the door which opens on to the stern gallery, to give himself some air. The ship is so still one would think it is in port, and the heat is unbearable.

'I think it comes from this Saint-Luperce fellow. I don't know exactly what he has said against you, but he seems to be on very cosy terms with the Admiral, unlike our commanders…Luckily for you I am the only one to be approved of by the Chevalier de Suffren. He liked the business with the tablecloth! I used that to mention your part in it, and added that I needed you as an officer of the watch. He was kind enough to give you a reprieve until we reach the Cape. You are authorised to resume your duties provisionally, as long as you remain on board *l'Annibal,* for which I have given my guarantee.'

Lieutenant de Galles allows himself a smile.

'I don't see anywhere else you could go!'

'Do you have any idea what this Saint-Luperce has said against me, Sir?'

'The Chevalier de Suffren did not want to tell me, but I have made my own enquiries and I think it's related to the steel chest that you gave to Captain de Trémigon. Saint-Luperce went aboard *le Héros* the day after the battle. That same evening he came back with a chit from the Admiral giving him permission to remove the chest and take it to him. It seems that it contains a fortune in diamonds that Saint-Luperce was to take to Hyder Ali Khan, in order to strengthen our alliance with him. He will accuse you, you and Captain de Trémigon, of having misappropriated the treasure for your personal benefit.'

That was not expected, for sure! I am speechless! So Saint-Luperce did know about the existence of the diamonds. And he knew they were in my charge. But how is that possible?

'It's absurd!' I say eventually.

'Does this chest really contain diamonds?'

'The equivalent of twelve million pounds worth of diamonds.'

'Twelve million? That is a lot!'

'Yes! That's why I was ordered to talk about it only with Captain de Trémigon, and not even you. In principle, Saint-Luperce ought never to have known about the existence of this treasure. I don't know what has happened. In any event, his accusation won't stand up. It will collapse as soon as we reach Port-Louis. Do you remember the letter from the Minister for Monsieur d'Orves and Monsieur de Souillac, which Captain de Trémigon showed you in front of me? Its contents will absolve me completely.'

'You say this letter came from the Marquis de Castries? Saint-Luperce is making out that the chest was entrusted to him by the Comte de Vergennes. I know that the Chevalier de Suffren is on middling terms with the Marquis but gets on very well with the Comte. Saint-Luperce will play on that, you can be sure. The game's far from won, but I believe you and will support you. I won't allow this Saint-Luperce to sully the name of Captain de Trémigon.'

*

During the following weeks we had variable winds, often with flat calms, always with an overcast sky and storms accompanied by rain and squalls that pushed us in every direction. We held a rough course south-south-west across the Atlantic, tacking laboriously to make our southing.

Roblet changed my dressings twice a day. Monsieur Boucher himself examined my wound each time and expressed his satisfaction. The scar above my left breast oozed considerably at first, but then, according to the medical terms used by the Surgeon, 'the cellular and vascular buds developed and a discharge of good quality appeared at the surface'. It was by then 6th May and we crossed the Line in eighteen degrees of longitude. Men wounded in the Battle of Porto Praya continued to die daily and we could not escape the burials on that day, just as on any other. It would not be true to say that there was a joyous mood aboard, but sailors are too attached to their traditions for the Bonhomme Tropique not to appear at dawn at the main topsail to name all those crossing the Line for the first time. A barrel full of water was placed on the quarterdeck, with a plank across the top. All the 'ignorant' officers had to take their turn sitting on it. Those who paid up well just had water thrown at their head, while those who were less generous had the plank pulled from under them, dumping them in the water. It cost each of us an écu – about six pounds. The bath was nonetheless welcome, as Neptune had decided to let the sun shine that day and the heat was once again overwhelming.

I had taken up my duties once again. With Lieutenant de Kermadec now second captain, I became watch officer and moved back to the wardroom. I fetched my personal chest. Everything was in order inside; Saint-Luperce had not even tried to open it. My fifty gold louis were still safe inside their purse, along with the copy of the key to the steel chest, still wrapped the same way in a handkerchief. Nobody knew that I had it. Contrary to what I had thought, Saint-Luperce had known exactly what he was doing when he tore the other key from my neck. He must have thought that Captain de Trémigon had taken his copy of the key with him on his final voyage to the bottom of the sea, and that it was he, Saint-Luperce, who possessed the only key. How had he managed to find out that I was to escort this fortune in diamonds to India? I reviewed all the people who knew of the existence of the treasure and the role that I was going to play in this affair: my grandfather, my uncle, Monsieur de Fleurieu, Monsieur de Sartine, the Comte de Broglie and the Marquis de Castries. That was plenty of people but they were all sworn to secrecy and beyond suspicion. To that list I had to add, of course, the King and the Comte de Vergennes. Could it be that the latter had been so imprudent as to entrust this secret to such a dubious character as Saint-Luperce? I had trouble believing it but could see no other explanation.

I continued to present myself at the infirmary twice a day so that Monsieur Boucher could check on how well my wound was healing; a new skin was gradually covering the scar on my chest. The weather was still wet and squally, with a heavy swell from the south but not much wind. We continued to tack south-west as best we could and on 24th May we started to see lots of seabirds, especially frigate birds. I had already seen these at Martinique – a bird about the size of a wood pigeon with a white belly, completely black back and long tail feathers. The next morning, nineteen days after crossing the Line, we raised the island of Trindade on the starboard bow, and a little while later, the rocky islets of Martin Vaz to the south.

The island of Trindade is lost in the ocean about six hundred miles east of Brazil. It is only four miles long and scarcely a mile and a half wide – a little chain of bare mountain, uninhabited, rocky and dry, a series of ragged peaks and arêtes rising a thousand feet above the sea. As for the islets, they seem even more desolate, spikes of volcanic rock, giant basalt teeth seeming to leap straight out of the abysmal depths. We bore off between Trindade and the islets, not being able to pass to windward, leaving the latter close to port. This place is the realm of the seabirds, which we could see wheeling endlessly around the steep, dark cliffs, their piercing cries mingling with the ceaseless sound of the surf.

By the end of May I had healed completely. I could now use my left arm without any trouble and, as Monsieur Boucher was pleased to say, that proved that the ball had not hit 'any important nerve of the brachial plexus'.

We still mostly had days of variable winds with squalls and rain, but after the island of Trindade we started to head south-east. As officer of the watch, I had to think carefully when having to report our course in the ship's log, as we had crossed the Line and the sun's position in the sky had changed. The air gradually became cooler. It was not really cold, but I found it more comfortable to wear my jacket over my waistcoat. On 9th June, in 35 degrees of latitude south and 13 degrees of longitude west[18], we started heading due east on port tack, hard on the wind. For the first time I saw the big white seabirds with a wingspan of nine feet

---

18 From the Paris meridian.

or more. They are called 'Cape sheep', as their size makes one think of the quadrupeds. We fell into steady west and north-west winds, which allowed our five ships to make a formation of two columns, slicing through the long blue swell, its peaks whitened by breaking crests.

Under clearer skies and in a bigger and bigger sea our speed regularly increased, with the result that *l'Annibal's* towline often parted, forcing the towing vessel to wear ship and come across, beam on to the swell, to pass us a new cable.

On 19th June, under an overcast sky and with an easing wind which in no way reduced the strong swell, we once more met large numbers of seabirds, in particular a kind that Lieutenant de Galles called 'Velvet sleeves'. He said that this showed we were close to the Cape of Good Hope and the Agulhas Bank.

For my part, I thought these birds were close cousins of the gannets I had often seen around the coast of Brittany. *Le Héros* immediately ordered *le Sphinx* and *le Vengeur* to reconnoitre ahead, but when they returned they has still not sighted land. We took soundings but did not find bottom. To be on the safe side, despite this, the Admiral had us heave-to on starboard tack to wait for daylight.

By dawn the wind had freshened from the west-north-west. *Le Héros* signalled for us to get under way once more, and almost immediately, the lookouts aloft reported that they could see land to the east-north-east. Later, as we approached the coast towards eight-thirty in the morning, our pilots were able to recognise Table Mountain and below, a little to its right, Lion's Tail. These two mountains overlooked Cape Town and Table Bay.

Table Mountain is higher, and the first thing one sees. Its summit really is as flat as a tabletop. The Lion's Tail is so called because it prolongs a rocky peak called the Lion's Head, and because the shape and colour of these two, taken together and when seen from the sea, resemble a giant lion, lying down and facing the Cape of Good Hope twenty miles further south.

At that time there were still flagpoles on the head and tail of the Lion, and the colour of the flags was based on a code determined every two years by the directors of the *Vereenigde Oost-Indische Compagnie*, the V.O.C., and which enabled ships arriving at the Cape from Europe to identify themselves. The Dutch had given us their code and we could see with our telescopes that the flags were definitely blue. However, when *le Héros* sent up the appropriate recognition signal, accompanied by three cannon shots, there was no reply, an absence of reaction that concerned us greatly.

Was the colony still in Dutch hands? Was it possible that the English had got there before us?

In any event, there was no question of us stopping in Table Bay, as the anchorage is dangerous from May to September, on account of the north-west winds, which can blow at storm force and from which there is no protection. We therefore headed east-south-east in order to round the Cape of Good Hope, which is situated at the end of the chain of mountains which extends south from Table Bay. The Chevalier de Suffren intended to anchor in Simon's Bay, which was on the west side of a huge bay which the English call False Bay.

Everyone's telescope was fixed on the coast. For many days we had been reduced to salted meat and dried vegetables, and every one of us was joyful at the idea of soon putting foot on land. For me it was a sad thought that I would be confined on board. Towards two in the afternoon, we rounded the Cape of Good Hope. *Le Héros* immediately raised the square flag, as from here on our commander was now due all the honours and prerogatives of a full Admiral. The crews shouted *Vive le roi!* several times and there was general rejoicing aboard, apart from me, of course. The Chevalier de Suffren now had the right to call a court martial and, in the worst case, have me put in irons or in prison somewhere, while awaiting written approval from the Minister.

Continuing on the same course in the west-north-west wind, we arrived within sight of the rock called Bellows Rock, about a mile off the Cape of Good Hope itself. We could see it from a good distance on account of the ceaseless breakers around it. There is another rock to the north-east of Bellows Rock, called the Anvil, but whose position was not firmly established in 1781, as it was not always uncovered. We knew only that it was about two miles to the east-north-east of Bellows Rock and that the *Colebrook*, an English Indiaman, had foundered on it three years earlier. For that reason we made a long detour east, with the sheets slightly eased, before daring to come back onto the wind and head up the east side of the Cape of Good Hope towards the anchorage at Simon's Bay. We had by then lost our leading wind and had to tack all evening to get into False Bay.

The cable with which *le Sphinx* was towing us parted again as night fell and the Admiral signalled to anchor where we were. Towards three in the morning, the wind went round to the north-north-east and freshened, with squalls and rain, forcing us to pay out a lot more cable to keep off the nearby coast to our west. Despite that, *le Sphinx* had to abandon her anchor and sail off to give herself some space, so that at dawn there were just four of us at anchor. At half-past nine the Admiral signalled to us to make sail and took *l'Annibal* under tow.

At six o'clock we entered Simon's Bay, still towed by *le Héros*, and anchored in ten fathoms on a sandy bottom, under a grey, rainy sky. The bay was almost empty, with only one ship that raised the Danish flag on seeing us arrive.

A boat put off from the shore, braving the gusty wind, and made straight for *le Héros*, now permanently flying the Admiral's pennant at her mizzen topmast.

*

Simon's Bay anchorage, Tuesday 31ˢᵗ July 1781.
Lieutenant de Galles has warned me that we have been summoned to see the Chevalier de Suffren at nine o'clock. I was expecting this, as an officer from *le Héros* came to get my logbook for Ship's Lieutenant de Moissac, who is in charge of the investigation concerning me. Lieutenant de Galles told me that he was surprised it was not Captain de Ruyter Werfusé who had been assigned to this task, adding that it was probably because the latter was now the Flag Captain, following the Chevalier de Suffren's elevation to full Admiral on rounding the Cape of Good Hope.

We go together in the Captain's gig, the same one I had shared with Captain de Trémigon at Brest. I have scarcely had time to shave my jaw and put on my braided uniform. I was going to take my sword but Lieutenant de Galles tells me to leave it behind. It is not yet a court martial, just a preliminary enquiry. Is that a good sign? In any case, I will soon know how the Admiral wants to deal with me.

Overnight, the wind has gone to the east and cleared away the clouds. It has now dropped almost completely and the sun is shining. For once the wide waters of False Bay are not streaked with whitecaps and boiling foam; the surface is as flat as a mirror.

We have now been anchored at Simon's Bay for forty days, and during this time we have had mainly north-west winds and a grey sky, rain and squalls which have forced us into difficult manoeuvrings, as our anchors break free when we yaw, despite the sandy holding. Otherwise, the climate is not unpleasant, about the same temperature as it is at home in September.

Simonstown is comprised of no more than a fort, the commander's and governor's houses, a market hall, a café, a few shacks, and a jetty for ships' boats. The place is overlooked from the west by a chain of steep mountains whose peaks reach to more than fourteen hundred feet, and which forms a protective barrier against the prevailing winds, but hides the evening sun. The main attraction of the place is that it provides a safe haven during the winter, but is less than thirty miles from Cape Town, from which everything necessary can be obtained. The latter is reached by an excellent road that passes to the east of Table Mountain, on the edge of the plain between False Bay and Table Bay. This is of no use to me, as I am confined on board permanently.

Do not think, however, that I have been doing nothing during all these weeks. We have been working night and day putting new masts in *l'Annibal.* One was taken from *les Trois Amis,* one of the ships of the convoy and the others were shaped by our ship's carpenters from timber that the Admiral had sent by sea from the Cape.

La Fortune and most of the ships of the convoy have rejoined us. We are only missing three, who we hoped have decided to carry on alone to the Île-de-France. The Comte de Conway, commander of the Pondicherry regiment, has managed to land almost all the troops destined to defend the Cape, and so the place is henceforth well defended against an eventual British attack.

Commodore Johnstone has also arrived, but too late. He has consoled himself by seizing five richly laden ships of the V.O.C., who at the wrong moment had taken shelter in a bay on the west coast north of Cape Town. This action was well worth his share of the prize! English warships have also been seen over the last few days behind the Île Robin[19], the northern limit of Table Bay, opposite Cape Town. The Admiral has twice held councils of war with the commanders of

---

19 The then French version of Robben Island, meaning Seal Island ('robben' being Dutch for 'seals').

his ships, to discuss whether it would be opportune to attack them or not. Perhaps he regrets his precipitousness at Porto Praya. If he had taken the time to give precise orders to his ships' Captains, rather than throwing himself at the anchored English without warning, we may have had a decisive victory, given that circumstances were in our favour. In the meantime, judging from the rumours that I have heard, he is perpetrating a disgraceful injustice against his subordinates, whom he is holding solely responsible for his defeat. He has even made it be known, loud and clear, that he will be writing to Versailles to demand sanctions. This is causing distress to all those concerned, or at least those who are still with us, Captain de Trémigon and Monsieur de Cardaillac having paid for their commander's impetuosity with their lives. Captain de Forbin, of *le Vengeur,* has in particular been singled out for criticism, despite being the Chevalier de Suffren's cousin. On the other hand, Lieutenant de Galles' credit is riding high, which is lucky for me.

When we arrive on *le Héros'* deck I can hear the clanking of pawls and the sound of voices from the foredeck. I can see men turning around the small capstan to sway up the fore topmast. A Bosun is shouting orders in Provençal.

A Ship's Lieutenant of about thirty years of age receives us on the quarterdeck. He is in a braided dress uniform but without a sword or high collar, and so is not the officer of the watch. He responds to my salute with a brief nod, but speaks to my commander in a friendly tone. He does not introduce himself. I presume that he now must be the first lieutenant, given the cascade of promotions that has hit the officers of this ship.

'You are punctual, Lieutenant de Galles, which is just as well as the Admiral has decided we will sail in an hour with the other three ships, to get supplies from the Cape. *L'Annibal* will stay here with the convoy until we sail for the Île-de-France. The Admiral will give you your orders as soon as we have finished with your Ensign. He is waiting in the Great cabin. Follow me, please.'

There are plenty of people in the narrow confines of the wheelhouse. I can hear that here too they are speaking Provençal. The conversation falls silent as we arrive, and they all seem to look at me with hostility. As far as I can tell, Saint-Luperce must have done all he can to prejudice them against me.

'Could you just excuse me for a moment,' says the Ship's Lieutenant politely, 'I have to get the file I have prepared for this business.'

He opens the door of one of the little officers' cabins giving onto the wheelhouse. While we wait, some supernumerary servants come out of the narrow passageway where the rifles are kept, carrying what looks like the leftovers from the Admiral's lunch. When we enter the Great cabin it is empty except for the jacket of a dress uniform adorned with the wide braided stripes of an Admiral thrown carelessly over one side of the box seat in the middle of the aft end of the cabin, beneath the stern windows. Through them we can see the Chevalier de Suffren smoking a cheroot on the stern gallery. The Ship's Lieutenant signals to us to wait, and we remain standing there in silence, in front of the big circular table in the middle of the cabin. On it is an inkwell, some quills and writing paper. The Admiral eventually throws what remains of his cheroot overboard and comes into the cabin. He is so huge that I wonder how he gets his paunch through the doorway. He has made the effort to put on a dress uniform to lend some weight to the occasion and has retained the scarlet braided waistcoat which he wears under his jacket but has relaxed a little by rolling up the sleeves of his shirt over his huge arms. Without a word he lets himself down onto the box seat.

'Good day, Galles. Come and sit here. I have just written a request for you to be promoted to Ship's Captain. Begin, Moissac.'

I have only met him once but I could never have forgotten his nasal voice and an accent so strong that one might say that he overdoes it purely to satisfy his need to provoke people.

Lieutenant de Moissac sits down at the table and places in front of himself a quarto volume in a brown binding and a cardboard folder labelled with my name. As for me, nobody has spoken to me, and so I remain standing, facing the *Lord God Almighty*.

'Admiral, gentlemen. I will begin by reading, if you so wish, articles 1245 and 1246 of the King's Naval Regulations of 25th March 1765,' says Lieutenant de Moissac, 'but I must start by stating that we will be touching on subjects which are State secrets, and that all those present are bound to respect this, including the accused.'

For the first time the Chevalier de Suffren raises his eyes to look at me. His eyelids are still half-closed, forcing him to push out his triple chin in an exaggerated way, which gives him an overbearing, disdainful look. His knitted brows rise suddenly in semi-circles behind his nose and he opens his mouth to speak but changes his mind. He does not take his eyes off me; something about me seems to intrigue him.

The Ship's Lieutenant opens his quarto book and finds the articles he wants in the three hundred pages of this famous *1765 Regulations for the Navy*, better known as *Choiseul's Regulations* and which, apart from some additions in 1776 and 1778, is still in force.

> *'Article 1245. A port commander or a commander of the fleet or a squadron can arrest any officer who has committed a grave dereliction and is required to inform the Secretary of State for the Navy as soon as possible, so that he may receive the King's instructions. Article 1246. No officer will be court-martialled without an order from the King. However, in cases where speed is of the essence, a port or fleet commander may hear witnesses to ascertain the truth of the facts, which he will then report to the Secretary of State for the Navy who will apprise him of the King's intentions.'*

Lieutenant de Moissac puts down *Choiseul's Regulations* and takes up the folder with my name on it and which, I can see, contains my personal logbook and several sheets of paper.

'We are met here to investigate the case of Monsieur Laforest-Dombourg, Ship's Ensign of the King aboard *l'Annibal*, following testimony made against him by the Chevalier Tallebau de Saint-Luperce, Agent Extraordinary of the Minister, sent by the Comte de Vergennes, Minister and Secretary of State for Foreign Affairs. The Chevalier de Saint-Luperce has stated that he was required by his Minister to present himself aboard *l'Annibal* at Brest to take charge of a chest containing diamonds of an estimated value of ten million pounds. This fortune had been raised from the Royal Treasury and was to be put in his charge to take to the Nabob Hyder Ali Khan, our Indian ally, in exchange for his support in the campaign we are about to launch in that country against the English. However, when he presented himself to the commander of *l'Annibal*, in order to take possession of the chest, as instructed by the Minister, with the approval of His Majesty, Captain de Trémigon made out that he had never received such a chest and refused to listen to the Chevalier de Saint-Luperce's protests. The Chevalier does not know exactly what scheming the Ship's Ensign has been party to, in a business way above his rank and his competence, but he believes he has discovered that *l'Annibal's* Captain and Ship's Ensign Laforest-Dombourg had been plotting together to divert the King's goods for their own profit. His proof is that he found the said chest amongst the personal belongings of the Captain, and that the Ensign was carrying, hidden in his clothes, a copy of the key to the chest. Does the accused recognise the case against him?'

I prepare to answer when the Chevalier de Suffren cuts me off with a calm voice, devoid of the hostility expected under such circumstances.

'I have seen you before! Where was it?'

'At Versailles, Sir. Six months ago, in Monsieur de Fleurieu's office. We had come from the Marquis de Castries, who had just entrusted me with ensuring that the chest of diamonds got to the Île-de-France.'

My reply does not seem to be what he was expecting.

'I do remember, but that's not what I was thinking of. I have seen you somewhere else.'

His voice has softened. He remains silent for a moment, then, without warning, shouts loudly, making us all jump.

'A mission like that! For a know-nothing Ensign! Jesus Christ! You think I'm going to swallow that! In any case, you're a bad liar! It's the Comte de Vergennes who was in charge of this business! The Navy Minister has nothing to do with it!'

'I beg you to excuse me, Sir, but you are wrong. It is the Marquis de Castries who was directing this operation because it had been started by Monsieur de Sartine. Monsieur de Vergennes was only involved later on. I would also add that, although at first it had been envisaged that the diamonds would be offered to Hyder Ali Khan, the Ministers and the King eventually decided to offer them to the emperor of the Marathas.'

The Admiral is certainly not used to being contradicted and his face starts to go the colour of his waistcoat. I suspect that this is not good for me, but what can I do? I'm not going to lie just to please him!

'Good God, Ensign! How dare you invent such nonsense! You will make your case worse!'

'It is the truth, Sir, with all respect to you. Moreover, since you have the chest, you will have seen that it contains a safe-conduct from the King in my name and a sealed letter from the Navy department addressed to Messieurs Souillac and d'Orves, as well as a letter of introduction from the Minister that I presented to the late Captain de Trémigon, which he unsealed in my presence to read. All these documents confirm that I am not making up anything.'

The Chevalier de Suffren turns to his Lieutenant.

'What's all this nonsense? A letter for that fool d'Orves? Have you seen such documents, Moissac?'

'Absolutely not, Sir.'

'Well I'll be damned!'

The Chevalier de Suffren taps his foot like a wild boar preparing to charge and shakes his jowls. I pull my head into my shoulders at these new signs of an impending storm.

'If you will allow me, Admiral,' then says Lieutenant de Galles, in his calmest voice, 'I certainly did see Ship's Ensign Laforest-Dombourg hand two letters to Captain de Trémigon. He showed me one which was indeed addressed to the Governor of the Île-de-France. I was present when he read the letter addressed to him.'

Ship's Lieutenant de Moissac carefully notes down everything said. The Chevalier de Suffren gets out a big handkerchief to mop his brow, calming down as quickly as he had got angry. His brows are still furrowed and he seems to be considering matters. In the silence one can hear the scrape of the quill on paper.

'This is anything but clear! Where is Saint-Luperce?'

'He is next door, Sir. I asked him to wait in his cabin under the poop.'

'Go and fetch him!'

While Lieutenant Moissac carries out his order, the Chevalier de Suffren examines me again.

'Laforest-Dombourg…hmm.'

The hostility has gone from his voice.

'I knew a Laforest-Dombourg at Louisbourg, in the old days, when I was first lieutenant aboard *le Dauphin Royal,* in La Motte's squadron. He was in command of a merchant frigate belonging to his father. I saw him again at La Rochelle. War had been declared and he wanted to sign up in the King's Navy as an auxiliary. We had a drink together ashore. He had no pretensions and could never be bought. A good seaman too. He beat us to La Rochelle and *le Dauphin Royal* was a fast ship!'

'That was my father, Sir. He died in the King's service in 1771.

The Chevalier de Suffren looks at me for a long time, saying nothing. He is almost smiling. He is no longer the same man.

'I think you resemble him, now that I look at you more closely. Sacré bleu! I was twenty-six! We don't get any younger!'

We are interrupted by the return of Lieutenant de Moissac, accompanied by Saint-Luperce. The latter has lost none of his swagger! He carries himself as well as when I met him at Versailles. He is half a head taller than all of us and still wears the same ironic little smile at the corner of his mouth. Lieutenant de Moissac reads aloud my statement and that of Lieutenant de Galles.

Saint-Luperce shrugs.

'Trémigon and Dombourg were accomplices, Admiral. They played their little scene, brandishing papers in front of Lieutenant de Galles. In reality there was never any letter from the Minister!'

'And what do you think of this statement as regards the Marathas? I can say that that would suit me, as the Malabar Coast is sheltered from the north-east monsoon and you can operate there for the whole year.'

'Admiral! I have known India for twenty-five years and can speak most of the languages of this vast country. Although I am more of a diplomat, I commanded Hyder Ali Khan's artillery, for which he was most grateful. I then spent nearly four years at the court of the Emperor of the Marathas at Poona. And what has this young Laforest-Dombourg ever done, may I ask? He knows nothing of India. I would add that he gained entry into the Marine Guards by means of false certificates of nobility, he schemed with the Comte d'Estaing to be promoted to Ensign, which did not stop his last commander from throwing him ignominiously off the frigate on which he had served since the beginning of the war. He is only good for duelling, and is known as a unworthy swordsman, having been imprisoned at least twice for that. So, Admiral, how much weight does the word of this young schemer carry against mine? Which of us is to be believed?'

I am totally taken aback by Saint-Luperce's dishonesty. At first I am speechless at such cunning, before feeling a mounting anger that I have trouble containing.

'Well, then, Ship's Ensign,' asks Admiral de Suffren in his nasal voice. 'What do you say to that?'

'It is pure slander! This man is a liar and a fraud!' I shout.

I have an urge to throw myself on Saint-Luperce, but I luckily manage to hold myself back and continue.

'I do not understand how Monsieur de Saint-Luperce can dare to lie with such self-assurance, when all you need to do is ask the Marquis de Castries and the Monsieur de Fleurieu about me. They will both confirm that I am telling the truth. As for the diamonds which I am supposed to have wanted to steal, they do not come from the Royal Treasury, but were hidden in the house of my maternal grandfather, the Baron de Kermean, who knew nothing of their existence. It is me who found them and who, in agreement with my grandfather, decided to give them to the King, when we could just as easily have kept them without anyone ever knowing. That, amongst others, is the reason why the King wanted to entrust me with this mission. I swear it, Sir! Ask the Minister! All I ask in the meantime is to continue serving the King and doing my duty.'

I have trouble stopping myself from shaking. My left hand searches for my sword, which luckily I had left on board *l'Annibal*.

'It is quite pathetic,' sneers my adversary. 'This poor lad is clearly just trying to buy time. Don't listen to him. I'm sure he'll desert at the first opportunity. If I were you, Admiral, I would leave him here and put him under a good escort on the first ship bound for Europe. Choose well those who will guard him. He even dared to challenge Colonel de Guypair, commander of the Neustrie regiment!'

Hearing that, the Chevalier de Suffren pushes out his lower lip between his jowls, with a doubtful expression, all the while examining me carefully under his half-closed eyelids.

Lieutenant de Galles once more intervenes.

'Admiral! When I asked Ship's Ensign Laforest-Dombourg to go with me, at the risk of his life, to rehoist the white flag at *l'Annibal's* stern, he did not hesitate for a second. Leave him to me, Sir. I will keep an eye on him and will take personal responsibility if ever he tries to desert the ship I command.'

'What do you think, Moissac?'

'Upon my word, Sir, this case seems more complicated than I thought. In any event, we cannot judge and condemn Ensign Dombourg without having asked the Minister about him, without forgetting too that there is the question of the late Captain de Trémigon's posthumous reputation. And consider too that the winds are north-west in October, which will slow down the next ship to leave for Europe. It will take at least a hundred and twenty days for a good frigate to bring Versailles' answer to the Île-de-France. By then we would certainly have left for Bengal, and at least another fifty days would be needed to catch us up from Port-Louis. In the best case, we would not have a reply from the Minister within six months.'

Saint-Luperce starts to speak again.

'Gentlemen, you do not need to wait six months. With Monsieur de Vergennes' agreement we have sent a secret agent to the Nabob. His mission is to escort the diamonds with a troop of cavalry from our point of disembarkation to the Nabob's camp, as the roads inside the country are not safe in wartime. He was sent off at the end of last year and must by now already be with Hyder Ali Khan. As soon as we have arrived he will contact us and confirm that I am telling the truth.'

'Why on earth do we need a wretched secret agent to escort our chest?' replies the Admiral, always ready to get annoyed. 'As if we haven't got enough soldiers and officers for that!'

'Of course, Admiral, but they won't have the necessary knowledge of the country and its peculiarities. And don't forget that this started as a secret mission. The man we have recruited is called Barrad Amzer.'

'I'll be damned! A foreigner too?'

'Not at all. Rest assured, I only know his *nom de guerre*. He's a former soldier with Lally-Tollendal's India campaign. We fought together when I was an honorary Volunteer in that contingent. I lost contact with him after the fall of Pondicherry in 1761, as I joined the Nabob's army while he offered his services to the Peshwa of the Marathas. I met him again at Poona when I myself was a King's Minister there. He came back to France with me and I presented him to the Comte de Vergennes. Barrad Amzer is greatly experienced in Indian warfare and speaks the local dialects. We gave him funds with which to recruit a small group of Maratha horsemen with which he would come to meet me, thus assuring discreet protection of our gift, until we can give it to the Nabob in the name of the King. He is a most trustworthy man!'

*

My interrogation finished following this last speech from Saint-Luperce. The Chevalier de Suffren gave us both permission to leave and kept back Lieutenants de Galles and de Moissac in order to discuss things with them and give them their orders for the following days. I came out of the Great cabin on the heels of the man I would from then on consider my worst enemy. I would have liked him to have turned round to look at me, as I would have laid down a legitimate challenge to him in front of all those present in the wheelhouse. This would no doubt not have helped matters for me, but I would have felt better. Luckily he was housed in one of the cabins under the poop deck, which he went straight into, closing the door behind him without looking at me. All that remained for me was to wait for Lieutenant de Galles outside on *le Héros'* deck. None of the officers or petty officers dared speak to me and moved out of my way, looking somewhat uncomfortable, it seemed to me. I had the impression of moving along inside an invisible bubble. This was no doubt the result of Saint-Luperce's scheming.

I leaned my elbows on the rail above the ship's ladder to watch *l'Annibal's* gig tied up twenty feet below me, in which our Breton sailors were also awaiting the return of their commander. The weather was changing, with the wind coming back to the north-west. The morning's fine spell had been short-lived and grey cloud foretelling rain and showers were gathering above the peaks overlooking the Simon's Bay anchorage. I thought it likely that the plans to sail to Table Bay would have to be put back.

The fresh air made me feel better and I was able to reflect more lucidly on the conversation which had just taken place. Although it was hard for me, I had to admit that Saint-Luperce's slanders in respect of my departure from *l'Astrée* and my bad reputation were not completely unfounded. They rested, alas, on the rumours circulated by the Marquis de Castries in order to hide the existence of the diamonds from his friend Necker, the Minister of Finance. Saint-Luperce probably knew that it was a fairy story invented out of necessity, but he would have found it easy to pretend to believe it. However, that was of secondary importance. How could he assert, with such self-assurance, that the Comte de Vergennes, and by extension the King himself, had ordered him to take personal charge of the diamonds? He knew perfectly well that this was false, especially as he had without doubt seen my safe-conduct signed by Louis XVI, and the letter for Monsieur de Souillac, even if he had then, in all probability, destroyed them. He must therefore know that his position would be fatally untenable once Versailles had replied to the Chevalier de Suffren on this point. Could he really believe himself protected by the Comte de Vergennes? Certainly, the reports of the agents who had spied on Saint-Luperce in Paris, which I had read in the folder left in Monsieur de Fleurieu's steel cabinet, seemed to suggest that Saint-Luperce was playing a double game on behalf of the Department of Foreign Affairs. I found this difficult to believe. Wasn't the Comte de Vergennes one of the King's most loyal servants? But there was something even more surprising! Everything I had learned about Saint-Luperce's past in India, from Admiral des Roches to Doctor Rollin's *Memoir of Hindustan*, indicated that he had got on the wrong side of Hyder Ali Khan, who would no doubt want to take revenge on Saint-Luperce if he ever turned up again. The Nabob was not known for his kindness! Why would Saint-Luperce want to throw himself into the jaws of the tiger when he probably already knew that the Ministers wanted to send him to the Marathas, with whom he was on excellent terms? Logic suggests he must have seized this unhoped for opportunity to enhance his value, what with all this talk of Poona and his successes with the Marathas. But this did not make sense! He must surely have read the letter from the Marquis de Castries to the Vicomte de Souillac, the only written proof on this side of the world that the King's government was shifting its policy in India towards the Marathas rather than the Nabob. Could he have destroyed it without reading it? And what about this Barrad Amzer? Where did he appear from? He must have been sent by the Department of Foreign Affairs rather than that of the Navy, but why had nobody said anything about it to me in Versailles?

Once back on board *l'Annibal*, Lieutenant de Galles told me that the Chevalier de Suffren had eventually agreed to his request. I would be allowed to continue to serve normally, but confined on board at all times, the responsibility of the Lieutenant, until the Admiral had received a positive response about me from Versailles. According to my commander, Lieutenant de Moissac considered me to be sincere, but that did not necessarily mean that Saint-Luperce was an impostor. There may be some misunderstanding between the Navy and Foreign Affairs Departments. Versailles was so far from the Cape. As for the Admiral, he was keeping to the facts: Saint-Luperce had arrived at Brest carrying an authentic letter signed by the Comte de Vergennes, while I was unable to provide the least proof to support my position. All the same, Lieutenant de Galles believed that he had spotted a degree of benevolence towards me on the part of the Chevalier de Suffren. He put this down to the fact that my father had started out in the Navy as an Auxiliary Officer before becoming an Officer of the King's Ships.

'Saint-Luperce,' said Lieutenant de Galles, 'was mistaken in thinking that his attacks would totally prejudice the Admiral against you. It has actually caused the opposite, as the Chevalier de Suffren, although he is a product of the Toulon Marine Guards, has always had a weakness for middle-ranking officers who have risen purely through their own merit, like your father. Also, he found it very amusing that you had the audacity, or the presumptuousness, to challenge to a duel an Army officer as well known as the Comte de Guypair.'

I escaped, therefore, an unpleasant imprisonment or a premature return to France. I was sure of being supported by the Monsieur de Fleurieu when it came down to it. I had confidence in him, but I would have to wait six months or even longer. Six months without going ashore! This campaign would perhaps be over by then and I would return home only knowing the Île-de-France and the Indies through my telescope from the deck of my ship.

The next night, when I was off watch, I had once again the nightmare in which I heard Flaharn's voice in the Jewish cemetery at Savannah. This had not happened since I had disembarked from *l'Astrée*, even though I had subsequently learned from my friend Vernon that Flaharn was not dead when I had seen him in his tent and that he was perhaps still alive somewhere, probably the Americas. I dreamed too of the pieces of flesh stuck to my soles when I had returned from the attack on the Springhill redoubt. All this was mixed up with images of the Battle of Porto Praya. From that night onwards I often had this kind of nightmare, always beginning with Flaharn. At first this was worrying to me, but I tried to think through what was happening. I spoke about it to Roblet, without mentioning Flaharn's name and without telling him exactly why these fantoms haunted me at night. My medical friend told me that these kinds of recurring nightmare were not uncommon. Other officers and men were sleeping badly since the Battle of Porto Praya. He had even talked about it at length with the ship's Chaplain. No! What he found more surprising was that it had not happened sooner. Maybe it was because of the very particular nature of my wound. He told me that he wanted to talk about 'the seeming miracle that had made such an impression on our Breton sailors'. He asked me if I had thought myself dead at that moment. 'Maybe,' I had replied. In fact, I didn't remember it very well. All I knew was that I thought I was going to die but it had not scared me in the least. That was maybe the reason for my 'immunity', Roblet eventually concluded, but the question that needed to be asked was why the nightmares had started again straight after appearing in front of the Chevalier de Suffren. Was I afraid of the Admiral, without realising it?

I had not been mistaken with my weather forecast. During the night of 31st July to 1st August the wind strengthened considerably from the north-west, with rain and squalls. It looked as if we were in for a real blow and so the Admiral postponed our departure for the Cape. *Le Héros, le Sphinx, le Vengeur* and *l'Artésien* waited until 3rd August before sailing. The wind had dropped so much that they had to have themselves towed by their ships' boats, then let go a light anchor to hold position against the turning tide. It took them two days to get out of False Bay and another six days under sail to get to Table Bay once they had weathered the Cape.

On 15th August a frigate arrived from Port-Louis with a letter from the Comte d'Orves for the Chevalier de Suffren. Lieutenant de Galles himself took it by road to the Cape, where our ships were loading provisions for the crossing to the Île-de-France, while at the same time preparing to ride out another blow from the north-west in the exposed waters of Table Bay.

We still had no news from France. We entrusted our mail to ships leaving for Europe, praying they would not be captured by the English. I wrote to Maria Kirwan and to my grandfather, telling them that I was fine, in case they were worried on hearing news of the bloody Battle of Porto Praya. I said nothing about the accusations against me. In any case, I had never said a word to Maria Kirwan about the diamonds entrusted to my parents by the late Marquis de Kersalaun.

On 25th August all *l'Annibal's* officers rose early and donned their dress uniforms to go to Cape Town for a dinner and ball organised by the Comte de Conway to celebrate the day of Saint Louis. I remained alone on board, regretful at missing this event and the Dutch ladies who would no doubt be adorning it. That would have put me in a better mood! All the same, my bitterness was softened by the confidence shown in me by my commander in leaving me in charge of his ship and by the kindness of the crew towards me. I had not noticed this until Roblet had spoken of it. I thought that the sailors aboard *l'Annibal* liked me because the longest-serving amongst them remembered that I was with them at the Battle of Grenada. Moreover, although I was not of Breton descent, I spoke their language a little, having been born at the mouth of the Scorff and Blavet rivers and having passed my youth at Vannes. What I had not noticed was that my rapid recovery had assumed a miraculous side to it, given that they thought I had been killed by a musket ball straight to the heart. They thought, quite simply, that I brought good luck. I began better to understand why, when I gave an order, it was always carried out with a promptness and good humour not accorded so easily to other officers on board.

On 3rd September 1781 *l'Annibal* left Simon's Bay with the five remaining transports and rejoined the other ships of the squadron at the Agulhas Bank. The latter is so called because the compass needle there shows some variation, not pointing exactly north[20]. Cape Agulhas is the southernmost point of Africa.

After several days the weather turned to rain, squalls and the occasional thunderstorm, which persisted for most of this long and unpleasant voyage. Our pilots followed Monsieur d'Après de Manneville's *Instructions sur la Navigation des Indes orientales et de la Chine*[21]. These recommend sailing east between the *observed* parallels 35 and 36 degrees until reaching an *estimated* longitude of 55 degrees. In principle this ought to have assured us of strong westerlies, but we had many instances of light and variable winds from the north-east and south-east. These meant we had to tack laboriously in a sea which retained its big westerly swell, the whole time in rain and sometimes hail, as the temperature had dropped noticeably. We had four topmen injured by lightning but no dead to report.

After 2nd October, having reached an estimated longitude of 55 degrees, we began to head up to the north-north-east. We then sailed north-east to 20 degrees of latitude, that of the Île-de-France, by which time we were in 61 degrees of longitude, estimated, which is that of the Île Rodrigues. The tropical heat had returned and all that remained was for us to head west along the 20th parallel. Some thought we might head north to pick up the Île Rodrigues, but we did not do that.

Drawn on a chart, this circuitous route may seem long and the curve out to the east a waste of time, in the eyes of those unversed in navigation,

---

20 Translators note: *Agulhas* (*Aiguille* in French) is Portuguese for a 'needle'.

21 Translator's note: *Instructions sur la navigation des Indes orientales et de la Chine*: 'Instructions for Navigating the East Indies and China'. The standard French navigational work of the time, referred to in the French Navy as *D'Après*.

but at least one is sure, by using this method, of minimising the effect of mistakes in the estimation of longitude, while being confident of arriving at one's destination.

We often had a fresh wind, which would have enabled us to sail, if not quickly, at least at a more convenient speed had we been able to spread all our canvas, but we were constantly having to put in reefs or clew up the topsails in order to stay with the transports, who were dragging along at less than three knots. Sometimes we even had to heave-to completely to wait for the fleet. These constant changes of speed, and the frequent rain, were tiring for our sailors, and after a month scurvy started to appear amongst the crews. On 7th October, *l'Artésien* and *le Vengeur* were authorised to leave the convoy and put on all sail to get to the Île-de-France. It had become a question of life and death for those who were most ill.

At dawn on our fiftieth day from Cape Agulhas, in a fresh easterly, *le Sphinx* and *le Héros* at last signalled land ahead. Climbing in the rigging I could see the Île-de-France with my telescope, forty-five miles away on our port bow, with mountains crowned in cloud at its centre and four smaller islands to its north. The weather had become overcast and rainy.

In the evening *le Héros* fired rocket signals to bring the fleet together and signalled to us to hold the wind on starboard tack to wait for morning.

The next morning the sun had returned, and we received the order to tack all together and bear off under all sail towards the islands which were now easily visible from the poop deck. To get to Port-Louis we had to pass through these islands in a channel laced with submerged rocks and breakers, before going around the island's north-west point, called Gunners Point, as there is a battery there.

At eleven in the morning our squadron and its convoy anchored in fifteen fathoms in front of two buoys marked with small flags which mark the entrance to the port. These are situated at the end of the Coopers Reef, a flat island on the port hand side of the entrance channel to Port-Louis. On the other side of it we could see the masts and rigging of numerous war ships and commercial craft inside the port.

L'Artésien and *le Vengeur* had already arrived, as well as two of our merchant ships that we had not heard from since the Battle of Porto Praya. During the afternoon our ships were towed into the channel, also marked on each side by flagged buoys. *L'Annibal* stayed outside with the transports.

We spent almost six weeks at Port-Louis on the Île-de-France. I am unable to describe either the town or the island, as I could only see them from the decks of the two ships to which I was assigned during this whole period. Port-Louis looked like a big town built on a small plain enclosed by high mountains covered in yellow grass and sparse bushes, and overlooked by the spiky, rocky crests of the peaks. The charm of the Île-de-France, where the Comte de Lapérouse, my former Captain, had met the lovely Mademoiselle Broudou, whom I had got to know at Brest, was to be found, as well as in its climate, in its delightful society. I could hear my fellow officers praising the balls and concerts – for it seems that everyone on the island is a musician – and the hunting and fishing parties, all in the best of company. They spoke also of the *Camp Malabar* where, it seemed, a good time could be had drinking coffee and punch, while talking with the friendly half-caste ladies, each one prettier than the other and each one easy of access. I consoled myself with the thought that the pleasures I could have tasted at this *camp* – on the Île-de-France they talk of *camps* rather than *quarters* – would certainly have been spoiled afterwards by the remorse I would feel when thinking of Maria Kirwan.

I said that I had been assigned to two ships. *L'Annibal* had, in her turn, been towed into the port as far as the Fanfaron Hole, a recently hollowed out basin named after the stream that flowed into it. The facilities here enabled us to replace the jury masts installed at Simon's Bay with a rig more fitting for a ship of the line. As I was confined on board, I had on more than one occasion stood in as officer of the watch for my luckier shipmates able to go ashore to taste the many delights of this idyllic port of call. They were grateful to me for this, but I could not stand in for them right to the end, as I soon had to leave *l'Annibal* for *la Pourvoyeuse*, a frigate permanently stationed at the Île-de-France. This was the indirect result of an argument which pitted the Chevalier de Suffren against the Comte d'Orves and the local Naval officers.

Having arrived at Port-Louis, the Chevalier de Suffren was still Admiral, by the special grace of the King, as he had rounded the Cape of Good Hope, but he was no longer the commanding officer. He was required to put himself under the orders of the Comte d'Orves, for whom he had little respect. We knew that the Chevalier had not hidden his bad mood at having to replace his brand-new flag with a blue and white pennant to distinguish his ship from *l'Orient,* the only ship now allowed to carry an Admiral's insignia. Moreover, he had waited three days before bending to this demand of protocol.

We also knew he had said privately – although everyone knows that everything is repeated amongst the officers of a squadron – that he hoped his superior, who was not well, would *slip his cable* before the end of the campaign, thereby ceding his place. The Admiral had even been heard saying that this 'happy circumstance' would allow us to achieve 'great things' in India.

I do not know whether the Comte d'Orves got wind of these words and if that had an influence on his actions, or whether his illness had already weakened his judgement, but the fact is that he decided that as Lieutenant de Galles had only been a Ship's Lieutenant for four years, he could not continue in command of *l'Annibal,* a sixty-four gun ship. For a long time he had been promising a command worthy of his rank to Ship's Captain Boudin de Tromelin, the Port-Louis commander, who had excelled himself in directing the works to create the Fanfaron Hole. This nomination sent the Chevalier de Suffren into a rage against Captain de Tromelin, especially as the latter had the temerity to belong to the Breton nobility.

For his part, Lieutenant de Galles kept quiet on the matter. I even think he perfectly understood the decision of the Comte d'Orves, with whom he had previously sailed, and was embarrassed to have become the subject of a controversy. Eventually my captain gave up the command of *l'Annibal* to move to *la Pourvoyeuse.* As he had promised the Chevalier de Suffren to keep an eye on me, I had to follow him.

La Pourvoyeuse was an 18-pounder frigate, build ten years earlier in L'Orient. She was a little bigger than *l'Astrée* and *l'Amazone* and like them had twenty-six gunports. But she was not as fast or as manoeuvrable as the 12-pounder frigates. Moreover, she was not copper-bottomed but had been studded with nails prior to being sent to the warm waters of the Indian Ocean, which slowed her down even more.

So I was confined aboard her and, as I no longer had the safe-conduct signed by the King, or the letter addressed to the Governor of the Mascarenes, it was out of the question for me to ask to see the Vicomte de Souillac. Nonetheless, I did hear reports of what was being said at the officers' meetings at the Governor's residence, thanks to

Lieutenant de Galles, who had become a friend and who had taken me into his confidence.

According to the orders received from the King, our commanders were preparing an expedition with the double aim of *destroying as much as possible of the English naval and commercial power in this part of the world* and *protecting French and Dutch settlements.* The Comte d'Orves had proposed an initial attack on Trincomalee on the island of Ceylon, which the English had just taken from the Dutch. This had the advantage of giving us a port, were we successful. Moreover, from here, depending on the intelligence we received, we could at the last moment choose between two strategies: either concentrate our efforts on the Coromandel Coast and the Bay of Bengal, or operate on the Malabar Coast. The east coast was impracticable for us from October to December, an account of the north-east monsoon, as the only sheltered harbours during this period were in English hands. Moreover, since the fall of Pondicherry, we no longer had any place where we could disembark troops. The west coast of India was more sheltered and in case of need we could count on the supportive neutrality of the Portuguese Governor of Goa and on the Mysore ports.

The Chevalier de Suffren, perhaps recalling what I had said to him, had asked whether we should rely on the Marathas rather than Hyder Ali Khan. The Vicomte de Souillac had then turned to Saint-Luperce, the advisor sent to him by the Comte de Vergennes, who said that the Marathas were too fickle to have confidence in. He had impressed those present by saying that he knew Nana Fernis, the Prime Minister of the Maratha empire, personally, and that he said one thing, thought another, and always ended up by ceding to the highest bidder. Saint-Luperce had contrasted him to the Nabob, saying he was the master of the Carnatic, headed a formidable army, hated the English as much as we did and that there was no force in India that would provide us with a better alliance than his.

Lieutenant de Galles also told me that Saint-Luperce had asked him to stop me saying anything to anybody about the treasure that he was charged with delivering to the Nabob. Apart from us, the Chevalier de Suffren and Lieutenant de Moissac, only the Vicomte de Souillac and the Comte d'Orves had been made aware of it. Saint-Luperce had also told Lieutenant de Galles not to trust the General in charge of our land forces for the future expedition, the Comte Duchemin, nor

Monsieur de Canaple, his aide-de-camp, as if they got wind of the existence of the diamonds they would do everything possible to divert some of them for their own profit, they being in India solely to enrich themselves.

All this left me puzzled. I wondered once more why Saint-Luperce was so keen to see Hyder Ali Khan again. He obviously could not mention the letter to the Vicomte de Souillac from the Marquis de Castries without admitting that he had stolen it from me and lied about me, but he could easily have jumped at the chance to once more shine at the Maratha court. I ended up by wondering whether, despite his dishonest conduct as regards me, he was in fact motivated by an odd but sincere patriotism. Maybe he really did think that an alliance with the Marathas would be a bad thing and that Hyder Ali Khan was a better potential ally. Perhaps he had decided consciously, despite the personal risks involved, that in the interests of the King he would push our commanders to make an alliance with the Nabob. After all, wouldn't he win favour with the latter, considering the royal gift that he was bringing him?

8

We sailed for India on 7th December 1781. We had eighteen ships of war: three 74-gun ships, seven 64-gun ships, a 54-gun ship – *la Pourvoyeuse,* two 12-pounder frigates, a small frigate carrying a battery of 8-pounders, a corvette, a fast lugger and a fire ship; as well as ten transports.

The squadron and its fleet were carrying the land forces under the command of the Comte Duchemin: three thousand men not counting the ships' garrisons.

The Comte d'Orves had decided to follow the route recommended by the Chevalier de Grenier for a November to April passage, following his hydrographic expedition ten years earlier, and whose conclusions were adapted in d'Après de Mannevillette's *Instructions sur la navigation des indes orientales.*

We had generally moderate but constant winds and fine weather. As we progressed north it grew hotter and hotter. *La Pourvoyeuse's* main task was to sail up and down the columns of the fleet and the convoy, repeating the Admiral's signals. These were mainly ordering the ships at the head to slow down and those at the tail to put on more sail. We crossed the Equator on 13th January 1782. Nine days later *le Héros* chased and captured a 50-gun English ship called *Hannibal,* which was immediately rebaptised and absorbed into the squadron as *le 'Petit' Annibal,* to differentiate her from the 64-gunner *l'Annibal.*

This initial prize was soon augmented by many more as we sailed towards the Bay of Bengal. Eventually our 12-pounder frigates and corvettes were bringing in twelve a day, but they were mostly small local boats carrying provisions to Madras. We took everything that was worth taking: rice, corn, vegetables, as well as sails, rope and any useful spars. We kept any boats which could sail well, but they were mostly very poor craft called *sampans* or *pariahs*. Our shipwrights either made a hole in the hull or set fire to them to sink them. I was reminded of the voyage I had made around the British Isles under the Comte de Lapérouse, right at the start of the war. The English sailors were treated as prisoners of war. These black seamen, who are called *lascars*, were at first shared amongst our ships to help work them, but they were of no use. For religious reasons, they would only eat food cooked by themselves and preferred to die of hunger than eat what was on our plates. They were more of an encumbrance than anything else. The Admiral had decided to free them, which eventually happened, but we could not do it immediately as they would have warned the English of our arrival.

On 3rd February the Comte d'Orves, whose health was deteriorating, handed over command to the Chevalier de Suffren, who immediately took charge. At dawn on 6th February, land was sighted in the distance and was identified as the mountains of Pulicat. This was followed by several days of flat calms.

*

Pulicat anchorage, Saturday 9th February 1782.

I am suddenly woken from my usual nightmare. I force open my eyes, wondering where I am. I think that I have shouted out loud. My heart is beating so strongly that I feel as if I have a drum in my chest and I am short of breath as if from some great effort. I sit up on the edge of my bunk and look around, trying to pull myself together. I am still affected by my nightmare and for a few moments think I am still aboard *l'Amazone,* off the coast of Georgia.

The frigate is completely still. We anchored towards four in the morning at the end of my watch, which had begun at midnight. Land must be to starboard. It runs north to south and we had calculated we were about six miles off when we dropped anchor, but it was completely invisible in the dark.

At four o'clock in the night, as there was no wind and the current was pushing us back where we had come from at about two knots, *le Héros* fired a rocket to get our attention and hoisted a combination of lights telling us to: *let go a light anchor.* The ships at the rear of the convoy had not been able to decipher the order. I had Lieutenant de Galles called, who decided to let us drift down on them, repeating the Admiral's signal, while firing rockets. We are three days from the new moon. The land was in darkness but the sky was clear and the moon's thin crescent was shining like silver in the starred vault. We let go the anchor once we were sure that the signal had been seen by everybody, by which time we were halfway between the squadron and the convoy. While *la Pourvoyeuse* faced gently south in the current, Lieutenant de Galles asked me to have a sounding taken. We were in fifteen fathoms, at the edge of a reef that stretches three miles out to sea. Mannevillette's *Instructions* say not to go beyond the ten-fathom line, as the bottom rises very quickly after that. I turned in and we have not moved since.

It is still dark in the orlop, where my cabin is situated, but a faint light falls on the steps of the main companionway to the gundeck; day is breaking. Although not truly cool, the temperature during the night has been relatively bearable. Once day comes it will be another matter. I have sweated a lot, mainly on account of my nightmare.

I am once more at Savannah. I see Flaharn's huge body stretched out on his belly in the tent, his nose on ground soaked in his blood, making a dark circle around his head. The body gets up and turns towards me. Only half its face is left, its remaining eye shining with a devilish light. It gets bigger! It asks me where I have hidden the diamonds. I want to run off but I cannot move. In my nightmare I always end up buried to the neck in the Jewish cemetery at Savannah, a living corpse amongst the cross-less tombstones. Flaharn laughs and calls to his accomplice, Jakar. I know him by his turban and his blue waistcoat striped in silver. This surprises me. I thought that he too was dead and that it was he who killed Flaharn. They are no longer at odds with each other? I remember then that Flaharn is not really dead. They are talking in a language I don't understand but that I recognise anyway: the language of the lascars we have just taken on board; the Tamil language of the Coromandel coast. Flaharn had met Jakar in the north of Hindustan and I know, in the absurd logic of my dream, that they

I woke at the moment that Flaharn had translated for me what they were saying: they were going to torture me just as they had tortured Avelus de Kersalaun.

I am soaked, my shirt and drawers sticking to my skin. I will have to wash myself down before dressing. I put a towel and a clean shirt under my arm and go barefoot up the companionway to the quarterdeck. The sky is quite blue and cloudless, the sea a mirror reflecting the brightness of the sun already above the horizon to port. Day comes quickly in the tropics! It is starting to get hot.

The frigate has not moved and is still lying the same way with all her canvas brailed up. The coast is just five miles off to starboard, closer than we had thought. It is slightly veiled by the morning mist but I can make out, with the naked eye, a green line of palm trees and coconut trees which delineate a beach of white sand stretching north and south as far as I can see. The place is deserted; there is only one lone seaside building visible, which seems to have been overrun by vegetation and abandoned. The countryside behind is quite flat, but in the distance, on our beam, a mountain pokes through the mist, while to the southwest, a ridge runs inland. The European sailors call it Pulicat Mountain.

What takes my eye above all is a merchant frigate anchored between us and the coast, which we did not see in the dark when we anchored last night. We have not yet raised our colours and she must take us for an English squadron, as she is still happily flying the Red Ensign at her stern. Nobody has warned her of our arrival; the result of the Chevalier de Suffren's tactic of ordering our frigates to capture every single vessel encountered at sea, down to the smallest *pariah*. The Ensign who is officer of the watch turns his glass towards our ships two cable lengths ahead and I see that *le Héros* and *le Sphinx* have just launched their boats. The sunlight reflects off the bayonets of the riflemen stood between the rowers, the latter pulling as if their lives depended on it. The boat from *le Sphinx* wins the race and the English flag is soon struck.

The morning clearing of the decks starts. Hammocks are folded and stored in the netting, the deck is washed with seawater, running through the toes of the laughing, quietly joking men working their swabs. Two men on the foredeck operate the small, fixed pump which pulls seawater from the bow to fill the buckets for the cleaning squad. I approach and ask them to pass me one. I strip off, lean over the bucket and douse myself thoroughly. A little later I will probably feel salty but for the moment it does me good. In any event, our fresh water is rationed. The hum of conversation and supressed laughter suddenly stops. Surprised, I stand up and see that the sailors around me have stopped working. They are all looking at me strangely. I wonder whether I have broken some rule of protocol, then realise that they are all staring at my chest. Like an idiot, I too lower my head to look. My wound has healed well, but I now realise how repulsive it still is. I am ashamed at having imposed this awful sight on others, even if I did it without thinking. I put my towel around my neck to hide my torso as well as I can and beat a retreat to the main companionway hatch, but I cannot hide the entry wound on my back and feel the sailors' eyes following me. The young Volunteer beside the officer of the watch turns his head away sharply when our eyes meet, and as I go down the ladder I hear him ask his superior 'How can he still be alive after such a wound?'

*

On 9th February, towards four in the afternoon, the ship *l'Orient* put her flag at half-mast and crossed her yards. We knew immediately what that meant and had it confirmed that evening: the Comte d'Orves had passed away, carried off by a dreadful disease against which he had never ceased to struggle since our departure from the Île-de-France. We awaited the order to accord him the honours prescribed in the Regulations for an Admiral who has died at sea while exercising his command… *the embarked troops will stand to arms in each of the ships in the division he commands and there will be fired thirteen cannon shots…*

But the Chevalier de Suffren was not a man to be bothered by this sort of detail, especially as regards somebody he did not appreciate while he was alive: there were no honours, they being postponed for better days. *L'Orient's* chaplain read a prayer in the ship's Great cabin, in front of the assembled officers, and the Comte d'Orves' body was passed over the stern rail. As the proverb says: *roses bloom not on the sailor's grave.*

Three days later, when we were still in a flat calm, the Chevalier de Suffren summoned Lieutenant de Galles, along with several other ships' captains, aboard *le Héros*. On his return, Lieutenant de Galles told me to prepare my sea chest without losing a minute, as he had been ordered to take over another ship immediately and I of course had to go with him, given that he had promised the Admiral to watch over me.

The *Lord God Almighty* – he had not yet acquired the nickname the *Fat Caulker* – had decided to redistribute several positions within the squadron. This was not the first time he had done this, nor would it be the last. He no doubt considered that he could more easily impose his authority on his subordinates by keeping them permanently fearful of being relieved of their command at any moment. This was simply the first stage in the ordeal known later as 'Suffren's martyrs'. Moreover, the Admiral was capable of writing to the Minister demanding sanctions – anything from retirement without a pension to imprisonment. This of course allowed him, at the same time, to reward his 'good' captains by giving them the commands he had just taken from the 'bad' captains. This was how Suffren's system worked.

On this occasion the system dealt with three Ship's Captains and five Ship's Lieutenants, amongst whom was the 'bad' Captain de Werfusé. The Chevalier de Suffren had previously assigned him to take command of *le 'Petit' Annibal* after we had captured her, but now he was to be replaced by the 'good' Lieutenant de Galles. Captain de Werfusé was therefore demoted, leaving a ship to take command of a frigate, while Lieutenant de Galles was rewarded by taking his place. It was thus that I found myself, overnight and without warning, third lieutenant aboard the little 50-gun English ship captured by *le Héros* when we were still in the same latitude as Sumatra, just north of the equator.

Le 'Petit' Annibal, which our sailors also called *l'Annibal Anglais,* was not much longer than *la Pourvoyeuse,* but she had two decks, the first with eleven gunports a side for 24-pounders, the second with twelve 12-pounders a side, plus six 6-pounders on the fore and after decks. She tended to make some leeway when on the wind and was an average sailor off the wind, despite being coppered like all the English ships, but was in a good enough state when captured to be immediately included in our line of battle. A makeshift prize crew of sailors, petty officers and officers taken from all the ships of the squadron had been put aboard. As one would expect, the commanders asked to provide the crew had not handed over their best men. As a garrison, a company of Foreign Naval Volunteers had been taken off one of the convoy's transports. These were in fact horseless hussars from the Lauzun Legion, transformed into infantrymen for the occasion. They were part of the land force to be disembarked under the command of the Comte Duchemin. Amongst themselves they spoke German, their officers were Irish and Polish, and orders were given in French.

The English sailors from the original crew had been divided amongst our vessels once they had been taken prisoner. They had nonetheless had time to destroy or damage much of the ship's apparatus before leaving. Captain de Werfusé told us that this had caused him a lot of trouble at first, but everything was in order now. He had also inherited a female passenger, the young wife of an English infantry officer, but he had finally obtained permission to have her transferred to one of the ships of the convoy, so as she would not be in the way should we meet the enemy. In truth, the ship left to us by Captain de Werfusé was not yet ready to take her place in the line. There was still much to do to improve her manoeuvring and her fighting, to teach the gun crews, to take on board and stow a full store of ammunition; all the while sailing in waters controlled by the Royal Navy, a squadron of which we could happen upon at any time. Luckily Lieutenant de Galles was capable of meeting the challenge.

I had the impression, during this period, that our commander was asking more of me than the other officers, to the extent that I felt it was unjust. I was several times tempted to complain but thought that without Lieutenant de Galles' protection I would perhaps be sent back to France under guard, or worse still, I might find myself in prison in Port-Louis. For two days I worked around the clock and slept little. When I was able, I threw myself on my bunk, in the heat of the 'tween deck, only to be wrenched from my sleep by the two ghosts which haunted me every night: Flaharn and his accomplice Jakar. The latter, almost every time, had started to look like Saint-Luperce. It was only Flaharn who scared me during these nightmares; Jakar, as Saint-Luperce, did not really frighten me, a fact I thought about once I had woken, breathing hard and covered in sweat. The real Jakar was dead. I had witnessed his last breath. But what about Flaharn? I would have liked to have asked my friend Roblet for his opinion on this, but he had remained aboard the previous *Annibal*. There was nobody on board with whom I could confide. Apart from Lieutenant de Galles, I knew none of the other officers, as they were all from the Île-de-France station. My captain and I certainly talked freely to each other, as we shared secrets unknown to the others, but it was not the same as with Roblet.

I finally came to understand why Lieutenant de Galles had made me work so hard outside my normal watches when he said that he was happy that circumstances had allowed him to keep me with him when he left *la Pourvoyeuse*. He said that he would very much have liked to put me in charge of the main battery, but that would have elevated me to first lieutenant, which was not possible as I was both the youngest and had the shortest service.

'However,' he added, 'I have more confidence in you than in any of the others. They do not have your experience under fire and have been having a soft time of it on the Île-de-France since the start of the war. And – keep this to yourself – I have been given the worst of them.'

He added that the men of the crew had picked this up and that he had been pleasantly surprised to see that I had more authority over them than any of the other officers. The Lieutenant was unaware of the real reason for my so-called 'authority' over our sailors, as explained to me by Roblet. In fact, as *le 'Petit' Annibal* had taken on men from all the ships of the squadron, we had some former sailors from *le 'Grand' Annibal,* who had explained to their shipmates that it was fortunate to have me on board, as I would bring good luck to the ship. Sailors are always ready to believe this sort of nonsense. I kept my little secret to myself.

Lieutenant de Galles told me that the lugger *le Diligent* had been sent to Pondicherry to land Lieutenant-Colonel de Canaple, who had been ordered to make contact with Monsieur Piveron de Morlat, the King's envoy to Hyder Ali Khan. The Chevalier de Suffren had suggested to Saint-Luperce that he join this expedition but the latter had preferred to stay on board *le Héros.* On hearing this I wondered whether this was because Saint-Luperce did not want to leave the diamonds unguarded, or whether he feared a hostile reaction on meeting the Nabob. My commander said that in any case, relations between Canaple and Saint-Luperce were not good. There was rivalry between them. Lieutenant-Colonel de Canaple was not a soldier by training. The Comte Duchemin, who had wanted him by his side, had given him this rank because of his knowledge of India. Like Saint-Luperce, Canaple had been an adventurer and secret agent in India, he spoke several local languages and had carried out missions on behalf of Monsieur de Sartine. Above all, he had spent time in Hindustan as adviser to the Moghul's Grand Vizier.

The light breeze at the end of the north-east monsoon strengthened again and we had a fair wind which allowed us to sail up the coast, past the Dutch fort at Pulicat, towards Madras. On the basis of information obtained from the native sailors on our various prizes, the Chevalier de Suffren thought that the anchorage would be empty. When the frigates sent to reconnoitre reached Madras, they could see nine English ships of the line and two frigates anchored less than three miles off Fort St. George. The Admiral had the squadron form a line of battle, leaving *le 'Petit' Annibal* and *la Pourvoyeuse* to guard the convoy. As night was falling, we anchored where we were, in twenty-eight fathoms, still in the same order.

Madras, which unfortunately I would soon get to know, was split into two parts built along the coast. To the south, beside the mouth of a small river which bends round to the north, enclosing part of the town, were the Fort St. George and the *White Town*. These were protected by brick walls edged with bastions, half of which faced the sea and were laced with cannons aimed at the harbour. To the north and north-east, the *Black Town* was more extensive but much less well defended. The Madras roadstead, like that of Pondicherry, was really no more than a seasonal anchorage outside a bar which only the local craft, the *masula*[22] boats, were able to cross to get ashore. This 'roadstead' became impractical and even quite dangerous at the height of the north-east monsoon.

Seeing us arrive at a distance, the English had changed their orientation, bringing themselves broadside on in front of the fort. The main question was whether they were within range of the fort's guns or not, and opinions were divided on this point. *Le 'Petit' Annibal* had been reintegrated into the line of battle and, remembering the impetuousness with which *le Héros* had charged like a wild boar at the enemy ships at Porto Praya, I was convinced we would attack. The ships had long since been cleared for combat, the line had been formed, we outnumbered the English and the north-east wind favoured us. Instead, the Chevalier de Suffren ordered his ships to heave-to and called all the commanders

---

22 Translator's note: *masula* boat: called a *chelingue* in French, from the local word *salangu*. They were specifically designed to negotiate the surf off Madras and along the Coromandel Coast.

aboard *le Héros* for a council of war.

When he returned on board, Lieutenant de Galles told us that we would not be attacking, as the Chevalier de Suffren considered that it would be too dangerous. He had decided to go down to Pondicherry or to Porto Novo to put the land forces ashore. We also needed to take on water urgently. So in the afternoon we ran before the wind along the coast, on port tack, still in the moderate north-easterly that blows at the end of the monsoon. Before nightfall, at five in the evening, we could see the English weighing anchor and heading seawards on starboard tack. The Admiral signalled to us to come up to windward on starboard tack too, which took us well away from the coast. He then signalled the 12-pounder frigate *la Fine* to reconnoitre ahead, and *la Pourvoyeuse* to pass to leeward of the squadron and sail between us and the coast with the convoy she was protecting. Eventually we were ordered to douse all our lights. Did the frigate captains misunderstand their orders? By the next morning we were alone on the sea, nearly fifty miles off the coast, with no idea where the convoy was. As for the enemy, the Admiral was convinced that they had returned to their anchorage under the protection of the Fort St. George cannons.

During the morning the frigate *la Fine,* who was still sailing ahead, signalled that there were ships of war to the south-west. By afternoon we were sure it was the English squadron. Rather than return to Madras, it had slipped between us and the coast during the night and was now, in fact, chasing our convoy. The Chevalier de Suffren ordered our fastest ships to put on all sail and go to protect the endangered convoy. Seeing our advance guard arrive, the English broke off their chase and came beam on to the wind, heading south-east, to form a line of battle and wait for us. Thanks to this, most of our transports were able to get away, except for a ship carrying the rifles and artillery of the Lauzun Legion, along with their campaign equipment. We could see her being towed by the English squadron once we had rejoined the advance ships. She was called *le Lawriston* and was well known to the crew of *le 'Petit' Annibal* as our garrison had been seconded several weeks earlier from the troops she was carrying.

Our studded ships, slower than those sheathed in copper, took a long time to gather together and we were unable to form a line of battle before dusk. The Chevalier de Suffren ordered the frigate *la Fine* to keep him informed of the enemy movements during the night, to enable him to manoeuvre in such a way as to be able to attack the next morning.

＊

At sea, sixty miles to the south-east of Sadras, Sunday 17th February 1782.

Day has arrived but the sky is completely covered by a layer of dark cloud. In contrast, the sea seems very clear, with its almost luminous blue-green reflections. The weather feels thundery, the air hot and heavy, and the faint breeze from the north-east scarcely ruffles the surface of the water. The last time we streamed the log we counted just two knots.

The nine enemy vessels that we caught up with last night are in a single line about six miles to leeward, on our starboard side. Like us, they are heading south-east. With an eyeglass we can sometimes make out the flags at their sterns, when the weak breeze manages to make them flutter. They are blue, quartered by the Union Jack, but we are too far away to see the latter. The English are holding their line, beam on to the wind on port tack, with a half cable's distance between each ship, except for the last two, who are falling behind with *le Lawriston* in tow.

As for us, we certainly have the advantage of the wind, but our ships have become separated during the night because of a signalling mistake. The Admiral had ordered the ships at the head of the line to light three stern lanterns, so that those behind could see where they were. Unfortunately, the signal also means *all come up to the wind at the same time* in the list we were using since leaving the Île-de-France, and some of the ships at the rear of the squadron headed off east, hard on the wind, in the dark. Luckily the wind is so feeble that the misdirected ships have not managed to go far, but in these conditions it will take a long time to collect everyone together. Without this unfortunate mistake we could have begun to chase the English and cut them off. There are more of us, and every moment lost is to their advantage. Their commander, Admiral Hughes[23], is well aware of this, old fox that he is.

---

23 Translator's note: *Admiral Hughes:* Admiral Sir Edward Hughes RN (c.1720 – 1794). He spent a lifetime in the Royal Navy, having joined the service at the age of 15. He was a veteran of Anglo-French naval conflict, having been with Boscawen at Louisbourg and Saunders at Quebec. Having commanded the East India Station from 1773 to 1777, he was soon after sent back as Rear Admiral with a large naval force to protect British interests against the French.

By eight o'clock, *la Pourvoyeuse* has rejoined us, along with *les Bons-Amis*, one of the transports. I also see that *le Diligent,* sent to Pondicherry to land Lieutenant-Colonel de Canaple, is back with us.

We are cleared for action. My place is on the poop deck, beside our commander. My task is to read the Admiral's signals, while overseeing the 6-pounders on the foredeck and poop deck. *Le Héros* is sending up flags to the masthead one after the other and as there is not enough wind to stretch them out and they stay stuck to their halyards, I have trouble reading them before they are taken down. However I have clearly made out a blue and white chequered flag over a blue flag with a white saltire; the Chevalier de Suffren must have ordered them to be left at the main topmast head until the latecomers have arrived. It is the signal for *natural order of battle.* Apart from this signal I have to guess, without having the time to really see the successive colours and designs of most of the flags sent up without respite at the whim of the Admiral: *Keep together! Repeat all signals! Put on more sail!* The last signal is even repeated again, together with the numbers of the three offending ships, ours included. When I pass on its meaning to Lieutenant de Galles he shrugs, pointing out with a resigned gesture to our sodden sails hanging from their yards.

After several hours, by which time it is late morning, the squadron manages to form something resembling a line of battle. But so much time has been lost. Knowing the Chevalier de Suffren as I do, he must be fuming. We are in sixth place, astern of *le Héros* and ahead of *l'Annibal.* We are well hemmed in by these two 64-gun ships, which is reassuring if we have to fight in this order. We are still six miles from the English, on a parallel course: same heading and same tack.

'Why are we waiting and not bearing down on them?' murmurs Lieutenant de Galles beside me. 'With twelve against nine we're sure to wipe them out. But if we carry on like this, especially with this falling wind, we'll never overtake them by nightfall. The chance will have been lost!'

As if he had heard this, the Admiral at that very moment sends up a signal ordering us to *bear off to the south-east a quarter south one after the other.* A well-timed squall hits us. I see the curtain of rain that accompanies it bearing down on us on the port bow. The sea beneath it is covered with whitecaps, advancing at the same speed. Our sails fill with a snap, the blocks start to groan and the sound of the hull slipping through the water can be heard from one end of the ship to the other. We feel the deck coming to life beneath our feet. The Admiral immediately uses the squall to send up new flags, easily visible this time, ordering *le Bizarre,* at the head our line, to *head south-south-east,* and to the rest to *make all sail* and follow her.

But the English under our lee are hit by the squall in their turn, and take advantage of it by all bearing off together and running downwind in line abeam, turning their sterns to us and moving quickly away. After the initial moment of surprise, *le Héros* reacts with a flurry of successive flags which snap in the wind: signal *to l'Artésien to come up astern* – I wonder why, *to the whole squadron to bear off south; to the second division to make all sail;* and, to finish, the final bouquet: *bear off south-west all together,* followed by *change from line astern to line abeam.* Our ships pivot as one, the yards are braced and our twelve bowsprits make a powerful quarter turn to starboard. We find ourselves in line abeam, yards squared to a following wind, following the English.

Then the wind falls; the squall has passed. The sea, ruffled just a moment ago, goes calm once more. There are no longer any white crests, just a short-lived swell that gently rocks us.

Midday has passed. Ahead of us the English are still running before the wind in line abeam. The return of calmer weather has disordered them a little, but they nevertheless manage to stay relatively well aligned and maintain a regular spacing. When I point this out to Lieutenant de Galles he says it's because they are all copper-bottomed.

'It's why their ships sail in a similar way, even with the wind from astern, when it's difficult to regulate your speed. It gives them a big advantage over us, with our mix of coppered hulls and studded hulls that don't slide through the water so easily. Going to windward or with the wind on the beam it's not so obvious, but once you are running everything falls apart. Look at the result!'

The line abeam that we formed not long ago is now just a memory. *Le Sphinx, le Vengeur* and *le Héros,* all copper-bottomed, are far ahead, with the faster *le Héros* even overtaking the other two. We are astern of them, a little to their starboard. *Le 'Petit' Annibal,* although coppered, sails less well, but more quickly than our studded ships. *L'Orient,* number two in our natural order of battle, is astern of us slightly to port, and *Le Bizarre,* an old ship and in principle our number one, is even further astern. As for the ships of the second division, they make up a separate group far astern on our starboard quarter.

We hear rolls of thunder in the north-east, and a new squall gives us a favourable boost, as the English are still becalmed. Seeing us sailing faster, however, they close up, turning to port to form a line of battle again, hard on the wind on port tack, waiting for us stolidly, while releasing *le Lawriston*, who drifts slowly off to the south. Now, our own line widely spread, we are rushing down on a solid block of nine ships, well aligned and each a half cable from the other.

The breeze persists and seems to want to last longer than before. *Le Héros* makes use of this by coming up a little to the wind, to port, to follow the direction of the English line. The squall has now reached the latter, which is moving across ahead of us, from starboard to port. *Le Héros* again sets her mainsail and foresail, which had been brailed up for battle and surges ahead of *le Vengeur* and *le Sphinx.* At the same time she runs up another onslaught of signals: *Put on sail! Attack the enemy at pistol range! Form a line of battle in order of speed!*

Le Sphinx and *le Vengeur* unbrail their lower sails too and alter course to put themselves in the wake of *le Héros*, who is charging diagonally towards the centre of the English column. We do the same and follow them. *L'Orient,* to port of us, has trouble executing the movement. This time, I think, the *Lord God Almighty* has committed himself and nothing will stop him. I am seized by the general excitement that usually precedes a battle, but despite myself, I feel my stomach knotting unpleasantly. I cannot stop myself thinking of the bloodied deck of *l'Annibal* at Porto Praya. Today things are certainly different, as we have numerical superiority, but as we get closer, I can see that there are three 74-gun ships facing us. I hope that we won't end up side by side with one of them when we have finished running down their line; *le 'Petit' Annibal* would be biting off more than she could chew.

The Admiral sends up a new signal preceded by the numbers for *l'Annibal, l'Ajax* and *le Flamand: overtake the enemy to leeward to bring them between two lines of fire.* These three ships are still far astern, and I tell the Master Pilot beside me which flags to raise to repeat the order for them.

The Admiral fires a cannon shot at the last ship in the English line to test his range, but he seems to me to be still too far away. He curves round a little, coming up to windward, approaching the enemy at an angle, and fires his first broadside. He then sails along the opposing line, alternately coming up to windward then paying off to get closer, before sailing a parallel course and firing nonstop. When he arrives at the enemy Admiral's ship, recognisable by the blue flag at her masthead, he brails up his lower and topgallant sails to slow down his speed. *L'Orient*, who was to one side, works her way into second place between *le Héros* and *le Sphinx*. We follow them, fifth in the order, astern of *le Vengeur*. We are no longer overtaking the English, and end up side by side with their last ship. Luckily for us it is a sixty-four armed with 24-pounders, like us.

Firing has started here and there. The sound of the explosions is deafening, the smell of gunpowder as intoxicating as ever. But we are at about half cannon range, not at all within pistol shot. I wonder why the Chevalier de Suffren has changed his mind. It is not like him to stay so far off! But I can no longer see *le Héros* through the smoke and there are three ships between us.

The wind has once again fallen away completely, leaving no more than a mild beam-on swell that has the opposing lines of battle rolling gently. The sky grows ever darker. Big raindrops start to create circles on the sea around us. Our Master Pilot tells me that this is unusual weather for the time of year hereabouts. In any case, it's a real tropical deluge that falls on us, and within a few moments we are soaked to the skin. Thank God it is not cold.

The action really gets going from here on. There is broadside after broadside and the smoke of battle, made heavy by the humidity, creates a thick fog that the light wind cannot budge. It is still raining; water streams down the sails and rigging, drums on the deck and pours out through the scuppers. The smoking barrels take on a varnished sheen. In these conditions it is difficult to use the linstocks, but in any case, our 6-pounders are at the limit of their range. With Lieutenant de Galles' agreement I gather all my gun crews together and take them down to the main battery where I help the Ship's Lieutenant in command to divide them up. The men behave well. It is true that the battle does not have the kind of intensity it would have were we within pistol shot. We take more cannonballs in the rigging than in the hull. Is it the distance or the poor visibility that that is forcing the English gunners to raise their sights? In any case, it is not at all comparable to what I experienced on the main gundeck aboard *l'Annibal* in the Battle of Grenada, in July 1779, when we were taking full 36-pounder broadsides straight in the hull.

When I go back on deck nothing has changed; we are still face to face with the English rear guard. Astern of us, *l'Annibal* and the second division look as if they are waiting for us to move forward so they can replace us. *L'Artésien* and *le Bizarre* have arrived and taken up their places in the line, the latter having a brief collision with *le Sévère*. It is certainly difficult to manoeuvre in this calm. *L'Artésien* comes up to the wind from time to time, desperately slowly, so that her guns can fire obliquely at the rear of the enemy, but this takes her further away, forcing her to bear off again to get closer, equally slowly. The ships astern of her are condemned to inaction. I think that if the wind does not return it will be difficult for them to pass to leeward, as they were ordered. It would be better to keep running along the English line, thereby stealing their wind and enabling us to engage them with all our forces.

Eventually the three ships of the second division fall off to starboard, leaving the line with the clear intention of executing the Admiral's order by joining battle to starboard of the English column. The first is *l'Ajax*, formerly of our now defunct India Company, a studded old tub bought by the Navy and refitted as a 64-gunner. She moves forward to starboard of *l'Annibal* then loses way, her wind taken by the latter. I say to myself that if she continues to drift as she is, she will be unable to get back to windward to take part in the battle. Captain de Tromelin must think likewise, as he signals to her to take her place in the line again. Another ship sets off at a snail's pace, also to try the same manoeuvre. I recognise her by the vermillion stripes along her gunports. It is the old *le Flamand*. She moves forward towards the starboard quarter of the English rear guard, but so slowly that she is overtaken by *le Brillant*, a handier sailor. This 64-gun ship is commanded by Captain de Saint-Félix. I remember his name as it was he who was commanding the frigate *la Fine*, which left Brest before us and which was one of the ships on which the Minister was thinking of putting me. Captain de Saint-Félix's ship manages to get to leeward of the 64-gunner we have been fighting with since the start of the battle. I can see her on our beam on the other side of the English ship. *Le Brillant* really is within pistol shot and is so close to her adversary that I fear that any of our cannonballs passing over the latter will damage her rigging. Once in position she starts to fire off broadsides with a remarkable speed and regularity. The Englishman's fire weakens and stops completely after an hour. *Le Brillant* breaks off combat, as her jib halyard has been cut, seemingly by a cannonball, but she is replaced immediately by *le Flamand*, who puts the *Exeter*, as the English ship is called, out of the battle for good. However, our ships cannot push further along the lee side of the enemy line, as the opposition bears off each time they see them coming. The wind is too weak for us to risk falling off so far as to be unable to rejoin the battle. Our second division is stuck at the rear, away from the action, on account of the lack of wind in which to manoeuvre.

With night falling, the rain eases and a sailable wind at last gets up. The ships at the head of the English column, who thus far have also been unable to do anything, due to the lack of wind, wear ship to starboard to come to the aid of their rear guard. *L'Annibal*, along with her still intact division, prepares to meet them. We are at last going to reap the benefit of our superior numbers. But at that moment *le Vengeur, le Sphinx* and *le Héros all* tack and pass us on starboard tack, signalling to us to break off from the battle. I do not understand what is going on. We repeat the signal, tack and follow them. After some hesitation, *l'Annibal* and the others follow. The battle thus ends with a feeling of incompleteness.

*

We had two killed and a dozen wounded, one badly, who died a few days later. These losses could be considered light for a naval battle.

Once of the two dead was a young sailor from Vannes who had served under me when I commanded the 8-pounders on *l'Annibal's* quarterdeck. He was a bit rough but had a good heart. I had once acted in his defence before leaving our former ship and was moved by the genuine pleasure he showed when I arrived on board *le 'Petit' Annibal*. He was called Kermovan, was twenty years old, and had survived the Battle of Grenada. He had been there on that memorable day in December 1779, when the Comte de Lamotte-Piquet, along with *l'Annibal*, had at Martinique recorded one of the most glorious days in our naval history. He had come out of the Battle of Porto Praya unscathed. All that while he was still so young, to finally fall in this action that would later be called the Battle of Sadras, despite it having taken place well out to sea, and closer to the latitude of Pondicherry than Sadras.

Having broken off the action, our squadron gathered itself around *le Héros* and hove-to on starboard tack until ten the next morning. By dawn the weather was superb, with a light north-easterly. Before making sail, the Admiral called his commanders aboard. When he returned, Lieutenant de Galles merely said that we were heading for Pondicherry. *L'Artésien* took us in tow so that we could repair our badly damaged rig. We had to change our topmasts and fish the mizzen mast.

I was always anxious to know what frame of mind the Chevalier de Suffren was in, as my future depended in part on his mood, and usually Lieutenant de Galles was happy to share his feelings on this. I was therefore surprised by his silence, which he only broke two days after the battle. I was beside him on the poop deck. We were on our own, leaning on the rail. It was just after dawn, we still had the same light north-easterly, the weather was fine and the lookouts had just spotted land about ten miles to the west-south-west. *L'Annibal*, who was sailing astern of us, lowered her flag to half-mast and we could see the white jackets of the detachment of riflemen from her garrison presenting arms on the quarterdeck of our former ship.

'Has an officer died on *l'Annibal?*' I asked.

'It must be Monsieur le Berre,' replied the Ship's Lieutenant. 'He was amputated at the thigh yesterday and must not have survived his wound.'

I stayed silent, remembering Le Berre, an auxiliary officer from L'Orient.

'I wonder what the Admiral will say,' continued Lieutenant de Galles, sounding disillusioned.

Hearing this, I looked at my commander, who understood my silent question.

'Yesterday the Chevalier de Suffren was furious with Captain de Tromelin. He accused him of treason and cowardice, in front of everyone. Then he went from anger to withering sarcasm, which he does so well. He made fun of *l'Annibal's* Captain because he had nobody killed on board, while there were about thirty killed in the squadron. If it were not such an unworthy thing to boast about the number killed, I would say that *le Héros'* losses were no greater than ours, and that, although the Admiral makes out he was fighting closer than everyone else, the only one who really got within pistol shot of the enemy was my friend Saint-Félix. Moreover, more than two thirds of our dead and wounded were on *le Brillant,* which was hardly surprising!'

'And what did Captain de Tromelin say?'

'What is there to be said against the wrath of the *Lord God Almighty?* He rode it out until the end of the squall. But the most interesting thing is that this time there was no announcement about asking for sanctions. I don't know what to make of that.'

'You think that Captain de Tromelin is not really guilty, then?'

'You remember the wind we had the day before yesterday during the battle?'

'There wasn't much.'

'You can say that again!'

We were off the coast at Pondicherry. Lieutenant de Galles told me that *le Diligent,* whom I had seen join up with us again on the morning of the 17th, had taken Lieutenant-Colonel de Canaple back on board *le Héros.* The pretend Lieutenant-Colonel had not wanted to disembark at Pondicherry because, he maintained, the unfortunate inhabitants of the place dared not fly the French flag out of fear of English reprisals.

The squadron anchored at dusk more than ten miles off the coast, in eleven fathoms. As regards Pondicherry, all I could see through my telescope was a small reddish hill crowned with a few trees, surrounded by a low, black landscape. I did not miss much, as I was later told that it was no more than a shapeless town with a few beautiful houses amidst a pile of ruins, and that its fortifications had been completely razed.

Early the next morning *le Héros* was approached by several local boats which must have set out during the night, given the distance we were from the coast. I could see a type of brigantine and a *kattumaram*[24]. This is the name for a craft made of three logs, about fifteen to twenty feet long, lashed together with rope and driven by an enormous sail attached to a mast. The latter is balanced by an outrigger. These *kattumarams* are crewed by Indian locals who often act as messengers between the land and the ships anchored out to sea. These sailors are usually soaked up to the neck and so carry the papers entrusted to them in specially designed hats.

---

24 Translator's note: *kattumaram:* A Tamil word meaning 'logs lashed together'. The craft described by Laforest-Dombourg would in modern terminology be called a 'proa' rather than a 'catamaran'.

Our frigates, which had been anchored closer to the land than us during the night, came up to the stern of the Admiral's ship to get their orders. At six-thirty *le Héros* made the signal to weigh anchor and head south-south-west, except for *la Subtile,* who turned round to heave-to off the Pondicherry bar. Lieutenant de Galles told us we were going to Porto Novo.

At midday *la Subtile* caught us up. She was towing fifteen *masula* boats, each tied to the other in her wake. These *masula* boats are flat-bottomed, with no framing, their planks sewn together with cord made from coconut fibre, rather than nailed. They are usually powered by a dozen oarsman and although the topsides are five or six feet high, they are so flat and light that they float in just a few inches of water. These boats, together with their Indian rowers, had been provided by the authorities at Pondicherry, at the request of the Admiral, so they we would be able to get ashore. The whole of the Coromandel coast is battered by continuous surf that over the centuries has created an unbroken bar of sand on which the sea breaks permanently, even at high tide. This renders everywhere on shore inaccessible by European ships' boats, apart from Porto Novo from time to time.

For the next two days we ran down the coast with a moderate north-easterly on the port quarter, following astern of *le Diligent,* who was taking soundings ahead of the squadron. The weather was fine, the sea calm, and we stayed just over three miles offshore on the ten-fathom line. The land here is low-lying, edged along its whole length with a beautiful beach and dunes. We could see that it was well forested behind its fringe of sand. We fired a salute as we passed Cuddalore, a former Dutch post taken by the English at the start of the war, and arrived within view of Porto Novo in the afternoon of the 21st. We anchored in seven fathoms with a muddy bottom, two miles off this settlement at the mouth of a river.

*

Tuesday, 26th February 1782, at anchor off Porto Novo.
It is now five days since we anchored two miles off Porto Novo, or *Parangipettai,* as the Indians call it.

It is one in the afternoon, the hottest hour of the day. Except for the officer of the watch, the captain and myself, the rest of *l' Petit*

Annibal's officers have been allowed to go ashore to visit the country. This morning they managed to cross the bar in the ship's boat, as it was high tide, but the wind has strengthened since and I worry that they won't be able to get back so easily.

Until now nobody has been put ashore apart from the sick. The Army battalions with all their baggage and artillery have not moved. Like me, they are confined to their ships, condemned to inaction while waiting for the order which does not come. I don't know why.

As I am off watch with nothing to do, I have climbed to the main topsail to seek out some coolness in the breeze. To keep my hands free, I have brought an old soldier's haversack. Inside I put the late Doctor Rollins' *Memoir of Hindustan.* This will give me the impression that I will be visiting this country, forbidden to me but in plain sight. I have also brought my telescope, to try to at least see the countryside a little more closely.

The weather is fine and the sky completely clear; the shadows have not yet started to lengthen. The sounds of the wind in the rigging, and of the sea slopping against the side of the hull, are overridden by the permanent roar of the line of breakers between us and the shore. Porto Novo is built on the left bank of the Vellar river, also known as the White River, behind a sandbank on the other side of a sort of lagoon. You have to go up the estuary to see the houses properly; all I can see are roofs amongst trees. To the left of the river mouth, however, to the south-west, and clearly visible six miles inland, I can see four extraordinary structures rising out of the greenery. From my viewpoint they look like huge soaring towers shaped like pyramids with their tops sliced off. They are the porticos of the famous Chalembron[25] temple.

I see a boat pull away from *le Héros,* who is anchored nearer the shore than us. I pay it no attention and go back to reading Doctor Rollin.

India being a perfectly healthy country of modest habits, limited work and good quality food, bodies are vigorous and strong. The proof of this vigour is in the huge population of Hindustan and, in addition, the habits practised by the Indians are of great help in maintaining their

---

25 Translator's note: *Chalembron:* now known as Chidambaram.

I hear the ship being hailed and stop my oh so edifying reading, which has me dreaming of the beautiful landlady in the Chaussée d'Antin. The boat which I saw leaving *le Héros* has arrived alongside, and our officer of the watch is welcoming aboard on the side deck a visitor wearing a work uniform with the epaulettes of a Ship's Lieutenant. The arrival asks to see the captain and the two set off towards the quarterdeck. I start reading again.

They bathe all the time – that reminds me of the bath I had seen in Doctor Rollins' room in Paris. *They bathe from childhood, every day and in every season…*

Someone shouts from the deck below.

'Monsieur Dombourg!'

It is only when repeated a second time that I realise that it is my name being called. I lean over the topmast trees once again and see the officer of the watch at the base of the mast, his head raised towards me.

'The captain wants to see you! You have been summoned by the Admiral!'

I hear properly this time. The Admiral! Jesus! What's going on? I hurriedly put my things in the haversack, throw it on my back and slide down one of the main topmast backstays. As I am bare-footed and wearing just a shirt, I run past the officer of the watch, who does not seem to appreciate my fanciful dress, but paying him no attention, I take the steps of the main companionway four at a time to go and dress. I put on my braided jacket, red breeches, a pair of washed and ironed stockings and, after some reflection, I buckle on my shoulder belt with its sword. When I return on deck, tricorn hat under my arm, the Ship's Lieutenant has already left and the bosun of the captain's gig is getting his men into the boat, which is permanently tied alongside the ship's ladder when we are at anchor. I am preparing to follow them when Lieutenant de Galles appears at the entrance to the wheelhouse and signals me to join him. When the two of us are alone in the Great cabin, he keeps the door shut and speaks to me in a low voice.

'Ship's Lieutenant Bolle came to say that the Chevalier de Suffren wants to speak to both of us.'

'Bolle?'

'He is in charge of the general supply of the squadron, but he is also a man trusted by the Chevalier de Suffren, an important fact, given its rarity.'

'So his confidant is no longer Lieutenant de Moissac?'

'He left this morning with Monsieur de Piveron, the King's representative at the Nabob's court, who had come to see us, and with Lieutenant-Colonel de Canaple. The cannon salute last night was for Monsieur de Piveron. According to the official declarations they are going to present the compliments of our Generals to Hyder Ali Khan. But in reality, Lieutenant-Colonel de Canaple will be communicating to the Nabob the conditions to be imposed by the Comte Duchemin. Hyder Ali Khan will be told that until these conditions are met, the Comte Duchemin will not disembark with his army.'

'Is that why we have been waiting here doing nothing for nearly a week?'

'We will probably have to wait for another week, until they get back, as long as the Nabob accepts the conditions, of course. To have come all this way for this! The Chevalier de Suffren is in a permanent rage! He had planned on landing our soldiers as quickly as possible so that he could launch a joint land and sea offensive to retake Nagapatnam[26]. Things are currently in our favour. Once the English learned that we were intending to disembark here, they decided to launch a pincer movement on Porto Novo, with one column coming from Madras in the north, the other from Tanjore[27] in the south. Tipu Sahib[28], Hyder Ali Khan's son, totally defeated the force from Tanjore, while the Nabob has pushed back the northern column to the fringes of Madras, where he is holding it at bay. So we have free reign throughout the Carnatic. You can see that the Admiral has every reason to be unhappy and we could not be called at a worse moment! You know what he's like in a bad mood! You did well to put on your dress uniform.'

'But what does he want of us exactly?'

'Lieutenant Bolle couldn't tell me because I don't think he knows himself.'

---

26 Translator's note: *Nagapatnam:* Now known as Nagapattinam, but also referred to as Negapatam in relation to the naval battle between the French and English which took place there (see below).

27 Translator's note: *Tanjore:* Now known as Thanjavur.

28 Translator's note: *Tipu Sahib:* Also known as Tippoo Sahib, Tipu/Tippoo Sultan, and the Tiger of Mysore.

We are welcomed aboard *le Héros* by Ship's Lieutenant Bernier de Pierrevert, a nephew of the Chevalier de Suffren and well-liked in the squadron. He takes us to the Great cabin where his uncle is finishing his lunch. It is the third time I find myself in the presence of the Admiral. The first time, at Versailles, he was wearing town clothes, had taken trouble over his appearance in view of his meeting with the Marquis de Castries, and had acted most unpleasantly towards me, to say the least. Our second meeting had taken place during our stay at Simon's Bay, and the Admiral was probably wearing for the first time his Admiral's dress uniform, with braid everywhere, which he had had made before leaving Brest, knowing that he could put it on once we had passed the Cape of Good Hope. During this second meeting with the redoubtable *Lord God Almighty,* an unexpected tenderness, when he recalled the memory of my father, had shown through his thick boar-like hide. That had moved me.

Today, it is rather the *Fat Caulker* who receives us. His grey hair, swept back over his uncovered brow, is gathered into a short pigtail tied with a length of twine. There is no braided jacket, no scarlet breeches this time, but a rough linen shirt soaked in sweat, stained trousers, half unbuttoned and overhung by his paunch. Contrary to Lieutenant de Galles' prediction, the Admiral receives us without any ceremony, inviting us to sit at his table and asking his steward to serve us each a glass of wine to tide us over while we wait for him to finish his meal. He is eating a sort of Indian ragoût with rice which he rolls in his fingers to dip it in the sauce. He then wipes his hands on his napkin and rubs them on his breeches.

'I asked Saint-Luperce to get me a local cook and by God he's good! A bit too spicy sometimes…'

He pours himself a glass of wine and signals to his steward to clear the table. While the waiters rush around, the steward takes a box of cigars and a chandelier out of a sideboard. He strikes a flint and lights one of the candles, which he places in front of the Admiral. The latter opens the box and selects a cheroot which he lights with the flame, inhales and blows out the smoke while leaning back in his chair.

I glance at my captain. He is as taken aback as I am!

'Until today, Laforest-Dombourg,' the Chevalier de Suffren eventually begins, once we are alone, 'I took you for an impostor, a *pasto-messorgo* as they say where I come from. And that troubled me, d'you see, because I remembered that your father was not of that ilk…'

The Chevalier de Suffren draws on his cheroot, taking his time.

'Why did you not tell me last time, at the Cape, that you knew this Barrad Amzer?'

'But I don't know him, Sir.'

'It's all very odd! Yesterday when I mentioned the name to Monsieur de Piveron, it meant nothing to him either. He asked me who he was and told me that he believed he knew the names of all the Frenchmen serving in the Nabob's armies. When I asked Saint-Luperce about it, he told me that his Barrad Amzer commands a small troop of Maratha horsemen. According to him he must have looked like an Indian, and so Monsieur de Piveron could very well have not noticed him amongst the thousands of men gathered permanently at the Nabob's camp. In any case, this morning, after Monsieur de Piveron had left with Lieutenant de Moissac and Lieutenant-Colonel de Canaple, we had a visit from the Governor of Chalembron. Hyder Ali Khan uses the temple as a huge storehouse in which he keeps ammunition, food and grains under the guard of a sizeable garrison. The Governor had been ordered to put himself at our disposal. He was accompanied by two of the Nabob's trusted men, at least that's how they were presented to me. One of them brought us a puzzling message from the no less puzzling Barrad Amzer. This Barrad Amzer had learned that we were coming here and let us know that he was setting out with his troop to reach a discreet meeting place where he would wait for our delegation. He would then escort it to Arcot, where the Nabob had recently set up camp. That's where Moissac and Piveron are heading. Once Barrad Amzer has reached the meeting place he will send a guide to bring our envoys to him. Barrad Amzer's messenger who came with the Governor of Chalembron did not seem to know what was really going on, or at any rate did not seem particularly interested to know. The Comte Duchemin was at the meeting with his interpreter, who also had no reaction. He answers to the sweet name of Rajapa but, strictly between us, I trust him no more than his foot-soldier of a master.'

The Admiral leans back and takes several puffs on his cheroot before continuing. I am hanging on his every word.

'And there, in the middle of their pidgin, I clearly heard them mention the Chevalier de Saint-Luperce, and you too: Ship's Ensign Laforest-Dombourg. You should have seen Saint-Luperce's face! He had understood well enough as he speaks their language fluently and he tried to have me believe I had misheard. But I asked Rajapa, who confirmed it: you really are mixed up in this business!'

The *Fat Caulker* gets up and goes out onto the gallery to have a last pull on his cheroot before throwing it overboard. I try to find an explanation for what I have just heard, but am unable to. Having sat down again, the Chevalier de Suffren turns to me.

'What do you know exactly?'

'I swear, Sir, that this surprises me as much as you, even if it works to my advantage here.'

'Saint-Luperce wanted to get rid of you at any price! Lieutenant de Moissac was right, as usual! It must be the result of these deplorable Court rivalries, about which I know nothing, between the Marquis de Castries and the Comte de Vergennes. I say again, I deplore it, but since that's the way it is, I'm going to play the little Solomon and put an end to all this secrecy!'

The Admiral gets up and goes into his cabin to pull the cord for his bell, which we hear ring in the passageway. When he comes back his steward is already there.

'Have Monsieur Saint-Luperce come here.'

When the latter enters, I watch him for signs of annoyance, but he looks fine. Still the same unconcerned and casual look, the ironic and disdainful little smile at the corner of his mouth when he looks me up and down.

'Gentlemen!' begins the Chevalier de Suffren, with his Provençal accent, 'I well know that you are both zealous servants of the King. Monsieur de Saint-Luperce has acted as his ambassador, successfully, as we know. As for young Laforest-Dombourg, I do not forget his good conduct under fire. Rivalries for which you are not responsible have set you against each other. But we are far from France and we must remain united in the face of the enemy. You are both patriots, so please shake hands like good comrades.'

Saint-Luperce immediately offers his hand to me. I have to admit that I had to force myself to take hold of it.

'That's better!' continues the Chevalier de Suffren. 'This is what I have decided. Saint-Luperce, you will go immediately to Chalembron to wait for Barrad Amzer's envoy. Since you speak their language, you will use the time in getting to know the Nabob's subordinates. Monsieur de Piveron told me that amongst them there are agents in the pay of the English. It would be useful to be able to identify them. It's you who have the key to the chest and you can keep it. I trust Laforest-Dombourg, of course, but he won't need it. As for you, Laforest-Dombourg, as soon as the sea is calm enough to cross the bar without capsizing, you will go ashore with the chest and also wait. I will ask the Comte d'Hoffelize to give you a sergeant and ten riflemen from the Austrasie regiment to protect you and the chest until you leave. I will tell him that it contains piasters to be changed into local rupees. It would of course be safer to keep it on board, but the squadron may have to sail at any moment should the English Admiral put to sea. Unfortunately, I can't ask d'Hoffelize to have the chest escorted all the way to Arcot without first discussing it with Duchemin. That's a pity, as I would be happier if our treasure were escorted by the brave men of the Austrasie rather than by unknown soldiers.'

'Don't worry, Admiral,' Saint-Luperce replies immediately. 'Barrad Amzer has the full confidence of the Comte de Vergennes, as well as mine. His men are Maratha horsemen who have a deserved reputation of being honourable. Barrad Amzer has them well in hand and our diamonds will be safe with him, that I guarantee.'

'I would like to believe you. But why does he not come all the way to Porto Novo so that we can entrust him with the treasure immediately?'

'It would waste time. The road from Porto Novo to the meeting place is safe. The English are contained by Hyder Ali Khan to the north and Tipu Sahib to the south. There is no risk.'

'It's true we cannot provide an escort without first talking to Duchemin.'

He then turns to me.

'Monsieur Laforest-Dombourg, I'm also going to give you personal letters to deliver, one for the Nabob and one for Monsieur de Piveron. I am relying on you each being successful in your missions. I hope that this will put an end to the Comte Duchemin's and his brother Chenneville's nonsense; nonsense which has annoyed Hyder Ali Khan and could cause him to abandon us and seek a treaty with the English behind our back. We would look like idiots: off the coast with no land support!'

9

Wednesday 27th February 1782, former trading post of Porto Novo.

I go ashore the day after our meeting with the Chevalier de Suffren. There is still a big sea running and our Master Pilot, who has long experience of India, advises me to take the ship's boat as close as possible to the bar and then shout for a *masula* boat to come and fetch me. I have my sword at my side and a purse full of louis and ecus strapped under my shirt, so as not to lose it should we capsize; last night a boat from *le Bizarre* got caught beam onto the waves and filled instantly, with two drowned. My main aim at the moment is to reconnoitre the place and make preparations for staying there; I will return aboard *le 'Petit' Annibal* this evening.

In today's sea a European boat would certainly break up if it hit the sandy sill of the bar, but the *masula* boat I board has no framing and is lined by loosely tied planking which is so flexible that the boat simply bends to the waves, robbing them of their force. I admire the skill with which our oarsmen manoeuvre their shapeless boat through the wall of foam. Having ridden the rollers, the *masula* boat weaves between the low sides of the estuary, in what are now calm waters. The little town of Porto Novo appears on my right. It is made up of several long warehouses, low but elegant from a distance, and harmoniously arranged in geometric order amongst the trees.

We pass along a sandy riverbank on which are drawn up several *kattumarams* and reach a jetty where other *masula* boats are tied up, and where a large crowd seems to be awaiting my arrival. I have scarcely put foot ashore when I am surrounded by Indians, many of them half naked, shouting and pushing their way to reach me. I know, as I have been forewarned, that news of our arrival has spread through the countryside, and that many people from Pondicherry, quite destitute and in a state of extreme distress, have hurried *en masse* to Porto Novo, where they are waiting for us as if we were the Messiah.

This should be to my advantage, as it gives me the opportunity to find amongst them a good *dubash* who speaks French. I have read in Doctor Rollins' *Memoir* that in India it is impossible to do anything without a *dubash*. He is a sort of steward and general factotum who, as well as his own language, speaks that of his employer. Hindus in general have such a low opinion of foreigners that it is impossible to trade directly with them. *Dubashes,* on the other hand, will do so as it is one of the privileges of their caste that they can deal with us directly. They profess to be honest and faithful, but have one fault in common, that being that their vanity increases with the quality of the person they serve. They feel better the higher the rank of the person they are attached to and I have to admit that mine is on the modest side, even if my purse is well provided. I am thinking about this as I go ashore, but after a few steps I feel terribly ill. My head starts to spin, and the ground gives way under my feet. I stagger on like a drunken man, searching vainly for somewhere to sit down. Luckily one of the men pressing in around me has the presence of mind to take my arm to help me and takes me, there being no benches to sit on, to a boat pulled up ashore that I can lean against. I realise then that I left Brest in March 1781 and that having been confined on board, it is almost a year to the day since I last set foot on *terra firma.*

The man who of his own accord has taken charge of me, without any ado drives off the crowd, delivering blows left and right with his cane, all the while delivering a discourse which I don't understand but which does the trick, as we are quickly left in peace.

'Would you like me to fetch a doctor?' my rescuer asks in excellent French.

He is between thirty-five and forty, a little taller than me, with a round coppery face and features similar to those of a wealthy bourgeois

European. He is wearing a turban of white muslin bound tightly above his ears from which hang gold rings decorated with rubies. He is sporting magnificent black moustaches, their ends carefully twisted, and is wearing a long-sleeved waistcoat, also white, in gauze muslin, without pockets, and attached by ribbons crossed in front. His legs are covered by breeches of sorts, they also in white.

I hurriedly tell him that it is nothing and will pass. I am just a sailor unused to being on land. I worry above all that he may think I have had too much to drink, as I know that the Indians despise whites who get drunk. I don't know whether he understands me but he seems relieved by this explanation. When I tell him I am looking for a *dubash* he reacts immediately.

'My name is Ana Sami Ranga Pillai. One of my uncles was *dubash* to Dupleix[29] and my father was *dubash* to the India Company. In Pondicherry my family were all *dubashes* before the war.'

I tell him that my father was a captain in the India Company.

'Are you a captain?'

'I'm an Ensign of the King's Ships and have the means to pay you.'

He sighs.

'You are very young, but with times such as they are, I ought not argue. You are the first Navy officer to come ashore too. I come here every day and have no idea whether there will be any other officers needing my services. You seem to be an honest young man and I think we could get along. Do you intend to stay for long?'

'I will be spending several days at Porto Novo then will be travelling for a while inside the country.'

'Well then, you'll need a house, a cook, servants, a palanquin and boys and at least one pawn.'

I ask him what all that means and he explains that a palanquin is a sort of very comfortable bed on which Europeans can travel without getting tired, the boys are the *coolies* who carry it, and the pawn is a kind of herald who runs along in front of the palanquin to clear the way. As I am of modest rank, one will be enough. I reply with a laugh that I would rather travel on horseback than on a bed and that I don't need a herald, but a tough bodyguard capable of fighting off bandits

---

29 Translator's note: *Dupleix:* Joseph François Dupleix (1697 – 1763). At one time Governor-General of the French territories in India.

and tigers if necessary. I also tell my future factotum that I will have considerable baggage to carry and that he'll have to arrange food for the ten soldiers and their sergeant who will be guarding me at Porto Novo before I set out on my journey.

Ranga Pillai replies that he can get me a little Coromandel horse and its tack for a hundred and fifty rupees, a pair of oxen for fifty rupees, a cart to carry the baggage, food for the men and the horse, a cowherd, a Moorish groom, called a *cavaler,* and his assistant, the first to prepare food for the horse at each stop, the second to go foraging. He will enlist a good cook, a woman to carry water, a young servant, called a *rappia,* and will finally seek out the kind of bodyguard I asked for. He calculates that the whole lot will cost two hundred and seventy-seven rupees, including a month's wages for each of my employees. I show him my purse and he chooses thirty louis, rather than ecus, explaining that it would be better to trade the gold pieces for silver rupees. I give him a bit more so as to have a supply of local money. As for the house, it will not cost anything, but will need to be cleaned.

I understand what he means as soon as we enter the town. All the houses, which looked fine from a distance, are deserted, their interiors ravaged by war. Some walls show signs of having been burned, and there is no furniture, no windows; everything has been destroyed or pillaged. The former Danish trading post, a group of buildings forming a square facing the landing stage, has already become our campaign's field hospital. Ranga Pillai takes me to a building further away, deep in woods facing the lagoon and the sea. It is the former French trading post.

Before leaving the *dubash* I ask him to have six leather purses made for me. I give him the size and shape and ask him to have them filled with shells. He asks no questions and shows no surprise, merely proposing, for a few pennies more, to fill the bag with cowries, to which I agree. I ask him how many days he will need and he replies confidently that everything I asked for will be ready by tomorrow.

I am not at all at ease. When Saint-Luperce comes back he could unlock the steel chest at any time and spirit away the diamonds with nobody stopping him. Maybe he already has. I have a sudden idea that I adopt without much reflection: I will steal the diamonds myself and deliver them to Monsieur de Piveron. Although I shook Saint-Luperce's hand in front of the Chevalier de Suffren, I still mistrust Monsieur de Sartine's former agent as much as I ever did. I think again about the 'English spy' at *Les Porcherons*. At the time I thought that Saint-Luperce knew nothing about the treasure and that the fact that Doctor Rollin was to replace him in India did not constitute a strong enough motive to have the doctor assassinated. But I have since learned, to my cost, that Saint-Luperce knew perfectly well that it was a matter of twelve million pounds. Who told him, I do not know. The description given by the waitress at the inn does not correspond to Saint-Luperce, but there is nothing to disprove that they were accomplices.

*

During the following days the strong winds and big seas continued. On the Thursday *l'Orient's* sloop capsized and lost four men trying to cross the bar. For several days it was impossible to go ashore. I made use of the time by polishing the riding boots I had not put on since riding from Versailles to the Bastille. I had to wait until Monday 4th March before being able to take the chest of diamonds safely ashore in *le Héros'* big ship's boat, helped by my escort. I was afraid that Saint-Luperce may already have come back to Porto Novo, but he was still waiting at the Chalembron temple for the emissary from the mysterious Barrad Amzer. He had just sent a message with an Indian to say that he had learned we were waiting for him at the former French trading post, and that we should be ready to leave as soon as he rejoined us. This would be one evening, as at this time of year it was better to travel at night.

The *dubash* had fulfilled his promises. Two white oxen with pointed horns, along with a little grey horse with a groomed coat and hocks were tied up and hobbled in the courtyard. The house had been roughly furnished with adequate matting and some chests. The grooms and cowherd were attending to their animals, and the cook, somehow forewarned, had prepared a meal of excellent fish for me and the Austrasie riflemen.

I had told Ranga Pillai that I did not want a pawn but a true fighter capable of defending me against my enemies and 'against tigers'. The last phrase was no more than a figure of speech, a metaphor appropriate to the country which had fascinated me for so long and which I was now in for the first time. I had only meant that I did not want some mercenary who looked the part and no more, but the *dubash* had taken my words literally and the Indian he had drummed up for me actually introduced himself as a 'tiger hunter'.

This killer of a singular type of big game did not use firearms of any kind. He carried a cutlass with a very wide and very thick blade, honed to razor sharpness. On his left arm he wore a small round shield about six inches in diameter, bound in leather and decorated with leather studs. That was his whole arsenal. He was bare to the waist, his loins covered by no more than cotton drawers that hung down to mid-thigh. Around his head he of course wore the length of cloth wound as a turban, which the Indians never take off. He carried everything else, his food and belongings, in a piece of cloth a couple of yards long, called a *dupatta*. He had dark skin and was not very big but was stocky, with muscular shoulders and torso, and sinewy legs. He went barefoot. His calm and resolute look pleased me immediately. I noticed too a small cross attached to a string around his neck, which also increased my confidence. He told me himself that his name was Thomas Moutou and that he had been raised a Christian at the French Catholic mission at Punganur. I would soon learn that these were the only words of French he knew. Otherwise he spoke Tamil and Telugu, and on a command from Ranga Pillai in the latter language he unrolled his *dupatta* on the ground and pulled out the six leather purses I had ordered. He opened them all so that I could confirm that they were filled with cowries. After he had closed them, I put them away with some show in my old soldier's haversack, which I had brought along especially for this purpose. I was surprised that the *dubash* had not touched the purses. He seemed to have an aversion to leather.

During the morning there was an unpleasant incident to which I should have paid more attention. Hearing shouting near the entrance to the trading post, I went to find out the cause of the disruption and came across my man Thomas Moutou brow-beating a repulsive-looking individual: long-haired, completely naked, penis hanging free, his body caked in ash. Ranga Pillai, he too alerted by the noise, reproached my tiger killer, who went off cursing. The creature then started to talk in an agitated way, pointing at me, then turned on his heels and went off. I asked Ranga Pillai who the miserable fellow was and what he had said. The *dubash* took a while to reply, seemingly embarrassed.

'He is a *sannyasi*, a penitent, a holy man. But I've never seen this one here before. It is true that some of them are fakes, though that is very rare.'

'But he said something about me, didn't he?'

'He said you should abandon your journey and go back to where you came from as quickly as possible, if you don't want to die soon.'

'Do you have a lot of these types here?' I asked.

'You mustn't laugh at these things, Sir. I don't know whether he is one, but we have sorcerers who have real powers, like making somebody ill, or even killing them from a distance. I once saw one kill some chickens just by looking at them!'

I had had the steel chest placed in my room. That same evening, having told the watchman who guarded my door no to let anyone in, I opened it with the key that I had covertly kept. I had hoped, without much belief, that I might find the letter for Monsieur de Souillac and my safe-conduct, just as I had left them, placed on top of the six leather bags I had acquired at Mesquer to hold the diamonds. Instead, I found a square of painted linen that the Marathas call a *chite*, seemingly put there to protect what was underneath. I was going to lift up this piece of cloth when a sudden thought stopped me: why would Saint-Luperce have wanted to protect leather bags inside a locked chest? I studied this piece of Indian fabric more closely before touching it. It had been placed any old how, seemingly at random. The edges of the cloth had been pushed down along the sides of the chest. Looking closely I found that scarcely visible marks had been made on the cloth with a lead pencil, each mark corresponding exactly to the corners of the chest. That reminded me of my mission at Saint-Malo, when spies in the pay of the English had used one of my absences to search my room at the inn; I had discovered it because they had left an unfinished painting on my table in the wrong position; I was painting a lot at the time. Saint-Luperce was not a beginner. His behaviour in Paris, as described in the reports of the policemen who had followed him on the orders of my uncle, showed that he was aware of the methods used by secret agents and spies and that he was a very careful man. He had told Lieutenant de Moissac, I remembered, that he had found on me a copy of the key to the chest held by Captain de Trémigon. Later he had also told everyone that *l'Annibal's* unfortunate Captain held the other copy and that it must have been left on his body when it was consigned to the sea. But apparently Saint-Luperce was not totally sure of this. Somebody else may have got hold of it. One never knows! He hadn't thought it necessary to transfer the treasure into another chest, no doubt as he would no longer be the sole keyholder, but he had all the same thought it a good idea to take some precautions.

Pleased with myself at having discovered Saint-Luperce's little trap, I pulled off the piece of *chite*, to find that my letters were no longer underneath. They had certainly been destroyed as I had thought. On the other hand, the bags of diamonds I had filled at Kermean were all there. I compared them with my bags filled with cowries. They had approximately the same weight and volume, but the bags which had just been made at Porto Novo were cut from freshly tanned leather and were still moist and flexible. They also smelled more strongly than those from Brittany. I carefully emptied the contents of the latter onto an unfolded sheet and stuffed the cowries into the old leather bags, which I then replaced into the chest in the same way they had been. I put the square of Indian cloth back meticulously, exactly as I had found it at the start, and locked the chest. As for the precious diamonds, I put them into the new bags, making sure not to drop any of them. I put everything into my old soldier's haversack, along with the Chevalier de Suffren's letters for Monsieur de Piveron and the Nabob and the rest of the King's travelling money given to me when I left Versailles, some of which I had changed into rupees.

No doubt I ought to have thought about things a little longer before taking this risky course of action. I could have my haversack stolen from me, or lose it. Above all, I risked being accused of attempted theft if Saint-Luperce prematurely discovered the substitution and denounced me. Nobody would believe I intended to deliver them to Hyder Ali Khan as agreed. From now on my fate depended on chance alone; I would not rest easy until we reached the Nabob's camp. I was deliberately putting myself into a delicate position and I knew that I had only myself to blame. I ended up by thinking that if, by misfortune, I fell under suspicion, it would be better if I did not have the copy of the key in my possession. I went and threw it into the sea as soon as I got up the next morning. The dice were cast and there was nothing I could do to alter my plan. That was my then state of mind. Had I been able to read into the future, I may well have thought differently.

In any case, I had made these dispositions just in time, as Saint-Luperce arrived the same evening together with the man sent by Barrad Amzer.

Saint-Luperce was at ease riding a superb bay mount, called a Maratha horse. It was a gift from the Governor of Chalembron, who had also supplied him with three grooms. It needed at least that many to look after such a steed. His companion, the guide sent by Barrad Amzer, was riding a smaller but less highly-strung mount. This wild warrior was sporting a thick beard under his aquiline nose. His eyes were blue and his skin colour almost as light as mine, given that I had been at sea for a long time. He was wearing a sort of wide-sleeved tunic, above which a beige woollen stole was thrown proudly over his shoulder like the toga of a Roman emperor. The strip of cloth forming his turban was sewn together from pieces of different colours and was wrapped around his head with one end hanging down to his waist. A sturdy dagger with an ivory handle and an eight-inch blade was slid under his belt and at his side was a sword. To finish, a large calibre musket with a barrel shorter than the norm was slung across his back.

Seeing him, Ranga Pillai, whom I had told that he was a Maratha horseman, whispered in my ear that he was not at all a Maratha, but a Rohilla from the north of Hindustan.

'The Marathas usually have a spear and a round shield, but he's a Pathan mercenary! Moreover he speaks northern Hindustani. The Marathas have their own language, which is different. And then the Marathas worship Brahma Vishnu and Krishna, but the Rohillas, as we call them here, are Mohammedans.'

Saint-Luperce began by saying that it was too late to set out that night and that we would have to travel by day to get to our rendezvous on time. The meeting place was a former inn a day's march from Porto Novo. I forewarned the *dubash* to be ready to leave at dawn and went back to find Saint-Luperce opening the chest with his key. Seeing that, my heart jumped and I felt faint. Luckily his back was to me and he did not notice. I saw him lift the lid and look under it closely. Satisfied by what he saw, or perhaps bothered by my presence, he closed it immediately and relocked it before turning to me.

'Do you still intend to come with us?'

'That's what the Chevalier de Suffren ordered, isn't it?'

'He didn't really define your role and I think you have mostly fulfilled it by looking after the chest while I was away. In your place I would go back on board.'

'I'm very sorry but I don't think that is what the Chevalier de Suffren intended.'

'As you wish. You won't be able to say that you weren't warned!'

This sounded strangely like a warning and made me think of the one the *sannyasi* had already given me that same morning. It worried me so much that I began to regret having taken the diamonds out of the steel chest and above all, having thrown away the key. In any case, on account of that, I had no choice but to carry on.

We were ready to leave at daybreak the following morning. The wind had gone round to the west. This land breeze was weaker than the usual north-easterly off the sea at the end of the monsoon, but it was a scorching wind. Ranga Pillai came to say it was unwise to travel in this furnace and Saint-Luperce agreed. Even his redoubtable Pathan had no objection. Luckily the sea breeze came up at about ten in the morning and our little caravan was able to get under way.

As we left Porto Novo a group of men and women came to join our procession. These were the friends, mothers, brothers and cousins of our servants. Ranga Pillai introduced me to his wife, who I thought was young and pretty. Everyone was going to accompany us on our expedition; apparently this is the custom in India. I shared with Saint-Luperce my discomfort at these unforeseen reinforcements. He too seemed annoyed but eventually decided to let them do as they wished, adding that we had no responsibility for them and that they were free to come and go. I think now that later he would deeply regret this. He wasn't so bad. Only Thomas Moutou and my groom were unmarried. All these poor folk thought that they were going to escape their daily misery for a while and were so happy! My heart bleeds when I think about them.

Saint-Luperce was riding ahead with his Rohilla guide, while I followed on my little Coromandel horse. It was a pleasant mount and quite docile, although a stallion. It reminded me of our Breton hacks, and was elegant too. Unfortunately, I was not going to have the chance to get to know it well. My groom walked beside me. Being a *cavaler* is the most prized job amongst servants. His role is to wash the horse, care for it and exercise it. He must also be a good runner as it is supposed to be a point of honour never to let the horse out of his sight, even when its owner takes it into battle. The *cavalers* are honest and faithful, and mine did not deviate from this rule: he had been looking after his horse for three years. Thomas Moutou and the *pallegara*, as the assistant grooms are called, walked behind me. Then came the cart, on which the *dubash* and his wife were sitting alongside the cart driver. This cart, which carried the chest, our baggage, our tools and provisions, was drawn by the two oxen that Ranga Pillai had bought for me. They had a collar on their shoulders to which was attached the yoke, and they usually went at a trot, and were as dashing and alert as horses. The driver controlled them from his seat by means of a rope passed through their nostrils. The women and families of our servants carried up the rear, bearing baskets on their heads.

I was carrying the haversack with its precious cargo on my back and was soaked in sweat. Seeing this, Thomas, who of course thought it contained inexpensive cowries, ran up alongside me and indicated that he wanted to carry it for me, to relieve me of the burden. He was already carrying an earthen pot on his shoulder, his *dupatta* containing his provisions, a leather bag I had not seen before, and his strange shield. At first I refused but he made so much noise that Saint-Luperce turned in his saddle to see what was going on, so I handed over my load in order not to raise the latter's suspicions.

Going by the sun, we were moving to the north-west. The countryside was flat, with little vegetation apart from some hedges and bushes. Everything was wilting under the sun, despite the easterly wind. It was the time of year when the Carnatic was at its driest. From time to time we crossed dried up river beds. As long as we were still close to the coast, there was a little water in these fords, but it had come in with the high tide and was brackish. After that there were just a few stagnant pools in the hollows of these meandering watercourses which could turn to raging torrents as soon as it rained. I could nonetheless see a number of artificial ponds held in by dykes built by an industrious people so that they could have the water necessary for cultivation for the whole year, especially for that of rice, which is the daily bread of the inhabitants of this part of India.

I could see all around me fields laid out and worked by hand, but they all seemed abandoned; the countryside looked desolate and empty, with no animals. I only saw vultures circling here and there in the sky and, once, a huge snake at least ten feet long, with a dark grey back and a dirty white stomach. It was coiled up by a roadside bush and seeing us arrive, lifted its head a foot and a half high, inflating its neck. Our procession gave it a respectfully wide berth. Ranga Pillai said simply that it was a *nagapambu*[30].

Eventually I asked the *dubash* how the country had been so laid to waste.

'It's Hyder Ali Khan,' he replied. 'The harvests have been cut down while still green to feed his horses, the grain stores pillaged to feed the thousands of people following his army, the villagers and animals which have not been killed have been deported to Mysore, which belongs to him. Everything else had been burned down or destroyed to stop his enemies benefitting from it. There is now famine everywhere in what is a rich and prosperous country. From Madras to Pondicherry you'll only see dead or dying.'

The only woods we could see were those planted by man to shade the villages, called *toppoos* by the Carnatic Indians and *taupes* by the Europeans. These *toppoos* were mainly made up of two kinds of tree: tamarinds, whose fruit is used by the Indians to make a sauce for their ragouts, and another very strange tree that I saw for the first time, whose branches stretching out from around the trunk planted themselves in the ground again, creating columns under its thick canopy. My *dubash* told me this tree was an *aalamaram*[31].

These villages, which in India are called *aldeias*, from a Portuguese word, were all abandoned, their roofs burnt. All that remained were ruined earthen walls, blackened by fire; the only inhabitants were monkeys, jackals and snakes.

Night had long since fallen when we arrived at the inn, called a *chaudhury*, where we were to wait for Barrad Amzer and his escort. These *chaudhuries* are a kind of hostelry for travellers, founded by rich donors as an act of charity. They are everywhere in India and always built near a pond or well in the middle of a small wood. Usually they are looked after by an Indian paid for by the donor of the *chaudhury* but, like everything else here, this one was abandoned, although it had not been destroyed, having extremely thick walls. The main building was divided into small, vaulted sections inside which we arranged ourselves. Torches were lit; Saint-Luperce and I had the use of a lantern made of tin, with a yellow wax candle, that I had borrowed from *le Petit Annibal's* Master Gunner.

---

30 Cobra

31 Banyan.

While my cook prepared supper I went to look for my tiger hunter, having lost sight of him in the darkness when we arrived. This was especially worrying given that on his back he was unwittingly carrying the equivalent of twelve million pounds worth of diamonds. I saw women coming and going with pots that they were filling in a nearby pond. They had lit little fires everywhere outside the building to cook rice. The *chaudhury* was built in the middle of a wood and the shimmering light from all the fires played on the trunks rising from the ground. One could have been in a church lit by candles. But as for Thomas Moutou – no sign!

I went towards the oxen and horses which I could see in the torchlight in the middle of the wood. Our two horses were each tied to two stakes with a long rope around their necks and their back legs hobbled. The Indians did not use head stalls. My *cavaler* was cooking a kind of lentil that is used in place of oats in this country. I tried with gestures to ask him if he knew where my bodyguard had gone, but without success. As a last resort I looked in all the rooms of the *chaudhury*, and ended up finding my *dubash*.

'Moutou?' he replied. 'I sent him to sleep outside. I even forbade him to sleep in the woods surrounding us, as it is too close to us.'

'But by what right?' I asked, indignant.

'He has no caste, Sir – a *dalita!* Even though I admit he is clean and does not smell, unlike other *pariahs,* I cannot allow him to stay here. Everyone would be angry with me.'

I did not insist. Having read Doctor Rollin's *Memoir,* I knew the importance of the caste system in India. I returned to the room where mats had been laid down for Saint-Luperce and me. As I arrived, I could hear him talking in Tamil to my cook. He did not sound in a good mood.

'Ah, there you are! Where have you been? I'm dying of hunger. I've not eaten today, and your stupid cook was refusing to serve me until you got here.'

The cook brought us rice with a spicy local sauce. Saint-Luperce had asked him to make tea for us. At first, we ate in silence. I was too taken up with the thought of Thomas Moutou wandering about in the wilds with my haversack to want to talk about anything.

'You should not have come!' Saint-Luperce said suddenly.

'Why not?'

He shrugged without answering, not looking at me. He seemed nervous, even worried. Was it because he was concerned about his next meeting with Hyder Ali Khan? I knew that he had lied to everybody in maintaining that he was on good terms with the Nabob. And who was this Barrad Amzer, who seemed to know me but whom I did not know? When we were being questioned at Simon's Bay, Saint-Luperce had said that he had known him in India, at Pondicherry, with Lally-Tollendal, and also at Poona, and that he was an agent of the Comte de Vergennes. According to the Chevalier de Suffren, he had seemed surprised to learn that my name had been mentioned in the letter from Barrad Amzer and had immediately tried to push me aside. But why? What element of truth was there in everything he had said right from the beginning?

'You told the Chevalier de Suffren that the escort provided by Barrad Amzer would be made up of Maratha horsemen,' I said.

'Yes…and so what?'

'Well, our guide is not a Maratha. He's a Rohilla.'

'Did you find that out all by yourself?'

'My *dubash* told me.'

'He's correct. What difference does it make?'

I had to admit that I had no answer to that. Nonetheless, I had the very clear impression that this was a delicate subject that unnerved Saint-Luperce. He had always maintained to everybody that his agent would come to escort us with Maratha horsemen. We knew nothing about it and he had no reason to lie to us about it. And there we were with a Pathan! That was perhaps what was worrying him, and he did not dare let me see his disquiet. I lay down in my mat. I had put my saddle at the top to act as a pillow and also to have the two pistols in the saddle bags close to hand. I checked the powder charges in the breeches before stretching out. I had decided to sleep fully dressed, my boots on and my sword at my side. I had tried in vain to convince myself that Saint-Luperce had merely wanted to frighten me. His repeated warnings, following on from the incident with the holy man the day before, were concerning me. Before going to bed, my roommate went out with the lantern and put it down, still lit, outside the door, so that it would attract the mosquitoes and keep them outside.

I had thought that the Indians would be keen to get some sleep after the tiring journey, but that wasn't the case: they stayed awake. I could hear them chatting, laughing and even singing until midnight. I had trouble getting to sleep. I was thinking about Thomas and was praying that he had not made off with the diamonds. I had read that the *pariahs* were the lowest of the low in India. If I had known he was one of them I would certainly not have entrusted my precious haversack to him.

*

Inland in the Carnatic, a day's journey to the north-west of Porto Novo, Thursday 7ᵗʰ March 1782.

I have finally fallen asleep, despite all my worries, and am woken by a noise that seems to interrupt my slumber. I think it is a horse neighing. I lift myself up on an elbow to listen. Saint-Luperce is sleeping soundly. All seems calm. I begin to wonder whether I have been dreaming, when I clearly hear our horses snorting outside. I tell myself that perhaps there are jackals hanging around our animals and that my trusty *cavaler* will get up and chase them off, but it starts again. I stand up, wondering whether to take my sword to stab the jackals, but I leave it, thinking it will be better to try to frighten them or throw stones at them; I have heard that there is rabies in the area and I don't want to take the risk of being bitten.

Everyone is asleep in the *chaudhury,* and the night is dark. We are at the last quarter of the moon and the celestial vault is party hidden by the foliage of the *toppoo.* The line of the horizon is clearly visible to the east, heralding the dawn behind it, and this weak light is enough for me to find my way. I go through the trees to the spot where I saw our horses yesterday. I had not realised that this wood is composed of a single giant *aalamaram.* It is decidedly cooler than at Porto Novo and there is a lot of dew, soaking my boots.

I reach the horses, who seem nervous. Moving closer to them I stumble against a body lying on the ground. Alarmed, I get down on my knees and recognise my *cavaler,* lying on his stomach. If I did not know that Hindus do not touch alcohol I would think that he is dead drunk. I turn him over and lift him by the shoulders. His head falls back in a strange way. It is still too dark to see properly what the matter is, but when I lean closer to have a better look my heart jumps: his throat is slit from ear to ear. He is still warm and hot blood is running over my hands. His heart has stopped beating and there is nothing I can do for him. I turn round to go back to the *chaudhury,* with a single thought in my head – to retrieve my pistols and my sword. I have completely forgotten Thomas and the diamonds.

'Halt!'

A massive figure stands silhouetted against the crescent of light from the east. I can make out the barrel of a musket aimed at my chest and I hear clearly the sound of a gun being cocked. Other shadows appear in front of me, barring my path to the *chaudhury*. My assailants are big, bearded, their turbans like pumpkins in the dawn light. They are draped in woollen shawls – Pathans!

'Laforest-Dombourg! You have forgotten me, I would wager. It is a great pleasure to see you again after all this time.'

That hoarse voice! I would like to think I am still in my usual nightmare, but the blood of my brave *cavaler* sticking to my hands tells me I am fully awake. I recognise this huge body, the mighty shoulders, the light but implacable carriage. He is dressed like an Indian, with a dark blue sleeveless tunic falling to his knees and split for horse riding. On his head is a white turban. His fine face, that of a hero of antiquity, as handsome as his soul is black, is now wound in a leather band that covers his left eye, but it is him alright! Flaharn! I cannot believe it. My nightmare has become real. How is it possible? By what magic is he now in India? I thought he was either dead or in the Americas, at the other end of the earth.

'I only had one fear, d'you see? That you would not come! I'm going to get my diamonds back but my pleasure would not have been complete without making you pay for everything you have made me suffer. That's the only reason I mentioned you in my message.'

His message? So he's Barrad Amzer?

The sun rises. I hear women screaming inside the *chaudhury*. The Pathans round up my Indians in front of the building, beating them with sticks. Only the men are there. Poor Ranga Pillai's face is covered in bruises and somebody has already ripped off his ruby earrings. Flaharn gives an order in Hindustani and his mercenaries, or at least those not busy with the women inside, line up in front of their prisoners and load their muskets. Saint-Luperce, who speaks Hindustani, has understood.

'Declercq! For the love of God, don't do that! Let these poor men go! They are only servants!'

The noise of the shots makes me jump and drowns out Saint-Luperce's voice. The executioners move forward and finish off their victims with their daggers. Several Indians have escaped the salvo and try to flee, but five or six Rohillas jump on their horses and set off after them, sabres at the ready.

'You would have preferred them to go to Porto Novo to warn the French? That they alert your great friend Hyder Ali Khan, so that he cancels our passes?' says Flaharn in a mocking tone. 'We have the whole of Mysore to cross. The dead do not speak!'

'But – we are no longer going to Madras?'

'Why Madras? You really thought I was going to give my diamonds to the English?'

Flaharn bursts out laughing and turns to me. He is still holding me at gunpoint.

'As for you, my little friend, you will envy that lot their fate. My good man Babar Khan will take special care of you. He will kill you slowly by the end of the day. He's even better at that than Jakar, curse him!'

He points to a Pathan at his side. It is our guide from yesterday. I have the impression that Saint-Luperce is not happy at these words. He gives me a sad look, reproaching me for not having taken heed of his warnings. At heart he is not so bad; compared to Flaharn he is just a choirboy.

'Come with me and I'll show you the diamonds,' says our choirboy, no doubt with the worthy aim of buying me some time.

'Ah yes! My diamonds! If you knew how long I have been chasing after them!'

Flaharn gives another order to his men and follows Saint-Luperce into the *chaudhury.* I am pushed to the ground by iron fists and my hands and feet tied together by leather lanyards tightened behind me. Rohilla warriors come out of the building and replace their comrades, who in their turn go inside. The women's screams start again, even louder, but are eclipsed by a huge roar coming from the room in which I have spent the night. I can easily guess what has happened: Saint-Luperce has opened the steel chest and they have found what is inside. Despite the horror of my situation, I cannot help smiling, especially when I hear Saint-Luperce being called a scheming bastard and a string of other names. Flaharn comes out with Saint-Luperce at his heels and strides towards me.

'It's him, I'm sure of it! You've been had, Saint-Luperce! I told you not to trust him! It's because of him I lost my eye!'

He delivers a few angry kicks at me which lift me off the ground and have me crying out in pain.

'But how could he have opened the chest? I took his key!'

'He had another one! You don't know him! I want it found right now!'

He gives his men another order. My bindings are cut, my boots pulled off, along with my breeches and all my clothes. I am left naked as the day I was born. Flaharn flings my clothes at Saint-Luperce.

'Search that lot well! I'm sure you'll find the other key!'

'But what's the use of finding it? It's the diamonds we want!'

'Do what I tell you! I want it back! I'll deal with the diamonds. I'm sure he knows where they are and he'll soon tell me, don't you worry!'

He gives another order in Hindustani and two Pathans climb onto the cart that came with us from Porto Novo. They get down again with spades and head out of the *toppoo.* Flaharn and I follow him, or rather Flaharn follows them while two of his men drag me brutally behind him. We leave Saint-Luperce on all fours searching through my clothes. I have the impression that he was not expecting this and that it is all too much for him.

We come out of the edge of the *toppoo* into the sunlight. The sky is blue and the sun is already high over the horizon to my right. I am as naked as the holy man at Porto Novo whose warnings I had made fun of, and am trembling like a leaf, though not from cold.

The day is already warming up. The dew has dried on the grass and on the bushes of the flat savannah that stretches before us. I can see the edge of another wood about half a mile to the north. It is not a *toppoo* but the green beginnings of a real forest. The road towards it is scattered with little groves of coconut palms and thick bamboo. I think to myself that I will never get as far as the edge of the woods and will never know what an Indian forest is like. I will die here and, according to Flaharn, will suffer before I do. If I were able, I would kill myself now, without hesitation, just as Avelus de Kersalaun had done at the Brest jail, even if it is unworthy of a Christian. The idea of pain frightens me more than death.

The two Rohillas are digging. It can only be for me. I begin to hope that my end will be quicker than I thought. When the hole is finished, the two giants who brought me here lift me up, carry me over the pit and drop me in it. They hold me firmly while their companions shovel earth around me. Their grip hurts me. I am soon completely buried apart from my head, which I can't even turn. They have buried me facing north. They pile in the earth carelessly and the iron of the spades hits my forehead and ears several times. Flaharn leans down to me.

'Listen well, Laforest-Dombourg. If you tell me where my diamonds are, I will free you and let you leave.'

I don't believe a word of it. As soon as I have told him he will kill me. I close my eyes, saying nothing.

'Just as stubborn as ever! Well then, if that's how you want it! Here's what I propose: I will give you two hours to think about it. If by then you don't want to help me, Babar Khan will take out your left eye with his dagger. That will make things even between us. I'll then give you another two hours and he will take care of your right eye. If that is not enough, the ants will come to busy themselves with the holes where your eyes were, and then you will beg me to finish you off. I have plenty of time.'

He goes off, or rather disappears from my view. I cannot keep watching him as my head is locked by the earth which imprisons me. I can see nothing but the unreachable edge of the forest and the pure sky. I think of Maria. Will she ever know how I died? Will she be told that I disappeared like a miserable wretch in the depths of India? Will my memory be sullied by accusations of having stolen the diamonds? I regret not having been killed at the Battle of Porto Praya. It was all so simple in *l'Annibal's* orlop: I had accepted my fate.

I hear heavy footsteps, those of the mercenary left to guard me. He walks in front of me and stops to consider the countryside. He is as wide as he is tall, with huge calves and big bare feet in leather sandals. He is carrying a musket on a sling over his right shoulder and his woollen Pathan shawl is rolled on his left shoulder. He turns round. His pumpkin-shaped turban presses down on his thick eyebrows and his jet-black beard spreads from under his nose like the blade of a knife. I cannot see his eyes. A kind of grimace pushes up his moustache and displays his teeth, as if something has suddenly amused him. I look at the dagger stuck in his cloth belt: a long blade, pointed, narrow and thick. Is that what they're going to gouge my eye out with? When Flaharn returns I will tell him that Thomas Moutou has the diamonds. They haven't found him. I hope that he is now far away and that they will never catch him. Flaharn will be furious and perhaps will kill me straight away. All that remains is for me to pray and ask God to forgive me for having ignored Him when things were going well for me.

My guard walks behind me and I have the impression that he has stopped behind my back. I wonder what he is up to. A stream of hot liquid hits the back of my head sharply and my torturer bursts out laughing. His laughter suddenly transforms to a groan and at the same time I hear a thud similar to that of a meat chopper hitting a quarter of beef. The Pathan's body falls down on my head. I can no longer breathe. Somebody pulls aside the heavy weight which is suffocating me. It is Thomas Moutou. He lays his bloody cutlass on the ground and gets hold of the spade the diggers have left. His movements are precise and powerful and his face impassive. I wonder how he can be so calm while Flaharn and his gang are close by and could come at any moment without warning.

The Pathan's body is lying on its stomach. His back has been completely split open by the terrible blow dealt by Moutou. The sight is so awful I start to vomit. While I try to get my stiffened and paralysed limbs moving again, Moutou grabs the Pathan's sandals and shawl and hands them to me. He then goes to get his things left at the edge of the *toppoo*. I try to lift the body as I would like to have his dagger and rifle, but when Moutou returns he hands me the soldier's haversack, takes my hand and pulls me after him. He is right; we must not stay here. Flaharn and his henchmen could arrive at any moment. We must run as fast as possible to the edge of the forest I had seen, to hide ourselves. Instead of that, my saviour pulls me towards a wide flat field a short way from the *toppoo* and the dyke holding the pond for the *chaudhury*.

'*Nelloo*,' he says in a low voice. We are in a rice paddy dried out for the harvest. The area is covered with stalks of rice straw lying flat. Thomas stops in the middle of the field. We are clearly visible and close to the *chaudhury*. I wonder whether he has gone mad. He makes a space in the straw by running his palm over the bare, slippery earth and signals me to lie down. He covers me with the yellow shawl taken from the Pathan and I hear him throw armfuls of straw over it. He then slides under the shawl beside me and we remain there motionless. Just in time! Angry shouts tell us that the Rohillas have found the body of their companion beside the empty pit. Some minutes later we hear the thunder of many hooves on the dry earth. Gently raising an edge of the shawl I see the Rohilla horsemen galloping off along the track that leads north. The troop divides into two. The half commanded by Flaharn plunges straight into the forest while the others start to search the groves one by one. I admire the wisdom of my guardian angel: we would have been caught immediately had we tried to escape that way.

It is now getting very hot and I am sweating under the woollen cover, my perspiration mixing with that of my saviour. To that is added the disgusting smell of urine emanating from my hair, but it is that which has saved my life: I will learn later that Moutou had spent a long time hidden in the branches of the *aalamaram* waiting for the opportune moment to attack my guard. It was only when the latter had relaxed his vigilance in order to urinate on me that my tiger killer had been able to use the moment to even the score.

We stay thus until the evening, not daring to move. The heat between the woollen shawl and the scorching earth becomes unbearable in the middle of the day. I have not seen Saint-Luperce leave. He is still there and has kept some Pathans with him. We have a close call when they bring their horses and mine to the pond to drink, not far from our hiding place. I scarcely dare breathe. If they find us Thomas cannot do much with his cutlass, against their rifles.

When they light their fires at nightfall we stand up so as to slip away while their eyes are still dazzled by the glare from the fires, but the sound of horses coming from the north forces us to throw ourselves down again. Flaharn and his men have returned emptyhanded from their manhunt. They stop at the edge of the *toppoo* and I hear Flaharn giving orders to his men in a loud voice. Thomas must have understood what he said as he grabs me by the arm and squeezes it hard, signalling me to get up. Behind us I can hear the horsemen dismount. They are leading their horses by their bridles towards the pond, cutting across the rice paddy straight towards the spot where we have been lying just a few moments ago. We make off towards the other side of the field. I have a strong urge to run but that would be the last thing to do. Luckily there is not much moon and the stamping of the horses stops the Rohillas from hearing us.

*

We walked for hours in the darkness without stopping. At first we went straight across the countryside, before Thomas picked up a track heading west, as far as I could tell from the stars. He seemed tireless. I clung on to my haversack, which he had taken back to put on his back along with his bundle. I was so exhausted from the stresses of the day and the bad night before that I think I fell fully asleep, pulled along by him and not stopping walking. After a period of time I had no means of measuring, he eventually consented to stop and I fell to the ground. I rolled myself up in the woollen shawl, dirty and smelly as it was, got my haversack back from my saviour and put it under my head before falling into a deep sleep.

I dreamed that I had scabies and that my whole skin was irritated by a painful itching. When I awoke the impression persisted and lifting my blanket I found that my naked body was covered in ants. I leapt up to brush them off. I thought that I had been lucky that this had not happened the day before, but then reflected that the soil of the dried up rice paddy had been too hot during the day and too hard, whereas now it was probably the warmth of my body on the cold earth which had attracted the insects.

The sun rose and Thomas Moutou, squatting on his haunches beside me, watched me wordlessly, his dark face still as impassive. Clothed in the single piece of cloth around his loins, he seemed insensible to the dew and cold of the dawn. I wondered how he had managed to sleep. He held out his gourd and I realised that I had not drunk or eaten for twenty-four hours. The water was cool. He let me drink and after I had handed back the gourd he brought something out of his *dupatta*. I thought at first it was a half round of Dutch cheese but turned out to be a kind of loaf, although not made from wheat or corn flour. He pulled off two pieces and handed me one.

'*Keveroo,*' he said.

It had an insipid taste which reminded me of cinders or sawdust, but I was too hungry to complain. He got up and I followed him without a word. What else could I do? I was totally naked, hungry despite the *keveroo*; my dirty hair, dusty and saturated with urine, was falling in a dishevelled mass on my shoulders and in front of my eyes. I was conscious of the fact that my appearance must have been as repulsive as that of the holy man I had seen at Porto Novo. I did not know where we were going, I was lost with no interpreter in a country I did not know and whose language I did not know. I was as destitute as Job while carrying on my back a fortune capable of provoking every kind of greed.

Moutou took the dusty track that we had followed during the night. The day grew hotter as the sun rose in the sky. The heat, at first pleasant after the dawn coolness, gradually became overpowering. We were walking west across a wide plain covered with dried grasses and clumps of sparse bushes surrounding groves of coconut trees and palms. The horizon in front of us was barred by the peaks of a chain of mountains that had not been visible the day before.

Towards midmorning we reached a cultivated area that seemed to have been spared the war. Stacks of carefully arranged stalks stood in the middle of the fields to protect the last harvest. The path passed beside a pond held in by a dyke. I immediately stopped and with signs made it known to Moutou that I wanted to dive into the water to wash myself. He nodded his head in agreement, then suddenly changed his mind, his face darkening. He pointed out a cloud of dust rising above the track behind us and we ran to hide in the nearest grove. I was about to throw myself to the ground but my guide, ever watchful, held me back and with his cutlass cut in half a nasty little viper scarcely more than a foot long and perfectly invisible in the grass, except to a practised eye like that of my bodyguard.

'*Viriampambu!*' he said, indicating that we could now lie down with no fears.

We were just in time. I could now hear the characteristic sound of a troop of riders arriving at a canter: Flaharn and his band of mercenaries. They passed in front of us without stopping, thank God. I counted about thirty of them. Flaharn and Saint-Luperce were riding at the head of the column. Two horses without riders, one of which was mine, were held by bridles at the rear. I wondered what had happened to the oxen. Once they were far enough away, Moutou stood up at the edge of the grove to keep watching them. They were heading to a big village quite close by, which I had not yet had time to spot. This village, or small town, was surrounded by a low earthen rampart with no ditch. The houses inside must have been of modest size, as from where we were only a central tower and the portico of a little temple were visible. The settlement was built at the crossroads formed by the intersection of the track we had been following and a bigger road running from south-west to north-east. I could not see all the gates to the town, but there must have been at least one for each of the roads, or tracks, arriving there.

The sudden appearance of a group of mercenaries spread panic amongst the people of this peaceful area as, despite the distance, we could see men and women running from several directions to take refuge in the town, whose gates were shut just before Flaharn arrived there. We saw him advance alone on horseback to the east gate, to parley with the guards. He must have used convincing arguments as the heavy wooden doors were eventually opened for him and his band of assassins.

We waited for a long time, hidden in the edge of the grove. Moutou seemed annoyed. Eventually, after two or three hours, the Rohillas and their chiefs came out by the north-east gate and disappeared at a canter in that direction.

'*Gingee!*' said my companion, indicating the road taken by the Rohillas. '*Caadam anjoo!*' he added. Or at least that is what I think he said.

I had in any case recognised the name Gingee, a place long ago fortified by the Marquis de Bussy when he was in India during the preceding wars. As far as I knew, this fortress had since been occupied by Hyder Ali Khan's troops. Flaharn and his men seemed to have decided to go back up north, perhaps to rejoin the Nabob's army, to which they were attached. I knew Flaharn too well to believe that he had given up on 'his' treasure. Saint-Luperce must have told him that Thomas Moutou had escaped the massacre and that it was probably he who had rescued me. Flaharn was aware, given how well he knew me, that I would try to fully complete my mission by taking the diamonds to Hyder Ali Khan. He had therefore thought it better to await my eventual arrival at the Nabob's camp rather than to try to find me in the vast Indian countryside.

Moutou pointed to the town and had me understand that he was going there and that I should wait for him. I held him back and got some rupees out of my bag. Showing him my naked body, I indicated that I wanted him to buy some clothes for me to give me a more decent appearance. He seemed to understand what I was trying to tell him. After he had gone, I swam for a long time in the pond and washed the woollen shawl which had served me so well. I then went and sat on the dyke to dry off, naked as a new-born baby, and waited for my guardian angel to return.

There was nobody about. Flaharn and his nightmare band were already far away. I felt better for having bathed myself. The piece of *keveroo* bread, as Moutou had called it, tasteless as it was, had eased my hunger. I could now start to put my thoughts in order after the terrible time I had just had. I now knew how Saint-Luperce had known about the existence of the diamonds and how he had been able to guess that they were in my charge. It was Flaharn, of course, who had told him all that, and not the Comte de Vergennes or somebody in his Ministry, as I had mistakenly thought. Despite my precarious position, I was greatly relieved to know that there were no traitors in my King's entourage. But how had Flaharn and Saint-Luperce managed to meet, given that the latter had been imprisoned in the Bastille after returning to France after several years in India, while the former had stayed in the Americas? In fact, I had already heard a part answer to this question, from the lips of Saint-Luperce himself, but I was still too disturbed by the memory of the dangers from which I had just escaped to be able to reason things out properly.

When he returned, Thomas Moutou began by pointing at the town and delivering a lively speech. I did not understand a word, but judging by his sign language, he was strongly advising me not to go there as it would be dangerous for me. He then pulled out from his bundle some things which he had bought for me. Firstly, there was a sort of waistcoat with long sleeves, of the same kind worn by the unfortunate Ranga Pillai, but in plain cotton. Once I had put this on, he showed me a long piece of cloth of the same material, for covering the lower body, which he helped me arrange in the Indian style. It is wrapped around the waist underneath the waistcoat, then one of the ends is brought between the legs to the front, while the other is tucked in behind. The result is that one thigh is entirely covered, and even part of the leg, while the other is only half covered. Finally, he took on the job of creating a turban for me, from a piece of muslin about thirty feet long and half a foot wide. Having knotted the two corners of one end around my head like a sort of skull cap, he wound it around, sometimes horizontally, sometimes diagonally, all the while taking care to keep my hair tight underneath. Once he had finished, he stepped back to consider his work, with evident satisfaction; with my sea-going tan I must have looked like a real Indian.

My companion then began a new speech, in a calmer tone than before, finishing with these words: '…Abbot Perrin, Punganur, French Catholic Mission'.

'Punganur?' I asked.

He pointed to the north-west.

'*Punganur, caadam, naappadu!*'

I took it from this that Punganur must be in that direction, at an unknown distance, but that it must be important and my companion was prepared to lead me there. I had no way of calculating how long it would take for us to get there, but I at least had the assurance of finding there a missionary priest who could interpret for me and give me some information. In any case, my only other choice was to try to return to Porto Novo, which perhaps was closer, but where there may now be nobody left.

10

Our journey was to be long and hard.

We started out heading west, although Thomas Moutou had indicated that Punganur was to the north-west. I had no idea where we were going, nor was my guide able to tell me, as we had no common language. As long as we were on the plain, we walked at night and slept during the day. Moutou kept well clear of the towns and villages, only approaching them to buy food, and even then the strict minimum: a pound or two of cooked rice that he wrapped up in a corner of his *dupatta,* and some salt. However, like all the *pariahs,* he was not vegetarian, fortunately for me, and he enhanced our usual diet with a kind of fairly tame pigeon, abundant in the woods, that he caught cleverly with a small net. These birds, about the size of one of our thrushes, and apple green, were so tender that they could be cooked easily on a simple fire of twigs or straw lit beside the track.

I realised quickly enough that Moutou was doing his best to avoid any meeting with the people of the country. So we always slept outside under the stars. I thought at first that it was because of his status as a *pariah,* a caste rejected by all the other castes, and I thought that, as I was travelling with him, I too ought to pass myself off as a *pariah* in the eyes of others. But it was more than that: whenever he had no choice but to go into a town, he always left me in a discreet spot out in the countryside, where he told me to wait.

'*Aabattana,*' he would repeat, raising his arms to the sky, if I tried to follow him. He never let me go with him. I also noticed that from then on he left his big cutlass and his shield before leaving me, but always kept his mysterious leather bag with him.

After some time, however, I contracted a bout of dysentery, forcing Moutou to find a roof under which he could care for me. He took me to some *pariahs* he knew in a little hamlet of mud cottages built at a respectful distance from the nearest village. The *pariahs* do not have the right to live too close to other Indians, who consider their proximity a bigger stain the higher their own caste. I have even seen that *pariahs* have to cover their mouths with their hand when passing noble people, as if their breath risked poisoning them.

These fine folk installed me in their little house and went to sleep outside so as not to disturb me. I was lying on a plank in a small windowless room which during the day was lit only by the sunlight coming in through the door. But I was safe from the dew which is very heavy in this part of India. Moutou stopped me from eating, forcing me to drink rice water the whole time. After three or four days of this diet, or maybe five or six – I don't really know – the sickness went and I was able to start eating more solid food to build my strength before leaving.

Once we had reached the mountains called the Eastern Ghats, towards which we had been walking for what seemed like an eternity, Moutou kept well clear of the roads and passes which are most used, and the easiest. Instead, we constantly wound our way up and down rocky paths and along the edge of steep cliffs where the smallest misstep would have us falling into oblivion. This meant we had to travel by day, in order to see more clearly, and light a fire at night to keep away wild animals and snakes. This, alas, did not protect us from ants! The temperature was relatively pleasant but by dawn we were always soaked by the morning dew, as if we had slept in a bath. We were advancing too slowly for my guide's taste, who often had to stop to wait for me.

We passed through forests resounding with the cries of monkeys, where the bamboo trunks were as thick as our poplars and birches, and where the undergrowth was thick with bushes whose sharp thorns tore our clothes and stayed embedded in our skin until evening. We then reached the Deccan plateau and Moutou turned north. I had long since lost count of the weeks and even had no idea what month it was, but looking up I could see more and more cloud along with the south-west monsoon.

One fine day, towards midday, with the sun at its zenith behind a screen of grey cloud, we reached a fortified town set on a plain surrounded by hills and mountains.

'Punganur!' said my companion.

Since morning we had passed through several heavily inhabited and lively *aldeias,* and had seen the countryfolk trampling the mud in fields which had been flooded to prepare for the rice planting. Carts loaded with sugar cane were going to and fro on the roads, pulled at a trot by the agile Indian oxen. This land had been spared the war whose damage I had witnessed while crossing the Carnatic.

The crenelated ramparts of Punganur were composed of a number of round towers set at regular intervals. It all seemed well built and of recent construction. We entered through a gate carved in a somewhat Gothic style and guarded by soldiers carrying spears and ancient flintlock muskets. They looked easy-going and seemed happy just to watch those going past without checking them. There was no tollgate here as at Paris: the authorities did not charge a tax for entry or ask for voluntary contributions. Once through the gate, I found wide avenues of houses, all single-storeyed except for a temple and the prince's citadel. The whole area was drowned by a huge, groaning crowd amongst which cows, big chickens with longer claws than ours and various domestic animals moved around freely. Piles of rubbish released pestilential smells much stronger than those of Paris which had so much disturbed me. Giant bats were flying around the pyramidal, statue-covered towers of the temple, just as jackdaws fly around our own belltowers.

The presbytery and church of the Catholic Mission were on the east side of the town, beside an artificial pond and not far from the walls. The presbytery house had a little vegetable garden in the European style just beside it, otherwise it resembled all the other houses of the town: brick built with a roof of palm wood covered in scalloped tiles. There were no windows on its four outside walls but the latter were surrounded by a terrace of flagstones and columns supporting an extension of the roof. This formed a veranda crowded with people who seemed to be living there with their families as if at home.

The room behind the sole door seemed to be a reception room. It too had another door, opposite the entrance, which opened onto the interior, as did the windows, through which I could see a paved courtyard surrounded by a similar veranda as outside, giving the look of a cloister.

My arrival set off quite a stir and once I was inside I was surrounded by a great crowd of people, either standing or on their haunches, all talking at the same time. Moutou himself stayed on the street from where he was shouting a long speech, probably introducing me. I was deafened by the shouts and noisy exclamations and obviously could not make out the sense of it. After a while everything went quiet and I saw, coming in from the inside courtyard, a giant bearded man in a brownish cassock: the Abbot Perrin! I was immediately overcome by the calm and quiet authority that emanated from the giant missionary, the only European for thousands of miles around, living with the Indians in the depths of the Deccan. For his part, the Abbot did not hide his surprise at the arrival of a young Frenchman dressed like a Hindu and with several weeks of growth on his cheeks.

*

Punganur, Tuesday 14th May 1782.
Flashes of lightning light up the night but the rumbles of the thunder are muffled by the din of the torrential rain falling on the roof tiles. The paved courtyard is overflowing, the excess water running through the reception room into the street. The latter, where during the day I saw children splashing and laughing, despite the rubbish drifting along, has been transformed into a river. I meet the Abbot Perrin again in the room he uses as his study at the end of the courtyard, with its plank laid across trestles, two candle holders, a chest for records and two rattan armchairs. The Abbot serves me an infusion made from long pepper and saffron, which he calls *mulligatawny*[32]. He tells me that this drink strengthens the stomach, makes you perspire and 'freshens the skin', eventually stimulating the vital spirits and bringing happiness.

'Your adventure is unbelievable. You were lucky that Thomas Moutou was at Pondicherry and that you were able to employ him. I send him there with my correspondence for the Bishop.'

---

32 Translator's note: *mulligatawny:* from the Tamil words *milagu* – a pepper, and *tanni* – water. Later to become the basis for the famous soup.

The Abbot points to a leather bag on the chest, which I recognise as the one Moutou carried throughout our long journey, never being parted from it.

'I had not intended to enrol him in my service,' I say. 'It all came about because of a joke I made. My *dubash* wanted to find a pawn for me, but I had replied that I would rather have a 'tiger killer'. Poor Ranga Pillai had taken this literally, and after a search, found me one. But he unwittingly saved the life of your disciple, and mine too, by forbidding him to sleep in the *chaudhury* as he was a *pariah*.'

'That was indeed lucky, but nothing unusual. My main problem here is the caste system. You know I had to take it into account when building my church? I had a little wing built beside the sanctuary, with the main roof extended to cover it. That's where I put my *pariahs*. They have a view of the altar and the sanctuary but are kept out by a small wall that they dare not cross. So they have access to the sacraments without being under the same roof as my faithful. Without this ruse I would have lost my *shudras*, a higher caste that I had so much trouble converting.'

'Is that why,' I ask, 'Moutou always stopped me from going with him into the few villages we approached?'

'Partly, yes. But there was another reason,' replies the Abbot. 'If you had been seen with him you would have been recognised. Thomas told me that the man you call Flaharn, known to the Indians as Sher Sahib, a name he got in Hindustan, circulated your description, including the scar on your left cheek, around all the local dignitaries, while spreading the rumour that you had been tricked by a *pariah* who had subverted you from your mission to Hyder Ali Khan. All the Mysore governors have been ordered to arrest Moutou and take you to the Nabob's camp, by force if necessary, but treating you well and keeping you safe.'

Of course, I thought. Flaharn is not stupid. He's not going to ask that I be arrested and searched so that somebody else can find the fortune he still hopes I am carrying. He thinks that there is a reasonable chance that I would be happy to be taken to Hyder Ali Khan, especially as, not speaking Tamil, I would not be sufficiently informed to be on my guard.

'But how,' I ask, 'did we manage to get into Punganur without any problem?'

'Because we are not under the same authority. Although Punganur is on the edge of Mysore, its Raja is close to the Marathas, so Hyder

Ali Khan handles him carefully. He is busy enough dealing with his enemy, the Carnatic Nabob, and the English who support him, without bearing down on the Marathas. As you will have seen coming here, this is a peaceful region. Its prince is cherished by the people as his sole wish is to make them happy. But it was not always so. Fifty years ago, the then king of Punganur was at constant war with his neighbours. When he conquered somewhere he would have its ruler and his family decapitated. He enjoyed playing with the heads while parading through the streets of Punganur. So much so that eventually his enemies attacked this town and completely destroyed its ramparts. They have since been rebuilt. The Hindus wouldn't hurt a fly, but when they make war they are pitiless with the humans who are unfortunate enough to be their enemies.'

So it would be better to be an insect rather than a man in this country? I listen to the Abbot Perrin's words with my mind elsewhere. Flaharn has reassumed the *nom-de-guerre* that had made him famous in the north of India. He must be well established in the Court of Hyder Ali Khan to be able to give such authoritative orders to the town governors of Mysore. The name Barad Amzer must have been invented solely for the benefit of French Ministers, perhaps by Saint-Luperce, he too being accustomed to using assumed names. And, thinking of Saint-Luperce, I suddenly remember the other name he had used when speaking to Flaharn on the day of the attack on the *chaudhury*.

'So you are carrying a fortune in diamonds,' says the Abbot, interrupting my thoughts.

'Twelve million pounds' worth, Father.'

'All that for the tyrant Hyder Ali Khan!'

'It's for the Nabob to maintain our soldiers and sailors with, and to keep him from going over to the English, Father. The Chevalier de Suffren is relying on it. I also have a letter from him for the Nabob which I have to hand over to Monsieur de Piveron.'

'I have just read in the Bishop's letter brought by Thomas Moutou that the Chevalier de Suffren has given the poor people of Pondicherry enough to feed two thousand people for quite a while. Some merchants, unworthy of being called French, have hidden their reserves of rice in order to speculate on human misery. I will do everything I can to help this benefactor of the poor. If there were a thousand Suffrens in India there would be no sign of famine.'

I remember that the Chevalier de Suffren had sent *la Bellone* to cruise in the Bay of Bengal and capture any merchant ships carrying rice or food for Madras, then unload these prize cargoes at Pondicherry to be distributed amongst the local population. All this had done was to shift the problem, as our ally Hyder Ali Khan had laid waste to Madras as well as Pondicherry. I decide there is no point telling my host all this. After all, it was good military tactics and honourable on the part of the Admiral.

'Monsieur de Piveron is a friend of mine,' says the Abbot. 'I will find out where the Nabob is currently camped and once the rains have stopped, I will accompany you there. I am well known and that is more sensible than letting you go alone. Hyder Ali Khan likes the French but the same cannot always be said for those around him. This Sher Sahib, or Flaharn, as you call him, must be well established in the Nabob's Court; well enough to pose a real danger to you. Even if, as you say, his real aim is to get hold of the diamonds for his own benefit rather than Hyder Ali Khan's.'

'You say that Hyder Ali Khan is a tyrant but at the same time a friend?'

'I said only that he likes the French very much. So, for example, he has at my request stopped his own lieutenants and governors from persecuting a small community of the faithful that I converted and which lives in the forests of Gingee. He himself is a Mohammedan, but only because this is the religion of the princes who came from Persia after the Mongols. Although he makes sure he follows the heavy practices of the Koran, I don't think he has any God other than himself, his own pleasure and his own interests. He prefers the wines of Bordeaux and Madeira to the promises of the Prophet and is happy to let his soldiers and people practise Ramadan. He attends the mosque but he could just as well enter the Indian temples or go to Christian Mass. He sends flowers to be offered to the Indian idols and lets French missionaries have land to build their churches. If this interests you, I can let you read a short memoir I have written about this extraordinary man.'

'That would interest me a lot. I'm very grateful. When do you think we would be able to leave?'

'As soon as I have up to date information and as soon as the rains stop. They don't last long in this part of India, unlike in Goa, for example. You'll have to get some different clothes. I don't have any European clothes here apart from my cassock, which is not very practical for travelling on horseback, which I do often. For that I have had myself made a set of clothes similar to those worn by nobles here, but less elaborate. I chose them in white, which is the colour for funerals here but also for important people. Indians do not like black. I'll have some ordered for you. You say you are a sailor. Would riding be difficult for you?'

I reply that nothing would please me more and that I've done enough walking for the moment.

'So much the better, otherwise I would have ordered a palanquin for you, but that is more expensive. I'll also have a pair of boots made for you. Good! I imagine you're tired. I'll show you your room.'

The Abbot Perrin has prepared one of the four rooms surrounding the little courtyard of his 'presbytery' for me. The veranda around it is very practical as we can get there without getting soaked by the deluge of water falling from the skies. It is crammed with men and women sitting with their backs to the wall, or standing, for its whole length, under the roof extension. They are chattering or chanting to the frenzied rhythm of several drums or empty chests whose sound is coming from the reception room and which I have not heard before because of the rain. Children sleep on the floor, rolled up in their *dupattas*, insensible to the racket.

'They will spend the night here. I made them come out so that you can have the room and sleep, but I'm afraid they won't be quiet until midnight. It's their habit and you'll have to get used to it.'

We enter a room about twelve feet long by twenty-four feet wide. A mat and chest covered with embossed leather have been placed in one corner, along with two vases. They are the only furnishings.

'All those people outside normally sleep here?' I say in surprise.

The Abbot laughs softly.

'Yes indeed! That's a lot of people, isn't it? You were probably surprised when you arrived here at the number of people living in the town, when there are only low houses like this one, with wide avenues and half the space taken by squares, temples, ponds, palaces and the Prince's gardens. That's because twenty or thirty Indians live in a space which at home would be no bigger than a doorman's room. But they sleep just as well outside, have no fear.'

The missionary lifted up his candleholder to inspect the ceiling and the corners of the room.

'Good! You won't have any undesirable bed companions.'

'What are you talking about?'

'*Pambu kapell*! One of the most dangerous snakes in the world. When the rains arrive, they are happy to take shelter in houses and like to curl up in your bed. Otherwise you can find them on door handles, in toilets, kitchens, anywhere. The respect shown them by the Indians allows them to do all this. If one bites you, you'll die in half an hour. You are not allowed to kill them – they are gods! They even have their own temples and priests who feed them. I think the noise from my boarders has scared them off. But I see you won't be totally alone.'

The Abbot illuminates what look like two little lobsters with their pincers, remarkable for their tails which are curled back as far as their heads. They run off at the speed of light to hide in a darker part of the room.

'Scorpions. Those are young, not very dark yet. They are not as dangerous as the older, blacker ones. They are getting out of the rain too. But don't worry! They only sting if you crowd them or put them under pressure. Their sting is rarely fatal anyway.'

What charming company! Once my host has gone, I stretch out on my bed and roll myself up in a cotton sheet which I find there, to protect myself against my unattractive roommates. Sleep does not come despite the accumulated tiredness of my long journey. I have never felt so lost and uprooted since coming ashore in this extraordinary country. The heat is not a problem, rather the strange music mixed with the drumming of the rain on the roof. I cannot identify the instruments or the number of musicians. They are certainly percussion instruments, their sound sometimes dull and deep, sometimes as light and clear as a pair of cymbals, continuing without respite.

Declercq! That was the name Saint-Luperce had used when talking to Flaharn as the Rohilla mercenaries were preparing to assassinate Ranga Pillai and the servants he had engaged for me. I have not had time to think about it much during my odyssey on foot across the Carnatic and the Deccan. But now that I am at a distance from the business, for the time being at least, it pains me to think of all those poor people. My spine tingles thinking about what I myself would have gone through without the heroic intervention of Thomas Moutou.

Declercq. This name was mentioned in the file my uncle had left in Monsieur de Fleurieu's steel cabinet. It was quoted in the report signed by Inspector Binet of the Sixth Office of Public Security in Paris. It was one of the two men with whom Saint-Luperce had had a secret meeting near the Palais-Royal. I well remember the description given by the hotel keeper: 'about fifty, very tall, a leather band over his left eye'. There is no possible doubt! I had not made the connection at the time as I thought Flaharn was dead, but everything coincides. It was he whom Saint-Luperce met in December 1780 in Paris, eighteen months ago. Apparently, according to the file I had seen, Flaharn, alias Declercq, was therefore an agent of the Insurgents recruited by Doctor Baldock. But what were the Americans doing in India? Had Flaharn told them about the diamonds and offered to steal them on their behalf? Had they agreed to betray us for that? It seems absurd. I remember as well that Saint-Luperce had talked about going to Madras and that Flaharn had made fun of him about it. But Madras is the English trading post and aren't they the enemies of the Americans? Everything is confused inside my poor head. I no longer understand anything!

*

I had insisted on paying for my meals. Abbot Perrin had at first refused, but once I had said that it was for the benefit of his poor, he had agreed. From time to time we could pick vegetables from his garden, but his cook mostly prepared a ragout made of water, spices, salt, garlic, some liquid butter and meat that resembled mutton, everything accompanied, of course, with rice.

'This meat is from the same animal as your boots!' the Abbot said to me when we were eating one of these ragouts. 'I'll wager the shoemaker will be round to take your measurements before the evening.'

As I wasn't clear what he meant, he added, 'I bought a brown dog, which we are now eating, so that the shoemaker could make your boots from its hide.'

'We're eating dog?' I shouted out, unable to help myself.

The Abbot laughed.

'Forgive me, but I couldn't resist it. It's only the Europeans who call them that. I don't know why. In fact, it's a kind of sheep covered in hair rather than wool, with hanging ears. I paid the shoemaker in advance. He killed it and I let him have half the meat and hide. Tomorrow you'll have a new pair of boots in 'brown dog' hide. They of course won't be

259

as long-lasting as a pair made at home, as the leather will not have had time to mature, but they'll be enough for riding to the Nabob's camp.'

He served me tea, saying that the local Indians did not drink it much, as it was not cultivated at Punganur. He had to have it brought in and he explained that he drank it with every meal.

'It gives me the chance to boil some water and hide its taste, as the only water available here is kept in open reservoirs in the town. Every kind of nasty thing gets into it, the locals bathe in it, wash their clothes in it and happily throw their rubbish in it. I couldn't say that anything bad has resulted from this, but for myself, I try to avoid drinking it as it comes.'

I was in fact called during the afternoon, as my shoemaker was waiting for me in the street. Shoemakers are all *pariahs*, otherwise they would not be able to kill animals for their hide. This one obviously did not dare enter the house and I had to go out to be measured. He had no measuring instrument, instead taking my feet one by one in his hands and manipulating them. My boots came two days later and were a perfect fit although, as the Abbot had said, the freshly tanned leather did not seem very strong.

It still rained from time to time but there were now some good clear patches and Abbot Perrin told me we would soon be able to leave. While we were waiting he told me that Thomas Moutou had been called to hunt a man-eating tiger which had killed two women and a child in the surrounding countryside. If I were interested, Moutou would be happy for me to go with him. The Abbot told me that this happened from time to time. When a tiger was badly wounded when fighting with other tigers, so that it was not strong enough to go after its usual game, it would start attacking country folk, soon getting a taste for this easy prey. I jumped at the chance to see my lifesaver at work and was happy to go and meet him again. It was thought that the lair of the tiger in question was in a small ravine to the east of the Punganur principality. The sky was clear when we arrived early one afternoon at the place indicated. Leaning over the edge, we could see the fine animal stretched out in the sun right below us. It was the first time I had seen a tiger and it seemed huge. I remembered the dramatic story of a hunt told to me by Flaharn in Brest. This unnerved me, but my companion seemed quite confident. He signalled to me to stay at the edge and armed only with his little shield and his cutlass, he jumped quickly down to the bottom of the ravine, shouting to wake up his formidable adversary, then walked straight towards it with a strong and measured step. The tiger, seeing him, raised itself on its front paws and let out a terrible roar which chilled my blood. As Moutou continued to approach him slowly, his eyes fixed constantly on those of the animal, the latter suddenly raised itself to its full height and began to beat its flanks furiously with its tail. Moutou nonetheless kept on straight for it with a deliberate step. When he was as close as could be, I saw the tiger lay itself flat, preparing to spring. Moutou stopped dead. The huge cat lifted its head, roared once more and sprang, but the *pariah*, alert and twisting his back, took the paws of the furious beast on his shield, drove his cutlass into the tiger's stomach as it passed over him, fell to the ground and rolled away into the grass. The tiger tumbled onto its back. Moutou, who had stood up again, then ran at the tiger and quick as lightning sliced its throat with his big cutlass, then sprang back to put himself out of range of the terrible claws. The tiger died there and then. Seeing that it was no longer moving I rejoined Thomas Moutou at the bottom of the ravine. Everything had happened so quickly. The wound in the animal's stomach was terrible to behold, having reached the lower part of the heart and cut its intestines. The hunter, still as calm as ever, began to skin his vanquished enemy with quick and precise movements. He soon finished. Rolling the skin carefully, so as not to damage it, he put it on his back and we took the road back to town. The skin would be cured and presented as a trophy to the Raja of Punganur. I realised how lucky I was to have taken on such a bodyguard. I was more than ever convinced, after what I had just seen, that nobody else could have rescued me from the hands of the Pathans as he had. I thought sadly of poor Ranga Pillai, who had found such a man for me, despite his aversion to *pariahs*.

When we got back, Abbot Perrin told me that he had received news about Hyder Ali Khan from merchants coming from the Carnatic. The Nabob had laid siege to Permacoul, a place about thirty miles north-west of Pondicherry. The French soldiers had joined up with him after taking Cuddalore from the English.

'I suggest we leave next week,' the Abbot said. 'I'll forewarn my parishioners that they will have to make do without me for a while. I'll take you first to see my friend Monsieur de Piveron and then I can visit my community at Gingee.'

'I thought,' I said, 'that Gingee was a fortress taken by the Marquis de Bussy during the last war, and that there are only soldiers there.'

'You are correct. My faithful are not at Gingee itself. They have taken refuge in thick woods to the south. Gingee was once the capital and the seat of a Raja whose power stretched to the edge of Tanjore. Its centre is surrounded by a walled stronghold flanked by towers. Three miles away there are three mountains on which forts have been built. The town which is also called Gingee is situated on the plain between these mountains. It was taken by the French in 1750, by scaling the mountains during the night and putting explosives on the gates. It's considered to be the strongest fortress built by the Indians.'

I was somewhat nervous at the idea of finally meeting this Nabob Hyder Ali Khan, about whom I had heard so much nonsense in France, and so I was happy to lose myself in the Abbot Perrin's little memoir. When lending it to me, the missionary told me that he himself had met the Nabob in December 1781, having accompanied Monsieur de Piveron when the latter had been named as the King's envoy to Hyder Ali Khan.

'I was able to write this document thanks to details provided by Monsieur de Piveron, who had collected them at the Nabob's Court. I have known André Piveron for a long time. We both experienced the difficult trials of the last siege of Pondicherry, under Monsieur de Bellecombe. We both then stayed on there to look after our compatriots during the English occupation, and were both recalled to the Île-de-France at the same time. When Monsieur de Souillac, Governor of the Mascarenes, appointed my friend as the King's envoy to Hyder Ali Khan, I myself was due to return to Punganur, and we both landed at Goa.'

*

Punganur, Friday 24th May 1782.
No rain has fallen for several days. The sun beats down on the roof tiles, but the temperature is bearable. I have installed myself in the Abbot Perrin's work study, to immerse myself in the biography of the great Nabob I am soon to meet. I admit that the missionary has scared me by referring to him as a tyrant…

…Hyder Ali Khan was born in the kingdom of Mysore, into a little-

known Mohammedan family. His father, Fath Sahib, was commander of the five-hundred strong guard to the Raja of Mysore, and Hyder Ali Khan took over the same role after his father's death. When Monsieur Dupleix made a treaty with the sovereign, on condition that he provided five thousand horsemen for the French, Hyder Ali Khan, burning with an ambition for glory, asked to command this force. This was granted to him. He demonstrated such bravery and zeal for the French that Monsieur Dupleix, on sending him back home after the war, gave him a present of two cannons and wrote flatteringly about his conduct to the Raja of Mysore. A man deemed capable of command by the French could not fail to be of interest to this ruler. He showed great confidence in him and gave him ever more honours. Hyder Ali Khan fully justified the belief in his ability. Disliking rest and inaction, he used his force to harry the neighbouring princelings, regularly offering newly conquered lands for his master to add to his territory. Idolised by the Raja he served so well, he became an object of jealousy for the First Minister, who did everything he could to get rid of him. But Hyder Ali Khan was a step ahead of his enemy. When he saw that his downfall was inevitable, he raised a revolt, not only against the Minister, but also against his own sovereign.

The unfortunate Raja had made him the general of his cavalry. This emboldened him, as a general had the right to have the gates of all the towns opened. Hyder Ali Khan marched quickly on Bangalore, the second city of the realm, took the city's treasure and used it to raise an army. This enabled him to capture the country's capital, Seringapatam[33], where he imprisoned the Raja in his palace. To make imprisonment more bearable, the Raja was accorded every pleasure except that of ruling.

After that, he behaved to the neighbouring princes and to the people of Mysore as if the Raja had given him the right to govern. He did everything in the name of his prisoner: it was the Raja who wished, ordered, made peace, or declared war. However, when he dealt with the Europeans or with the Moghul, it was in his own name.

When the Raja died in prison, Hyder Ali Khan enthroned his son, but kept him in the serail. He did show him to the people dressed in full

---

33 Translator's note: *Seringapatam:* Now known as Srirangapatna. The Treaty of Seringapatam, 1792, ended the Third Anglo-Mysore War.

royal regalia. By this means he misled the supporters and allies of the House of Mysore and suppressed any reprisals. Without realising it, the people became accustomed to seeing only Hyder Ali Khan.

Hyder Ali Khan is bold and unbelievably active. Although personally exposed to every danger, he never forgets his pleasures and his harem accompanies him on the battlefield. It is said that he can speak twenty-two languages, despite never having learned to read. He can dictate letters to six people at a time on different subjects and in different dialects, while six other secretaries read letters to him to which he must send replies. He demands a detailed account of what is going on in the country and his camp, and can remember all the facts and figures.

Hyder Ali Khan has to overcome many obstacles to maintain his hold on the crown he has usurped. The Marathas, the English and the peoples he has subjugated form a formidable net around him. He sees around him the inheritors of the throne he has stolen, who are to be more feared the more they are loved. He constantly sows division amongst his enemies in order to pick them apart one by one. He hands out gold freely to quell the anger of some and when under too much pressure makes treaties advantageous to himself only.

His main focus of attention is his army. It is the sole source of his strength, but its loyalty cannot be guaranteed. To avert any threat, he concentrates ceaselessly on his soldiers. If he had no enemies, he would besiege a mountain. His troops are always campaigning and he is always amidst them. If he loses a battle he makes up for it by attacking a weaker neighbour. If his empire is constrained at the south, he extends it to the north. Moreover, Hyder Ali Khan's armies do not ruin his finances. For him it is a kind of saving to maintain a hundred thousand fighters: friends, enemies and neutrals all contribute to the troops. Everything they touch belongs to them: grain, animals, fowl, even men. Everything is taken.

Let us look at his administrative policy. As he is constantly at the head of his armies, almost always out of the country, and taking with him all the forces which could defend him, he lives in fear of foreign invasion, uprisings, fraudulent governors, and more than all that, the emigration of his people, abandoning their land and so depriving him of his riches. Our cunning man uses all his mind and intelligence to make sure his ship of state does not founder on these reefs. All the neighbouring princes being vassals, they have to provide him with a certain number of soldiers. Sometimes the minor potentate has to command his own contingent in the army. Nothing is cleverer than this policy since, as well as these auxiliaries being also hostages which ensure the loyalty of their masters, Hyder Ali Khan places them in the front rank in battle, thereby preserving his own troops, and ensuring that those who die by the steel of his enemies constitute a loss for his rivals rather than for himself.

It is impossible to conceive all of the measures that Hyder Ali Khan takes to discourage fraud on the part of his town and provincial governors. Anyone appointed to an important post sends him wives, brothers and children as hostages and surety for their loyalty. Pity those whose relative does not do his duty! In addition, every governor has somebody watching him closely. This is more dangerous as there is a strong incentive to find evidence of wrongdoing: if the observer can prove that the man he is charged with watching is at fault, whether it be by not advancing the interests of the Nabob sufficiently forcefully, or by being too hard on the people, or in some other way, he takes the place of the accused. The latter first receives a punishment of a hundred lashes with the cane and then is stripped of all his belongings. Then, if it is a question of an ordinary peccadillo, he in turn is given the job of watching over his accuser. One can imagine how motivated he is to do his job.

Nothing is more exceptional than the way in which the usurper ensures that he holds onto his conquests: he moves the people from towns he has captured to places far removed from everything they know and where they are completely under his control.

*

Having read this surprising text I asked the Abbot Perrin about the size of the Nabob's army.

'First there's the cavalry, which gives him a hundred thousand men and is his main force. He also has powerful siege artillery that he uses very well. But for his hundred thousand cavalrymen you also have to include an equal number of servants who look after the horses. The infantry must have about the same number of men but it is not completely regimented.'

'That must create an impressive camp.'

'Even more than you think, as all the soldiers receive as pay rations which are enough to feed their complete household, which therefore follows them everywhere: wife, children and sometimes their mother and father. Imagine too, as well as the horses and camels, the oxen required to carry all the baggage of such a multitude. And don't forget the elephants. Including the areas for the horses and for the animals for pulling loads and for food, the circumference of Hyder Ali Khan's camp must be as great as the walls of Paris. And although the army often changes position, these movements are done in a remarkably orderly way. It is true that the huge plains in this part of India make these movements easier. The camp is a moving city whose buildings always retain the same place and orientation. The army has to move all the time, not solely for tactical reasons, but mainly because it exhausts the countryside on which it lives. Is it any surprise that after that the Carnatic is in a state of famine!'

'You wrote in your memoir that the Nabob keeps a precise tally on all his soldiers.'

'That is true, but it does not mean that he controls all of them. Within the army there are also foot bandits and mounted bandits, an Indian version of Tartar mercenaries. They have no rules or defined ways of manoeuvring, or any knowledge of military tactics, but they know how to rape, pillage, burn, massacre the children and disembowel the women. Nothing more is asked of them. They move around in packs, with no discipline, preceding the main army the way lightning precedes thunder. Your Flaharn must command a band of this type. You can imagine that within Hyder Ali Khan's huge camp he must enjoy a certain level of independence, which could make him very dangerous for you. That's why I am keen to accompany you. Without an interpreter you would be quite lost when arriving at the Nabob's camp. You could fall in with somebody malicious who takes you to Flaharn rather than to Monsieur de Piveron.'

'But are you not afraid of him?'

'In principle, no! I have been to the camp several times, and as I told you, it is always laid out the same way, so I know my way around it. As soon as we arrive, I will go straight to Monsieur de Piveron's quarters, without any problem. There will be no risk as he will immediately ask for an audience with the Nabob. If we need to, we can also put ourselves under the protection of the French soldiers. There is a French military corps in Hyder Ali Khan's army. Did you know that? My friend de Piveron discovered this when he arrived last December. Monsieur de Souillac thought it was made up of deserters and partisans, but their officers showed him mission orders signed by a Field Marshall in Versailles. Their presence must have been kept secret as war had not been declared, which is why successive Governors in India had not been told.'

At Mass the following Sunday I saw Thomas Moutou in the *pariah* section. I could see a rather pretty young woman at his side and some smiling children who seemed to be theirs. Until then I had always thought he was unmarried.

Although I would very much have liked Thomas Moutou to accompany us, as I had developed great confidence in him, having seen how he confronted a tiger, the Abbot Perrin said it would be dangerous for him as his description had been given by Flaharn to several Governors dependent on Mysore, at the same time as mine. He nonetheless wanted him to be called to Punganur before I left so that I could say farewell to him. I was sad at leaving this brave man to whom I owed my life and to thank him I gave him a purse containing all the rupees I had left, to which I added several gold louis for good measure.

We left on the 29th May, the Abbot and I on horseback, followed by three servants on foot who were to look after our horses and the ox which was carrying our baggage. I was dressed in an Indian horseman's outfit which the Abbot had acquired for me: trousers in the local style and above them an *angui*, a tight tunic to which were sewn skirts reaching to the ankles. However, I did not wear a turban, the Abbot having given me one of his own hats, in black felt with a large brim, which made me look like a Breton country curé.

The shortest route would have been to the north-east, but the missionary told me that the main pass in that direction gave onto the Carnatic plain at a valley that led to the town of Vellore, which was in English hands. Tipoo Sahib, Hyder Ali Khan's son, was skirmishing in the area and the surrounding countryside was rife with armed bands like Flaharn's. It was never good to fall into their hands, whether friend or foe. As we were carrying a huge fortune in our saddlebags, the risk was too great. We therefore went south along the eastern edge of the Deccan plain, as far as a watercourse that passed through the

Eastern Ghats to the Carnatic plain. The Abbot Perrin told me that it was called the Penna and reaches the sea close to Cuddalore. The countryside looked quite different from when I had come the other way with Thomas Moutou. The yellows had been replaced by every shade of green. The rice paddies in particular were magnificent, the streams had become torrents and the rivers I had crossed with dry feet were now overflowing.

It took us four days to reach the Penna. The river flowed east, growling its way through a narrow pass surrounded by forest-covered mountains. We took three more days following a track on its left bank. The Abbot Perrin had intended to make a stop on the evening of 5th June on the north bank of the Penna at a small town called Tirukoilur, where the road to Gingee starts. However, on that day we were stopped by a group of soldiers who asked to see our *radari,* or passports. The Abbot had told me that in normal times one could travel freely throughout India, without any checks, but the rules had changed because of the war. He had a document which he presented to the soldiers. Unfortunately, none of them could read, so we had to wait while they took it to their General, who lived in a little fort overlooking the valley. This meant we had to spend the night camped there, waiting for the great man's response.

The next day towards midday, when we had finally reached Tirukoilur, whose temple we could see on the other side of the river, we came across a large number of Mysore infantrymen who had stopped beside the Gingee road. We greeted then as we passed, but just as we had overtaken them, one of their chiefs, who must have been some sort of junior officer, barked an order. We were soon surrounded by a band of moustached fellows with bare calves and pancake-shaped turbans, all pointing their spears at us in perfect order. The Abbot was not in the least disconcerted, lecturing them in a haughty, even arrogant, tone that took me quite by surprise. I watched as he dismounted and followed the men who had stopped us towards a palanquin laid down in a copse beside the road. I stayed on my own, still mounted, amongst these warriors who were looking at me without the least kindness, white eyes rolling in their bronzed faces. I admit that I was not at all at ease. I was worried that the Abbot, by his tone, had greatly irritated this crowd of unfriendly killers which surrounded me. After what seemed like a long time, the missionary finally came back, mounted his horse and wordlessly rode it forward towards the soldiers, who moved aside to let us pass, along with our servants and baggage.

'What did they want?' I asked, when we were a little way off.

'Their commander asked who I was, where I was going, and on what business.'

'I really thought they were going to do us harm,' I said. 'How did you answer?'

'In good Tamil, I said to him 'I am not going to your enemies and for the rest, I do not answer to you!''

'You said that?'

'The Indians are often like that. You can be sure that if they had felt for a second that I was not sure of myself, they would have wanted to know more about why we were here and asked to search our baggage. Can you imagine his face and his reaction if he had discovered we were carrying a fortune in diamonds? Whereas by acting as I did, he must truly have believed that I could have caused him trouble if he had insisted. However, we had better not sleep outside tonight as they are going in the same direction. If they catch up with us beside the road this evening, I'm not so sure we could extricate ourselves so easily, especially knowing what you are carrying in your haversack. We'll stop earlier than intended in a fortified village called Pandarom Shutri, where we can find a *savadi*, a sort of communal building where we can spend the night. We will be better protected there than in the open countryside.'

Towards five in the evening, we arrived at Pandarom Shutri, a small town surrounded by earthen ramparts, with its low houses, temple and a crenelated keep in its centre. It looked very like the town near which Thomas Moutou and I had stopped and which Flaharn and his bandits had entered before taking the road to Gingee.

That evening, as the servants prepared food for us and our horses and while we were sitting on the outside veranda of the *savadi*, peacefully smoking our cheroots, we saw coming towards us along the street an old man wearing a fine muslin *angui* as white as his beard. With him was a moustached man in his prime, although a little tubby, wearing a scarlet *angui* embroidered in gold thread and with a big sabre at his side.

'This is just what I wanted to avoid,' said the Abbot. 'The little old man is the Governor, a Brahmin. You'd think butter wouldn't melt in his mouth, but I know him. He's a cunning old rogue. As for the other, he's the head of the troop we met at midday. Nothing good will come of this sudden meeting!'

After the usual greetings, they went with the Abbot into the reception room found at the entrance to houses in this region. I followed them. They arranged themselves on cushions while the hostel keeper rushed off to bring a *hookah*. I was present for the long conversation. Not understanding the language they were speaking, I tried to guess what was being said by watching the faces of the speakers, but it was no use; the Indians do not show their feelings. All the same, I understood that they were talking about me, as I thought I heard my name mentioned several times, despite the accent.

'It's just what I thought,' said the missionary once they had left. 'The Governor knows who you are. Your Flaharn, or Sher Sahib as he calls him, although they are Hindustani words, not of his language, has spread your name everywhere, and also described the scar on your face. Flaharn had it be known that he does not want you harmed but anybody who finds you must take you to him at the Nabob's camp. The Governor has spoken to the commander, or *thalapathi* as he's known, and proposed joining forces with him.'

'I thought I heard my name, by I didn't feel any hostility towards me.'

'There was none, and my impression is that nobody had been given any reason to be hostile towards you.'

Obviously, I thought, Flaharn wants me brought to him in one piece, along with my diamonds. It is very cunning of him. Without an interpreter I would only have understood that they wanted to take me to the Nabob's camp, and I would have gone along willingly.

'In that case, could we politely decline their invitation?'

'I tried. There were polite but firm. They will use force if necessary, I fear. I am convinced that the Governor has no idea why Flaharn wants to see you, and that the two of them know nothing about the diamonds in your bag, but you can be sure that Flaharn will have offered a good reward and they will do anything to earn it.'

'And what did they say about you?'

'I am known around here, as I travel a lot. They didn't know I was with you. They had only been told about Thomas, saying that you were accompanied by a despicable *pariah* who should be killed. They asked me whether I knew him and I lied. It was as well I did not bring him.

They said that they had nothing against me, that I should continue on my way without waiting for you, and that they would guarantee my safety much better than I would be able to. But I can't abandon you now.'

'In principle,' I said, 'they have not been able to contact Flaharn and there is not much time left for them to do so. The main thing is to get to the Nabob's camp as quickly as possible. Once there we will be out of danger.'

'Don't you believe it! You are right in that there is little chance of Flaharn attacking you on the road. It's what could happen once we have arrived at the camp that worries me.'

'You think we won't be safe there? Didn't you say that your friend Monsieur de Piveron would have us protected by the French soldiers serving Hyder Ali Khan?'

'Yes! If we could have moved freely, if we had been free to join up with him and put ourselves under his protection as soon as we arrived at the camp. But the Governor and his friend the commander will want to take us straight to Flaharn and I can't see how we could stop them. I could leave you with them at that point and run off to alert our compatriot, but that is risky as we could do nothing against Flaharn's band without having first seen Hyder Ali Khan, even if we did manage to get to the colonel of the French horsemen. And the camp is like a huge town; we would need a long time to find Flaharn's tent if we didn't know where it was.'

'Could we not slip away from our escort tomorrow? We have horses and they are on foot.'

'You won't be on horseback, but in the commander's palanquin. They have decided to have you carried with him, under the pretext of honouring you, but really to keep a better eye on you. He's called Dhuraisingam, a Hindu.'

I searched desperately for a way out. Kill the commander in his palanquin and ride off as fast as possible with the Abbot Perrin? I could not ask a priest to be an accomplice to a murder. In any case, I had no weapons and was not a killer.

'Could we try to leave quietly tonight?'

'Alas, no. We are in a walled town and the gates are closed and guarded at night. And to think I believed we would be safer here! Even if we could get over the walls without being stopped, we would be on foot. I have learned that the Nabob's camp has moved to the north of Gingee, near Chetpet. We would have at least thirty-five miles of flat land to cross, probably with horsemen chasing after us. Thomas Moutou might be able to avoid them in these circumstances, but not me, and you need me, if only as an interpreter.'

I thought for a while. Maybe all was not lost. There was still one solution.

'Father, you said that they would allow you to move around freely?'

'Absolutely.'

'So take the bag of diamonds and the Chevalier de Suffren's letter and leave tomorrow morning. On horseback you'll go quicker than us. You can get to Hyder Ali Khan's camp with enough time to give him the treasure and come back to meet me with an escort and one of the Nabob's officers who can get the commander to release me.'

'You're right. I'll leave at dawn with one of my servants, who can take your horse. I'll tell the others to wait for me here with the ox. I will pick them up on my way back.'

The Abbot stopped for a moment to think.

'I have a better idea. I won't go straight to the camp. I'll first put the diamonds in a safe place. I won't need to make a big detour.'

'Are you afraid of being robbed by bandits on the way?'

'Anything could happen but that's not what I'm thinking about. It's impossible to give a present directly to the Nabob, or even a letter, though that would be easier to hide. Piveron would have to hand over the diamonds to dignitaries, who would open them in front of everybody and then present them with all ceremony. If, as I fear, Flaharn has informants at the heart of the *darbar*[34], he could find out that he has lost his treasure and nothing could stop him from taking his revenge on you before we find you. He holds a deadly grudge against you, and if I understood you correctly, that's why he arranged the ambush that Thomas Moutou rescued you from.'

I shivered, remembering that Flaharn had arranged for me to come with Saint-Luperce solely so that he could take his revenge on me, and that had he not found the chest empty, he would have tortured me immediately, as he had intended. Thomas Moutou would not have been able to stop him.

---

34 From the Persian *darbar* meaning 'the door of affairs' i.e. the Court.

'Let's see! The camp is to the south of Chetpet,' continued Perrin. 'I should be there by tomorrow afternoon. Piveron will ask for an audience immediately. He is able to see the Nabob at any time of the day or night, and the latter trusts him enough to allow us a private interview. We will tell Hyder Ali Khan what is happening, he will have Flaharn arrested before he has realised anything, and we will come to escort you along the road. You should be arriving at the outskirts of the camp towards six in the evening, but we will have met you well before that – by about five, I think. We'll then ask Colonel Bouthenot to provide us with a troop of French horsemen to retrieve the diamonds from their hiding place. You yourself will give them to the Nabob.'

'And where are you thinking of hiding the treasure?'

'I'd prefer that you don't know that for the moment. I'll tell you later. But I guarantee that it will be safe. Trust me.'

I did not insist, having understood. If by any mischance I fell into Flaharn's claws and he tried to make me talk, I would not be able to tell him. But this was an unlikely possibility, at least if everything unfolded as the Abbot had related.

✳

On the plain to the south of Chetpet, Friday 7th *June 1782.*

Our troop has set out at dawn. We have made several short stops to change the bearers of the palanquins and let those who require it attend to their natural needs, but the soldiers have eaten nothing since their morning rice.

As arranged, I am travelling in commander Dhuraisingam's palanquin. The Governor of Pandarom Shutri follows in his personal palanquin. It is obvious that he does not want to miss out on his share of the cake promised by Flaharn to all those who bring me to him. All the same, I feel no hostility towards me. Dhuraisingam is even quite considerate, often asking me, in a friendly and concerned way, whether there is anything I need. At least that is what I assume, as I can't understand what he is saying.

I no longer have a watch, as it was taken from me by the Rohillas, but I think it is now well past five in the evening. The Abbot Perrin had reckoned that by now we would not be far from the Nabob's camp, but nobody has yet come to meet us. This is starting to worry me!

Our procession suddenly stops moving; something is going on. Dhuraisingam leans out and speaks with the bearers, who lower the palanquin to the ground. He gets out and I follow him. I look first towards the front of the cortege, hoping to see the horsemen who will save me, but the road ahead of us is empty. I can see a long way in that direction, as the countryside is flat apart from a distant chain of mountains to our left. Behind us the track we have been following snakes through the high vegetation of the savannah, from which emerge occasional blocks of rock and groves of straight-trunked palm trees. We have passed well to the west of the outcrops which surround the Gingee fortress. The soldiers call out to each other along the length of the column, their voices echoing in the evening quiet. They are leaning on their lances and seem to be discussing something to the right of us. That's where the commander is heading, and I go round the palanquin to follow him.

We pass a few bushes. The Carnatic plain is spread before us. An unpleasant smell hits me and I see a huge strip of land trampled and ploughed up by thousands of hooves. Parallel ruts have been carved out by several lines of heavily loaded carts moving along abreast. It is the track left by the Mysore army, at least four hundred yards wide, coming from Gingee in the south-east and heading north. I can see the corpses of several oxen, abandoned on the spot, their stink mixing with that of the animal dung. There are also a few human bodies. Vultures fight with jackals over the remains of their macabre feast.

Dhuraisingam does not seem especially interested on this morbid sight; he is looking north and seems annoyed. He gives an order and the column moves off again, keeping the track left by Hyder Ali Khan's hordes to our right. Rather than getting in his palanquin, the commander trots quickly to the front, past the ranks of marching soldiers. Two hundred yards further on, the track left by the huge army disappears into an immense circle of torn-up earth which stretches as far as the eye can see in every direction. We pass piles of rubbish and more animal corpses. We can spot the places where the oxen and horses were tethered, by the clouds of flies swirling around above heaps of dung. The ground still bears the marks of the huge tents erected there recently. The Nabob's army has struck camp!

*

It took us almost an hour to cross the devastated and now deserted heart of the Mysore armies' old encampment. At the northern edge we found the track left by the marching multitudes, and halted there. Night had fallen. I had the impression that the Governor wanted to continue on to the Nabob's new camp without stopping, but the wiser military man knew that his men needed to rest. Our meal was meagre and made me think of those I had taken with Thomas Moutou during our long journey: a handful of rice with a bit of salt; water flavoured with garlic and pepper. The commander shared his meal with me, while the Governor kept his distance: he was of too high a caste to soil himself by contact with a vile European.

We set off before dawn. A thin crescent moon more or less lit up the track left by the Nabob's army, but we could have followed it by nothing more than the smell of the animal carcasses in various states of putrefaction that littered its progress. I had not slept much during our stop, being too anxious. The good Abbot Perrin had not foreseen that Hyder Ali Khan's army would move again so soon after shifting from the Gingee region. I hoped that this unforeseen movement would not upset the plan we had made before separating.

From then on I had no idea how far we would have to travel to reach our goal. I was afraid of arriving at night, as it could make matters difficult for the horsemen who were to come to meet us and take me into their protection. The new day gave me some reassurance on this latter point and I relaxed a little. Being so tired I eventually fell asleep, rocked by the gentle sway of the palanquin.

*

The Nabob's camp, south of the Arni fortress, Saturday 8th June 1782.

Loud voices shout orders and the earth trembles beneath the marching feet of a huge troop. Woken suddenly by this noise, I lean on one elbow to look around us.

'*Mysore iravunam!*' says Dhuraisingam to me, pointing out the soldiers manoeuvring on the plain. They are wearing blue jackets and red turbans and are armed with lances and old muskets. It is a battalion of Mysore sepoys doing exercises. We have just arrived at the Nabob's camp. In sudden alarm I stand up on my bed in the palanquin. Nobody is paying us any attention. The orders I can hear are in the local language, given by Indian officers; there is nothing to be hoped for there. Why have the horsemen who were to protect me not arrived? What has happened to the Abbot Perrin? What has he done with the cursed diamonds?

Our column continues on, passing between numerous areas marked by stakes and ropes, where hundreds and hundreds of oxen are grazing. I see camels too, and further off, some elephants. It is the first time I have seen them! In other circumstances this would have excited my curiosity and interest, but I am too worried to pursue it. We then enter a crowded avenue like that of a big city, except that the houses are here replaced by huge tents. The soldiers' tents are big enough, but there are also some magnificent ones whose poles carry gilded orbs and crescents, and which are no doubt the private residences of chiefs and princes. There are even shops made from canvas and a bazaar, as in a real town. We are moving through a huge and disparate crowd, including women and children. Everybody steps quietly to the side as our advance guard approaches.

The tents are precisely aligned and everything has a good sense of order. However, rubbish is strewn everywhere over the ground; the only ones devoted to clearing the refuse seem to be the vultures which circle overhead and glide down to head height to fight over the most interesting scraps, watched indifferently by the passers-by.

Increasingly alarmed, I see that the sun is already high in the sky and it is almost midday. We arrive at a huge square in the middle of which has been built a six-foot high palisade at least a mile in circumference. Three tents as big and as high as our own storeyed houses dominate this area. Above them are orbs and crescents much bigger than those I have already seen and which shine so brightly that they must be of pure gold.

'*Napab Hyder Ali Khan Sultan Pahadur*!' says the commander, pointing to the three tents.

I scarcely have time to see the canvas gateway to the enclosure, with its battery of two field cannons, a banner planted in the ground and a squad of foot lancers. Our column turns to the right and moves away immediately. I seize the commander's arm and he recoils, visibly shocked by this disrespectful contact, but I am too alarmed to worry about that.

'Hyder Ali Khan!' I say. 'I want to be taken to the Nabob!'

Dhuraisingam shakes his head and makes a speech in which I think I hear the words '*naam kalunkal pirandjeu nampar Sher Sahib cella.*'

He utters all this with a smile, no doubt believing that he is making me very happy, but I have heard the words '*Sher Sahib*'. I think to myself that the Abbot Perrin and Monsieur Piveron de Morlat must have been held back, that they are at this very moment talking to the Nabob about me, so close to us in the big tents, not suspecting that I am passing right beside them and being delivered into the claws of my worst enemy. I cannot allow myself to be lead like a lamb to slaughter! I have to escape now; it is my last chance! The commander has no suspicions about me. I will jump out of the palanquin. The crowd is so dense at the spot we are passing that I may be able to lose myself in it to escape my guards. I think about it: we have turned fully to the right from the location of the Nabob's tents. They are at the end of the street just behind us, but if I try to escape that way the soldiers of the escort will stop me immediately. We are still moving along. I see a gap between two tents to our left. Now's the moment! I jump to the ground, barge past one or two people and throw myself into the narrow canvas corridor. The commander is taken completely by surprise and I am already well away before I hear the men being alerted.

I come out into a road parallel to the one I have just left, which must also lead to the enclosure with the Nabob's tents. The soldiers are now if full pursuit. They have bare legs, while I am wearing an *angui*. It may be a beautiful item of clothing, but it is not made for running in. I will soon be caught if I stay long in this new street, which is almost deserted. I hare off in the right direction but duck into the first passageway I see on my right. I take a few more strides then stop to catch my breath. It feels like the beating of my heart is going to explode my thoracic cage. My old wounds from Porto Praya are hurting. My clothes are soaked in sweat and I have lost my hat. I hear soldiers calling to each other in the road I have just left. Thank God they did not see me turn off and so don't know where to look for me. I set off again and find myself at the crossing of several narrow corridors lined by walls of canvas. I try to get my bearings in this maze. We arrived at the camp from the south, marched straight on, and once we had arrived at the Nabob's Court we had turned right. I decide to go left. I am out of sight in this row of narrow passageways, but I can see, or rather feel, that I'm not the only one to appreciate the quietness here. The soil is littered with turds covered with flies which take off and buzz all around me. So as not to smell the strong odour rising from the ground in this spot, sheltered from the wind and transformed into a furnace by the Carnatic midday sun, I have to breathe with my mouth open, thereby risking swallowing one of these disgusting creatures. If anybody finds me here there is nowhere I can hide. I slowly get my breath back but I have trouble keeping a cool head, fearing at any moment that my pursuers will appear from an alley and cut off my route. I worry about going past the central enclosure, and count the tents. At the fifth I see a passageway to my left and I slide into it. A miracle! I am just opposite the canvas gate to the Nabob's residence, defended by its two cannons. There are ten or so guards there, fine men, all tall and well-built. They are wearing red turbans, and are wild-looking with long moustaches which reach to their temples. They are carrying a kind of short sabre and silver-bladed lances decorated with ribbons and black ostrich feathers. As I approach them I hear shouts to my left. Dhuraisingam's soldiers have just caught sight of me and are running in my direction.

'I am French. I want to see the Nabob Hyder Ali Khan!' My pack of pursuers arrive, shouting at the guards in Tamil.

'Monsieur Piveron de Morlat!' I shout. 'I am a friend of Monsieur Piveron de Morlat, ambassador of the King of France!'

The Nabob's guards look at each other, hesitating. I think for a moment that I am saved. Then they lower their lances to my chest. The soldiers of my escort come up to me and surround me. One ties my hands behind my back and I am dragged to the street, where the commander's and the Governor's palanquins are waiting.

Seeing me being brought to him, the commander firstly admonishes his men for having bound me, or at least that is what I assume, as they quickly release me. I have the impression that the Governor disapproves of this move, but the commander takes no notice. He invites me to get into the palanquin with him and posts three lancers on each side in case I try to escape again. We cover a long distance before arriving at the eastern end of the camp, just before the savannah which stretches away as far as the horizon.

The Governor and the commander go into the last tent on the left and come out with my living nightmare: Flaharn! He is followed by another cursed soul, Babar Khan, our old guide from Porto Novo who, doubtless without knowing it, has replaced the unfortunate Jakar whom I saw die at Savannah. On an order from his chief, the terrible Babar goes back into the tent and returns with several well-built Pathans who surround me and drag me roughly along with them. I have time to notice the surprise on the commander's face. I don't think he expected a reception like this. The tent is very big, with a cloth partition that must enclose Flaharn's private quarters. In the common area the ground is covered with rugs and mats, along with horse saddles and pots for all the movables. Muskets and sabres are hung up or placed everywhere against the canvas sides of the tent. We wait inside while Flaharn finishes talking to the Governor of Pandarom Shutri. Two Pathan warriors stand each side of me, holding my arms. They have recognised me and are clearly burning with desire to take revenge for the death of their fellow soldier, sliced in two so beautifully by Thomas Moutou. No doubt they are adequately fearful of their chief to await his orders. The talking outside goes on and on. I can mainly hear Flaharn and the Governor. The latter seems very angry at first, but quickly calms down as he realises who he is dealing with. I hear feet stamping and orders as the troop which brought me here goes off.

Flaharn comes back into the tent and plants himself in front of me. He stares at me right in the eyes and suddenly, without warning, slaps my face hard. My head is pulled to one side by the force of it.

'Laforest-Dombourg! I have just lost a hundred rupees for nothing! Where are my diamonds?'

I search for something to say and a second blow, stronger than the one before, forces my head in the other direction. My lip has been split and I feel the taste of blood in my mouth. The Pathans hold me in an iron grip. I get the feeling they are enjoying this.

'My baggage was left at Pandarom Shutri,' I finally say.

Instead of replying he gives an order to his henchmen, who rip off all my clothing. This is becoming a habit! Flaharn looks at the scars on my torso.

'Porto Praya,' I say.

'I should have seen it the other day, but I wasn't paying attention. You are maybe more fragile than I thought. I'll have to bear that in mind. I want to make you talk, not kill you, at least not straight away,' he adds with an ironic smile. 'I'm going to have you dealt with in a manner suitable to your state.'

He thinks for a while and then delivers a long stream of orders to his men. Two of his bandits go to fetch four ramrods. They clear the ground of the carpets around us and push the iron shafts deep into the earth. They attach leather ties to my wrists and ankles and stretch my bindings to the four improvised stakes. I end up spreadeagled on my back, completely naked and at the mercy of my torturers. For good measure they attach a hemp rope to the stakes holding my wrists and take a turn around my neck, squeezing my Adam's apple. A mercenary brings a bucket full of cloudy liquid and Flaharn dips a piece of muslin used to clean their rifles into it.

'I told Babar to prepare a secret little potion for you which will loosen your tongue. In the meantime, to whet your appetite, we'll give you a taste of the water from our oxen's drinking trough.'

On the word from Flaharn, they throw the wet cloth over my face. One of my torturers grabs me by the hair and roughly pulls my head back, while his associate sits squarely astride my midriff, compressing my stomach, and slowly pours the contents of the bucket over the cloth. I try first to keep my lips tight but the liquid runs up my nostrils. The pain is unbearable and I open my mouth to breath in some air but the instead breathe in the thin cloth, which sticks in my throat. I suffocate, I choke, I am drowning. A black veil covers my eyes.

When I come round I am still spreadeagled on the ground. I don't know how long I have been unconscious. Flaharn is leaning over me.

'Stay with us, Laforest-Dombourg. We have hardly begun. Damnation! I thought you were stronger than that! Right, now let's be serious: what have you done with my diamonds?'

I don't reply because I don't know what to say. Why didn't the Abbot Perrin send the soldiers who were to protect me? And Monsieur Piveron de Morlat? Did the Nabob refuse to listen to him? Is he annoyed with his French auxiliaries? What's his name again, the French colonel? Bouthenot, that's it…

Flaharn is growing impatient. 'Be reasonable. Why give yourself so much trouble just for the Nabob? He's nothing but a tyrant and usurper, after all, and he already has mountains of diamonds in his treasury. What difference does it make to you if I have them instead of him? He already has plenty which he doles out to all his guests. Why play the hero? You think you'll get a medal? You really are so naïve!'

He watches me for a few moments, no doubt waiting for me to react. Then he shrugs with a sigh, saying again that I am so stupid.

'Fine! I hope you are thirsty, as that excellent fellow Babar is going to give you his own special treat!'

I see the awful Babar arriving, with a terracotta pitcher in his hands. An underling kneels down and traps my head between his knees. With one hand he pinches my nostrils and with the other opens my jaw. Flaharn's lieutenant starts to pour into my mouth a kind of brandy so strong that it feels as if I am swallowing fire. I cough. He pours faster to empty the pot. My mouth overflows and once again I lose consciousness. When I come round, everything seems to be dancing around me. I seem to be floating underwater. When someone talks their voice echoes strangely in my head. He weeps, he shouts. This lasts for a long time, going on and on, until I realise that the voice is mine. My head is spinning and I want to be sick. Just as I feel as if I will pass out again, I am untied and lifted up. My stiff legs buckle beneath my weight but strong hands keep me upright. My wrists are bound with rope and I am dragged along like a sack, my feet no longer touching the ground. Flaharn hits me in the stomach with his strong fists to bring me round, to the extent that I start to groan.

'It's not yet bedtime, Laforest-Dombourg! You are lucky! The cordial which the fine Babar has so graciously given you has made you a little more talkative, but not enough. But you mentioned an interesting name...'

I feel sick and my whole body is in pain, but I am much more alert now. They have hung me by the wrists under a kind of gallows erected at the end of the tent. Some oil lamps have been lit. I have no idea what time it is. Night must have fallen a long time ago, as most of the Pathans are already sleeping.

'You spoke about both Piveron de Morlat and Bouthenot,' continues Flaharn. 'That's not the most important thing for me, but as I think you said you were expecting them to come to your aid, I thought you may be interested to know that they are no longer in the camp. They left with the Nabob and his cavalry almost a week ago. The English wanted to attack the Arni fortress. Yesterday we could still hear cannon fire from that direction. The Nabob sent a message to say that the English were withdrawing towards Madras via Wandiwash[35] and that he was

---

35 Translator's note: *Wandiwash:* now known as Vandavasi, and scene of the Battle of Wandiwash, 1760, a pivotal engagement in which the French, commanded by Lally-Tollendal, and suffering from a lack of naval and financial support, were heavily defeated by a British force under Sir Eyre Coote. The battle effectively established British supremacy in India.

pursuing them. He also ordered us to make camp here and wait for him. But I don't think they will be back by tomorrow. Perhaps the day after?'

Despite my weakness this news is like a hammer blow. I can't hold out for another day! If I knew where the diamonds were I would tell Flaharn right now so that he can kill me immediately.

'But you also talked about a certain Abbot Perrin. That's what interests me! The little rat who governs Pandarom Shutri completely forgot to mention him. Who is this Abbot Perrin? Is he the one you have entrusted my diamonds to?'

I don't know what to say. My mind is too disordered. What can I say without putting the missionary's life in danger? My silence annoys my executioner, who once again starts pummelling my stomach with his fists. The dirty water from the trough, combined with the rotgut, have started a bout of dysentery, and Flaharn's furious blows do the rest: I can do nothing, and feel my bowels emptying themselves, although I have not eaten since yesterday. A nasty smell spreads through the tent, waking the nearest Pathans and bringing protests from them. Flaharn chuckles.

'What a little pig you are, Laforest-Dombourg. You are offending the sensibilities of my men. They are very delicate, don't you know? I'll have to put you outside, otherwise they'll knife you during the night. It's late and you've tired us all out with your stubbornness. We'll talk later. Use the time to think. Today we have been gentle with you, but my patience has its limits. Tomorrow, if you refuse to help me, it will be a different story. You will curse your mother for ever having given birth to you.'

He has said that deliberately, having killed my mother himself, and being well aware that I know it. He wakes his men and says something to them in Hindustani. Muttering, they untie me. I instantly fall to the ground. They dress me in my *angui,* without which I have nothing to wipe myself with. Under their chief's orders they pull my scaffold out of the ground and take it out of the tent. I remain sitting on the ground. On another order from Flaharn one of the mercenaries brings me a bowl of cold rice. He spits in it before placing it in front of me. That greatly upsets Flaharn, who unleashes a mighty blow with his fist, full in the face, which has the recipient recoiling two paces under the shock. He is no weakling, but Flaharn is as strong as Hercules. That's how he has always imposed his authority. The other Pathans, now well awake, burst out laughing, slapping their thighs. Flaharn picks up the bowl and throws it in the face of his victim, swearing at him. The man goes off and comes back with another bowl. He grimaces as he touches his nose, which to me looks completely broken. His comrades make fun of him, laughing.

I force myself to swallow a few mouthfuls. I have to eat with my hands. The Pathans who took the scaffold out come back and report to Flaharn. I am pulled off the ground and dragged outside. We go around the tent. Two Pathans have lit torches to give some light. I can see the wooden posts stuck in the ground in the corridor between the neighbouring tents.

'While you are here,' explains Flaharn, 'you won't be visible from the street when it gets light and in the meantime you'll have some shelter from the wind.'

I remain all alone in the dark. They have tied my two hands together and passed around another rope which secures me to the frame from which I am suspended by my wrists. My feet are not on the ground but they too are tied to two supports of the gallows. I can put my weight on these to relieve my arms. I have no idea what time it is but feel it must be after midnight. I had remained unconscious for a long time after Babar's devilish potion. I wonder whether I will be strong enough to hold out until dawn. I would like to die before then, as I am so fearful of what awaits me. I would like to escape into a deep and beneficial coma which would cut short my suffering and from which I would never waken, but nothing brings it on. I can feel the night breeze passing between the tents. Despite everything I can hear the plaintive cries of the jackals as they call to each other while marauding around the camp. I cannot even sleep, as once I start to doze my body slumps either forward or backwards, pulling my arms, and the pressure of the ties on my wrists wakes me up.

*

The first thing I could smell was the dew. They had tied me up facing east and in front of me at the end of the corridor between the tents I could see a small section of horizon lit up by the nascent dawn. The Pathans were snoring loudly but I thought I could also hear quiet steps coming from the street on the other side. They stopped for a good while and I thought I had imagined it. Then there was a groan close by, as if from a pig having its throat cut, and the silence was broken by a shout of surprise that finished as a death rattle. There was then a gunshot, followed immediately by a sustained salvo. A battle was going on in Flaharn's tent. Several musket balls came through the canvas and I could smell powder. Someone spoke in Hindustani, with a begging tone. There was one final shot. I distinctly heard someone shout 'Weiterziehen!', and the same voice continued on, 'Stop firing! I need prisoners!'

The cool of the morning was soon replaced by the usual intense heat of this climate. Peace had returned inside the big tent, from where could be heard the sound of voices conversing. In my state of fatigue I did not at first realise that I could understand some of what was being said: they were talking in a mixture of German and French. I would have like to call for help but I was too weak to shout. My hearing was still good, however, and I recognised the voice of the Abbot Perrin. They had finally come to my aid! Having wanted to die before Flaharn had me fetched for more torture, I was now afraid that they would find me too late. My anguish reached its height when I saw European soldiers passing to and fro at the end of the corridor where I was tied up, and could do nothing to attract their attention. They were wearing boots and scarlet French uniforms. They were no doubt those famous hussars, or dragoons, about whom my uncle de Kermean had spoken at Brest, and the Abbot Perrin at Punganur. I could see them perfectly well but not one of them thought to stop and look in my direction. To add to my misfortune, huge clouds of flies had risen with the sun. They landed on my hands, feet and neck, and stuck to my face. The only defence I had was to shut my eyes and mouth and weakly shake my head. I scarcely dared to breathe.

I was finally saved thanks to the numerous vultures which fly above the camp from dawn in search of anything edible. Nothing escapes their sharp eyes. One of them, having seen me from on high, and no doubt wanting to check that I was dead, glided down and landed at my feet with a loud clacking of its wide wings. One of the horsemen, intrigued by the appearance of this scavenger, came to see what had attracted it. Thus was I found.

I remember little of what then happened. When I came round properly, two days later, I was lying on a proper bed, with real sheets, in a tent with a double wall of painted canvas and a floor covered with carpets. I had been dressed in a cotton robe and washed from head to toe. An incense burner was smoking softly beside me on a small ebony table inlaid with pearl, filling the air with a discreet perfume that held at bay the stink of the camp outside.

Hearing me move, a young girl sitting at the other end of the room, and whom I had not noticed, got up and came to stand at the foot of my bed, saying a few questioning words in Tamil with a very gentle voice. She really seemed to expect an answer from me, and we looked at each other in silence for a long time. She had a pleasant face and fine features, light brown skin and a small diamond attached to a ring in one nostril that gave her a mischievous look. Her black hair hung down her back in a heavy plait and she was wearing a dress of light gauze over a sort of short-sleeved white bodice that came up to her neck. As I said nothing she went out, no doubt to tell someone that I was awake, coming back shortly afterwards followed by a European of about fifty and an old, white-bearded Indian. They listened to my chest, while talking to each other in Tamil.

'Forgive me for not introducing myself straight away,' said the Frenchman. 'My name is Rousseau, previously Surgeon-General to the troops of the India Company, and this is Arivu, an empirical doctor, versed in the traditional medicine of this country. We are both in the service of the Nabob and we complement each other very well. You had us very worried! I think you are through the worst, but you must still be patient, as it will take you a long time to recover your full health. You are going to have to make do with little food, and drink only rice water for a fair while. Especially no wine! I am the first to deplore this, as your mental state is very important and privations are not good for that. I have already seen patients whom I thought to be cured fall into a deep apathy and a fatal indifference to the world to the point of letting themselves die, with medicine being of no help. But you are young and there are more than the pleasures of the table to life! I think that Nadanamani will be of great help to you as far as that is concerned. You are a lucky man!'

I did not immediately understand what he meant and the strange look on my face made him laugh.

'Nadanamani is a special consideration from the Nabob, who greatly appreciates what you have done. I would very much like to be in your place.'

His Indian colleague said a few words to him in Tamil and he became serious again.

'Arivu is most impressed by the scars you have on your chest and back. We can see that it is a bullet wound, but I don't understand how you could have survived it.'

'It is a souvenir from Porto Praya…' I began.

He stopped me with a hand gesture.

'You will tell us later. I don't want to tire you too much at the moment as you will be having visitors.'

A little later the Abbot Perrin arrived at my bedside, along with two visitors whom I found quite intimidating: Messieurs Piveron de Morlat and Bouthenot – a diplomat and a soldier. The diplomat must have been a little under forty. He spoke with polish, calm and distinction, but also showed the ease and hardiness of a man used to danger. The soldier seemed to be of the same age, perhaps a little younger. He was wearing a scarlet coat with fawn tabling, and although he had always been talked of to me as a Colonel, he had on his left shoulder the silver epaulette of a cavalry Captain, with only fringes and no pips. His face and hands were heavily weather-beaten from ten years in the saddle in India. With his dark eyes and lively gaze, he looked particularly intrepid, almost wild. He spoke with the unpretentious and clipped manner of a soldier.

They had begun by asking how I was. I had replied that I still felt very weak, that I was not in any pain, but was above all troubled by what I had just been through. I told them that I still had difficulty believing that it was over. Saying this, my voice failed me and I started shaking so violently that they were within an inch of leaving immediately. Monsieur Piveron said that he would call Doctor Rousseau.

'Please stay, gentlemen!' I cried. 'Don't leave me on my own! It does me good to talk about what I have been through, and I also need to know what happened and how everything finished. Have you given the letter and the diamonds to the Nabob? What has become of Flaharn?'

My three visitors looked at each other and the diplomat addressed me.

'I have read most of the letter to Hyder Ali Khan, telling him it was written by the Chevalier de Suffren. Anything from your Admiral is most appreciated at the moment! I also spoke to him about the diamonds, making clear, as it says in the letter, that the gift is to compensate him for his promise to maintain the troops who disembarked with the

Comte Duchemin. The letter and 'gift' came just at the right moment to improve our relationship with the Nabob at a most delicate time. Moreover, he was most interested to hear that you are a naval officer from the Chevalier de Suffren's squadron and he will no doubt want to see you once you are better. Although I do wonder how one could have entrusted such a mission to a simple Ship's Ensign…but there we are! You haven't come out of it too badly, all the same. But as for an audience with the Nabob, don't count on it too much.'

'You have given him the diamonds then, Sir' I asked.

It was the Abbot Perrin who responded.

'I am leaving for Gingee today to fetch them, with Colonel Bouthenot and a troop of his hussars. They will bring them here so that Monsieur Piveron can present them to the Nabob. I'll use this opportunity to say farewell to you, as I will stay in Gingee to deal with my parishioners before returning to Punganur. I'll go via Pandarom Shutri to collect my brave servants. But I owe you an explanation as you must have thought that I had abandoned you. Even though it was not my fault, I feel very guilty, thinking of everything you have suffered on account of my powerlessness.'

'More than anything, I would like to know where the diamonds are,' I replied. 'You see, they have been a real curse for more than ten years, first for my parents and then for me. I will never be at peace until I know that I have truly got rid of this burden.'

'Do you remember my portable chapel?' the Abbot asked me, rather than give a direct answer.

'You mean the little varnished wooden chest with one handle like a suitcase? If I remember correctly it was on the back of your ox.'

'That's it! I had taken it with me when I left Pandarom Shutri on horseback on the Friday morning. Inside it I put an altar stone, ciborium, chalice, cloths and everything necessary for celebrating the Holy Mass. There is plenty of spare space, and even a double bottom. I poured all your diamonds any old how amongst my holy utensils and closed up the portable chapel, which has a single lock. I gave it to my parishioners at Gingee, telling then that it contained holy spirits and that they must on no account try to open it. I'm sure they will have respected my orders and looked after it as if it were a prized possession.'

The Abbot Perrin paused for a moment, and, as I did not reply, continued on.

'I'm coming to what happened. Having left Pandarom Shutri I stopped at my community at Gingee at eight in the morning and stayed there for a while. I expected to arrive at the Nabob's camp beside Chetpet towards four in the afternoon. As you know, the army had struck camp. I followed its track and arrived here on the Saturday night. I went straight away to see Monsieur Piveron de Morlat, only to learn, not only that he was away for a few days, but that he had gone with the Nabob, who had taken his cavalry on a campaign against the English. Nobody could tell me when he would be back. Not knowing which way to turn, and unable to do anything on my own, I decided to go and ask help from the Court first thing in the morning. I told the entrance guards that I needed to see Vennagipendet, the Nabob's Deputy. He's the one I know best in the Nabob's entourage, as it's he who was designated by his master to deal with me in matters to do with the relationship between my communities and certain governors. Anyway, he was there but the rascal made me wait for hours. When he finally deigned to see me, and after I had told him that I need his help against Flaharn, the name meant nothing to him, and he replied quite rudely that it was a problem between the French and that he had had a bellyful of our problems. Finally, he told me how badly he thought of the Comte Duchemin and all his promises, when the troops he commanded had done nothing since their arrival but whose upkeep was costing the Nabob dearly...'

'My dear friend,' interrupted Monsieur Piveron, 'this is extremely interesting to me, especially as you had no need of an interpreter for this conversation. You ought to have mentioned it to me earlier. I beg you not to leave before you have recounted to me in detail everything that Vennagipendet said. However, now is not the time for that!'

'As you wish,' replied the Abbot Perrin. 'So, at that point,' he continued, turning towards me once again, 'when I had come out from my audience, I learned from one of the guards that you had been arrested in front of them by Dhuraisingam's sepoys.'

'I thought you were there!' I exclaimed.

'Alas! If I had not been held up by that fruitless audience with Vennagipendet, I may have been able to stop you being taken off. However, leaving the Court, I met the Governor of Pandarom Shutri. He was furious at only having been given a hundred rupees as a reward for his efforts and I was at least able to get from him the location of the tent where you were being held prisoner. Luckily Monsieur Piveron returned earlier than expected on Sunday morning, well before dawn, and I explained the position to him. He immediately called Colonel Bouthenot and asked him to follow me with his men, whom I guided to the Pathans' tent.'

'Were it not for the ceaseless activity and energy of the Nabob, we would never have returned in time to save you,' said Monsieur Piveron. 'On the eighth of June, after following the English for three days with a series of marches and counter marches, and having fought all day, Hyder Ali Khan had us set off at nine o'clock in the evening. Instead of letting his men rest we marched all night. Moreover, as I am well thought of by the Nabob at the moment, I myself was able to take the decision to send Colonel Bouthenot and his hussars to save you, without getting prior permission from the Court.'

'Monsieur Piveron is too modest,' added Colonel Bouthenot. 'He has omitted to say that the reason he is so well thought of at the Court is because the night before he had saved the Nabob's life!'

'Oh, I didn't do much, but I don't regret having seized the opportunity,' said the diplomat. 'Hyder Ali Khan, careless of danger as usual, was standing all alone on a dike and I saw that the English were aiming two of their cannons at him. I rushed to push him down just before the cannon balls arrived right where he had been standing. That made him laugh, as none of his courtiers would have dared to manhandle him in that way, even to save his life, as they are so afraid of him.'

'Unfortunately, Flaharn escaped,' said Bouthenot. 'We didn't find him immediately. He heard us coming and had the time to slice through the outer canvas of his tent with his sword and get away.'

'We don't even know if he has left the camp,' added Monsieur Piveron. 'It seems that he has accomplices inside the Court. A most strange character! He came to the Nabob last December, a little before me, with a little band of Rohilla mercenaries that he had apparently recruited himself, using his own money, in Rohilkhand, in the north of Hindustan. He was passing himself off as a Belgian adventurer by the name of Declercq. Talking of which, the Chevalier de Suffren had asked me to look out for a certain Barrad Amzer. Would that be the same man?'

'Indeed,' I replied. 'The name Barrad Amzer had been mentioned to us by an accomplice of Flaharn, a man called Tallebau, who styles himself the Chevalier de Saint-Luperce and who was recently entrusted with a mission by the Chevalier de Suffren.'

'I saw that this Tallebau de Saint-Luperce is mentioned along with you in the letter from the Chevalier de Suffren that the Abbot Perrin gave me on your behalf. He had been asked by the Minister to present your diamonds to the Nabob with all pomp. That had greatly surprised me as Hyder Ali Khan would probably have had him arrested and executed had he been so bold as to present himself. In any case he did not come, luckily. Naturally I did not read that part of the letter to the Nabob. Do you know where he is?'

'No, Sir, and I was going to ask the same question,' I said. 'We left Porto Novo together and the last time I saw him he was riding with Flaharn and his band of mercenaries on the Gingee road. There's no doubt that they were in cahoots and had planned to steal the diamonds. Do you know him?'

'Not really. I was at Pondicherry when I heard from Monsieur Law de Lauriston, a little over twelve years ago, that he had asked the Governor of the Île Bourbon to have this Saint-Luperce arrested and sent to France in irons. He was accused of being an English agent. At the time he would have been paid at the Siege of Madras for encouraging desertion, not just amongst the European soldiers serving Hyder Ali Khan, but also the sepoys in our garrisons. I then caught sight of him in Monsieur de Sartine's office when I returned to France in 1770. To my great surprise, moreover, as I thought he was in the Bastille. He was preparing to return to India in great secrecy. I then heard him spoken about by Colonel de Montigny last August, when I made the crossing from the Île-de-France to Goa. The Colonel was going to Puna on a mission similar to mine here. He told me that Saint-Luperce had been the King's envoy to the Marathas before him and that when he had returned to France he had been sent to the Bastille once again. This was not at all reassuring for Montigny, who had to replace him at Puna. So, he has been released once again from the Bastille to be sent as an envoy to the Nabob? It makes no sense!'

I perhaps ought to have said that Saint-Luperce had managed to mislead the Chevalier de Suffren and the Vicomte de Souillac, but that would have meant getting into complicated explanations, and I was too tired. It would also have meant explaining that in reality the King and the Marquis de Castries had decided to deal with the Marathas rather than the Nabob, and that would no doubt have displeased the diplomat, whom I did not want to upset for no reason. In any case, there had been no turning back for a while; the dice had been thrown once the Vicomte de Souillac and the late Comte d'Orves had decided to send the King's squadron to the Coromandel rather than the Malabar Coast.

As he left, the Abbot Perrin noticed the presence of the young Indian girl who was standing discreetly at the end of the room, no doubt waiting for the visitors to leave before making her appearance. Monsieur de Piveron noticed his look.

'She's a dancer from the Nabob's Court. Their supervisor buys them when they are four or five years old, choosing the prettiest, and has them taught singing, dance and music. Hyder Ali Khan had her sent here to serve as nurse to Ensign Laforest-Dombourg. He chose her personally and said absolutely no payment must be made to her supervisor.'

Bouthenot burst out laughing.

'Her supervisor! Madame pimp, you mean! She'll be very put out! Usually, you have to give her a hundred rupees for a night with one of her boarders, on top of the diamond given to the girl when she leaves in the morning. And moreover, beneath her innocent looks, Nadanamani is the star of her high-class bordello!'

'I thought it was something along those lines,' said the Abbot. 'I have had parishioners come to me to beg me to protect a child who has taken the Nabob's eye. And you know what becomes of them? Once they are eighteen, they are sent away and all they can do is serve as a *devadasi* in the temples consecrated to carnal love. On condition, of course, that the Nabob has paid a dowry to the Brahmins who run these establishments, supposedly holy but in fact the hotbeds of vice in this country.'

'Oh, come on, Father,' said the Colonel. 'At least they don't have husbands who beat them, and the *devadasis* are very well thought of. Their lot is not so bad, if you want my opinion. For sure, they have to put up at the start with being branded on the chest with a hot iron, as a consecration to their divinity. That's probably why in public they wear more modest clothing than most of the good women of this country.'

'Colonel, you seem to know what you are talking about! Rather too well, I'm afraid,' said the Abbot, half joking and half serious. 'You lead a dangerous life and you should think a little more of your health. That goes for you too, my young friend,' added the missionary, turning to me. 'But you are in excellent hands with Arivu. You can ask Monsieur Piveron about him. He cured a man of an illness nobody had managed to treat before him.'

The Abbot Perrin's fears about my health were unfounded. At the beginning, anyway! I was in a state of extreme physical weakness, on account of another bout of dysentery caused, no doubt, by the tortures inflicted on me by Flaharn and a consequence too, I think, of the trials I had endured since leaving Porto Novo. I was confined to my bed and shut off in my tent for a long time. During this time Colonel Bouthenot often came to see me. He considered me a friend, and asked me about my campaigns in the Navy and kept me up to date with what was going on outside. The dancer accompanied our conversations by plucking the strings of an instrument almost as big as herself, which looked like a huge lute with two sound boxes.

The Colonel told me that there was another French officer in the service of the Nabob who, unlike him, had not been sent on his mission by Versailles, but had joined Hyder Ali Khan of his own volition with a strong partisan group of five hundred Europeans and five thousand sepoys that he himself had put together. He was a former staff officer of Lally-Tollendal who had stayed in India after the first capture of Pondicherry in 1761. His full name was Motz de la Sale, but he was known to everyone as Lallée. I would have liked to have met him, as he must have known Saint-Luperce and Doctor Rollin, but he was away on campaign with Tipoo Sahib in the Vellore region.

Bouthenot also told me that the relationship between Hyder Ali Khan and the Comte Duchemin was very poor, largely because the latter had refused to allow his soldiers to fight alongside our allies, while constantly asking for more money from the Nabob to maintain his troops. He was also asking for land which had not yet been conquered. This situation had been heavily exploited by the English, who had numerous agents in the Nabob's entourage. Monsieur Piveron strongly suspected that Vennagipendet was one of them, as he was doing all he could to sow discord between Duchemin and his master. Things had reached the point where Colonel Lallée had even had to go secretly one night to the French camp at Manjakuppam, near Cuddalore, to tell them that the Nabob was so exasperated that he was going to send envoys to Madras[36]. This had finally convinced Duchemin to join up with the Mysore army at Permacoul, but he had gone no further and the situation between him and Hyder Ali Khan was once again deteriorating. The Nabob had not yet ceded to the English advances, for two reasons. The first was the gift of diamonds which I had risked my life to help bring him; the second was linked to what he was hearing about the maritime activities of the Chevalier de Suffren, whom he admired as much as he distrusted the Comte Duchemin, who was eaten with jealousy at this. This was why, the Colonel explained, Monsieur Piveron had not wanted the Abbot Perrin to discuss in front of a sailor like me the criticisms made by the Nabob's Deputy.

'He was wrong not to let the Abbot talk to you about it,' Bouthenot said to me, 'as it was Vennagipendet who brought Flaharn into the Nabob's camp. That was confirmed by the Rohilla prisoners I interrogated. Flaharn had paid them in advance when he recruited them in Rohilkhand. He had equipped them and brought them here, and he was expected by Vennagipendet. The latter had used all his resources to have this band of mercenaries incorporated into the Nabob's army. They were specialists in reconnaissance and skirmishing and it's true that Flaharn's personality, his impressive strength, his violence and his cruelty had made a strong impression on Hyder Ali Khan's generals.'

I was alone for the following days. Colonel Bouthenot and his squadron had gone north, where Tipoo Sahib was going to confront an English column coming from Madras to resupply Vellore. Before leaving, he had told me that the Chevalier de Suffren had sent a letter to Monsieur Piveron announcing a victory[37] against an English squadron off the coast of Ceylon. Monsieur Piveron was impatient to read it to the Nabob. The situation was becoming more and more delicate as regards our interests, mainly because of the Comte Duchemin. Fortunately, the Colonel told me, with some cynicism, that the Comte had fallen seriously ill. There was a good chance that he would have to pass command to the Comte d'Hoffelize, the Colonel in charge of the 1st

---

36 Translator's note: *…he was going to send envoys to Madras:* presumably to sound out the possibility of an alliance with the English.

37 Translator's note: *victory:* The Battle of Providien, 12th April 1782, was the second engagement between the Chevalier de Suffren and Admiral Hughes. Although as indecisive as the Battle of Sadras, the English suffered considerably higher casualties.

Battalion of the Austrasie regiment. These were the elite soldiers of our little expeditionary force while we waited for the arrival, announced but always delayed, of the Marquis de Bussy with his reinforcements. The Comte was a real soldier who had distinguished himself during the Seven Years' War and whom Bouthenot greatly appreciated.

Shortly afterwards, towards mid-June, as I languished in the suffocating heat of the tent, which had to be kept closed because of the flies, and as I was admiring the pretty form of my nurse sitting beside my bed, and wondering if I would ever recover, I was surprised to see a visitor enter wearing the uniform of a Ship's Lieutenant. It was Lieutenant de Moissac! I don't know which of us was the most moved. He had left our ships anchored off Tranquebar six days earlier, with the Chevalier de Suffren's latest correspondence for the Nabob.

Before his Flag Captain had left, the Chevalier de Suffren had told him that he had just received the reply from Monsieur Piveron to his previous letter about the Battle of Providien. Amongst other things, the King's envoy had announced that I had eventually completed my mission, against huge odds, given that I had been betrayed by Saint-Luperce and Flaharn, *alias* Barrad Amzer. Not having had any news for all this time, the Admiral had long been wondering what could have happened to us. Depending on his mood, he said we had either been killed or had deserted with the diamonds. He had been greatly relieved to hear that the Nabob had finally received his 'present' and his letter, but had asked Lieutenant de Moissac to come and see me, to obtain more detail on the business. I told the whole story from the beginning: the slanders of Saint-Luperce, which I was perfectly aware of but against which I could not defend myself, there being no proof; the totally unforeseen trap set by Flaharn, from which I had escaped thanks to an extraordinary stroke of luck and the fidelity of Thomas Moutou.

I already knew that our squadron was returning from the coast of Ceylon, where it had once again engaged Admiral Hughes' ships, and that Monsieur Piveron had shared this news with the Nabob. Lieutenant de Moissac told me that this encounter had been as indecisive as the Battle of Sadras, but much more lethal: a hundred and thirty-seven killed and three hundred and fifty-seven wounded, some of whom had since died. All the same, he was pleased with how he had been received at the Court, finding the Nabob very supportive of the squadron.

Hyder Ali Khan completely approved of the Chevalier de Suffren's planned attack on Nagapattinam and had ordered his troops in the area to put themselves at the Admiral's disposal. He had said several times that he had a great desire to meet the Chevalier de Suffren and proposed that this meeting should take place at Cuddalore once our ships had returned from their campaign against Nagapattinam. On the other hand, he did not hide from Lieutenant de Moissac the fact that he really needed to have the same kind of relationship with our army, which had remained encamped at Villianur and had never joined up with his, despite repeated requests.

I was very sad to see Lieutenant de Moissac leave. I would have liked to have gone with him, as I missed the sea. Alas, I was still unable to stand.

My condition started to improve soon after the Ship's Lieutenant's visit. I tried first to walk by hanging on to the canvas sides of my tent. Seeing this, Nadanamani came to hold me up. She was smaller than me, but incredibly strong in the legs. When I mentioned this to Colonel Bouthenot, who had now returned, he said it was a result of the constant practice of Tamil dance. Thanks to her I made good progress and before long the Abbot Perrin's worst fears were realised. Once again, I had reason to feel guilty as regards Maria Kirwan. In my defence, I would say that my nurse had a body as luscious as those of the statues covering the temple walls and which had more than once piqued my imagination. I had been too close to death to have the strength to resist Nadanamani's extraordinary vitality. Once I could walk, I got better very quickly. By chance, it was at that moment that the Nabob sent one of his officers, accompanied by an interpreter. They brought me a present of a sumptuous Indian suit, to replace the clothes I had lost and announced that Hyder Ali Khan had summoned me to the Court for nine o'clock the following morning. I would discover later through Colonel Bouthenot that Monsieur Piveron had done all he could to stop this meeting, as he thought that I was too young, and of too low a rank, and that this could demean us in the eyes of the Nabob's Court dignitaries. The Colonel also told me that Nadanamani made a daily report on my progress to Hyder Ali Khan, and that was how he knew that I was now in a fit state to come to the Court. Hearing that, I felt myself blush from tip to toe. The Nabob had called me directly, without going through Monsieur Piveron. Had I been younger I would have rushed innocently to this prestigious meeting, but fortunately my time at Versailles had knocked some sense into me. I immediately went to see the Monsieur Piveron to tell him about the meeting. I believe that he was grateful for this, as he was a man as honest as he was descent.

There were three canvas tents inside the enclosure at the entrance of which I had been arrested by the guards at the beginning of June: one for the Nabob, one for his harem and the third for holding Court. It was into the last that Monsieur Piveron and I were taken. It was lit up, although it was daytime, and had galleries and columns covered in precious brightly-coloured cloths. The ground was laid with superb carpets covered in muslin. The exterior tent walls were also draped with muslin. The furnishings were so sumptuous that it felt more like a palace than a tent. Hyder Ali Khan was sitting at the opposite end from the entrance on a superb divan. He was dressed all in white, with a white silk bodice decorated with gold sprays, and his turban and belt were enhanced with magnificent precious stones and diamonds. We walked straight towards him and Monsieur Piveron stopped us at the appropriate distance. But Hyder Ali Khan, smiling, signalled to us to come closer, thereby demonstrating to his entourage that he was dispensing with protocol. The air was scented, and rosewater had been sprinkled on the ground. We were brought cushions and offered betel nuts, plates of fruit and other sweets. I could at last see close up this famous Indian prince about whom I had heard so much. He must have been about sixty. Although he was seated, I found him smaller than I had imagined. His face was ordinary, although sharp-looking, and his skin very dark, even for an Indian, but I understood the power he could have over men when I looked into his fiery eyes, bursting with life. With a laugh he reminded Monsieur Piveron that he had dared to touch him. He asked where my Navy uniform was and I told him that Flaharn had stripped me completely when they wanted to torture me to find the whereabouts of the gift which the King had entrusted to me. The Nabob then said that the chest wound I had sustained in battle was proof enough of my bravery. On hearing that, I could not stop myself from blushing once again, not just from modesty, but because I knew only too well how he had learned about it. Nadanamani had been impressed by the exit scar of the bullet which had wounded me, and which was so much bigger than the little entry hole on my back. Hyder Ali Khan asked me to tell him about the battle in which I had been wounded. I gave him a short summary of the Battle of Porto Praya, stressing above all the bravery with which our Commander had thrown himself into the middle of the anchored English squadron, thereby enhancing the Nabob's admiration for the Chevalier de Suffren. When it was time to leave, he presented me a beautiful diamond set in a ring, saying that it was nothing compared to those I had risked my life to bring him. I accepted it in the hope that I would live long enough to be able to give it to Maria Kirwan and so ease my conscience.

Now that I was recovering, and despite the pleasures to be had in Nadanamani's company, I was keen to return to the sea and my ship. The diamonds had been presented to the Nabob. My role in this adventure was over, even if unanswered questions remained. What had become of Saint-Luperce? Where had Flaharn gone? How had Flaharn, *alias* Declercq, American agent, having met Saint-Luperce in this capacity in Paris at a meeting organised by Doctor Baldock, been able to appear a year later in Rohilkhand in northern Hindustan?

At the beginning of July, the English agents redoubled their efforts to prise Hyder Ali Khan away from his alliance with the French. British ambassadors were received at the Court and this time the Nabob sent permanent envoys to Madras. At almost the same time we heard that the Chevalier de Suffren had put to sea, leaving the convoy at the Tranquebar anchorage, and that the squadron had returned to Cuddalore after another naval battle with the English off Nagapatnam. On this news, Monsieur Piveron became more than ever convinced that only the Chevalier de Suffren would be able to put an end to the negotiations now under way between the Nabob and the English. He left the camp hurriedly for Cuddalore, with the aim of telling the Admiral that a meeting between him and Hyder Ali Khan had to be arranged. I was now much better and would happily have left with the diplomat, but he had not forewarned me. He returned a few days later carrying a letter from the Chevalier de Suffren which described the Battle of Negapatam. The Nabob wanted it read to him immediately, after which he left for Cuddalore to meet the Admiral. He sent a message to his envoys in Madras, ordering them to break off negotiations with the English forthwith.

The King's ambassador also brought back a surprise for me: a parcel containing a complete Ship's Ensign's uniform, including a regulation sword. It was a personal gift from the Chevalier de Suffren to replace the uniform taken off me by Flaharn's Rohillas. With the parcel was a short and friendly message from the Admiral, saying that he was short of officers and look forward to having me back in the squadron.

Two days later, the Nabob's army prepared to move. It was the first time I had seen this enormous body get under way. Beneath the apparent chaos there was in fact considerable order. The evening before, flags had been planted close by to indicate the start of the next day's route. A man mounted on an elephant carrying two huge kettledrums crossed the camp, pounding a slow beat that could be heard from a great distance. He headed up the column with no break in his drumming, continuing in this manner for the whole day and the following days, thereby showing the direction to take. The elephant was accompanied by horsemen carrying banners and flags, and whose job was to mark out the new camp and show each part of the army its place. The infantry and cavalry marched in several columns, and everything non-military formed separate columns. Thousands of people of every age and sex were on the move. Veiled women dressed in white travelled in covered wagons pulled by oxen or horses. Then elephants passed, carrying their platforms, with mahouts astride their necks guiding them with an iron rod. Next came herds of camels carrying tents and equipment. Carts pulled by white oxen as big as battle horses formed other columns. The number of buffalos and oxen carrying loads was incalculable. This mass of men and animals made lines stretching to infinity across the flat plain of the Carnatic. It reminded me of a Latin text from Quintus Curtius describing the armies of Darius the Great, which I had read as a college pupil at Vannes: *this army is formidable for its neighbours; it shines with gold and silver; its arms and its vast machinery, its mass of peoples torn from their homes in every corner of the Orient, is dazzling, and he who has never seen its richness could ever imagine it...*

I was travelling in a palanquin which had been made available to me. It was the second time I had used this form of transport but this time I lounged all alone. Nadanamani had not come, and I would never see her again. I have often since wondered whether the seeds which I planted in her young body with such guilty ease had borne fruit.

11

The Nabob's armies, and the multitude which followed it, had set out on the morning of Sunday 21st July 1782, and marched without a stop for three days. They had a break on the Wednesday night, without erecting the tents. The Indians call this a *mocam*. They set off again the next morning and on Thursday 25th the huge canvas city was set up at a place called Bahour, about five miles north of Cuddalore. A troop of cavalry was immediately sent to the Comte Duchemin's French army camp at Mangikuppam, to escort the Chevalier de Suffren to the Nabob. This escort was under the command of two Generals of the Mysore army. Colonel Bouthenot had joined them with his elite squadron.

Hyder Ali Khan had simply moved about a hundred and fifty miles, with thirty thousand cavalry and foot soldiers, their followers and families, camels and elephants, buffalo and oxen, all that just to meet the Admiral!

At midday on 26th July, I saw the uncountable brightly dressed and armed cohorts of the Nabob gather together, on foot, on horseback, on the backs of camels and elephants, and form two lines of honour to welcome, with all ceremony, the Chevalier de Suffren and his entourage. I had been invited to Monsieur Piveron's tent to wait for the arrival of the great man. The camp was newly set up and the stink that usually pervaded its air and the clouds of flies which infested it had not had time to appear. Nothing was to mar this day of celebration.

The Chevalier de Suffren arrived during the afternoon in a palanquin, followed by several Naval officers from the squadron. Besides the escort provided by the Nabob, the Admiral was accompanied by a company of grenadiers from the Austrasie regiment and another from the Île-de-France regiment. The Comte Duchemin was unable to come as he was ill. Their arrival was greeted by the beating of drums and loud fanfares of trumpets and cymbals which echoed around the horizon. It had been agreed that the audience with the Nabob would take place that evening and that the guests of honour would wait for this in Monsieur Piveron's tent. The Admiral had put on his gold-braided Squadron Commander's jacket over a scarlet waistcoat, it too striped in gold, and red breeches stretched tight over his big thighs; the uniform I had already seen him in at Simon's Bay. It certainly was a magnificent outfit which made one forget the slovenly *Fat Caulker* whom we were used to. The Admiral was soon too hot under the implacable Carnatic sun, as the breeze from inland, sometimes from the south-west, sometimes from the north-west, brought a blast of burning air to the Coromandel Coast at the end of July. The Admiral was streaming with sweat and close to having a heat stroke when he got out of his palanquin in the furnace of the Indian afternoon. He took refuge in the shade of Monsieur Piveron's tent, and the latter advised him to take off his jacket until the evening's ceremonial reception, to save himself from the heat of the day. The others were encouraged to follow suit. As for myself, I only had the light work uniform brought to me by Lieutenant de Moissac and I had had the time to get used to the heat of the country. In any case, I was not invited to the evening's celebrations.

To accompany him, the Chevalier de Suffren had chosen his nephew, Lieutenant de Pierrevert, his Flag Captain, Lieutenant de Moissac, the Squadron Intendant, Monsieur Ravenel, the Ship's Captains de la Pallière, de Saint-Félix and de Cuverville, along with Ship's Lieutenants de Salvert and Pas de Beaulieu. I looked in vain for Lieutenant de Galles and wondered with some alarm whether he had been wounded or worse. Seeing me standing beside Monsieur Piveron in my Ship's Ensign's uniform, the Chevalier de Suffren greeted me with the jovial simplicity he could show when in a good mood, asking in patois "Ow be you? Be good t'see yer, ole chap.' I replied that I was in good health again and that my only wish was to be back at sea.

'That's lucky!' he said, now using French but keeping the Provencal accent. 'I saw in your record of service that you have already sailed aboard a cutter?'

'That's correct, Admiral.'

'Good! Lieutenant de Moissac told me your story and Monsieur Piveron wrote to tell me how pleased the Nabob was with you. I too am very pleased with you.' He turned towards Lieutenant de Moissac, who was following him.

'Moissac. I am giving *la Resolution* to Lieutenant Macé. I have to send her to Manila and he knows the route well. That means *le Diligent* is free. You will give her to Laforest-Dombourg to take the demoted Captains and my correspondence to the Île-de-France. Lieutenant Bouvet will transfer to *la Sylphide.*'

He went off, without giving me any further explanation, to talk with Monsieur Piveron and Lieutenant de Moissac in preparation for the evening's audience. I knew *le Diligent.* She was a former English corsair from Madras, sixty feet on deck and ninety tons burthen, rigged as a lugger, which had been attached to the Île-de-France since her capture. She wasn't clinker-built like the French boats of this type, as the English had coppered her for the Indian Ocean. She sailed well, although she was a little old. She carried eight little 4-pounder cannons, four on each side, and had been used as a corvette to hunt the *pariahs* and carry the Admiral's orders around the squadron. It was she who had disembarked Monsieur de Canaple at Pondicherry shortly after our landfall at Pulicat. She was commanded by Frigate's Lieutenant Macé, an experienced mariner who had sailed for many years with the India Company. I understood that I would have to leave the squadron to return to Port-Louis, and I was a little upset at having to abandon my comrades when the war was not yet finished. On the other hand, the prospect of going on board a ship as the sole master, despite her being as small as *le Diligent,* and for a voyage across seas which were little known to most French sailors, presented a most attractive opportunity for a young Naval officer. Nonetheless, the mention of 'demoted officers' had rung unpleasantly in my ears: as he said those words, the *Lord God Almighty* had let slip a hatred and anger which had not escaped me. I did not know what to make of it.

The Captains who were there crowded around me. They all knew about my punishment following the Battle of Porto Praya, as Saint-Luperce had made sure everybody knew about it. They knew too that I had gone ashore at Porto Novo, but had no idea why. They were intrigued as to why I was suddenly in the Admiral's good books and were clearly surprised to find me at Hyder Ali Khan's camp, especially Lieutenant de Salvert, who had already carried out several missions to the Nabob, and asked me, not without a hint of jealousy, what I had done to please him so much. I did not know whether I was allowed to talk about my mission and its aim, but I told them about Saint-Luperce's treachery, the dangers I had been forced to endure, and how I had crossed the whole of the Carnatic on foot during wartime.

Luckily my awkward explanations were interrupted by the arrival of Indian servants bringing baskets of fruit and refreshments. I took advantage of this to ask Captain de Saint-Félix what the Admiral meant by 'demoted Captains', and why Lieutenant de Galles was not there.

'You must know this camp well,' he said, not replying to my question. 'Could you show me around? I'd be interested to see what an Oriental army is like.'

'I'd warn you that we'll have to put up with the heat,' I said.

He said nothing and waited until we were outside before talking again.

'Lieutenant de Galles likes you very much and I believe I can tell you what I have on my mind in all confidence. He was not wounded. He's fine, but *le Petit Annibal* had only five killed and thirteen wounded at our last battle. The Chevalier de Suffren has an annoying habit of rating the value of his commanding officers by their ship's losses in battle. And so, my friend is not in favour and not, therefore, invited to the celebrations. It could be said that de Tromelin, on *le Grand Annibal*, suffered greater losses than *le Héros*, and he's not here either, but he has been out of favour since the start.'

'Which battle are you talking about?'

'The last one we fought, on Saturday the sixth of July, off Negapatam.'

'The Chevalier de Suffren talked about 'demoted Captains'. Is Captain de Tromelin one of them?'

'Not yet. He was talking about Captains de Cillart, de Maurville and Forbin. It all started with the business of *le Sévère*. Towards the end of the battle there was a sudden wind shift from south-west to south-

south-east. The Admiral signalled to fall off to port, but *le Sévère* and my ship *le Brillant* were unable to complete the manoeuvre. We had both suffered big losses and our rigs were in too bad a state. We ended up in the crossfire of several English ships. *Le Héros* and two other ships of ours came to extricate us, but nobody helped de Cillart. Some of his officers had been sliced in two by cannonballs, right beside him, and he wanted to strike his colours. It seems that his crew stopped him, but the English came the next day to claim *le Sévère* as a prize. When Cillart was summoned to *le Héros'* Great cabin to explain himself, the Admiral was in such a rage that de Moissac discreetly hid his pistols. The officers on board at the time evacuated the sailors who were on watch on the poop deck, so that they could not hear the Admiral shouting. Anyway, there's Cillart broken, and with the Chevalier de Suffren's report he risks facing the firing squad, no more, no less, once back in France.'

'And what about the other two?'

'Same as Lieutenant de Galles – not enough losses! It wasn't their fault! The English had the windward advantage but the ships of their rear guard, which were opposite *le Petit Annibal, l'Artésien* and *le Vengeur*, held back and fired from further off than the others. The Chevalier de Suffren has long since wanted to punish Maurville and Forbin, and used the opportunity provided by Cillart. Moreover, Forbin is a cousin of his. I suspect that the Admiral wants to play the upright Roman, not hesitating to punish a member of his family as an example, like in a Corneille play. He must think the King will approve. He wasn't happy with Forbin's conduct at Porto Praya either, but unlike you I wasn't there.'

I told him that at Porto Praya *l'Annibal* was surrounded by English ships and drowned in such thick smoke that we could see no more than thirty feet around us. We had seventy killed and a hundred and thirty wounded in less than an hour.

'Oh! Good Heavens!'

'Yes! The Chevalier de Suffren said it was all Captain de Trémigon's fault. What will happen to Forbin and de Maurville?'

'Lose their rank, dismissed from the Navy without a pension and, if the Admiral's recommendations are followed, at least for Forbin: prison!'

'Do you think they deserve it?'

'Me? No! I think the way they have been treated is a serious affront to the honour of all the officers of the Grand Corps.'

'And Lieutenant Bouvet?'

'For him it's different. Too old and sick. It seems he asked to be relieved of his command. *L'Ajax* missed the battle as she had been dismasted the evening before in a squall and he hadn't managed to repair her during the night. We have to admit that our ships are tired. He will have an honourable retirement, given his past service record. The Chevalier de Suffren likes former officers of the India Company.'

'That's why he likes me a lot,' I said. 'My father served there.'

'So much the better for you! My friend Lieutenant de Galles is next on the list. Then it will be my turn, and Captain de Tromelin's, of course. And naturally, the Admiral has redistributed the ships of the squadron each time. I'm transferring to *l'Artésien.* I do well out of the change of ship, but I can't help thinking that this constant revolving of commanders has a bad effect on the morale of the crews and particularly the officers.'

The evening reception was, as I heard later, very formal in the Indian fashion and lasted at least three hours, spent mainly exchanging compliments and gifts. Our officers were given purses filled with gold and silver pieces, as well as diamonds, and the Nabob was given gifts which the English had, it seems, intended for the Emperor of China and which were found on an East India Company ship captured by *la Fine.* Afterwards the Chevalier de Suffren went to spend the night in Monsieur Piveron's tent.

The next morning, at dawn and before the heat of the day, there was a big breakfast to which I was invited. I had had the time to get used to the local cuisine, but it was an unpleasant surprise for many of our officers, who did not expect such spicy dishes at the crack of dawn. Luckily there was plenty of fruit and sherbet drinks. The Admiral could eat fire and asked for more. He was going to spend the day at the camp discussing more serious matters than those of the evening before with the Nabob. I followed the ships' commanders and Lieutenant de Moissac, who were returning to Cuddalore and our ships.

I did not know Cuddalore at all, having passed by it on the way to Porto Novo, scarcely seeing it behind the dunes from the deck of my ship. The French had recaptured it from the English not long afterwards, but had soon abandoned it to set up their camp a little to the west, at Mangikuppam, on an airy hillside where the climate was more bearable. Cuddalore was enclosed by ramparts in the European style, with rounded walls and bastions, most of them facing west, towards the interior of the country. An arm of water running south-east from the ramparts gave onto the sea, but the bar which edged the Coromandel coast was much bigger and more dangerous here than at Porto Novo. Only local boats could cross it, and then only in good weather. The squadron and the convoy had anchored in eight fathoms at a reasonable distance from the surf which was unnavigable for our rowing boats, which had to wait outside for the *masula* boats. It was under these conditions that two weeks previously the six hundred wounded from the Battle of Negapatam had been put ashore.

This anchorage, in the open sea a mile and a half from a straight coastline running north to south, and devoid of any shelter, had no protection from any onshore winds or swells and was only tenable during the south-west monsoon. I hailed the small ship's boat from *le Petit Annibal.* Her sailors recognised me and came to fetch me. Our ships were anchored further in or further out depending on their draft and we passed by *le Diligent,* who was further inshore than the others. Her black hull, set off by an ochre stripe above her wales, stood out boldly against the bright sea. I had seen her before, but now that I looked closely, I could see that she had a strong sheer, rising noticeably to the bow and stern, and very evident tumblehome. Her bow was plumb, with no cutwater, and extended by a long bowsprit. She had a vertical foremast, but her mainmast and mizzen were raked heavily aft. I could see nobody on deck.

It was now five months since I had left *le Petit Annibal* at the Porto Novo anchorage. So many adventures had befallen me in the meanwhile that it felt like more than a year. At the same time, seeing once again a familiar ship and familiar faces, I wondered whether what I had been through was no more than part of my old nightmares, and whether I had really met Flaharn in flesh and blood. The ship and the men were worn out after six months at sea with three battles and no respite, but the good humour was still there. The men were happy to see me again, as was my captain.

I told Lieutenant de Galles that the Chevalier de Suffren had given me the command of *le Diligent,* and he congratulated me, saying at the same time that he would miss me. I told him that I would have Captains de Cillart and de Maurville, along with Forbin, as passengers, and repeated what Captain de Saint-Félix had told me.

'This whole business is troubling,' replied Lieutenant de Galles. 'The Chevalier de Suffren keeps us on the Coromandel coast, with no ports in which to unwind and repair our ships, and with no respite for our crews which are reduced more and more after each battle. This singlemindedness merits the admiration of the English. I recognise that there is merit in it: it requires an iron will and an iron fist to take a squadron to sea under such conditions. But when we fight, we don't know what his intentions are, or else he changes his mind in mid-flow, without forewarning us. Above all, he lacks patience. Our tired old ships all have different sailing qualities, as you saw at the Battle of Sadras. They need time to form a battle line, which is a shame, but there's nothing to be done about it. It's necessary if we want to concentrate our fire on the enemy properly. Every time it's the same: we start to line up patiently but then the Admiral can't wait any longer and rushes into attack with his ship without bothering to find out whether the whole squadron is able to follow him. He fights on his own, of course losing lots of men. Those who are close to him can fight beside him and are congratulated, but all those left behind and who, because of lack of wind, cannot get there before he breaks off fighting, are accused of cowardice or even treachery! So he accuses Captain de Forbin of behaving badly at Porto Praya because he arrived too late to join us in the heart of the battle, and was happy just to fire at the *Isis* and the transports. But what else could he do? And I'll tell you something: if Admiral Johnstone failed to get to the Cape before us, it's largely because he was held back repairing the damage inflicted by Forbin, on the *Isis* and above all on the ships of the convoy, which the English needed to carry their troops.'

I went down to the gun room, where my chest had been stored while I was away, and began to go through what was left in it. Luckily, I had not taken my telescope, or Doctor Rollin's manuscript, when I had gone ashore at Porto Novo nor, of course, my octant. I had lost my uniform during the attack at the *chaudhury*, but that had been replaced by the one sent to me at the Nabob's camp by the Chevalier de Suffren, along with a new sword. This uniform had belonged to a Swedish Ship's Ensign aboard *le Héros,* who was about my size but had been killed in the Battle of Providien. His shoes hurt my feet somewhat, but that was maybe because I had lost the habit of wearing them. Apart from my watch, my only real loss was the sword given to me by my uncle de Kermean from his time serving as a Musketeer in the King's Household.

He had given it to me when I had left for Brest in 1776 and I was very attached to it. However, the attachment was purely sentimental; Army and Navy swords were the same, but the one given to me by my uncle was inscribed on the blade with the motto of the First Company of Musketeers: *Quo ruit et lethum*[38]. It was even more valuable to me as the Corps of Musketeers had been disbanded many years previously. Colonel Bouthenot's cavalrymen had searched for it in the Pathans' tent but without success.

I was still going through the things in my chest when Lieutenant de Galles' orderly came to tell me that the Lieutenant was waiting for me in *le Petit Annibal's* great cabin, along with the squadron's Flag Captain. My first thought was that Lieutenant de Moissac had come in order to officially appoint me as commander of *le Diligent,* which surprised me a little as normally the Chevalier de Suffren would have called me aboard *le Héros* once he had rejoined the squadron.

'I'm sorry,' began Lieutenant de Moissac as soon as he saw me, 'but you can't have *le Diligent* as she has to be refitted. I decided to tell you this news myself, as it will no doubt disappoint you. I said nothing yesterday as I wanted to check beforehand. I have spoken about it with Lieutenant Macé, who has been in command of her up until now. Last June, returning from Batticaloa, where the Admiral had sent her, *le Diligent* met some big seas and made a lot of water. She had to be taken into an uninhabited creek in Ceylon to be careened and repaired. This was enough to enable her to rejoin us at our anchorage at Tranquebar, but she is once again making more water than she should. She's too old. Her planking and ceiling are tired. She might possibly be fixed by careening her again and pulling off her coppering, but what can be done in Ceylon isn't possible on the Coromandel coast, because of the bar. Moreover, her pumps are nearly useless. It would be suicide to try to cross the Indian Ocean as far as the Île-de-France with her in that condition. I'm really sorry about that.'

'So am I,' added Lieutenant de Galles, 'even though I'm glad to be keeping you.'

'I'll suggest to the Admiral that the packages are sent on *la Sylphide*, and to split the three demoted Captains and the remaining prisoners

---

38 Translator's note: *Quo ruit et lethum:* In reference to the Musketeer's helmet: *'Where it falls, there is death.'*

between *la Sylphide* and *le Maurepas,* one of our convoy ships that has to go back to the Île-de-France. In any case, Lieutenant Macé has kept his whole crew, to transfer to the *Resolution,* which was captured a month ago by *la Sylphide,* to take her to Manilla for wood, food, and more sailors if possible. We wouldn't have been able to give you men for *le Diligent.*'

I was of course disappointed, but having miraculously escaped from Flaharn twice, I had no wish to make my grave at the bottom of the Indian Ocean. And the thought of having responsibility for three Ship's Captains, who were prisoners and possibly the victims of a miscarriage of justice, had started to trouble me greatly.

'This prize, the *Resolution,*' I asked. 'I heard that she had belonged to Captain Cook?'

'That's right,' replied Lieutenant de Moissac. 'He made his second voyage in her and his third, from which he never returned. If you want to have a look at her you'd better hurry, as she sails soon.'

I thought to myself that as I no longer had to prepare for taking *le Diligent* to the Île-de-France, I may have time to visit the *Resolution* before her departure for Manilla. Not that there was anything especially remarkable about the ship, but the Comte de Lapérouse, my old commander, was a great admirer of Captain Cook. In his library he had a copy of the translation of Cook's first voyage, which he had given to me to read and I had a great desire to take in the atmosphere of the places where this great navigator had lived and thought – his cabin, the ship's wheelhouse and poop deck.

Towards eight thirty that evening, at dusk, a boat from *le Héros* came alongside *le Petit Annibal* to say that the Admiral was back and that he wanted to see me immediately.

The deck of *le Héros was* crammed with soldiers from the Austrasie regiment and sepoys who had been embarked for an expedition to Ceylon and who were taking advantage of the cool evening air. The officer of the watch took me through the wheelhouse to announce my arrival before withdrawing and leaving me alone with the Admiral. The Chevalier de Suffren was sitting on the box seat at the aft end of the cabin. He was in shirt sleeves and had taken off his pumps and red stockings so as to soak his feet in cold water. The sight of this huge fellow in such a posture could have been comical were it someone else, but nobody dared laugh in the face of the Admiral. I saluted him, therefore, greeting him correctly, and he told me to sit down, pointing to one of the chairs around the big circular table in the middle of the cabin.

'Are you still willing to take *le Diligent?*'

'Oh, but Lieutenant de Moissac told me…'

'For God's sake! Are you willing or not?'

'Yes, Sir.'

'Good. I've already warned Gautier, my Master Shipwright, and Maunier, my Master Caulker. They're waiting for you with their men and will go with you to *le Diligent* at five tomorrow morning. They're going to repair and caulk everything they can inside. They'll have a look at the ceilings and put in knees everywhere they're needed. And we'll change your pumps. There's a brig from Madras just captured by *la Fine, l'Hindou.* She's not worth much but her pumps are in perfect condition. They'll swap them with *le Diligent's.* I'm going back to the Nabob's camp tomorrow and returning on Tuesday. You will install yourself aboard *le Diligent* at five tomorrow morning to supervise the work and make an inventory of it. When I'm back you will come and report to me. And we'll see what we can give you as a crew.'

The interview was over and I rose to leave.

'You will be aboard *le Diligent* at five?'

'Yes, Sir.'

'Have you a watch?'

'No, Sir. As you know I was stripped of everything.'

'Open the top draw in that chest and take one.'

There were several watches in the drawer, some ornate, others not. I assumed they had been taken from the many English ships captured by our frigates since the start of the campaign. I chose one.

'Bring it here.'

He wound it and set it to the right time before giving it back to me.

The caulkers and shipwrights of *le Héros* worked day and night to get *le Diligent* into sea-going condition. They tried to limit the play in her bulkheads by reinforcing them with curved pieces of timber and iron pegged into the deck beams and ceilings; these were the knees. The old pumps were dismantled and those from the English brig modified and fitted precisely into the lugger. The workers were all from La Seyne[39]

---

39 Translator's note: *La Seyne:* also known as La Seyne-sur-Mer, a town to the west of Toulon, once famed for its shipbuilding.

and knew each other well, with some even being related. They spoke their patois, and French for my benefit. I was impressed by their skill and competence, but more than anything by their boundless devotion to the Chevalier de Suffren. The rig and sails had been changed before leaving the Île-de-France and were in good condition. The Gunner's equipment was complete except for rifles, but for the Pilot there was only a compass, the log and the flags, as Lieutenant Macé had taken everything else with him.

The Chevalier de Suffren returned the next Tuesday towards eleven. I had been watching out for him and was on *le Héros'* deck, beside Lieutenant de Moissac, when he came on board. He immediately signalled to us to follow him. The Flag Officer made his report: Lieutenant de Pierrevert, commanding *la Bellone,* had gone on reconnaissance with his frigate to Tranquebar, where he had found Monsieur de Launay, Commissioner-General of the Marquis de Bussy's land force, who had come to Ceylon on a local boat. He had immediately taken him to Cuddalore.

'When Monsieur de Launay told me that the Marquis de Bussy had arrived at the Île-de-France with reinforcements and that two ships would soon join us with the advance guard of the land troops, I took it on myself to send him to you immediately.'

'And you did the right thing. He arrived just in time to dispel the final hesitations of the Nabob.'

The Chevalier e Suffren was in an excellent mood and very pleased with his deliberations with Hyder Ali Khan. He had managed to persuade him to stay on the Coromandel coast with his army, despite the Nabob needing to go to the Malabar coast, where an English offensive out of Bombay was threatening the west of Mysore. Proper arrangements had also been finalised for providing food and pay to the French army. The Admiral then turned to me and I was able to tell him that the work on *le Diligent* would be completed by the Thursday. After that it would just be a matter of provisioning for the crew that I would be given, although Lieutenant Macé had taken the ship's armoury and all of the navigational equipment except the compass and log.

'You'll have twenty kaffirs, enough to handle a lugger. You won't have to fight, which is good, as you won't need a chaplain or a doctor for the kaffirs! For your second I'm giving you a Bosun's Mate, but he's as good as any officer. He's from St Tropez, like me! Best sailors in the world, for God's sake! What's more, he knows you and is quite happy to sail with you, even though you're a Breton.'

And the Admiral, obviously in top form, burst out laughing at my surprised look.

'He's called Perrin. He was in charge of *le César's* boat during the Comte d'Estaing's campaign.'

'Savannah!'

'Yes, indeed! Perrin told me that you had a rough time there. After coming back to France, he was at the School of Hydrography at Toulon and I took him with me on *le Zélé* once he had his certificate. Good! Moissac, go and see Perrin right now, help him choose twenty blacks, and make sure the Master Pilot also gives him a nautical almanac, sight reduction tables, charts and the usual calculation tables. As for a copy of *D'Après*, I have several here so I'll give Laforest-Dombourg one. I don't have any more clocks. Can you also choose an apprentice pilot, a volunteer if possible? That'll more or less complete *le Diligent's* officers. You'll give him an octant. With three of them they can at least take a longitude. Laforest-Dombourg will have to do some mathematics. Make a change from having fun with dancers.'

He turned towards me.

'Do you still have an octant?'

'Yes, Sir.'

'And your table of signals and repeats?'

'Yes, Sir, as long as they haven't changed since Porto Novo.'

'They're still the same.'

I was going to follow the Flag Captain out, but the Chevalier de Suffren signalled to me to stay and waited until we were alone before speaking again.

'Laforest-Dombourg! The first time I saw you at Versailles, Monsieur de Fleurieu had been very guarded when talking about you. I didn't realise it at the time, but you work for the Secret Service, despite your youth.'

I reminded him that I had told him at Simon's Bay that I had left a safe-conduct from the King and a letter for the Vicomte de Souillac in the steel chest, and that if he had trusted me rather than Saint-Luperce, none of this would have happened.

'Yes, I know – the Marathas! That's all in the past and we can't change it. I just wanted to say that as you have abilities in clandestine work, I too would like to take advantage of them. I will of course give you copies of my packages for the Vicomte de Souillac and a letter of recommendation to him. As I hope *le Diligent* will be quicker than *la Sylphide* and *le Maurepas*! Unlike Moissac, I'm not worried about you. My Master Caulker and Master Shipwright have not yet had time to report to me, but I have full confidence in them. They've been with me for years. Only a storm near the Mascarenes could really threaten *le Diligent,* but it's August. They can have storms there from November to May, but never in August. *D'Après* is very clear on this. However, I want to give you a more personal package, not for the Vicomte de Souillac, and not to be mentioned to him. You will deliver it to Squire Pascalis, a fellow-Provençal who is a merchant on the Île-de-France. And I'd like to congratulate you on your tenacity in carrying the treasure to the Nabob. It helped me a lot. I have mentioned this in my letter of recommendation to the Vicomte de Souillac.'

I now understood why the Chevalier de Suffren had been so friendly towards me and why he had made such an effort to have *le Diligent* repaired. It was not purely out of concern for me.

*

In the Cuddalore roadstead, Friday 2nd August 1782.
It is one in the afternoon, the sky is clear and the sea calm, with scarcely a ripple beyond the bar. Since morning there has been a light offshore breeze, hot but now going to south-south-west and freshening. Apart from us there are only three ships left at the anchorage – three prizes of which two will be staying here to be sold. The other will be sailing for Pegu, in the north of Sumatra. Our ships weighed anchor yesterday morning and went off hard to windward on starboard tack, along the coast towards Ceylon. They tacked at midday and anchored in the evening off Porto Novo. They must have left during the night as they were no longer there at dawn. I was delayed as I wanted to complete our provisioning with little limes, a large quantity of which I bought myself at the Cuddalore market. I read somewhere in a book about a voyage, Captain Cook's I think, that this fruit keeps well and is excellent for stopping scurvy. In principle I ought not to be worried: our voyage should not last more than two months and this campaign, although lethal, has given our crews plenty of time to relax in sight of

the coast, where the Nabob has always provided fresh food. But I don't want to take any risks.

'Start to raise the anchor, Monsieur Perrin.'

My second takes up the order. Sailors are sent forward to slot bars into the square holes at the ends of the wooden horizontal winch that is used instead of a capstan on small boats. We have a single anchor down. The cable, dripping with water, starts to come slowly aboard, soaking the foredeck planking as it moves to the regular clicking of the pawls in the early afternoon quiet. The whole crew is silent. This is a Naval regulation, but there is also something solemn about this solitary and discreet departure from an India where each of us, in his own way, has several times confronted his fate. The lugger starts to advance against the weak northerly current that runs along the whole of this coast.

I have had the men eat before leaving. At first I was worried about having to command some blacks, but they are very disciplined, and happy to escape the bloody carnage of naval battles and return to the Île-de-France and their families. Lieutenant de Galles has assured me that the colonists there are much gentler and more tolerant towards their slaves than those in the Antilles, and that their relationship with the kaffirs is relaxed and sometimes even friendly. Moreover, my sailors had been bought in the King's name in order to make up our crews before leaving Port-Louis, and the Chevalier de Suffren had emancipated them before entrusting them to me. There is nothing for me to worry about as far as they are concerned.

'Up and down!' announces the apprentice pilot in his singsong accent, leaning over the bow. His name is Daniel and he too is from La Seyne.

'Hold on!'

The wind has strengthened again and is now stronger than the current.

'Have the mainsail and jib raised, Monsieur Perrin.'

'Aye, aye, Sir. Hoist the mainsail!'

Three kaffirs haul on the peak halyard, four on the throat halyard. I watch the yard rising perfectly horizontal. Yesterday we took care to acquaint the men with the rig, with which they were not familiar, but they are applying themselves and are clearly keen to do the job well. I had the mainsail yard got ready to port of the mainmast and the fore and mizzen yards to starboard, as I was advised. In principle a lugger, like a *chasse-marée*[40], trims all its sails on one side, the leeward side, of the vessel. This means that on every tack everything has to be lowered to the deck, the halyards unhitched, the yards moved to the other side, and the halyards reattached, all of which is most inconvenient, given our big sail area and reduced crew. *Le Diligent,* having been used as a pursuit vessel, could not allow this kind of nonsense; she had to be agile and be able to tack quickly. Lieutenant Macé had therefore decided to sail with part of the canvas against the mast and the other part filled, so as not to have to change them at every tack. Instead of sheeting the mainsail, foresail and mizzen to the sides, they were permanently sheeted at the foot of the masts.

My second pilot Perrin is a solid chap, blonde, bearded and with a Provençal accent. He is constantly good-natured and I am happy to have him with me. He has given me a notebook in which I can keep my personal log. I had found *le Diligent's* log, along with everything needed for writing, in the commander's cabin, but I had completely forgotten to bring one for myself before leaving. Perrin and I had got to know each other in October 1779 during the Siege of Savannah. I was in charge of carrying despatches between the anchored squadron and our land forces. For that I had been given the Captain's gig from *le César,* a seventy-four gun ship which had come from Toulon with the Comte d'Estaing's

squadron. Perrin was in charge of this boat. He never knew what I went through while I was ashore, but I must have looked very strange when I returned. This must certainly have made an impression on him, according to what the Chevalier de Suffren told me.

'Raise the jib!'

The jib is hooked on to the traveller, which the kaffirs haul smartly to the end of the bowsprit. Three men are needed to raise the triangular sail, which snaps in the wind.

'Take the helm, Monsieur Perrin,' I say. 'I'll give my orders directly. Prepare to turn the windlass! Sheet to port! Helm up!'

The lugger moves off to port, pulling on her cable. It's the moment to turn the windlass hard to break out the anchor before the ship swings back onto the other tack.

---

40 Translator's note: *chasse-marée* (literally *tide-hunter*): a kind of Breton coastal fishing boat.

'Turn!'

My kaffirs bend to the bars, bare-chested, their muscled backs shining in the sun.

'Turn! Turn!'

'Anchor up and clear, Sir!' sings Daniel a moment later.

Le Diligent moves off hard on the wind, on starboard tack.

'Ready the foresail! Raise and sheet!'

I then have the main topsail set, then the mizzen, and the foretopsail to finish. The wind is now good and strong, and the lugger moves ever more quickly, heading south a quarter south-east. The apprentice pilot supervises the catting of the anchor. The flat Coromandel landscape slowly fades away astern. I have decided to take a seawards tack immediately and hold it for as long as possible. From what I have been told prior to sailing, the English squadron is still in Madras, but no doubt it will very soon head down to Ceylon once they hear that our Admiral has designs on Trincomalee. I want to get away from the field of battle as quickly as possible. *Le Diligent* has little powder and ammunition for its four-pounders and my crew cannot even handle all the cannons on one side simultaneously.

And so I leave India, where I had hoped for so much and where I almost lost everything. This departure, without fanfare, leaves me with a sense of something unfinished. Saint-Luperce was unmasked and my nightmare about Flaharn became reality, but I feel no further forward. I don't even know what has happened to the flamboyant Saint-Luperce. Is he still alive? As for Flaharn, I know now that he will always reappear *like a devil vomited from hell,* as the Marquis de Kersalaun had written in his tragic final message. He too had seen Flaharn well and truly dead on the paving stones of Chandernagore, just as I had later at Savannah. Now that the treasure of diamonds was out of his grasp forever, he will always be seeking revenge. At this thought I shiver, despite the heat. My nightmare will never be over! Flaharn was not the only actor in this story, though, so who was behind him? The Americans? I have difficulty believing this. The English? From what I heard at the *chaudhury* this seems unlikely. I think again about poor Duval, no doubt still languishing in secret in the Bastille, and about the poisoning of Doctor Rollin. I am convinced that everything is connected and that the answer to all these questions is to be found in India, but now I am leaving and don't know whether I will ever return. I don't know what is in the second package entrusted to me by the Admiral, the one I must not mention to the Vicomte de Souillac. Is it his personal correspondence? A secret letter for somebody highly placed at Versailles? He needed me and he certainly sweetened the pill to get what he wanted. But no matter, I don't hold it against him! Thanks to him I have my first command and I am happy with that, even if my crew comprises nothing more than a Bosun's Mate, an eighteen-year-old apprentice pilot and twenty Kaffirs. And it's likely that I will be returning to France. I have heard nothing from there since leaving Brest. I wrote to Maria Kirwan from the Cape and also from the Île-de-France. She has probably replied but there is a good chance that her letters have been sent to India along with the mail for the Chevalier de Suffren's squadron.

*

At first, I had mainly south-west winds, sometimes going to south-south-west. They were never strong, varying from a fresh breeze to a flat calm, and the weather stayed fine. We carved out our wake, lost in the intense blue of the Indian Ocean, tacking south. On 17th August, despite no change in the weather, we met a huge swell from the south-south-east, which worried me a little, but the next day the sea had calmed again. As we approached the Equator, we had squalls of thunder and rain alternating with flat calms. I crossed the Line on Tuesday 20th August, at an estimated longitude of 84 degrees and 17 minutes east of the Paris meridian. This put us in the eastern half of the Indian Ocean, with the nearest land the islands of Nias and Mantac, off Sumatra, about seven hundred miles to our east. I had to put up with calms and variable winds, with squalls and rain, mainly from the west, until the 24th August. We had encountered no other ships, advancing as we were in the middle of a great empty circle that moved along with us. The war, India, even the land, were no more than vague memories: we had left time behind. I had not felt like this on the outward voyage, and it was perhaps because I was now sailing on a small vessel with a reduced crew and was the only officer on board.

From 24th August, the winds went predominantly east and I could finally head south-west straight towards the Mascarenes. We still had good weather, with a fine sea and a settled wind. There were occasional squalls, but nothing to force us to reef down, and eleven days later we raised Rodrigues Island: a green strip, slightly higher in the middle, sitting on the ocean about fifteen miles off our starboard bow. This allowed me to adjust my course, and on the seventh of September, before nightfall, I picked out the distant and cloud-topped summits of the Île-de-France, directly ahead. Our approach was the same as last time. The wind fell away completely after Gunners Point, then went to a light north-north-easterly. On 10th September 1782, towards four in the afternoon, I anchored off Coopers Reef.

I immediately went to report to the Governor and gave him the copies of the Chevalier de Suffren's despatches. Just as the Admiral had predicted, I had arrived ahead of *la Sylphide* and *le Maurepas,* and the Vicomte de Souillac congratulated me on a good crossing. He read the letter of recommendation written for me by the Admiral and asked me about my stay at the Nabob's camp. That day he also told me that the Grand Master of the Order of Malta had sent the Chevalier de Suffren the insignia for the title of Bailli[41], and that these had been sent to him, along with letters from Versailles, on the cutter *le Lézard,* which had left Port-Louis in July. In conclusion, the Vicomte de Souillac told me that *le Diligent* was to be refitted and sold, and offered me the post of second captain on the corvette *la Nayade.* She had recently arrived from France and was to leave in the coming weeks to carry supplies of piastres and correspondence for the Chevalier de Suffren's squadron. The corvette's current second captain had been transferred elsewhere and they were looking for a replacement. This proposition was made most politely, but I well understood that it would have been very unwise of me to refuse it. Contrary to what I had thought, I was therefore going to find myself back in India very soon. I couldn't say whether I was happy to return there or disappointed not to be going home. In any event, I wouldn't have much time to discover the delights of the Île-de-France, of which I had been deprived during our first stop here.

I made a very pleasant discovery, though, when fulfilling the little secret mission entrusted to me by the Commander, or rather the Bailiff, as he would hence be known. His correspondent, Squire Pascalis, insisted on putting me up until my new departure for India. Thanks to

---

41 Translator's note: *Bailli* – Bailiff, in the historical sense of someone in charge of a Bailiwick, and a higher rank than de Suffren's previous title of Commander within the Order. De Suffren was from then on often referred to as *le Bailli de Suffren,* or simply *le Bailli.*

him, his wife and their two charming daughters, I was to be in clover during my brief stay in Port-Louis, despite the bad news that we would have shortly afterwards as regards the war and affairs of state. Nothing affected me personally as, just as I had predicted, my personal mail from France had gone to India. I wrote to Maria Kirwan and my grandfather, and my host proposed that he take care of my letters.

Just before my departure from Cuddalore, Monsieur de Launay had told the Chevalier de Suffren, who had passed it on to the Nabob, that the Marquis de Bussy was at the Île-de-France with a sizeable naval and land force, that he would be leaving at its head in December, and that in the meantime he had sent initial reinforcements for the India squadron. In fact, this advance guard was comprised of just two ships. They were accompanied by a small fleet of merchant ships carrying food and munitions, along with six hundred soldiers drawn from the Île-de-France and Île Bourbon garrisons, for want of anything better. This modest division had got away in good order and I must have passed it, without seeing it, in the Indian Ocean. However, the other reinforcements were still not at Port-Louis when I landed. They arrived five days later but were much smaller than expected. Several convoys which had left France the year before had either been captured or put to flight by the English as they left Brest. A final convoy, much smaller, and commanded by Ship's Captain de Peynier, had managed to get through the net and reach the Cape with just four vessels. They were escorting a fleet of thirty-five merchantmen carrying powder, cannonballs, food and military reinforcements, and which had been separated by bad weather. In order to get all his convoy together again, Captain de Peynier had stayed three months at the Cape, where he had had to leave some of the troops destined for India, through fears of another attack on the Dutch colony. He finally reached the Île-de-France in mid-September. Unfortunately, there had been a bad outbreak of fever aboard his ships. Of the three thousand two hundred soldiers and sailors who had left False Bay, already a hundred and seventy had died and eleven hundred and ninety-eight were sick when I saw them reach Port-Louis. The island's hospitals could not cope with so many unfortunates and the Vicomte de Souillac had sent some to the Île Bourbon on a merchant ship.

A few days later, a fast, copper-bottomed merchant brig called *le Duc de Chartres* arrived. She brought sad news: the Naval force commanded by the Comte de Grasse, together with which the Chevalier de Suffren's division had left Brest in 1781, had met Admiral Rodney's squadrons in the Saintes Channel south of Guadeloupe. Our ships were to leeward in a battle fought in a flat calm. The Comte de Grasse had been taken prisoner, *la Ville de Paris,* which I had so much admired at Brest, had been reduced to a hulk and captured, and *le César,* in which my second Perrin had served, suffered a massive explosion shortly after her capture, killing her French crew and the English prize crew.

Le Duc de Chartres had arrived at the Île-de-France with a cargo of wine, brandy and naval munitions. She was immediately purchased, along with her cargo, by the island's Naval Administration, and her captain given the provisional rank of Ship's Lieutenant, enabling him to stay in command of the ship, on behalf of the King, until the end of the war. The brig had belonged to some Marseille shipowners with whom Squire Pascalis had dealings. It was he who negotiated her sale to the Navy. He told me too that he was going to buy *le Diligent* and refit her for trading and coasting between Madagascar and the Mascarenes, under the command of Perrin. The Île-de-France was well positioned between China, Europe and our Indian trading stations, and an astute merchant like Squire Pascalis could make a fortune there, even in times of war.

The corvette *la Nayade,* which I was joining, was still on the Navy roll as an 8-pounder frigate. Our old 8-pounder frigates were now commonly referred to as corvettes, now that we had launched 12- and 18-pounder frigates. She carried a battery of twenty-eight 8-pounders. She was an old ship launched at Toulon in 1764, and given a copper bottom before being sent to the Indian Ocean. My new commander was Ship's Lieutenant de Costebelle, aged about thirty. Most of the crew were from Toulon. Despite my fondness for Bretons, I have to admit that the Provençals are easier to command. They drink less and are more accepting of formal discipline. We left Port-Louis at the end of September, carrying despatches and half of the sum of 25,000 piastres destined for the India squadron and which had been split between us and *le Duc de Chartres.* We knew that the Chevalier de Suffren intended to seize Trincomalee and to pass the winter at Aceh, in the north of Sumatra. As *le Duc de Chartres* was a much faster ship than ours, it was decided that she would go to Aceh, if this rendezvous spot was confirmed, while *la Nayade* would wait off the Point de Galle, where we would be able to find out whether Trincomalee had indeed been taken by the Chevalier de Suffren.

There was nothing remarkable about the crossing, except that it was not quick and we did not make landfall until December. The Point de Galle was in southern Ceylon. The Dutch had fortified it and made it into a considerable settlement. It sheltered a bay which formed a natural anchorage surrounded by a low, wooded coastline, used as a port since Antiquity. With the war on, this harbour had become the preferred landing place for anyone not English. The bay was crowded with merchant and transport ships, either waiting for orders or simply looking for information before carrying on towards Bengal or the Malabar coast. We saw Dutch, Danish and Portuguese ships, and of course French ships like ours waiting to join the squadron. *Le Duc de Chartres* had arrived a month earlier, despite leaving Port-Louis a day after us, and had already sailed on. We learned that Trincomalee was now in French hands but that the squadron had not yet returned from Aceh. The north-east monsoon was not quite over, and since we were in no hurry, Lieutenant de Costebelle decided to take things easy, at least until the end of the month. This was with the intention of resting his men, who had still not fully recovered from their initial voyage from France, and taking on board fresh water and provisions before leaving for Trincomalee.

I had been able to get to know my commander during the voyage. He had been a Marine Guard at Toulon and had served under the Chevalier de Suffren in 1773 when the latter was in command of the frigate *la Mignonne.* Lieutenant de Costebelle had already been on one campaign to the Americas and could have commanded a nice frigate in Europe, but hearing that the little *la Nayade* was going to India, he had fought tooth and claw to have her. Despite her reputation as a slow ship, he wanted to rejoin his former commander, whom he greatly revered.

During our stay, my commander, who liked hunting as much as my friend Vernon des Aulnes, which was no mean feat, joined up with the local Dutch notables who shared the same passion. He was certainly a good shot, as he brought us game several times: lots of hares and also wild pigs which the ship's cook prepared for the crew. While on one of these expeditions he fell badly and returned to ship on a stretcher, meaning we had to rig a hoist to get him aboard *la Nayade.* It turned out he had broken his leg. This happened shortly before we were due to sail and the ship's Surgeon and the Dutch doctors advised him to stay ashore to recover, but he would not hear of it. Our Surgeon dealt with his leg as best he could and we sailed for Trincomalee, arriving on the 20th February.

Trincomalee, in north-east Ceylon, was perhaps one of the most beautiful harbours in India, situated at the north-west end of a huge bay. As it was surrounded by hills in an otherwise flat coastline, it was safe and sheltered from every wind. The entrance was about three miles wide. Coming from the south, the first danger was the extension of a low wooded headland called the Pointe Sale. There was a shoal that was easy to avoid using the transits given in *D'Après* for rounding Pointe Sale. Nonetheless, we were unpleasantly surprised by the sight of a recent wreck of a ship of war laying on her side. She had been to an extent dismembered by the sea, and part of her rig had been salvaged, no doubt to be used again. Looking closely with my glass, I was sad to see it was *l'Orient*, the Comte d'Orves' flagship when he had left the Île-de-France. I told Lieutenant de Costebelle, who had dragged himself to the officer of the watch's bench to oversee our arrival at Trincomalee, ignoring the protests of the Surgeon and myself. We entered the big bay, having raised our white flag and made a gun salute to the forts, which was duly answered. The entrance passage to the proper harbour was only two cables wide, but with the east wind that was blowing that morning we were able to go straight in. We found ourselves in a spacious anchorage that could have held several squadrons.

On an island to port of the channel we could see a converted quayside, where a copper-bottomed war ship was hauled onto her side, with shipwrights and caulkers working on her hull. Inside the port there were just eight ships anchored: two frigates, an ugly tub of a ship and several merchantmen. The careened vessel was *le Vengeur* and I quickly recognised *la Pourvoyeuse*. The other frigate was *la Consolante*, which had been sent as a reinforcement from the Île-de-France in August before I left Cuddalore. The other ships were two Dutchmen and two prizes taken by our frigates, and a vessel flying the Portuguese flag, but which had been commanded by an Englishman who had entered the bay thinking Trincomalee was still in English hands, and which had been declared 'fair game'.

All this was explained to us by Ship's Captain de Cuverville, who had commanded *le Vengeur* since Captain de Forbin had been sent back to France. He told us that the Chevalier de Suffren had ordered him to leave Aceh on the previous 16th December and go straight to Trincomalee to have a leak repaired. He had been escorted by *la Pourvoyeuse* in case anything went wrong. The squadron was due to sail from Sumatra shortly after him. The Admiral intended to make his landfall on the Odisha coast and descend to Cuddalore, taking as many prizes as possible on the way. He had even sent *la Bellone* and *le Petit Annibal* to cruise in Bengali waters and intercept English merchantmen coming out of the Ganges.

The Trincomalee settlement had fallen at the end of August after a siege lasting several days and the garrison had surrendered without much of a fight. Shortly afterwards the English squadron had appeared off the coast and ours had put to sea to confront it. There was a battle, after which the English withdrew to the north. It was when returning to Trincomalee after this battle that *l'Orient* had gone aground on the Pointe Sale following a navigational error.

Captain de Cuverville told us that the Comte Duchemin had died from his illness on 12th August, and that Lieutenant de Salvert, de Suffren's nephew, who was commanding *la Bellone,* had been killed in a battle between his frigate and an English frigate shortly after I had left Cuddalore on *le Diligent. La Bellone* had been given back to Lieutenant de Beaulieu, who had then left her to take *le Petit Annibal,* and then temporarily entrusted to Fireship Captain de Joyeuse.

'Lieutenant de Galles no longer has *le Petit Annibal,* then?' I asked Captain de Cuverville.

I was getting confused by all this switching around.

'Captains de Tromelin, de Lalandelle, de Saint-Félix and de Galles all asked to be relieved of their commands after the Battle of Trincomalee. The Chevalier de Suffren sent them back to the Île-de-France on *le Pulvériseur*[42]. He was furious and very angry with them and wrote to the Minister and the Vicomte de Souillac to let them know. It's a fair bet that they will be heavily punished.'

This news upset me, and confirmed, alas, what Captain de Saint-Félix had confided to me at the Nabob's camp.

We left Trincomalee two days later in a light north-easterly. Lieutenant de Costebelle was suffering more and more, but insisted

---

42 Translator's note: *le Pulvériseur:* in fact, the ship's correct name was *le Pulvératiseur,* but in eighteenth century France, where orthography was fluid, she was usually referred to as *le Pulvériseur.*

on carrying on to get to the Chevalier de Suffren and complete his mission as quickly as possible. Our course took us well out to sea and the next day, not having seen our ships, we tacked towards the Point Pedro at the northern end of Ceylon. On the 24th we captured a local boat and were told that the squadron had passed the evening before, running south down the coast. We came off the wind immediately and by the 26th were back in harbour at Trincomalee, where our ships had arrived three days previously. I had a great deal of trouble dissuading Lieutenant de Costebelle from having himself lowered into our boat so that he himself could deliver our despatches and the chest containing the piastres. It would have meant him being hoisted aboard *le Héros* in a chair. I went in his place to take the deliveries to the Chevalier de Suffren.

Arriving on *le Héros'* poop deck, I presented myself to the officer of the watch who took me to the wheelhouse. There was already someone in the Great cabin, so I had to wait beside the Master Pilot and his assistants, who were on duty there. I could hear shouting through the door. I recognised the Chevalier de Suffren's nasal voice and he was talking so loudly that I could hear everything he was saying. He was angry because he had wanted the work on *le Vengeur* completed before he came back. Eventually the door opened and I saw Captain de Cuverville coming out. It was obvious he had just been dressed down by the *Lord God Almighty*, and he passed by, not looking at us, with a shrug of his shoulders. I had the impression that the Provençal sailors looked at him somewhat derisively, but without letting him see. It was always amusing for them to see an officer, and a Norman to boot, reprimanded by their beloved chief, but they knew that deep down the Admiral appreciated the bravery and fidelity of Captain de Cuverville, even if, once again, he had let his Provençal temperament get the better of him.

My welcome was quite another matter. Not only was the Chevalier de Suffren happy to see me again, but once he had read the letters which I had brought him, his mood grew even better. I hurried to present my commander's apologies, explaining why he himself had not been able to bring the packages entrusted to him.

'You can tell Lieutenant de Costebelle on my behalf that I am greatly touched by his zeal and will not forget it, but above all I would like him to take care of himself so that he is on his feet again once I have need of him. You can also give him my formal order that I am giving you provisional command of *la Nayade* so that he can go ashore and get well quickly.'

I also told him that I had carried out the task he had given me as regards Squire Pascalis. The Chevalier de Suffren then put out a call for Monsieur Ravenel, the Intendant-General of the squadron, and Lieutenant de Moissac, asked me for news about his friend, then bade me goodbye in the most friendly fashion, telling me to wait for my instructions from Lieutenant de Moissac before leaving the ship. I could see as I went out that the attitude of *le Héros'* men towards me was quite different from my first visit aboard this ship when I had been summoned at Simon's Bay. They were aware that I was now in the good books of their venerated commander.

While waiting for Lieutenant de Moissac I went in search of the supernumerary who looked after the personal mail, to ask him whether he had seen any letters for me. He told me that he had indeed seen plenty. They had arrived just after my departure and he remembered them well as he had sent them all back to the Île-de-France on *le Pulvériseur*.

Lieutenant de Moissac told me that Hyder Ali Khan had died in December, from an abscess in his back which he had waited too long to have opened by the French doctors looking after him. Learning this, the Comte d'Hoffelize had immediately gone to the Nabob's camp to restrain anyone who was opposed to Tipoo Sahib and to give support to Hyder Ali Khan's firstborn son.

Tipoo was at that time on the Malabar coast, where he had gone to oppose a strong English offensive against his country. Those loyal to the Nabob had sent him a message and he had returned as quickly as possible, enabling him to take over his father's treasure and possessions without any difficulty.

However, people were not as happy with the son as with the father. Tipoo Sahib seemed to have decided to recross the Ghats to go to the aid of Mysore. It would have been better if he had waited for the arrival of the Marquis de Bussy, but the latter had been expected for such a long time that it was hard to make the case for it. At his wits' end, Monsieur Piveron had come to Porto Novo, where the squadron had anchored on 12th February, to ask the Chevalier de Suffren to write a strong letter to the new Nabob to dissuade him from leaving. It was hoped that the Chevalier de Suffren could exercise as much influence over the son as he had over the father. However, this alone may have not been enough, and so the Admiral had it in mind to send Lieutenant de Moissac as an ambassador to the Court, in support of Monsieur Piveron, aboard *la Nayade.* I therefore had to keep the corvette ready to sail for the Coromandel at any moment. The English squadron was still at Bombay, waiting for the end of the north-east monsoon before returning to the Bay of Bengal.

*

Trincomalee, Sunday 2nd March 1783

The wind is light, from the north-east, and the ebb tide weak, and the weather fine but not yet too hot. We have heard the bugle at Fort Ostenburg sounding reveille at first light. The murmuring of birdsong from the greenery on the nearest coastline reaches us across the calm water. *La Nayade* is anchored at the south end of the inner harbour, with a small island, covered in bushes, ahead of us and, to starboard, the wooded slopes of Point Ostenburg, crowned by its fort and prolonged by a sea-level battery. We began hauling up our small bower anchor at dawn. It is now out and being catted to starboard. We begin to get our main anchor and the clicking of the capstan pawls echoes again along the gundeck.

My second in command, a Frigate's Lieutenant, shouts from forward that the anchor is up and down. I turn towards Lieutenant de Moissac, who is standing behind me on the poop deck beside the ship's wheel.

'Carry on, Monsieur Dombourg. You're the captain. Consider me your passenger.'

It is my first voyage in command of a corvette. I have many times had charge of square-rigged three-masted ships, as officer of the watch, but they are much more complicated to manoeuvre than a lugger or a cutter, and I always had a captain behind me. Lieutenant de Costebelle is still convalescing ashore. The squadron's Flag Captain came on board last night with a note from the Admiral saying I must 'always follow Lieutenant de Moissac's orders'. The Chevalier de Suffren had just received a message sent via a local boat from the Comte d'Hoffelize, saying that he had not manged to convince Tipoo Sahib to stay on the Coromandel coast but, to win time, had got him to wait for an officer from the squadron sent by the Chevalier de Suffren. Hyder Ali Khan's son would share with him his latest intentions if the Marquis de Bussy had still not arrived. The Chevalier de Suffren had immediately ordered Lieutenant de Moissac aboard *la Nayade*, to get to the Coromandel coast and from there to the Nabob's camp, with instructions to convince him to wait for the imminent arrival of the Marquis de Bussy.

The capstan is turned hard to break out the anchor. When I can feel that the anchor is free, I order the helm to be put right down and the corvette moves off, falling astern and turning off the wind to starboard. The jibs are raised. They flog for a moment and are then sheeted to starboard. The bowsprit carries on turning, the main and mizzen topsails fill with a loud bang, the wheel is brought back amidships, the fore topsail is braced round so that it fills and the corvette launches gently forward with the wind on the port quarter. We head for the passage between the fort battery to port and two wooded islands to starboard. The careening quay lies in an inlet between the two, and as we pass I see that they have brought *le Vengeur* upright before laying her on her other side. Everything is sheeted hard to port to pass the Île Ronde, a bush-covered rock with two or three palm trees at its summit, and which marks the western limit of navigation in the harbour.

We have to put in two more tacks to get clear of the bay, but there is all the room in the world for turning through the wind. It is always easier to leave an anchorage than to enter it. Going out, one can see where the dangers lie, whereas coming in one is constantly searching them out with the telescope and consulting *D'Après*, left open on the officer of the watch's bench, with a sword across it to keep it at the right page.

And so I will be returning to Cuddalore, my departure point I thought I had left for ever. Last night I had time to tell my whole story to Lieutenant de Moissac. At the Nabob's camp he will certainly see Colonel Bouthenot and can ask him on my behalf if he has any news about Flaharn or even Saint-Luperce. I would dearly like to know what has become of them.

*

Leaving Trincomalee, we crossed paths with *le Petit Annibal* and *la Bellone,* who were returning from their cruise in the Bay of Bengal. On the evening of 4th March, we dropped anchor at Cuddalore. There was no army garrison on the corvette, so I chose two sailors armed with rifles, sabres and pistols to escort Lieutenant de Moissac in the *masula* boat that came to take him ashore. We waited for eight days in the anchorage off Cuddalore. During this time we saw several sails passing, out to sea, either neutral merchantmen or some of our ships which had been cruising between Madras and Bengali waters and were going back down to Ceylon. As the English squadron had not yet returned from Bombay, our ships had had a clear field to capture whatever they could find between Calcutta and Madras. They must have sunk most of their prizes as we no longer had enough men to make up prize crews, but the cargoes of rice which were seized were a valuable addition to the provisions for the squadron.

Lieutenant de Moissac returned on board on 12th March, his mission unaccomplished. He had been told at Cuddalore that the French army was at the Nabob's camp at Chetpet. Arriving there after several days' journey, he found our own troops, but Tipoo Sahib and his army had already crossed to the west of the Ghats. The Comte d'Hoffelize had sent six hundred soldiers from the Île-de-France regiment with our Indian allies, while in return the latter had left us a force of twenty thousand men. Lieutenant de Moissac had therefore not been able to see Monsieur Piveron, or indeed Colonel Bouthenot, and so had entrusted his dispatches for Monsieur Piveron to a local courier and returned to Cuddalore.

All we could do was return to Trincomalee, but the return voyage against winds and current would take much longer than the outward voyage. Having left Cuddalore on the 12th, we still had the town in sight on the morning of the 16th. The same day, towards one in the afternoon, when out to sea, we saw several sails ahead, coming from the south and seemingly heading for the Porto Novo anchorage. A vessel looking like a ship of war broke off in our direction, clearly with the intention of giving chase. *La Nayade* would have found it difficult to escape, were it the enemy. Luckily, once she was close enough for us to read her signals, we could see that she was French, and I recognised *l'Artésien*. She signalled to us to join the squadron, and so we set course for Porto Novo, anchoring there that evening.

Lieutenant de Moissac was able to return to *le Héros*, and as Lieutenant de Costebelle had remained at Trincomalee, I continued on with my interim command of *la Nayade*. Our troops were landed with the squadron's rowing boats, which would have been impossible at Cuddalore. The next morning at dawn I was ordered to cruise back and forth off Tranquebar and watch the sea to the south, as the English squadron could be returning from Bombay at any time. During the afternoon our ships moved anchorage to Cuddalore to land our baggage, artillery, food and ammunition, using *masula* boats. As for me, I stayed at sea, cruising to windward of the squadron.

On Sunday 23rd, most of the squadron sailed from Cuddalore in the morning and headed south, leaving two ships and two frigates at the anchorage. There was a moderate breeze from south-south-east, but having put in a board seawards, our ships were forced to anchor off Porto Novo, where I rejoined them. When making my report on *le Héros,* I learned that the ships which had stayed at Cuddalore were *le Fendant,* a seventy-four recently arrived with the Marquis de Bussy, *le Saint-Michel* and the frigates *la Cléopâtre* and the *Coventry.* This light division, under the command of Ship's Captain de Peynier, was to cruise off Madras for two weeks, to try to intercept an English convoy on its way from Europe and whose imminent arrival had been revealed to the Chevalier de Suffren by his informants. The squadron left Porto Novo at three in the morning and by dawn we were off the temples at Chalembron. Once more we had to work hard against the current, tacking into light and variable winds from south-east to south-west. When the wind was stronger than the current we tacked out to sea and back towards the coast, but when it fell we could only anchor and wait for it, as otherwise we would be carried north by the current.

On the 8th April, we finally reached the strait between Ceylon and the continent and on the 10th in the afternoon, *la Bellone,* who was reconnoitring ten miles ahead of the squadron, signalled land ahead to the west-south-west. Several hours later she signalled that from the masthead she could see nine sails, then fifteen, then twenty-three and then twenty-eight, running to the north-north-west. It was without doubt the English squadron returning from Bombay to Madras. The wind was light, from the east-south-east, and the enemy too far away to have been able to see anything other than *la Bellone* and *la Fortune.* The Admiral decided to make all sail to reach the big bay at Trincomalee before the English discovered us. *Le Héros* signalled the squadron and the convoy to close up and head south-west as quickly as possible, while clearing for action. We reached the big bay before nightfall, but the wind having veered to the south-west, we anchored just outside the entrance, to the north of Pointe Sale, in twenty-six fathoms.

12

At dawn the next day the wind was still in the west, and the sea beyond the entrance to the bay devoid of sails. The English had carried on without stopping. We had just to wait for a favourable wind to weather Point Ostenburg and enter the harbour. At eight o'clock that morning, however, the officer of the watch came to tell me that a ship's boat was approaching, carrying a Ship's Lieutenant who was not Lieutenant de Costebelle. I put on my hat and went to the quarter deck to welcome this unforeseen visitor. Once the boat was tied alongside the corvette's little boarding ladder, I could see that the officer coming up towards me was not a Ship's Lieutenant but a Fireship Captain. It was easy to make this mistake from a distance, as the uniforms are the same, except that a Fireship Captain's jacket is edged with slightly wider stripes. The man who stepped onto the starboard passageway seemed to be about thirty-five, with a pleasant and energetic face.

'Fireship Captain Villaret de Joyeuse at your service, Monsieur,' he said, handing me a document. 'I am your new commander.'

I had never before met Captain de Joyeuse, having only seen him on the poop deck of *le Pulvériseur*, which he commanded from the Île-de-France, and more recently aboard *la Bellone*, when I had been cruising off Tranquebar. The document, signed by the Admiral and dated the previous day, said that *the command of la Bellone has been given to Ship's Lieutenant de Costebelle, and that of la Naïade* (written thus) *to Fireship's Captain de Joyeuse.* I remembered Captain de Cuverville saying that *la Bellone* had been given to Captain de Joyeuse 'provisionally'. I had also noticed that Lieutenant de Costebelle was a particular favourite of the Admiral. All the same, this sudden change was surprising, as up until then Captain de Joyeuse's conduct had been exemplary, and in no way justified taking a good frigate from him in return for an indifferent little corvette.

'Don't worry!' he added, having sensed my puzzlement. 'I've not been given *la Nayade* as a punishment. I'll explain everything to you. But before that would you be so kind as to assemble the crew immediately, so that I can speak to the officers, petty officers and crew all together. And have my chest brought aboard.'

While everyone was being called to the quarter deck, my new commander asked to borrow my glass and went to the stern to watch *le Héros* and the other ships of the squadron. Looking in the same direction I could see that there was an unusual level of activity on some of the ships anchored around us. Boats were being put in the water and loaded with barrels.

'The Admiral has ordered the ships to give us their water. They won't need it as they can get water ashore. Please hurry up with getting everyone together, as we'll have to transfer it into our casks once the boats are here.'

The new commander's speech to the crew was short. He told them that he was taking command of the corvette and that Lieutenant de Costebelle had been given *la Bellone,* as she matched his rank better. I would soon realise that this introduction was a clever way of reassuring our Toulonnais crew about the fate of their former commander, whom they greatly liked. Captain de Joyeuse then announced that we would be sailing that very day. The Chevalier de Suffren, he told them, needed a corvette for a delicate and difficult mission and had decided to entrust it to *la Nayade,* as the crew was made up entirely of his fellow Provençals, whom he knew were the best and would never let him down. At that point I ordered the crew to shout *Vive le Roi!* three times, which they did with great enthusiasm. Captain de Joyeuse asked the officer of the watch and the Chief Bosun to prepare the ship for taking on the water which was starting to arrive, then asked me to follow him into the great cabin. He closed the two doors behind us and the stern windows, which I had left open to catch the brief morning cool.

'The Chevalier de Suffren spoke most highly of you and said that I could trust you. So I'm going to tell you what our mission actually is, but you must keep it to yourself. Don't talk about it to anyone, not even the officers!'

'It's a highly secret mission, then?'

Captain de Joyeuse lived up to his name: dimples appeared on his cheeks, his brown eyes lit up, and he raised a sardonic eyebrow, his lips suppressing a silent laugh.

'If it were only that! Above all I don't want to discourage the crew. Believe me, if they knew what was in store for them, you would have had trouble getting a *Vive le Roi!* out of them, as you just did.'

He became serious again.

'Have you heard about Captain de Peynier's mission?'

'Yes. I was told the other day that he had been sent to cruise off Madras to intercept a rich convoy.'

'That's correct! A convoy escorted by a single fifty-gun ship. Captain de Peynier will be waiting for them with *le Fendant,* a seventy-four, *le Saint Michel,* a sixty-four, and two frigates, *la Cléopâtre* and the *Coventry;* four of our best ships. If they were to have the misfortune of crossing paths with the English squadron we saw yesterday, it would be an irreparable loss for us.'

'Certainly, but what has *la Nayade* got to do with all that?'

'It's very simple. The Chevalier de Suffren wants us to go and warn Captain de Peynier of the arrival of the English squadron and tell him to return to Trincomalee as quickly as possible.'

At first I thought I had misunderstood and asked Captain de Joyeuse to repeat what he had just said.

'But Sir,' I continued, 'the English passed us yesterday, and as we will be astern of them, and we are slower than them, how on earth can we overtake them in order to get to our division in time? Why not send *la Bellone,* who is much faster?'

'Because the Chevalier de Suffren said I was the only commander in the whole squadron capable of doing this successfully.'

'But in that case, why didn't he leave you with *la Bellone*?'

'Because he is sure that, whatever happens, the ship he sends will be captured, whether going or returning.'

'So if I understand correctly, you are the best commander in the squadron for getting captured.'

Captain de Joyeuse burst out laughing.

'He also told me that with you as my second, I will have more chance of success.'

'Success in being captured? I'm the best for that too? That's the second time that the *Lord God Almighty* has sweetened the pill when giving me a mission. But the first time was less dangerous. Our lives may well belong to the King, but such a sacrifice serves no purpose! We have no chance of reaching Captain de Peynier. We will be chased long before that, and as *la Nayade* is too slow we will either fight to the death or be destroyed.'

'We have a plan,' said Captain de Joyeuse. 'How much does *la Nayade* draw?'

'Fourteen feet at the most.'

'We'll stick to the Coromandel coast as far as we can and if we meet an enemy ship we'll seek out water shallow enough for us, but not for them. That way they can only fire at us from a distance, but not board us. We'll continue like that as far as we can towards Madras and hope that the sound of battle will reach Captain de Peynier's division and be enough to warn them. At least in this regard the Chevalier de Suffren is correct to say I have a better chance of success than all the others. I've been sailing small ships up and down the Coromandel coast for nearly ten years. I know every danger and every nook and cranny.'

We raised the anchor towards the end of the afternoon, in a fresh south-south-easterly. By five we had Point Pavillon at Trincomalee on our port beam and were heading north-west a quarter north at four knots with the wind astern. I had put on a brave face in front of Captain de Joyeuse, saying that our lives were at the disposal of the King, but deep down I was scared, and envied the other lieutenants on board who had no idea about the aim of our cruise. I believed that it would serve no purpose and wondered how the Chevalier de Suffren could have thought otherwise. During the night the wind fell away to almost nothing, but was still from the south-east, and we were being pushed along by the current. On the afternoon of 12th April, a good distance off, we passed Point Pedro, a low stretch of land which merged into the line of the horizon.

By evening, under a splendid sunset, we had the wind on the port quarter, heading north-west a quarter north, all sail set, including the studding sails, in a fresh south-west breeze, with Ceylon's most northerly point twenty miles or so on the port quarter and just visible from the masthead. We were sailing well, the weather fine, the sea calm, alone on the sea. Many of the off-watch sailors had collected on the foredeck in the evening peace to watch the sunset on our port bow. The whole length of the corvette's deck was bathed in a gentle, warm light which passed under the shadows of the sails trimmed above our heads. The only sound was the light and unceasing hissing of the water along the hull. Captain de Joyeuse came out of the main companionway and leaned his elbows on the port rail of the poop deck.

'We'll bring in the studding sails for the night. It's not obvious, but the current here is taking us quickly to the north-north-west. By dawn tomorrow we should be within sight of Negapatam, and if the wind holds, we'll be off Porto Novo by nightfall. So far everything seems to be going well.'

He glanced at the helmsman then leaned towards me and lowered his voice.

'Negapatam is in English hands. We might be in for a surprise at dawn.'

On the 13th April, at seven in the morning, we could see a large number of black specks ahead of us, which turned out to be boats, and at eight the watchman aloft reported that there was land to the west. This extremely low part of the Coromandel coast looked like no more than a light mist on the horizon. The fishing boats we soon found ourselves among were mainly *kalimarrams*, crewed by two men and carrying one or two triangular sails. To our great relief there were no other sails in sight. By nine we could see Negapatam's remarkable black temple, followed by the minarets of the Nagore mosque. By ten we were abeam of the latter, seven miles off and in twenty fathoms. Apart from a few small trading boats at anchor, there was no other sail in sight. For the whole afternoon we sailed up the coast, keeping seven miles off in six to seven fathoms, thereby avoiding the shallows that stretch out from the shore in several places along this part of the Coromandel. The low land offered no features whatsoever. By half-past four it became a little higher and wooded. Shortly before sunset, a gap in the woods, formed by the mouth of a river, enabled me to see, further inland, four high gate towers, which I recognised as those of the Chalembron temple; the river was the Kollidam, which reaches the sea six miles south of Porto Novo. Captain de Joyeuse set a northerly course, which we maintained through the night, taking regular soundings to keep us in fourteen fathoms, to avoid the Kollidam Bank, which extends about six miles from the coast. During the night we passed Porto Novo, Cuddalore and Pondicherry.

At dawn on the 14th April, at dawn, in a very light south-westerly, the watchman on the mainmast signalled a sail twenty or so miles out to sea on our starboard quarter, heading east-south-east. She looked like a man-of-war. We had passed each other during the night. A few minutes later the watchman signalled that the ship had tacked and was now heading north-north-west. We were under chase.

*

Coromandel Coast, six miles south of Sadras, Monday 14th April 1783, seven o'clock in the evening.

The English ship which has been chasing us since this morning has caught up with us. The sun has just fallen below the horizon to port. We have taken our evening meal early and cleared for battle at five-thirty. My post is on the foredeck, and our guns are commanded by first lieutenant Giraud, a career Frigate's Lieutenant. The gun crews are leaning over their guns on the gun deck, with their lighted linstocks in tubs within a hand's reach. Everyone on board is quiet, sensing the seriousness of our position. Captain de Joyeuse told them a few minutes ago that we were being chased by an English merchant ship from the East India Company, but everyone can see that rather than an Indiaman, what we have here is a merchant of sudden death. The wind is quite light, from south-south-west. This part of the Coromandel coast bends to the north-east a quarter north, so we were running up it with the wind astern at two or three knots, with the current carrying us in the same direction. Up until now the land has been sandy and flat, with few trees. It is still flat, but we have arrived opposite a thick grove of palm trees which extends to the north. Captain de Joyeuse knows that at this spot there is a shelf of sand which extends half a mile out below the surface. We passed the end of it, after which the Captain had us harden up to port, keeping close to the coast in five fathoms, before

334

once more bearing off with the wind astern. He was hoping that the Englishman following us several cables astern would hit the bottom, but her Captain is not stupid, and has adopted a course parallel to ours without trying to get any closer. From there he will not be able to board us, but will soon be on our starboard beam, with us well within range. The ship has two gundecks, each with thirteen gunports each side. Captain de Joyeuse thinks they are 24-pounders on the main gun deck and 18-pounders on the upper deck. So she has fifty guns, plus the lighter artillery on her foredeck and poop. I particularly take note of two long 9-pounders whose barrels face forward over her beakhead. They would usually have been used to slow us down by damaging our rig, but they have not been brought to bear, doubtless because they are so sure of capturing us anyway. Night is falling quickly, but we are three days from the full moon, there is not a cloud in the sky, and it will be as clear as daylight for gunnery. There is no chance of escape.

Our big white flag is flying at our stern. During the day we tried raising the English red ensign, but that did not deter our adversary. The Englishman is now abeam of us and brailing up his lower sails and t'gallantsails, so as not to overtake us. The light from the battle lanterns on her gundecks highlights the contours of her gunports. She too has cleared for action.

Captain de Joyeuse puts his loudhailer to his lips.

'You can commence fire as you see fit, Lieutenant Giraud. Don't forget to aim to dismast!'

The Captain has hardly finished speaking when I hear Lieutenant Giraud give the order to fire and our broadside lets fly as one. Almost immediately, a double belt of flame, dazzling in the half-light created by the moon, lights up the port side of the English ship. The sound of the explosions arrives at the same moment that I see the mayhem of 24-pound and 18-pound cannon balls hitting our starboard side. The English have aimed for the hull. While they reload, I can hear the first cries of pain from those first to be injured on the deck below me. Thick smoke and the smell of powder rises around us in the warm, humid air of the early evening. Our ten 8-pounders start firing again, one after the other, Lieutenant Giraud having told them to fire at will. There is no point trying to fire at a higher rate than the enemy, to try to knock him out before he does the same to us, as our weight of metal is insufficient to have an effect on our opposition. We are better to take our time and aim our guns very carefully at his rig, in the hope of doing enough damage to slow him down. The English ship lets off another complete broadside. Once again, I hear the thudding of 24-pound balls hitting our planking and sending shards of wood flying through the gundeck; but I also hear the rush of air of heavy projectiles passing above my head. They too are now aiming 18-pounders at our rig.

*

We ran side by side, hard in to the coastline, and for five hours fought nonstop. At midnight our rudder shaft was broken; not completely, but we would soon not be able to steer. Our rig was shot to pieces and would not hold out for much longer either. Moreover, our hull was riddled with holes and there was six feet of water in the hold. The corvette was starting to sink. We must have been about forty-five miles south of Madras, but we could go no further. There was no point continuing to fight. All that remained was for us to lower our colours, hoping that Captain de Peynier had heard the sound of cannon fire. We had thirty-four killed and seven guns put out of action. This time I had come out of it unscathed, as had Captain de Joyeuse. We approached our victor as best we could, and were thrown a towrope, while the unwounded sailors busied themselves with the pumps to keep *la Nayade* afloat. The English ship was the *Sceptre,* commanded by Captain Graves. Admiral Hughes had left her astern, to watch out for the arrival of our squadron. She must have been tacking back and forth in a crosswind off Cuddalore when we crossed paths with her.

Captain de Joyeuse and I were concerned about the reception we would get from the English. The year before, when I was still at the Nabob's camp, the Chevalier de Suffren had delivered some English prisoners of war to the Nabob. This had caused a great deal of indignation amongst the English, as Hyder Ali Khan had a much-justified reputation for cruelty. The Admiral had first proposed an exchange to the authorities in Madras and to Admiral Hughes, but his requests had been rejected. Despite our fears, Captain Graves received us very politely, had our wounded looked after, complimented us on our defence, and showed generosity and chivalry. We were taken to Madras and put ashore in *masula* boats, to be first confined in the prison at Fort St. George. After a while the officers were offered a less rigorous

336

regime in a house outside the fort, where the English had their country houses, on condition that we accepted that we were prisoners on parole waiting to be exchanged. We had the satisfaction of learning that Captain Peynier and his little division had escaped Admiral Hughes' squadron; but we had wasted our time, as he had left the Madras area of his own accord long before our desperate battle.

*

Madras, Saturday 17th June, 1783.

It is a quarter after seven in the morning. I am walking towards the sea along a wide avenue bordered with parks and gardens surrounding beautiful houses. This quarter is built on a small lush plain south of the slopes surrounding the Fort St. George. This is where most of the employees of the East India Company retire with their families in the evening, after their day working in the warehouses and offices inside the Fort. The sun has appeared over the horizon. The weather is fine but the wind is from the south-west and in an hour or two it will start to get very hot.

Yesterday I had been given a note brought to the house where I am staying by an Indian. This *billet doux* had been written in French, but with 'Fort St. George' written without an 's', the English way. It was unsigned:

If you would like to know the answers to all the questions you have long been asking yourself, come to the shore south of Fort St. George's south-east bastion at half after seven tomorrow morning.

I believe I know who has written this message. If the man waiting for me is who I think it is, I will have lots of questions for him. On the other hand, I don't see why he would want to help me, and I wonder whether he is acting in good faith. This thought worries me a little. As I am a prisoner on parole, I cannot carry any arms outside, otherwise I would at least have brought my sword.

I reach the end of the avenue and start to hear the dull roar of the sea, echoing and growing louder as I approach. I come out onto the shore of beautiful white sand that stretches along the coast as far as one can see. The beach is flat and wide, with just a slight slope at its edge, where the *masula* boats and *katimarrams* are hauled out. I can see merchant ships and *pariah* coasters in the roads, but few warships. I have heard that the English squadron has left for Ceylon in search of ours. It is said in Madras that Admiral Hughes now has eighteen ships in excellent condition and that he will eventually destroy the fifteen tired vessels of the Chevalier de Suffren. It is also said that a strong English army is preparing to attack Cuddalore, where our little contingent has taken refuge since Tipoo Sahib marched west, thereby abandoning it. I don't know to what extent I should believe all these rumours which are repeated to me with relish once it was learned that I understand English. It is true that the people here have good reason to hold a grudge against the French, as the latter caused them to suffer food shortages at the start of this year.

I turn left and walk along the beach towards the red-brick walls of the Fort St George bastions. I am not at all reassured. In the distance I can see a group of fishermen, simply dressed in loincloths and with turbans wound around their heads. They seem to be talking with a man dressed in European clothes: white breeches, shirt and stockings and his hair tied behind with a ribbon. He is wearing a wide-brimmed hat to protect his face from the sun. Seeing me, the man bids farewell to the fishermen and returns to the top of the beach to wait for me. He is not armed, and apart from the innocent group he was talking with, I can see nobody else anywhere on the shore. All my concern suddenly dissipates, and I even feel some pleasure as I approach the man who has invited me to this strange meeting.

'You seem to like the company of *pariahs*, Monsieur Saint-Luperce,' I say as I get near to him. 'Or should I call you Winslow?'

'The *pariahs*, as you say, are resourceful people. And you should know as well as anyone. You don't seem surprised to see me! How did you know that I also go by the name of Winslow?'

'I know a lot of things about you. As least as much as you know about me. However, I don't know how you got here.'

'I'm here to tell you that. But where did your knowledge about me come from?'

'From several people, but in particular the late Doctor Rollin.'

'Oh! You knew Rollin? He told you about me?'

'Yes, in a way. One could say that. Why did you have him killed?'

Saint-Luperce, alias Winslow, starts at this.

'Who told you that? I had always heard that he was in bad heath and died of an illness. If what you say is true, I swear I did not know and had nothing to do with it.'

I watch him carefully. His surprise is not feigned. He seems sincere.

'Why did you invite me to this meeting?' I ask.

'As I said in my note: to enlighten and inform you.'

'So I read, but why do it?'

'I have caused you wrongs and I want to make them good.'

I burst out laughing.

'Wrongs? I was almost tortured to death because of you, and you call that wrongs.'

'I was not responsible for that. It was not intended. You really ought not to have come with me. When I saw that you were mentioned in Barrad Amzer's letter I was surprised. I then remembered that Declercq hated you, though I didn't know why. I did everything I could to warn you.'

'You arranged the holy man for me?'

'Yes. How did you manage to replace the diamonds with cowrie shells without me seeing?'

I told him briefly that I had a second key, and he continued his explanations.

'I've had enough of the English. They've used me too much against my will and I'm going to bow out. It's the right moment, as the war is over. It's not yet official but the beginnings of a peace treaty were signed last January at Versailles.'

It's my turn to be surprised.

'So, everything I've heard recently in Madras about Admiral Hughes attacking our squadron and English troops preparing to attack Cuddalore, it won't happen?'

Saint-Luperce shook his head.

'It will, unfortunately. News of the peace has still not reached Suffren or Bussy. I don't think it's even reached the Île-de-France. The English are well-informed because they have rapid packet boats across the Mediterranean. They can reach Alexandria in a month. The despatches are then sent by couriers to Suez, then by sea from Suez to Aden, and then to Bombay. That's how Declercq got to India. I know he still wants to take his revenge on you and it's also to warn you of that that I wanted to meet you before leaving Madras. But to come back to your question, the French forces, and particularly the Navy, have caused the English too much trouble and they want to rid themselves of this menace before a peace announcement stops them. They now think they have the means to do it and won't pass up the opportunity.'

'You talked about Flaharn. Do you know where he is?'

'Flaharn?'

'You know him as Declercq, but his real name is Flaharn.'

'According to the English, who are annoyed with him, Declercq would be at Tranquebar, with the Danes, looking for a ship to Europe. After that terrible business that caused you such misfortune, which I regret, but could do nothing about, he decided to return to the Nabob's camp, where he was known as Sher Sahib. We parted then and I haven't seen him since.'

'You didn't want to meet again with your good friend Hyder Ali Khan?' I said with some irony. 'How strange!'

Saint-Luperce shrugged.

'Declercq was convinced that you would reach the Nabob to give him the diamonds. I didn't think you were capable, even with the help of the *pariah* who rescued you. I preferred to keep looking for you in that area. You were on foot, and we had horses. Eventually, as I couldn't keep searching on my own, I gave up and decided to return to Madras.'

'Flaharn was waiting for me at the Nabob's camp. I ended up in his hands again.'

I could not stop my voice trembling at the horrible memory.

'And you got away from him again! I couldn't believe it when I heard. You are an amazing man, Laforest-Dombourg!'

'How did you find that out?'

'The English have plenty of informers at the Nabob's camp.'

'The English! I know you have often been their agent, but what do they have to do with Flaharn?'

'He too was one of their agents. In reality, he was acting on his own account, but the English only discovered this recently.'

'I thought at first that he was with the Americans, as I discovered that it was Doctor Baldock who had him brought to Paris,' I say.

We are walking along a strip of sand forming a sort of isthmus between the mouth of a river and the sea and will arrive at the south-east angle of Fort St. George. The sandy path that we are following goes along the bank to the foot of the walls of the fort, up to a door in the fortifications called the Marine Gate. This door opens to a bastion facing the anchorage beside steps which lead down to the shore.

'Let's turn round,' says Saint-Luperce. 'if we continue on there is a risk of meeting people who know me. It'll be hot soon too, like an oven at the base of the ramparts. There are palm and mango trees at the other end, where you came from. We can find some shade over there. I want to tell you everything I know before leaving.'

We went back the way we had come.

'As you no doubt know I was sent to the Bastille again the last time I returned to France. A Doctor Baldock came to visit me in my cell, saying that Monsieur de Sartine wanted to take me back into his service and asked Baldock to cancel the *letter de cachet* which had been issued against me.'

'I know all that,' I say. 'My uncle, the Chevalier de Kermean, told me this unlikely story. Baldock was the head of intelligence for the Americans.'

'That's what he told me at our first meeting at the Bastille, and had me sign a paper saying I would tell him secretly about anything I learned once I started working again for the Ministry for Foreign Affairs and the Navy. Baldock told me that I would probably be given a mission to India and that this was his main area of interest. I should in particular keep an eye on the Chevalier de Kermean, who was also involved in this project, and I should tell Baldock everything your uncle was doing. It was not very honest as regards Monsieur de Sartine, but I had no desire to remain in prison, and moreover, my treachery was not so bad, as the Americans were our allics.'

'If I have understood correctly,' I say, 'you became a spy for the Americans.'

'That's what I thought at first. I had begun work at the Navy Department, and the Foreign Affairs Department, and was seeing Baldock regularly in Paris to pass on what I had learned. These meetings were secret and I had to take many precautions.'

'I know,' I said. 'Riding round in a carriage, secret letter boxes and so on.'

Saint-Luperce smiled gently.

'It's true that you know all that. It makes us colleagues, in a way.'

'Except that I have only served my King!'

'I was joking. I thought that I was spying for the Americans, until the day Baldock showed me the documents that the English had made me sign when I was working for them, here in India. He made it clear that if I was not compliant enough, he would be tempted to pass these incriminating proofs of my past to the French. I knew then that even in the best of cases I would be back in the Bastille, but in secret this time, or else it would be the rope or twelve bullets from a firing squad. Baldock then told me he was head of English intelligence in Paris. I was trapped!'

'Doctor Baldock! An English spy!'

'And a master spy, too.'

I am shocked. My uncle de Kermean was fooled from the start. Not completely, though: he had been right about Saint-Luperce.

'His cover was excellent,' he continued. 'He was supposed to be creating a network of informers in London, for the benefit of the Americans. In reality his agents all belonged to the English secret service. Baldock told me that the mission that was to be entrusted to your uncle was to take a substantial treasure of diamonds to Hyder Ali Khan, and that Monsieur de Sartine intended to send me in his place. I told him that I did not want to go to the Nabob, as I was sure he would have me executed. Baldock told me not to worry and for the moment I just had to keep him informed. He also told me that the Chevalier de Kermean had been in contact with Doctor Rollin and he asked me to try to find out why. But I didn't have time to find out much about this, as a few days later I learned that Rollin was dead. You told me he had been assassinated?'

'He was poisoned. I know that a man who was shorter than me, with a pot belly, an English accent and a good knowledge of the West Indies, had poured poison in his glass when they were dining together at the *Porcherons* bar in Paris.'

'But that's a perfect description of Baldock!'

Baldock! It must be him. I suddenly remember that my uncle had told me that one of his pseudonyms was *Griffiths*. Rollin had indeed given the name of his assassin to his mistress, but she had thought he was referring to *Greffier,* her house cat.

'How did he find out that my uncle was seeing Rollin?'

Saint-Luperce raised both his hands.

'Nothing to do with me! Baldock had your uncle followed, which led him to Rollin. I admit it was because of me that he discovered that

Rollin might be of interest to the French because of his past in India. Rollin had always been good to me, despite my ingratitude towards him. I owe him a lot. He even saved my life once. I'll never forget him. That's another good reason for telling you all I know. So! Baldock told me that he had managed to get the Chevalier de Kermean sent to America, and that I would certainly be proposed as his replacement, but that wasn't the case. You arrived at Versailles. I let Baldock know, just in case. Later he told me you were the Chevalier de Kermean's nephew, and that despite your youth you were in the King's Secret Service.'

'And what of Flaharn in all of this?'

'I met him in Paris at a secret meeting at the Palais Royal. Baldock had invited him along with another of his men, telling the Comte de Vergennes' officials that they were American agents. Everything was decided at this meeting. Declercq was going to leave for Bombay on the packet boats, recruit a band of mercenaries and offer his service to Hyder Ali Khan. As for me, the Comte de Vergennes told me I was going to the Île-de-France as an interpreter and adviser on Indian affairs for the Mascarenes' Governor-General. I knew that you would be an officer on the ship I was sailing on, but it was Baldock and Declercq who told me you would be escorting the diamonds destined for the Nabob. Although I was told nothing at the time, I thought that everything the English knew about the diamonds came from Declercq. He was to try to convince the Nabob's ministers that he was in charge of establishing a secret liaison between the French expeditionary forces and Hyder Ali Khan. It was agreed that he would contact me as soon as we arrived on the Coromandel coast. Of course, the reason for all this was to steal the diamonds. One aspect of the plan pleased me greatly. They told me that the treasure would be given to the Marathas, to support the peace talks the English wanted to have with their government. I hated Hyder Ali Khan. He was a deceitful, licentious tyrant, and I was happy to know that I was helping steal a fortune from him, and, what's more, giving it to my friends the Marathas!'

We arrive at the end of the avenue I came along before. We leave the shore, cross a grove of coconut and palm trees, and take refuge under a mango tree whose thick greenery protects us a little from the overwhelming heat starting to beat down on Madras.

'My task was somewhat complicated,' continues Saint-Luperce, wiping his brow with his handkerchief. 'Then there was this stupid battle at Porto Praya, where chance enabled me to get hold of the chest of diamonds.'

'I assume you read the letter I was to deliver to the Vicomte de Souillac?'

'Yes! I discovered that the treasure was destined for the Marathas and that the King did not want to play the Nabob's game. The intentions of Versailles and the King were excellent. By supporting the Marathas and operating on the Malabar coast, France could have gained a permanent foothold on the Indian continent. The Nabob would have sought an alliance with us of his own accord, without asking anything in return. Even the Moghul would have seen France as saviours! And I could have played a leading role in these politics. Instead of which I ruined everything! Believe me, I was mortified when I discovered that everything would have been better if I'd left you alone to do what you had to do. But what else could I do? The English had me in their grip and I had lied too much about you. It was impossible to rewind the clock. I had to keep praising Hyder Ali Khan while denigrating my friends the Marathas. I destroyed the letter.'

Saint-Luperce takes a few paces outside the shade of the mango tree under which we have stopped and leans a hand on the trunk of a coconut palm, all the while looking out to sea through the undergrowth. The sun is high in the sky and the heat of the offshore wind is stronger and stronger. It's as if we are swimming: every movement makes me sweat heavily. I can once again hear the regular deafening roar of the swell on the bar.

'There you are! I have told you everything I know. Now we must part.'

'Wait a moment,' I say. 'There is still one point that needs clarifying. Baldock gave testimony that resulted in the arrest of an innocent man called Duval, the captain of a corsair. Baldock provided information which was correct, but incomplete, about an intelligence operation we carried out in the Channel. I'd like to know exactly what he knew about it and who told him.'

'I never heard anything about that, but I always believed that all the information the English had about the diamonds, about you and your uncle, came from Declercq, or Flaharn, as you call him.'

Everything now becomes clear! Flaharn was cared for by the English at Thunderbolt. Once he was better, he had only one obsession: to get his treasure back. He must have thought that the English could help him, and so he had the idea of offering his services to them and telling them about the diamonds. I now understand why Baldock knew the names of Duval, and the Captain of *le Moucheron,* while knowing nothing about our deal with the Cornish smugglers. He was just repeating what Flaharn had told him. I remember Flaharn telling me in April 1778 that he was going to command *le Moucheron,* with Fireship Captain Le Meur as his second. But as the Comte d'Estaing had wanted to keep Flaharn with him, Flaharn had finally agreed to give details of his go-between with the Cornishmen, Duval, and Le Meur had been given command of the cutter. But Flaharn knew nothing about what we had done after that. I am happy to learn that Duval is innocent and that I will be able to have him released once I return to France. I will also be able to denounce Doctor Baldock and make him pay for the murder of Doctor Rollin.

'What will you do now?' I ask Saint-Luperce.

'Don't tell the English. I am going back to Poona and the Marathas. I have never felt so welcome as with them and in any case, there is nowhere else for me to go. Back home, the best that awaits me is the Bastille. As for the English, they don't need me any longer and are quite capable of handing me over to the French once peace is announced. They said I was a double agent! The Marathas are a proud, free people. Horsemen! Even their women ride. Their faces are uncovered, and they look boldly on the world, like their husbands and sons. The English will try to subjugate the whole of India and only the Marathas are capable of standing up to them. I want to stay with them and for at least once in my life fight to the end in good faith, for a cause I have chosen freely. I no longer want people saying I am a double agent!'

*

Two weeks after my meeting with Saint-Luperce, the Vicomte de Bussy found himself blockaded in Cuddalore by an army of four thousand European soldiers and twelve thousand sepoys commanded by General James Stuart and, out to sea, Admiral Hughes' squadron, with its eighteen ships of the line.

The Chevalier de Suffren rushed to the aid of Cuddalore from Trincomalee, with fourteen ships. The English hopes of obliterating our forces in India once and for all seemed about to be realised, but warfare is full of surprises. The Admiral managed to make a stop off Cuddalore to replenish his crews with soldiers and sepoys before confronting the English squadron, and the battle which took place on 20th June 1783 went in favour of the French, despite their numerical disadvantage. Admiral Hughes had to abandon his blockade and the Chevalier de Suffren remained in control of the sea. Our land troops, inspired by this success, went on the offensive with renewed vigour. The Austrasie regiment overran the main body of English troops in a memorable bayonet charge and the situation turned in our favour for the first time since the start of the war. Seeing this, the English sent a frigate with some representatives, to announce that the outlines of a peace treaty had been signed between France and England at Versailles at the start of the year, and that Versailles and London had jointly decided to put an end to hostilities.

On Wednesday 9th July, an English officer came to tell me that all prisoners of war currently at Madras were to be liberated and that I must be ready to embark on a ship which would take me to Cuddalore. He held out a long, thin object wrapped in cloth.

'I am pleased to return your sword, Sir.'

This was a surprise, as the English had already given me back the Regulation sword I was carrying when *la Nayade* was captured.

'From Mister Winslow, Sir.'

I asked him where Saint-Luperce was, and he told me he had not seen him for a week, but that he had entrusted my sword to him before leaving, asking him to return it to me as soon as an end to hostilities had been announced at Madras. My heart was thumping as I unwrapped it. I discovered a normal Regulation sword, but which somehow seemed familiar. I pulled the blade from its sheath and could then read, engraved on the steel, the motto I knew so well:

Quo ruit et lethum.

My war, for the moment at least, was over.

LIST OF MAIN CHARACTERS

Real historical figures are indicated by an asterisk*.

THE LAFOREST-DOMBOURG/DE KERMEAN FAMILY

Pierre-Marie Laforest-Dombourg	a young orphan
Anne Laforest-Dombourg	his younger sister
Ship's Lieutenant Jean-François Laforest-Dombourg	his father, lost at sea 1771
Madame Emilie Laforest-Dombourg	his mother, murdered
Baron de Kermean	his maternal grandfather
Chevalier Jean-Baptiste de Kermean	his elder maternal uncle
Father François de Kermean	his younger maternal uncle

NAVAL OFFICERS, ADMINISTRATORS AND POLITICAL FIGURES

*Antoine de Sartine	Secretary of State for the Navy
	ex-Lieutenant-General of the Paris Police
*Chevalier de Ternay	Squadron chief in the French Navy
	Witness at Laforest-Dombourg's father's wedding
*Marc-Joseph Marion Dufresne	India Company captain and explorer

also known as 'Macé'. Witness at Laforest-Dombourg's father's wedding

*Comte de Lapérouse   Naval officer and explorer
Witness at Laforest-Dombourg's father's wedding
*Comte d'Estaing   Served as both an Army General
and Navy Admiral
*Comte d'Orvilliers   Vice-Admiral charged with
rebuilding the Navy
At this time Navy Commander at Brest
*Marquis de Langeron   Army commander at Brest
*Etienne Bézout   Mathematician and examiner who wrote
the standard textbooks for Army and Navy cadets
Henri Vernon, Chevalier des Aulnes   Fellow-Cadet and friend
Ship's Captain David Flaharn   Laforest-Dombourg's nemesis
*Comte de Boulainvilliers   Naval officer and huntsman
*Dr Benjamin Franklin   Polymath and first US Ambassador
to France
*Chevalier de la Rozière   Military commander of Saint-Malo
*Comte de Broglie   Head of Louis XVI's secret service
*Chevalier de Fleurieu   Director of Ports and Arsenals
Fireship Captain Le Meur   Captain of the cutter *le Moucheron*
*Colonel Dumouriez   Soldier and expert in coastal defence
Colonel de Guypair   Soldier and writer on military tactics
(Based loosely on the real-life Comte de Guibert)
*Duc de Choiseul   Author of the Navy Regulations
*Vicomte de Rochambeau   Commander of French forces in America
*Comte d'Hector   Commander of the Port of Brest
*Marquis de Castries   Secretary of State for the Navy,
replacing Sartine
*Jacques Necker   Swiss financier, Minister of Finance
to Louis XV1
*Jean-Frédéric Maurepas   Ex-Navy Minister, Chief Adviser to
Louis XV1
*Chevalier de la Jonquière   Second captain of *l'Astree*
*Comte de Vergennes   French Foreign Minister
*Vicomte de Souillac   Governor of the Mascarenes

*Monsieur de Montigny   King's envoy to India

*Marquis de Launay   Governor of the Bastille

*Chevalier de Saint-Sauveur   King's lieutenant at the Bastille

*Chevalier des Roches   Rear Admiral, ex-Governor of the Mascarenes

*Pierre Lenoir   Head of the Paris Police, succeeding Sartine

*Captain de Trémigon/Trémignon   Captain of *l'Annibal*

*Lieutenant Morard de Galles   Second captain of *l'Annibal*, later an Admiral

*Ensign d'Aché   Officer on *l'Annibal*

*Lieutenant de Kermadec   Officer on *l'Annibal*

*Lieutenant Boissauveur   Officer on *l'Annibal*

*Claude Roblet   Surgeon's mate on *l'Annibal*

*Monsieur Boucher   Surgeon-Major on *l'Annibal*

*Father Tiburce   Chaplain on *l'Annibal*

Monsieur le Choquet   Surgeon-Major on *l'Amazone*

*Chevalier de Suffren   Admiral of the French Navy

*Lieutenant de Moissac   Suffren's Flag Captain on *l'Héros*

*Marquis de Bussy   Commander of French Army contingent in India

*Monsieur Law de Lauriston   Governor-General of Pondicherry

*Comte d'Orves   Commander of French forces in the Indian Ocean

*Comte Duchemin   Commander of troops on de Suffren's expedition

*Rear Admiral Sir Edward Hughes   Commander of the English India squadron

*Monsieur Piveron de Morlat   King's envoy to the Court of Hyder Ali Khan

Doctor Rousseau   Surgeon-General of the India Company

*Colonel Bouthenot   Commander of French attachment to Hyder Ali Khan

*Captain de Saint-Félix   Captain of *le Brillant*

MISCELLANEOUS CHARACTERS

Louis Duval   ex-merchant navy officer, go-between with Cornish agents

*Jean Régnier   Entrepreneur and shipowner from Granville, Normandy

*Mademoiselle Eléonore Broudou   Comte de Lapérouse's fiancée

Tallebau, Chevalier de Saint-Luperce   Adventurer and double agent

(Based loosely on the real-life Pallebot de Saint-Lubin)

Doctor Edward Baldock   Physician and spy

(Based loosely on the real-life Edward Bancroft)

Doctor Rollin   Army doctor

Monsieur and Madame Dutertre   Wine merchant and boarding house owners

Louis Le Gall   Maria Kirwan's relative, claimant to *La Dame au Paon*

*Hyder Ali Khan   Sultan of Mysore

*Tipu Sultan   his son

Ranga Pillai   Laforest-Dombourg's *dubash,* or general factotum

Thomas Moutou   Laforest-Dombourg's guide and bodyguard

*Abbot Jean-Charles Perrin   Catholic Missionary to India

Nadanamani   Courtesan at the Court of Hyder Ali Khan

ABOUT THE AUTHOR

Eric Gautier is descended from a long line of Nantes and Lorient shipowners and was born and raised on the south coast of Brittany. He has been a lifelong recreational sailor and amateur student of French maritime history. He served in the French army alpine regiment for more than thirty years, retiring with the rank of colonel. A talented artist, he has also produced illustrated monographs on the traditional fishing boats of Brittany.